An
Amish Gathering

LIFE IN LANCASTER COUNTY

Three Amish Novellas

BETH WISEMAN

BARBARA CAMERON

KATHLEEN FULLER

THOMAS NELSON
Since 1798

NASHVILLE   DALLAS   MEXICO CITY   RIO DE JANEIRO

Beth: To Carol Voelkel. Hold on to the dream, my writer-friend.
"Miracles happen to those who believe."
Barbara: To my daughter, Stephany, and my son, Justin
Kathy: To Trish, my everlasting friend

© 2009 by Beth Wiseman, Barbara Cameron, and Kathleen Fuller

Published in Nashville, Tennessee by Thomas Nelson. Thomas Nelson is a trademark of Thomas Nelson, Inc.

Thomas Nelson, Inc., books may be purchased in bulk for educational, business, fund-raising, or sales promotional use. For information, please e-mail SpecialMarkets@ThomasNelson.com.

Scripture quotations taken from the King James Version.

Publisher's Note: This novel is a work of fiction. Names, characters, places, and incidents are either products of the author's imagination or used fictitiously. All characters are fictional, and any similarity to people living or dead is purely coincidental.

CIP has been applied for.

ISBN 978-1-59554-822-1 (tradepaper)

Printed in the United States of America
09 10 11 12 13 14 RRD 6 5 4 3 2

Glossary

ab im kopp – off in the head, crazy
aenti – aunt
allrecht – all right
bensel – silly child
boppli – baby or babies
brechdich – magnificent
bruder – brother
bu, buwe – boy, boys
budder – butter
budderhaffe – butter dish
daadi – grandfather
daed – dad
danki – thanks
Deitsch – Pennsylvania Dutch language
demut – humility
Die Botschaft – a weekly newspaper serving Old Order Amish
    communities
dochder – daughter
dumm – dumb
eldre – parents
Englisch – a non-Amish person
fiewer – fever
fraa – wife
frack – dress
Gebottsdaag – birthday
geh – go
grossmammi – grandmother
guder mariye – good morning
gut – good
gut nacht – good night
halt – stop
hatt – hard
haus – house
hochmut – pride

hungerich – hungry

kaffi – coffee

kapp – prayer covering or cap

kich – kitchen

kind, kinder, kinner – children or grandchildren

lieb – love

lieblich – lovely

liebschdi – dear child

liebschen – dearest

maed – girls

maedel – girl

mamm, mammi – mom

mann – man

mauseschtill – mouse

mei – my

minutt – minute

mudder – mother

nachtess – supper

nau – now

nee – no

onkel – uncle

Ordnung – the written and unwritten rules of the Amish; the understood behavior by which the Amish are expected to live, passed down from generation to generation. Most Amish know the rules by heart.

redd-up – clean up

rumschpringe – running-around period that starts when a teenager turns sixteen years old

schpass – fun

sehr – very

sohn – son

snitz pie – dried apple pie

vatter – father

wasser – water

wie geht – how are things?

wunderbaar – wonderful

ya – yes

Table of Contents

A Change of Heart

By Beth Wiseman

Chapter One

LEAH FOLDED HER ARMS ACROSS THE SPIRAL NOTEBOOK and held it close to her thumping chest. She was late for supper. Again.

She eased her way up the front porch steps of the farmhouse and peered through the screen door. Her family was already seated at the long wooden table in the kitchen. She sucked in a breath and prepared for her father's wrath. Supper was always at five o'clock, and preparations usually began an hour before that. Leah was expected to help.

Her eldest sister, Edna, cut her eyes in Leah's direction as Leah closed the screen door behind her. Mary Carol scowled at Leah, too, and blew out an exasperated sigh.

"Sorry I'm late." Leah tucked her chin but raised her eyes enough to catch a sympathetic gaze from her youngest sister, Kathleen. Leah forced a smile in Kathleen's direction.

"Wash for supper, Leah." Marian Petersheim didn't look at her daughter but instead glanced at her husband, a silent plea for mercy on her face.

"Yes, ma'am." Leah rushed upstairs, stored her notebook in the top drawer of her nightstand, and quickly washed her face and hands. She tucked loose strands of brown hair beneath her prayer covering, smoothed the wrinkles from her black apron, and walked briskly down the stairs.

She slid in beside Edna on the backless wooden bench and bowed her head in silent prayer as forks clanked against plates. When she was done, she reached for the chow-chow and spooned a small amount of the pickled vegetables onto her plate. She helped herself to a piece of her mother's baked chicken and then eyed her favorite casserole. Leah loved the way Kathleen prepared the green bean mixture with buttered Ritz cracker crumbs on top, but the casserole was on the other side of her father, and she wasn't about to ask him to pass it.

Daed didn't look up as he swallowed his last bite of chicken and reached for another piece on the platter to his right. The father of four teenaged girls—Edna, nineteen; Leah, eighteen; Mary Carol, seventeen; and Kathleen, sixteen—James Petersheim ran the household with steadfast rules and imparted strict punishment when those rules were disobeyed. Every one of the girls had been disciplined with a switch behind the woodshed at some point in her life. Leah wished she were still young enough for the switch. It would surely be better than what her father was about to unleash on her.

She pulled a piece of butter bread from the plate nearby and glanced toward him. Leah knew he would finish his meal before he scolded her for being late. She dabbed her forehead with her napkin, unsure if the sweat gathering on her brow was due to nervousness or the sweltering August heat.

"Abner's *mamm* is giving us her fine china as a wedding present," Edna said after an awkward moment of silence. Edna and Abner's wedding was scheduled for November, after the fall harvest, and Edna often updated the family about the upcoming nuptials during supper. "It belonged to his grandparents." Edna sat up a little straighter, and her emerald eyes shone.

"Wonderful news," their mother said. "I've seen Sarah's china, and it's lovely."

Leah waited for Mary Carol to chime in. Her wedding was scheduled to take place in December.

Leah recalled her father pointing his finger at her and Kathleen. "I reckon the two of you best not be thinkin' of marrying until at least next year," he'd teased after hearing Mary Carol's news two months ago—news that came on the heels of Edna's announcement only one week earlier.

Mary Carol smiled. "I have something to share too," she said, glancing back and forth between their mother and Edna. "Saul's parents are giving us twenty acres to build a new home. Until that time, we'll be living with his folks."

Here we go, Leah thought. Jealousy is a sin, but Mary Carol was translucent when it came to her feelings about Edna. And if Leah were honest with herself, she'd admit that she, too, had often been jealous of their oldest sister. Edna was the prettiest of all of them, with silky dark hair and stunning green eyes. She'd gotten her figure early, too, and all the boys took notice of Edna by the time she was fourteen. The other three Petersheim sisters were much plainer, with mousy brown hair and nondistinctive dark eyes, and without the curves Edna was blessed with. And Mary Carol battled a seemingly incurable case of acne, always trying some new potion the natural doctor suggested.

"That's very generous of Saul's family." Their mother nodded toward the green bean casserole. "Kathleen, could you please pass me the beans?"

Kathleen complied, putting Leah's favorite dish within reach. After her mother scooped a spoonful onto her plate, Leah helped herself.

"Abner and I will be livin' in the *daadi haus*, since his grandparents have both passed on. Then when Abner's brothers and sisters are grown, we'll move into the main house, and his parents will move to the *daadi haus*," Edna said.

"Our *haus* will be new." Mary Carol flashed her sister a smile.

"But we will be able to live in our *haus* right after we're married," Edna scoffed. "We don't have to wait for a home of our own, and—"

"Girls . . ." Their mother's voice carried a warning. "This is not a competition."

They all ate quietly for a few moments. Leah could hear their dog, Buddy, barking in the distance, presumably tormenting the cows. The golden retriever was still young and playful and often chased the large animals unmercifully around the pasture, nipping at their heels. Several cows voiced their objection, which only caused Buddy to bark louder.

"Aaron asked about you," Edna said sheepishly to Leah.

"Why?" Leah narrowed her eyes. Abner's brother ogled her enough during worship service every other week. Now he was conversation for suppertime?

Edna shrugged. "It's the second time he's asked how you are."

"*Ach*. You can tell him I'm mighty fine." Leah squared her shoulders and raised her chin, hoping that would put an end to the subject of Aaron Lantz. He was Edna's age, a year older than Leah. He was Abner's only brother, and Leah could smell a fix-up from a mile away. She'd had plenty of them lately. Just because Mary Carol was getting married before Leah didn't mean Leah would end up an old maid at eighteen.

Just the other day, Amanda Graber had stopped by to personally invite Leah to attend a Sunday singing coming up this weekend at her home, mentioning that Abram Zook might be there. *Abram Zook?* No, no, no.

Her own mother had invited Stephen Dienner for supper two Sundays ago. What was she thinking? Stephen was a good six inches shorter than Leah. While her mother insisted that it was only a friendly gesture, Leah suspected otherwise.

"Aaron is such a fine boy," her mother said. She smiled warmly in Leah's direction. "And very handsome too."

Leah swallowed a bite of bread. "You've always taught us that looks don't matter."

"That's true, Leah. But we're human," her mother answered. Then she glanced at their father—a tall man with sharp features and brilliant green eyes like Edna's. His beard barely reached the base of his neck and didn't have a single gray hair amid the thick whiskers. He was handsome, indeed.

Her mother refocused on Leah. "I hear Aaron attends the Sunday singings. Maybe you should go this Sunday."

Leah rolled her eyes and immediately wished she hadn't. Her father's expression blazed with annoyance at her display. She dropped her head. "Maybe," she whispered.

"Actually . . ." Edna cringed a bit. "He's coming over with Abner for a visit later."

"Why? Do you and Abner need a chaperone?" Leah pulled her mouth into a sour grin.

"No, we don't. I thought maybe—"

"You didn't *think*. I don't care anything about dating. I never want to get married! Everyone needs to stop—"

"Enough!" When their father's fist met with the table, everyone froze. Leah didn't even breathe. They all watched as he pulled himself to a standing position. He faced Leah with angry eyes, but far worse for Leah was the disappointment she could see beneath his icy gaze. "Leah will clean the supper dishes," he said after taking a deep breath and blowing it out slowly. "Every night this week."

"Yes, sir." Leah pulled her eyes from his and laid her fork across the remainder of her green bean casserole.

"I'll help you," Kathleen whispered to Leah when their father was gone.

"No. It's all right. I'll get it." Leah began to clear the dishes.

"You girls will learn not to behave in such a way during the supper hour." Their mother rose from the table and carried her plate to the sink. "Your *daed* works hard all day long, and he doesn't want to listen to your bickering during supper." She turned her attention to Leah. "Brew a fresh batch of tea for Abner—and Aaron."

After their mother headed upstairs, Mary Carol and Kathleen went outside to tend to the animals. Edna lagged behind.

"You know, you might like him," Edna said. She cleared the few dishes left on the table and put them next to the sink. "Like *Mamm* said, he's very handsome, and he seems to have taken a liking to you."

"He stares at me during worship service. But other than that, he doesn't even know me." Leah rinsed a plate and put it in the drying rack. "He was shy in school, barely talked to anyone."

Edna reached for a dish towel, then picked up a plate and started to dry it. "That was four or five years ago. He's quite talkative when I have supper with their family."

Leah sighed. She'd much rather spend her free time upstairs working in her notebook, not making small talk with Aaron Lantz. Her story was coming along nicely, and she was anxious to get back to work on it.

"You missed a spot." Edna handed the plate back to Leah and grabbed another one from the drain. "Leah . . ." She put the plate back in the water. "This one is still dirty too." Edna shook her head. "I'm going to go clean up before Abner gets here. Maybe you should clean up a bit too, no?"

Leah blew upward and cleared a wayward strand of hair from her face. "I'm fine, Edna."

Her sister shrugged and left the room.

Leah finished the dishes with dread in her heart. Why couldn't they all just let her be? Now she'd be spending the evening with Aaron, a young man she barely knew and didn't really care to know.

Chapter Two

MARIAN PULLED HER LONG WHITE NIGHTGOWN OVER HER head, then removed her prayer covering and allowed her wavy brown hair to fall almost to her waist. She folded the quilt on their bed to the bottom. It was much too hot for any covers . . . maybe just the light cotton sheet for tonight.

Rays of sunlight beamed through the window as the sun began its descent. It was too early for bed, but Marian wanted to give the young people some time to themselves. She was glad when James followed her upstairs after their evening devotions. As much as she'd like to read for a while, she suspected James wanted to talk—about Leah.

Marian sat down on the bed and applied some lotion to her parched hands, then smoothed it up her arms, the cool cream a welcome relief from the heat. She was still wringing her hands together when James walked into the bedroom, his dark hair and beard still damp, his eyes filled with tiredness and concern.

"I don't know what to do about Leah." He stood in the middle of the room in only his black breeches.

Marian eyed her husband of twenty-one years. His broad shoulders carried the weight of his burdens. It was a sin to worry so much; that was one area in which James could learn from Leah. Their carefree, spirited daughter tested the limits at times, but Leah seldom allowed her worries to press down on her for long.

James inhaled a long, slow breath, and muscles rippled across a chest reflective of many years of hard work. "It's not fair to the other *maed* when Leah shirks her responsibilities."

"*Ya*, I know, James." Marian patted a spot on the bed beside her. "Sit. And we will talk about it."

James sat down and turned to face her. He ran a hand through her hair and twisted a few strands within his fingers. "So soft," he whispered.

For a moment his eyes suggested that they not speak of Leah, but instead communicate with each other the way only a husband and wife can appreciate. But no sooner did the thought surface than Marian saw two deep lines of worry form on her husband's forehead.

"I don't like these stories she writes," he finally said. His eyes narrowed. "They are of no use to her. I don't understand why she tinkers with such nonsense."

"James . . ." Marian cupped his cheek, raked a hand through his hair. "It's not nonsense to her. She has an imagination. That's all."

Her husband sat taller and scowled. "It will do her no *gut*, this imagination of hers. These tales she pens are a waste of time, Marian." His eyes widened. "And did you hear her at supper? She doesn't even want to get wed." He hung his head. "No fella I know would want to marry her."

"James," Marian huffed. "That's a terrible thing to say about your *maedel*."

He leaned back on his hands. "I worry that she will live with us the rest of our days." He grinned at Marian. "You, me, and Leah."

Marian chuckled, glad that he was making light of his worries. "No, James. She will not live with us forever. Leah is finding her way. You must give her time."

"She is eighteen. Of proper marrying age." He sat tall again and twisted to face Marian. "And what kind of *fraa* will Leah make?"

Marian shared her husband's concerns about Leah and thought about it often.

"She cannot cook. She does not sew well." James brought both hands to his forehead. "Leah has no hand for gardening, nor does she do a *gut* job cleaning *haus*. These are all things a fine Amish *fraa* must do. Instead, she writes fanciful stories that have no place in our world."

"Now, James. You know that there are several people in our community who are writers. A few of them have even sold stories to people who print such tales. And it is allowed by the bishop, as long as the stories are wholesome and in line with our beliefs."

"It is a waste of time and will not help Leah to find a *gut* husband."

Marian heard the clippity-clop of horse hooves. She stood up and walked to the window. Abner was pulling onto the dirt driveway leading up to the house, and Aaron was with him. "Maybe she and Aaron will come upon a friendship," Marian said. She twisted around and smiled at her husband.

James joined her at the window, and they both watched as Edna met the boys at the buggy. "Edna will be a fine *fraa*," James said. "And Mary Carol too. Even young Kathleen will make a *gut* wife."

Marian patted James on the arm. "Leah will make a home with someone when she's ready."

"Where is Leah?" James pressed his face close to the window and peered against the sun's bright rays.

"Hmm. I don't see her."

James grunted. "Probably writing in that notebook she takes everywhere. Maybe you best go tell her that company is here."

"There she is." Marian was relieved to see Leah slowly making her way across the yard toward Edna and the boys. "Everything will be fine, James."

James twisted his mouth to one side. "I hope so."

❧

Aaron stepped out of the buggy, waved at Edna, and then fixed his eyes on the lovely Leah. She was taller than most of the women he knew, but Aaron still towered over her by several inches. Her soft brown eyes, always brimming with curiosity, met briefly with his. He loved the way her two tiny dimples were visible even when she wasn't smiling, a detail that softened her expression even when she was deep in thought.

He remembered when he saw her walk into the small schoolhouse on their first day of class, her eyes twinkling with wonder and awe. She asked more questions than any of the other students, and everyone wanted to be her friend. It stayed that way until their graduation from the eighth grade, but Aaron never seemed to be in her circle of friends, nor did she seem to notice him at the Sunday singings when they got older. But he wasn't the shy boy of his youth anymore.

If he took into account everything that he knew about Leah, he should not be considering a courtship, no matter how much she intrigued him. From what he'd heard from his sisters, the girl was flighty and irresponsible, couldn't cook, couldn't garden, couldn't even use a needle and thread successfully. Yet his heart skipped a beat at the mere mention of her name.

"I brewed a fresh batch of meadow tea," Edna said as she batted her eyes in Abner's direction. "Let's sit on the porch." She swung her arm in that direction.

"Hello, Leah." Aaron got into pace alongside her. "*Danki* for inviting me." He smiled with enough hopefulness for both of them, but Leah's eyes widened with surprise. She twisted her head in Edna's direction, and Aaron knew he wasn't supposed to see the scowl on her face. *Too late.*

"Sure," Leah said when she turned her face back to his. Her lips curled upward, but it was a sorry attempt to rectify her initial response.

Aaron glowered in his brother's direction. A guilty expression flashed across Abner's face as he moved his shoulders in a shrug of innocence. Aaron had wondered why Leah invited him over, since he'd been trying unsuccessfully to get her attention. Twice he'd offered to take her home after a Sunday singing, and she'd politely declined. During worship service, he was guilty of letting his mind drift and trying to make eye contact with her. Nothing.

He'd get hold of Abner later, but for now he'd have to make the best of things and try to convince Leah that he was worth her time.

Aaron was the last one to walk up the steps and onto the porch. Four high-back rockers were lined up across the wooden planks, a small table between each pair of chairs. Four glasses of tea were waiting for them.

"Help yourselves," Edna said. She slid into the rocker at the far end of the porch, and Abner sat down in the chair closest to her. Aaron waited until Leah eased her way into one of the seats before he got comfortable in the rocker next to hers. He removed his straw hat, placed it in his lap, and reached for a glass of tea. Beads of sweat trickled from his forehead as he gulped the cool beverage, and he could feel moisture on his shirt, particularly where his suspenders met with the blue cotton fabric.

He raised his eyes above the glass. The others were swigging their tea as well. This was the hottest summer Aaron could recall. Or maybe he just thought that every year when the scorching August heat settled in. Leah was gazing above the rim of her glass toward the pasture. A dozen cows grazed in the meadow as the sun began to set behind one of the crimson barns.

The Petersheim farm was one of the oldest homesteads in their district. Five generations had grown up in the two-hundred-year-old house with its two stories and wraparound porch. The tin roof was painted the same color as the red barns, and a fresh coat of white paint on the clapboard masked the structure's true age. Over six hundred acres surrounded the house; James Petersheim was one of the few farmers who didn't have to supplement his income by working as a carpenter or in another trade outside of the community.

Aaron set his glass down and wiped his forehead with the back of his hand.

"Leah, did you know that Aaron works with Abner at their father's furniture store?" Edna leaned forward in the chair.

This is a pitiful attempt at small talk, Aaron thought as he waited for Leah to respond. *Of course she knows.*

"*Ya*, I did know that." She glanced briefly at Aaron, forced a half smile, then pushed her bare feet against the porch, sending the rocker into motion and her dark purple dress flowing at her shins.

"Abner said you like to write stories," he said cautiously. The subject had come up at supper one night when Edna was a guest in their home. Both Edna and Abner seemed to think such a hobby was a waste of time, as did everyone else at the table, including Aaron. But when Leah's eyes began to twinkle, Aaron was glad he had brought it up.

"*Ya*, I do." She twisted slightly in her chair to face him and seemed to come alive as her whole face spread into a smile. "Do you write? Stories, books, or maybe poems?"

She looked so hopeful, but Aaron didn't have time for such silliness. "No, I don't." As soon as her expression went grim, he added, "But I like to read—whenever I have time."

Her response came quickly. "What do you read?"

"I, uh—I read the Bible, mostly."

She gave a nod of approval, then shifted her weight back to an upright position, as she'd been before he sparked her interest.

"We're going to take a walk," Edna said. She stood up from her chair and waited for Abner to do the same.

Aaron waited until they were out of earshot. "What do you write about?"

Her eyes narrowed skeptically, as if she didn't believe he was really interested. He was interested in anything that would help him get to know Leah better.

After a moment, she said, "The *Englisch*."

"Huh?" *Surely that isn't allowed.* "You write stories about outsiders? Why?" He stared at her.

"Why do you find this so odd? They write about us all the time." She shook her head and sighed. "And most of the time, they don't get it right."

Aaron folded his arms across his chest and cocked his head to one side. "Then why do you think you can get it *right* about them? You don't know nothin' about living in the *Englisch* world."

"I know that many of them don't know God." Her voice was sad as she spoke. "I write about *Englisch* people who are trying to have a relationship with God. Maybe it will make a difference to someone someday, help them find their way to the Lord." She got a hint of mischief in her eyes. "And there's always a happy ending!"

Aaron had to admit, he was fascinated by her effort to help others find a way to the Lord through her tales, but it wasn't something they were taught to do. "The *Ordnung* doesn't teach us to minister to those outside of our community, Leah, if that's what you're trying to do with these books." He liked the way her name slid off his tongue. "I reckon it's not our place—Leah."

"Why?"

"It just ain't."

They sat quietly for a few moments, but Aaron still had questions. "Where do these stories of yours take place? In an Amish district or in the *Englisch* world?"

"In the *Englisch* world and in Amish communities. You don't have to be Amish to have a strong faith and a relationship with God." Her eyes glowed with a sense of strength and purpose, and while her efforts were misdirected, he'd never been more attracted to her. But had she forgotten the one thing that almost always divided them from outsiders?

"Leah, we believe that all things are of God's will. I don't think most of the *Englisch* share our faith, dedication, and interpretation of the Bible."

"They do in my stories when I'm done with them," she said smoothly. Then she winked at him and set his heart to fluttering.

"How many have you penned?"

"I'm working on my third. They aren't as long as full-sized books. I mostly write at night after Edna goes to sleep, by the light of a small flashlight. It takes a long time to write longhand. I know that some of the writers in our district have typewriters. Not electric, but I suspect it's still faster than using an ink pen and paper. Someday I hope to have one."

"It seems like it would be *hatt* to write about the *Englisch* ways."

"I'm still in my *rumschpringe*, so the rules are relaxed enough to allow me time in the city, just like you. I have two *Englisch* girlfriends that I meet for lunch, and they help me with things about their world that I don't understand."

"It's interesting. Your writing." Aaron rubbed his chin for a moment. He wanted to ask her if she'd be better off learning to cook, garden, and sew, but instead he said, "Who will read these books?"

She took a sip of her tea, then placed the glass back on the table and shrugged. "I don't know." Her eyes lost their sparkle for a moment. "Maybe my two friends. Clare and Donna. That's their names. I hope they'll read my stories someday. They are such dear friends, but they seem to struggle with their faith." She paused, and her eyes became hopeful. "Do you want to read one?"

His body became rigid as he straightened in the chair. *I reckon not.* Aaron could barely fit his chores and devotions into his day in time to get a decent night's sleep. Of course he didn't have time to read her ramblings. "I'd be honored to read one of your stories," he said.

Leah was instantly on her feet. "I'll give you the shortest one to start off with."

Thank You, Lord.

Wait. *Start off with?* Did she expect him to read all of them?

"This is wonderful." Her eyes gleamed as she spoke, and her

tiny dimples expanded as her face spread into a smile. "I'll be right back."

Aaron watched her dart into the house and wondered what he'd gotten himself into.

When she returned barely a minute later, he stifled a gasp as she handed him a stack of lined white paper bound by two rubber bands. It was almost two inches thick.

"No one has ever read anything I've written. This is my shortest story. About a hundred and twenty pages." She lifted her shoulders, dropped them, and grinned. "How long do you think it will take you to read it?"

What? Probably forever. "*Ach*, I reckon I could finish it by—"

"By the Sunday singing at the Grabers' this weekend?" Her voice bubbled with hope, but Aaron knew he'd have to disappoint her. It was already Wednesday.

"Maybe . . ." She drew out the word, and her eyes batted with mischief. "You could pick me up and we could go together, if you'd like. We could talk about the story on the way to the singing."

Aaron reminded himself that he wasn't the shy, bashful boy who'd watched Leah from afar during the school years. He'd just tell her that he was much too busy to fit her ramblings into his schedule. He had his work at the furniture store and his chores at home.

She flashed a smile in his direction.

"I—I think that sounds great, Leah," he said, then sighed.

It would be a long week. He hoped she was worth it.

Chapter Three

LEAH WAITED UNTIL SHE COULD HEAR EDNA SNORING in the other bed before she carefully opened the drawer to the nightstand in between them. She pulled out her notebook, pen, and flashlight, then propped her pillows behind her. Once she was comfortable, she pulled her legs toward her and rested the pad against her knees.

Edna would deny, up until her last dying breath, that she snored, but this time of year it seemed to be the worst. The natural doctor said she had allergies, and Edna took an herbal mixture to help with her condition, but it sure didn't help with her snoring.

She was glad Edna was sleeping. If she were awake, she'd just lecture Leah about how nonproductive her writing was, how she was never going to find a husband, and on and on. It wasn't that Leah didn't want a husband . . . she just didn't see what the rush was. She enjoyed her time to herself, and once she was married, there wouldn't be time for her writing. There was barely time now. Once she was married, she would have not only a husband but an entire household to take care of, and babies would follow. Leah looked forward to all those things. Just not quite yet.

She tried to ignore Edna's unsteady wheezing and focus on her story. She reread the last page she had written the night before, but she couldn't concentrate. Aaron Lantz's face kept popping into her head. He wasn't the quiet, timid boy she remembered from school, and even though she saw him at social gatherings these days, she'd never paid much attention to him before now. He seemed . . . nice. And not bad looking either. Leah knew she should be ashamed for taking advantage of him the way she had, blackmailing him into reading her story in exchange for a date to the Sunday singing.

Her heart thumped in her chest all of a sudden, and she began to feel a little panicked. What if he didn't like her story? And told her so. Or what if he lost it? It was the only copy she had. What if he mistook their date to the singing as more than just a casual get-together? She'd need to straighten this out with him tomorrow, make sure he understood that friendship was all she was interested in. And someone to read her stories. Screen them, so to speak.

She shook her head. Aaron would tell her that he liked what she wrote, whether he did or not, just because he was smitten with her. She should have picked someone else to test her work on. Aaron couldn't be objective if he liked her—in that way.

Leah had to admit, if she were in the market for courtship, she'd be flattered by the way he looked at her, the way his big blue eyes seemed to call out for her to notice him, give him a chance. His build was a pleasing attribute. Tall and muscular. His light brown hair was sun-streaked with sandy-red highlights, as if he didn't wear his hat a lot of the time. And it was cute the way his mouth had twitched on one side when he'd seemed to be nervous around her earlier.

Why all the thoughts about Aaron? She'd always thought he was handsome. Just rather . . . insignificant. She silently reprimanded herself for having such a thought, especially after he'd been so polite earlier.

Leah blew out a breath of frustration. Her thoughts about Aaron were keeping her from her writing, and her heroine in her story was starting to put her faith in God, and Leah wanted to elaborate on that. It was her favorite part of storytelling, when things started to lead up to a happy ending.

She put the pen to the paper and let her thoughts about Abigail Bennett flow.

Abby listened to the inner voice this time, a voice she'd heard before but never paid attention to, a whispering in her conscience that beckoned her to follow the path to salvation through Jesus Christ.

Leah stopped writing when Edna started to cough. She sure wished the doctor could give her sister something better to help her. It sounded like the air in Edna's lungs was mixed with tiny rocks that she was trying to clear from her airway by taking deep breaths and then forcing the mess out. Leah didn't understand how Edna could sleep through it, but she always did.

When Edna's snoring resumed, Leah was able to reconnect with Abigail. By the time she finished telling Abby's story, it was almost midnight. Four o'clock would come early in the morning, but it was worth it.

She smiled as she wrote out the words *The End*.

∽

Midnight? Aaron shook his head as he turned off the lantern on his bedside table.

He hadn't meant to read Leah's story until that late, but as it turned out, he couldn't stop turning the pages. He was fascinated by the main characters, two girls, one *Englisch* and one Amish. Lauren and Rose had nothing in common but the friendship they shared, and Leah's storytelling was tender and compassionate as the girls struggled to be friends, even though their families were less than approving.

Rose was tall, like Leah. She had brown eyes, like Leah, and if Aaron didn't know better, he would have thought that Leah was writing about herself. Rose was strong in her faith and ministered to her friend, but she didn't seem interested in learning the skills necessary in an Old Order Amish community. There was one particular scene where Rose was skipping through a field on a cool spring day, her arms stretched out to her sides like she was flying. Cool blades

BETH WISEMAN

of grass tickled her toes, and wispy wildflowers brushed her shins as she sang.

Running over. Running over. My cup is full and running over. Since the Lord saved me, I'm as happy as can be. My cup is full and running over.

It was a song they sang during Sunday singings, usually followed by a game of volleyball. Aaron pictured Leah as the one skipping and singing in the meadow, and it was a delightful picture in his head.

But what held Aaron's attention the most was the budding romance between Rose and a boy in her Amish community—Jesse. Aaron cringed and wondered what his friends would think if they knew he was reading a romance book. He'd sure never tell them about it. But in the story, Rose wanted Jesse to accept her for the free-spirited girl that she was, and Aaron couldn't help but speculate that this was the kind of mate Leah was looking for too.

Aaron was certainly intrigued by Leah, but his reservations ran deep about whether he could make a home with someone like her. When he watched Abner and Edna together, there was no doubt that Edna would make a fine wife. Several times she'd brought casseroles or snacks to complement the meal his mother prepared for them all, and everything Edna brought was delicious. She often commented about the clothes she'd sewn for her family. She also talked about what a fine cook her youngest sister, Kathleen, was, and how Mary Carol grew amazing vegetables in their garden. But when it came to Leah, she would take a deep breath. "Leah will find her way," she'd once said.

Aaron got comfortable atop the sheets and hoped for a breeze to blow through the open window in his room. The heat was stifling, but he knew sleep would come. Normally he didn't need to set the battery-operated alarm clock on his bedside table, since his body was programmed to wake up at four o'clock, but on this night he did.

~~⁄⁄⁄~~

Leah made it a point to be downstairs before her father. She helped Mary Carol, Kathleen, and her mother prepare dippy eggs, bacon, scrapple, and biscuits.

"Where's Edna?" Mary Carol asked as she stirred the eggs.

Leah yawned. "She was still sleeping when I got dressed."

Edna was always up early and helped with breakfast.

"She was coughing a lot during the night again," Leah said. She poured herself a glass of orange juice. "Can't the natural doctor give her something that helps her more?"

Mamm walked away from the skillet of sizzling bacon, pulled six forks from the drawer, and walked toward the table. "Maybe she needs to go for another visit with him and see about that."

Leah picked up a fork to flip the bacon as her mother placed the other forks on the table.

"I can finish that, Leah. Why don't you get the butter and jellies from the refrigerator?"

Leah sighed. Maybe if everyone would let her cook occasionally, she'd get better at it. But she was too tired to argue. She set the fork down on a paper towel on the counter, then moved toward the refrigerator.

As she placed a jar of rhubarb jelly on the table, she heard footsteps coming down the stairs.

"*Guder mariye*," *Daed* said. He entered the kitchen, kissed their mother on the cheek, and sat down at the head of the kitchen table.

"And good morning to you," Marian said. The girls all echoed the sentiment.

Leah wanted her father to be proud of her, the way he was of her sisters. "Kathleen, I'll be going with Aaron to the singing at the

Grabers' house this Sunday," she said as she set the butter on the table. "I was hoping you could show me how to make that Lazy Daisy Oatmeal Cake you make. I'd like to bring that." She glanced in her father's direction, pleased to see his eyes shining with approval.

"Uh, are you sure?" Kathleen asked. She pulled the biscuits from the oven and put them on the table. "I reckon that cake is a lot of work. Maybe you could take a lemon sponge pie instead?"

"Kathleen, I'm sure your sister can make the oatmeal cake," their father said. "You give her a hand." He reached for a biscuit, and it warmed Leah's heart when he smiled in her direction.

"*Ya, Daed*," Kathleen said.

Her mother sat down in a chair at the other end of the table from their father. "Did—did you and Aaron get along well?"

Leah waited until Kathleen and Mary Carol were seated on the bench across from her before she answered. "He seems nice." She let her eyes veer in her father's direction.

He nodded his approval.

They all bowed their heads to pray, but *Daed* spoke up only a second or two into the blessing. "Where is Edna?"

"Sleeping," Leah answered. *But I'm here, on time, and I helped.*

Daed smoothed his beard with his hand. "Leah, go and check on your sister before we continue with the blessing. She is never late to breakfast."

Leah stood up from the table. "*Ya, Daed.*" *No one says anything bad about Edna being late for a meal.* She grabbed one of the lit lanterns on the kitchen hutch and marched up the stairs, thinking how she could have used an extra hour of sleep.

Their bedroom was the last one on the right, at the end of the hall. "Edna, get up!" she said before she pushed the door wide. "Breakfast is ready, and everyone is already . . ."

Leah froze for a moment. Her bare feet seemed rooted to the wooden slats on the floor as she looked at her sister lying in the bed.

"Edna?" Her eyes filled with tears as she slowly moved toward her sister in the bed. "Edna!"

She grabbed Edna's shoulders and shook her. "Edna! Wake up!" Edna's mouth was slightly parted, and her face was the color of ripe blueberries.

She's not breathing. Please, God, dear God in heaven. Help.

"*Mamm! Daed! Mamm! Daed!*"

There was a stampede of steps up the stairs. Her father was the first one to enter the room. "Mary Carol, go to the barn and call 9-1-1!"

Daed's mouth was quickly on top of Edna's, forcing air into her lungs, after he tilted her head back and pinched her nose. His hands were trembling, but he kept the breaths steady. Thank goodness her father had training in CPR when he was a volunteer at the local fire department years ago. Leah thanked God that he apparently still remembered his training.

Mary Carol jetted from the room to do as their father instructed. Kathleen was starting to cry, and Leah reached for her hand and squeezed it in hers. *Mamm*'s face was as white as the cotton sheet beneath Edna, and Leah didn't think her mother was breathing either. Her fingers were clamped tightly against her lips, and her eyes were wide and fearful.

Dear God, save her. Dear God, save her. Leah prayed like she'd never prayed before. *I promise not to be jealous of Edna ever again. Please, God, save her.*

"*Daed!*" Leah yelled. "Make her breathe!" Tears rolled down her cheeks as she watched her father trying to pump life into Edna. "*Daed!*" she yelled again.

I love you, Edna. I love you, Edna. Please wake up. God, wake her up.

Chapter Four

SIRENS SHRIEKED IN THE DISTANCE, INTENSIFYING THE fear in the room as their father continued his efforts to breathe life into Edna. But when Edna began to flail her arms about, their father backed away. Edna began to gasp for air, as if there were a shortage in the room. With each deep inhalation, a tiny bit of color came back to her face.

They'd all subconsciously moved closer to the bed, and *Daed* told them to step back. "Give her some room," he said, holding his hands outward.

Leah had seen her father angry, even frightened, but nothing like this. Even in the midst of a crisis, he always showed a level of calm. She recalled a fire in the kitchen a few years ago when a lantern got knocked over at suppertime and ignited a small rug by the sink. The fire had spread quickly and scared them all, but their father stayed reasonably calm as the old kitchen floor splintered and glowed. He hadn't hesitated but quickly retrieved the fire extinguisher and put out the fire.

They'd all had accidents as kids, and once their mother even fell down the porch steps carrying a casserole dish. She busted her knee up good, and Lydia had watched her father run from the fields when he was called. But again, he'd handled the situation calmly. But *Daed* looked anything but calm now, and Leah knew that Edna had been dead. Somehow she just knew. And their father had brought her back to life. Their father—and God. *Thank You, dear Lord.*

Sweat trickled from *Daed*'s wrinkled brow and poured over eyes that were wild with a mixture of terror and relief. The sirens grew louder, and Edna continued to cough and gasp, but she was breathing. Leah let the tears flow full force. *If anything had happened to Edna . . .*

Mamm clutched Edna's hand and seemed to take over where their father couldn't. "Edna, dear. Breathe slowly. Help is on the way."

Edna's eyes sought relief from their mother, but she continued to inhale and exhale, each breath crackling into the room with effort. Leah heard footsteps bolting up the steps, and within seconds two men dressed in navy blue entered the room. They brought in machines and gadgets Leah had never seen before, and they instructed everyone to move away from the bed. The first thing they did was put some sort of mask over Edna's face, and her breath clouded the clear plastic in shallow bursts.

The men didn't say much as they worked on Edna, but after about fifteen minutes they said that they were going to take her to the hospital in the ambulance, and that there was only room for one parent to ride along. All eyes were on their father, but it was *Mamm* who stepped forward.

"I am going," she said, standing taller. Then she reached for Edna's hand and squeezed it tightly within hers. Leah wanted to go so badly she could hardly stand it, but she could see that her father wanted to go equally as much, and they'd said there was only room for one anyway.

"I am going also." *Daed* stood taller and spoke with an authority that challenged the men in uniform. "She is my—my daughter." His voice broke as he spoke.

The two men in blue glanced at each other. Leah thought they could almost be twins, brothers at the least—both short and stocky with thick crops of unruly dark hair. And the shape of their eyes, more round then oval, was similar.

"I guess we can make room," one of the men said.

Leah recalled her trip to the movies with Clare and Donna a few months ago. Her father would have been furious, but she suspected her mother must have known she was indulging in the freedoms of her *rumschpringe* when she saw Leah leave in Clare's car that day. In the movie, there had been a scene where an ambulance picked up a sick girl, and the girl died on the way to the hospital. Leah closed her eyes and squelched the thought.

The men popped up a sort of portable bed right next to Edna's bed, and *Daed* helped them get Edna onto it and down the stairs. Once they reached the first floor, things happened quickly.

"We'll get word to you soon!" *Mamm* yelled as she and *Daed* followed Edna and the men across the yard. Her parents crawled into the back of the ambulance with one of the men, and the door slammed shut. The other man in blue scooted into the front seat. For what seemed like an eternity, the ambulance didn't move. Leah could feel her heart pounding in her chest.

After a while, the ambulance eased down the driveway and onto the main road. Thin beams of sunlight speared through gray skies as dawn approached, but thunderous rumblings from far away lent confusion as to what type of weather the day would bring.

The men didn't turn the sirens on. No swirly, colorful lights either. Leah presumed this to be a good thing. No sense of emergency.

"Edna will be all right, no?" Kathleen turned toward Leah. She blinked back tears and her lip trembled.

Leah reached for Kathleen's hand. "*Ya*. She was breathing on her own."

"But it sounded terrible, like she was choking, and her face was so blue," Mary Carol said, sniffling. "I've never seen anything like that."

Leah knew it was her job to reassure her younger sisters. "But her color started to return, and she was breathing. If it were that bad, they would have turned on the sirens."

Then Leah recalled why they didn't turn on the sirens in the movie.

The girl was dead.

Aaron picked at his eggs and stifled a yawn.

"Aaron, I got up at midnight to go to the bathroom, and I could see a light shining from beneath your door," Annie said. "What in the world were you doin' up at such an hour?"

He was too tired to deal with his sister this morning. She had a way of talking to him that he classified as clucking. Her tongue met with the roof of her mouth in an annoying manner.

"Reading." It was true, although he sure didn't want to elaborate—that he was reading to impress a girl.

"At that hour?" Mary chimed in. "What were you reading?"

"Nothing that would interest you," Aaron said, hoping to halt the inquisition. He stuffed a piece of biscuit in his mouth.

Annie and Mary shuffled around the kitchen with his mother while Aaron, his father, and his youngest sister, Mae, waited for breakfast to be served. Five-year-old Mae had already placed jams, jellies, and butter on the table, which was her only job for breakfast. Aaron suspected Mae had been a surprise, even though his parents denied it. But Abner was twenty, Aaron was nineteen, Annie, seventeen, and Mary, fifteen.

Aaron yawned. This time he didn't try to hide it. It just took too much effort. He reached for the bowl of applesauce to his right and scooped a generous helping onto a buttered biscuit. Then he piled eggs on top and took a big bite, thinking there was no better combination in the world than applesauce, egg, and buttered biscuit. Now if he could just have a cup of coffee, he might make it through the day. But his mother didn't believe in coffee. "We shouldn't need stimulants to get us through the day," she'd say.

Ridiculous. Other families in their district certainly enjoyed coffee. He'd asked his father about it once, and his father quickly said, "It was the only rule your mother said she wanted to enforce when we got married, and I choose to abide by it." Then *Daed* had smiled. "Coulda been a lot worse things to give up."

Aaron knew his father liked to sip wine in the barn from time to time and even enjoy a cigar occasionally. But on this morning, nothing sounded better to Aaron than a steaming cup of freshly brewed coffee. A mocha latte would certainly work. He'd had plenty of those in town. Maybe he could convince his father to stop at the bakery on the way to the furniture store this morning.

After two more buttered biscuits with egg and applesauce, Aaron excused himself to milk the cows. As he strolled out to the barn, he couldn't stop thinking about Leah and her story. He was anxious to see how the tale ended, but didn't see how he was going to stay up another night reading. Then he thought about having Leah by his side at the Sunday singing, and just the thought gave him a burst of energy comparable to that from any cup of coffee.

✑

Leah, Mary Carol, and Kathleen tried to stay busy all morning, but when the storm finally rolled in midmorning with lightning that lit up the skies and thunder that shook the china cabinet, a sense of dread further settled over the girls.

"It's so dark outside," Kathleen said. She lit another lantern and took a seat at the kitchen table. Mary Carol was seated and chopping cucumbers into tiny cubes.

"What's that for?" Leah slid in beside Mary Carol and studied the cucumbers.

"A new recipe Kathleen is trying," her sister said, not looking up. Then she slammed the knife down on the table. "Why haven't we heard anything?"

"I don't know." Leah figured her parents would have sent word by now. She glanced at the clock on the wall. Ten thirty. "Everything must be okay, or *Mamm* and *Daed* would have sent someone to pick us up."

Kathleen twirled the string on her *kapp* with her finger, then jumped when another flash of light lit the room, followed by a clap of thunder that Leah could feel in her chest.

"Look! Lights!" Mary Carol jumped from the table and walked toward the kitchen door.

Leah and Kathleen followed her onto the porch where they were misted with cool rain blowing up under the rafters. Leah put her hand to her forehead and watched the car coming up the driveway. Another bolt of lightning caused them all to jump, but they stayed on the front porch and waited.

"I don't recognize the car," Kathleen said. "Do either of you?"

Mary Carol shook her head. Leah strained to see past the headlights glaring onto the porch. "It's one of those big truck-like things with a backseat."

"It's a Cadillac Escalade Hybrid," Kathleen finally said, relief in her voice. Not because she knew who was in the vehicle, but because she'd identified it.

Kathleen had a strange fixation with automobile makes and models. She even had a *Car and Driver* magazine hidden in her room. "Front engine, rear-wheel drive, and it will hold eight people. Zero to sixty miles per hour in 8.4 seconds."

Leah glared at her sister in disbelief. "Who cares!" she snapped. "It's not like you're ever going to have one."

Kathleen's lip turned under, and Leah shook her head and sighed. She was about to apologize, but then the car eased all the way into the driveway and cut the lights.

All three of them moved a little closer to the edge of the porch, peering through the downpour to see who it was. Hopefully, it was their parents with Edna. But Leah knew right away that it wasn't anyone from her family when she saw the brightly flowered umbrella pop from the open car door and a high-heeled brown boot step into the mud below.

Chapter Five

LEAH LOOKED AT HER SISTERS. "DO YOU KNOW WHO THAT is?"

A plump woman trekked up the driveway on her tiptoes, balancing a bag on one hip and holding her umbrella with the other hand. *Daed* had recently added gravel to the dirt driveway, but it was still a sludgy mess from all the rain this morning, and the woman's fancy boots were sinking with each step she took.

"I've never seen her before." Kathleen arched her brows, then whispered, "She's rather old. She can barely walk in them shoes."

"I don't know her either," Mary Carol said. "Maybe she has word about Edna."

The woman stumbled toward them with a wide grin stretched across a wrinkled face painted with bright colors. Her eyelids were covered in dark blue, and her lashes were long and black. A rosy streak ran high along each cheekbone, and her lips were the color of cherries. Puffy gray hair topped her head in a loose twist.

Leah took in the women's floral print dress, which hung below her knees and didn't seem to go with her boots. She looked like a walking bouquet of mixed flowers from Mary Carol's garden, planted in those dark brown boots. And as the rain blew under her umbrella and slapped across her face, she merely licked those red lips and kept trudging. Leah bit her lip to keep from giggling. *Who is this Englisch woman?*

"Hello, hello!" she yelled as she neared the porch. The woman's presence was a light amid the gray skies and pouring rain. "Your sister is fine!" The stranger seemed as delighted by the news as Leah,

Kathleen, and Mary Carol, who turned to each other for a quick hug.

"Thank the Lord," Leah whispered. Then she pulled away and returned her attention to the woman coming slowly up the slippery porch steps. Leah took the bag from her hand, gave it to Kathleen, and gripped the woman's elbow to help her up the steps.

"Come into the *haus*. It's awful weather out here." Leah motioned toward the open screen door that led into the kitchen.

The woman placed her umbrella on the porch, then dripped her way into the kitchen. Mary Carol and Kathleen followed.

"Sit down. Tell us about Edna. Can I get you a cup of hot tea or *kaffi*?" Mary Carol moved toward the kitchen counter.

The woman raised her bottom lip and blew upward to clear a strand of wayward hair. Then she pointed to her feet. "I knew these boots were the right choice for today. I got these at a little shop by my house last year." She smiled at Leah, then at Kathleen. "They're sharp, aren't they?"

Kathleen's mouth hung open, but she nodded her head.

"*Ya*, they are," Leah said. "Edna is all right?"

"*Ach, ya*. Your sister is gonna be just fine. Asthma. That's what she's got. Your folks will be bringing her home this afternoon." The woman dabbed at droplets on her bright cheeks with a white handkerchief. "The Lord whispered in my ear that the weather was gonna be terrible. I listen when the Lord speaks. Do you?"

Leah nodded, but she knew her expression must be a mirror of Kathleen's—dumbfounded. "Do you speak the *Deitsch*?" Leah asked cautiously.

"Oh, sure." The woman waved her hand dismissively at Leah, then slid onto one of the wooden benches at the table.

Kathleen narrowed her gaze. "How could you know how to speak Pennsylvania *Deitsch*?"

Leah didn't care how she knew. She was just glad that Edna was coming home, and she found this stranger delightful.

The woman's eyes matched the shadow on her lids, and they grew wide as she spoke. "Why, it's not that much different from German."

Kathleen sat down across from the woman on the other bench. "You know German?"

Following a sigh, the woman said, "And French, and Italian, and Spanish, and . . ."

Leah was still standing as she listened to her rattle off several more. *Who are you?*

"I'm Leah," she said when the woman finished.

"Nice to meet you, Leah." She smiled with a warmth that Leah found contagious.

Kathleen was still scowling suspiciously. "I'm Kathleen. How do you know—"

"Oh! Kathleen is the name of my neighbor. Kathleen Fontenot. She's French." She paused and glanced at Mary Carol. "Honey, did you offer me a beverage earlier?"

"Yes, ma'am." Mary Carol stepped forward a bit. "What would you like, some tea or *kaffi*? Or we have lemonade or milk. And, um . . . I'm Mary Carol. And—and what is your name?"

The woman popped herself in the forehead with her hand. "My manners! I'm Ruth Ann Lantz. But you girls just call me Auntie Ruth. Everyone does." She smiled again, revealing a perfect set of white teeth.

Leah didn't think they could possibly be real. She glanced at Kathleen. Her sister's expression was still one of caution, but a smile tipped the corners of her mouth. Mary Carol stood by the counter and waited to see what Auntie Ruth wanted to drink.

"Um . . . something to drink?" Mary Carol offered again.

Auntie Ruth twisted her mouth from side to side. Then she looked hard at Mary Carol. "A nip of brandy would be nice."

The girls all looked at each other. Leah took the lead. "I—I don't believe we have any brandy."

The woman sat taller. "Sure you do. Look in that bag. I brought my own. Oh, and I brought a meat loaf, cooked celery, and a chocolate shoofly pie." She pointed to the bag. "It's all in there. My niece sent it when she heard her future daughter-in-law was in the hospital. All except for the brandy. I added that myself."

"Abner's *mamm*?" Leah was having trouble connecting this woman to Sarah Lantz.

"Well, not just Abner's. There's Aaron, Mary, Annie, and little Mae too. But yes, I'm Sarah's aunt, on her father's side."

Leah nodded toward Mary Carol to pour Auntie Ruth a glass of brandy, although she'd never heard of anyone partaking in such a thing at this time of day. *So this is Aaron's great-aunt?* Then Leah remembered. She'd heard about this woman from others in the community. The odd aunt who visited the Lantz family twice a year. She'd left the Old Order before being baptized, and she always stayed with Sarah and her family when she visited.

"Please thank Sarah for us, for sending the food. That was very thoughtful." Leah watched Mary Carol set the glass down in front of Auntie Ruth. She was glad that her sister only poured a small amount into the glass, since Ruth was driving. Ruth gulped it down in one swig. Then burped.

"Goodness me!" She chuckled, then said, "Well, they weren't sure early this morning just how long Edna would be in the hospital, and Sarah wanted to help."

Kathleen looked somewhat disturbed by Auntie Ruth, and Mary Carol just looked confused. Leah thought the woman was a welcome relief from the fear that had gripped them earlier in the day.

"So can you tell us more about Edna?" Leah took a seat in her father's chair at the head of the table. Mary Carol slid in beside Kathleen.

"Evidently she had an asthma attack. A bad enough one that it caused her to stop breathing." Ruth puckered her lips and nodded her head. "Your pop saved her life, I heard them say."

Thank You, Lord. "We appreciate you bringing this food to us in this miserable weather." Leah rested her elbows on the table, then cupped her cheeks with her hands. "Where do you live? Are you just visiting your relatives for a while?"

"Honey, do you think we could eat now? I get the cramps when I don't eat by eleven. The doctor says it's a gastric problem." She arched her eyes at Leah, as if she hadn't heard a thing she'd said.

"I'll get you something," Kathleen said. She rose from the table, but not before cutting her eyes in Leah's direction and making a funny face.

"I live in Florida," Ruth finally said. "I come up here a couple of times a year, and Sarah and her family visit me once a year as well."

Leah knew several families in their community who vacationed in Florida, but she'd never actually met anyone who lived there.

"Were you, um . . ." Mary Carol hesitated. "Shunned?"

"If I was, can I still eat here with you?"

None of them knew what to say. Of course they weren't going to ask her to leave.

Ruth burst out laughing. "Gotcha, didn't I?" Then she quickly turned serious. "No, my dears. I wasn't shunned. I chose to leave before my baptism, that's all."

"How long have you been visiting your kin?" Kathleen asked.

Ruth yawned. "Just got here this morning. Drove all the way by myself. When I got to Sarah's, they'd just received the news of your sister." She shook her head. "Abner was most distraught. I drove the boy straight to the hospital and waited with him until we knew Edna was out of harm's way."

Kathleen placed a plate in front of Ruth, filled with meat loaf and creamed celery from Sarah and some homemade bread Kathleen had made the day before.

"*Danki, danki.*" Ruth dived in.

All the girls looked back and forth at each other.

"How long will you be staying?" Leah stood up, retrieved a napkin from the counter, and pushed it across the table to Ruth, in case Ruth wanted to wipe the creamed celery from below her bottom lip. Evidently she did not.

Ruth chewed a bite of meat loaf, and Leah tapped her finger to her chin. "You have a, uh . . . bit of . . ."

"Oh my." Ruth swiped at the splotch of celery. "*Danki*, dear."

"Ruth, I was wondering . . . ," Kathleen began.

"Auntie Ruth, dear." Ruth smiled warmly in Kathleen's direction, then kept eating.

Kathleen grinned. "Is it true that your Cadillac can hit zero to sixty miles per hour in 8.4 seconds?"

Mary Carol rolled her eyes. "Kathleen, why does it matter? I don't understand your need to know these things."

"Honey," Ruth said, "I can hit seventy miles per hour in seven seconds on the open road."

At the way her sister's face lit up, Leah knew that Ruth had won Kathleen over.

"Oh, sure." Ruth sat up a little taller. "Now, I best be getting back to Sarah and the girls. Aaron went on to the furniture store with their father, but Abner chose to stay at the hospital. He was sure shook up about your sister. I'm glad she's going to be all right." She stood from the table and pushed the bench back with her leg.

Leah suddenly remembered her concerns about giving Aaron her story. "Ruth—I mean, Auntie Ruth, do you think you could drop me by the furniture store on your way? I'd take the buggy, but I'm not sure about this weather." It wasn't raining anymore, but the sky was still gray and threatening.

"Of course, dear." Ruth scuttled across the kitchen floor and reached for her umbrella.

Kathleen stood up and folded her arms across her chest. "Why do you need to go to the furniture store and get to ride in the car?"

"I have some business to take care of." Leah didn't owe Kathleen an explanation. "But I'll be home soon. Probably before *Mamm* and *Daed* get home with Edna."

Kathleen got in step beside Ruth. "You never did say how long you were staying. Maybe sometime I could ride in your car?"

Ruth pushed the screen door open and walked onto the porch, and the girls followed. Ruth's expression grew serious. "I don't know how long I'll be staying. It just depends on—on how things are handled." Then she narrowed her eyes at the three of them. "Till the good Lord tells me it's time to go, I reckon."

"What?" Then Leah remembered the brandy. "*Ach*, do you want your brandy to take with you?"

Ruth shook her head. "No, you girls keep it."

Mary Carol giggled, but Ruth didn't seem to notice.

"What do you mean, you'll be here until things are handled?" Leah grabbed her shoes from the porch, sat down in the rocker, and laced them up.

"Oh, honey. It's a secret. I surely can't tell you." Ruth's eyes widened, then she turned away from them and headed down the porch steps.

"I'll be back soon," Leah said as she followed Ruth to the car.

And I bet I'll know what Auntie Ruth's secret is.

Chapter Six

LEAH HAD BEEN IN PLENTY OF AUTOMOBILES OVER THE years, but she'd never experienced anything quite like riding with Auntie Ruth. The woman knew one speed—fast. As they peeled onto the highway, Leah double-checked her seat belt as Ruth sped over a well-known speed bump, causing Leah to bounce in her seat.

"Oops," Ruth said, then chuckled. "Didn't see that coming. So tell me, Leah. Are you sweet on my nephew, Aaron?"

Leah quickly turned toward her. "What? No. No, we're just friends." *And barely even that.*

"He sure seems sweet on *you*," she said, batting her long lashes. "When I arrived this morning, I heard him mention your name several times. And later, in private, he told me you like to write."

Leah was surprised Aaron had shared that news with his aunt. "*Ya*, I do. I love to write stories about people turning their lives to God."

"What a glorious feeling it is to know that you are a child of the Lord." Ruth zipped around the corner, even squealing the tires. "This car can take the curves," she boasted. "I'll have to take Kathleen for a ride sometime. She seemed awfully interested in my car."

Leah rolled her eyes. "*Ya*. She loves cars, and none of us knows why."

Ruth's lips curled at the corners, but only a little. "Sometimes we just can't understand what makes a person tick, now can we?" Ruth looked at Leah as if she was the keeper of more than just her own secret.

"I suppose not." Leah stared straight ahead, very alert. "So, you said you don't know how long you'll be staying?" She couldn't imagine what this charming, odd woman might be keeping as a secret.

"Till it's time for me to go," she repeated, then sighed.

They arrived at Lantz Furniture much too soon for Leah, and there really hadn't been an opportunity to question Ruth about her secret. Ruth screeched to a halt in front of the store.

"*Danki* for bringing me," Leah said.

"You're welcome. It was very nice to meet you and your sisters. I'll let you tell Aaron and his father about Edna. I'm going to head back to the house to let Sarah and the girls know she is going to be all right."

"Very nice to meet you too. We will see you again, no?"

"I hope so." Ruth smiled. "Take care, my child of God. Keep writing your stories. You never know who you might touch someday."

Leah climbed out of the car, then hesitated before she shut the door. She wanted to tell Ruth how she felt this strange connection to her, how she wanted to get back in the car and spend the day with her, but she simply said, "Good-bye, Auntie Ruth."

༺⚬༻

Aaron carried the wooden rocker to the back of the store, tucked it in the corner, and hung a Sold sign on it. Ms. Simpson said she'd be back this afternoon to pick it up. His father would be glad the rocker sold, along with three others this morning. Seemed to be a popular style with the *Englisch*. There was nothing fancy about the oak chair, but it was larger than most, and Abner had constructed the seat in such a way that a person's fanny seemed to nestle right in.

Aaron wiped the sweat from his brow and raised the window in the back of the store to allow a cross breeze, wishing he'd done that earlier. Then he headed back up to the front in time to hear the bell on the door chime and see Leah walk in.

"How's Edna? Abner's at the hospital, but we haven't heard anything." Aaron stopped in front of Leah, thrilled that she was the one to deliver any news, but also concerned about Edna.

"She's gonna be fine. She has asthma. *Mamm* and *Daed* will be bringing her home later this afternoon." She smiled, but only a little, as if forcing herself.

"That must have been a real scare for your family."

"*Ya.*" Leah's expression confirmed that it was. She avoided his eyes, hung her head slightly. "She was an awful shade of blue, and—and she wasn't breathing."

Aaron stepped a little closer and leaned down a bit. "But she's all right now, no?"

Leah took a deep breath. "Thank the Lord."

"*Ya.*" Aaron glanced past her and out the glass window of the shop and noticed that the designated buggy area was vacant. "How'd you get here?"

Then a large smile swept across her face, and those tiny dimples came into view. Aaron smiled along with her. He couldn't help it. She looked awful pretty in her green dress, and her face was aglow about something.

"Auntie Ruth brought me."

His mouth dropped open. "*My* Auntie Ruth?" *Oh no.* Auntie Ruth was as fine a woman as had ever lived, but she was a tad—off. Aaron wondered what sort of conversation Leah had with his great-aunt.

Leah grinned. "I liked her very much. She wanted me to let you and your *daed* know that Edna would be all right."

Aaron was confused. Why would his aunt bring Leah here and drop her off, instead of just coming to tell him and his father herself? He opened his mouth but was unsure how to phrase the question.

"I asked her to give me a ride to come see you, so she dropped me off and asked me to tell you about Edna."

Aaron looped his thumbs in his suspenders and tipped his straw hat a bit. "Really? And why did you want to come see me?" Perhaps he'd made a fair impression last night after all.

"I—I just wanted . . . I wanted to make sure that you understood that we wouldn't be courting if we went to the Grabers' Sunday singing together." She shrugged. "You know, it'd be more like—like going as friends."

Aaron mentally pulled her foot from his gut. "Of course it's only as friends. I reckon it's a mite silly for you to think otherwise." He folded his arms across his chest and stood taller.

"No. I didn't think otherwise," she quickly said. "I just didn't want *you* to think it was anything more than a friendly ride together. You know how sometimes people tend to assume that a boy and girl are dating when they attend a singing together."

"If you're so worried about it, why did you ask to go with me?" He realized right away that his voice revealed more anger than he would have liked.

"Well, I—I thought we would talk about my story." She batted her eyes at him and smiled. "Have you read any of it?" Then her face grew still. No smile, only questioning eyes. She bit her lip and waited.

"Maybe."

"You did, didn't you?" She actually bounced in her black leather shoes, and the dimples were back.

He couldn't help but grin. "*Ya*, I did." He recalled the romance between Rose and Jesse. "Jesse just told Rose that he loves her." Aaron hated it when he blushed. That was something women did, yet he could feel his cheeks taking on an embarrassing shade of pink. But he felt a tad better when he saw Leah's cheeks matching his in color. She looked toward the ground.

"That's one of my favorite parts." Then she looked up and smiled. "What else? Do you like it? Am I a good storyteller? Are there any parts you didn't like? And what about—"

"*Ach!*" He pointed a finger in her direction. "We are supposed to talk about this when I'm done." *Plus, if I tell you now, you might back out of our Sunday date, which isn't a date.*

She twisted her mouth to one side. "Aaron?"

"Ya?"

"You won't let anything happen to my story, will you? It's the only copy I have, and I've worked hard on it."

He spoke with tenderness. "No, Leah. I won't let anything happen to it."

"And you like it so far?" Her eyes begged him to say yes.

"Ya. I do." *And I will finish it by Sunday so I can spend time with you.*

"Ach, gut!" She gave a little bounce again. "Then I will see you on Sunday."

Aaron nodded as she turned to leave. He was just about to get back to work when Leah spun around and faced him.

"Aaron?"

"Ya?" She walked back toward him, folded her hands across her chest, and pressed her lips together. "Did you know your Auntie Ruth has a secret?"

Aaron laughed out loud. "I reckon Auntie Ruth must have lots of secrets." He paused. "Why?"

Leah shrugged. "I don't know. She told my sisters and me that she has a secret. And that she'd be staying until things were handled. I just wondered what that meant."

Aaron scratched his forehead. "You can probably tell that Auntie Ruth is—is different. There ain't no tellin' what she might be talking about."

"She's very special. I can tell. I hope I get to see her again."

"She's special, all right." Aaron recalled the time Auntie Ruth told him where babies came from. At twelve, he was probably old enough to know, but it was the *way* she'd told him. *"Now, honey, here's how it works . . ."* Aaron cringed at the recollection. He was sure his parents would have doubled devotion time that entire year if they'd ever found out. But Auntie Ruth never meant any harm. She just had a funny way of doing things.

"How are you going to get home? It's a far piece if you plan to walk. But the weather is better, I reckon."

"*Ach*, I'm going to hold my thumb up and hitch a ride from the *Englisch*."

Aaron's eyes grew to the size of golf balls. "Leah! You can't do that. That's not safe for you—"

She doubled over, laughing, then looked back up at Aaron, dimples and all. "It was just a tease, Aaron. You're so serious. *Mei Englisch* friend Donna works at the bakery. She gets off work in about twenty minutes. I will *hitch* a ride with her. 'Bye now."

Leah waved and turned again to leave. Aaron shook his head. It was no wonder Leah took to Auntie Ruth so well. He suspected there was a tiny bit of Auntie Ruth in Leah.

☙

Donna pulled into the driveway and put the car in park. "Are you sure you don't want to meet me and Clare at the movies later? We can pick you up near the road, like we did last time."

"No. *Danki*, though." Leah looked at the large family buggy pulled up next to the spring buggies. "My parents are home from the hospital with my sister, and tonight would not be a *gut* night to get caught sneaking out."

"I'm glad everything is okay with Edna. And you'll be in your *rumschpringe* until you're married, so I feel sure we have *plenty* of time to go out another night."

Leah giggled at her friend's use of Pennsylvania *Deitsch*—and at her implication that Leah wouldn't be married for a long time. "You're still not saying it right," she teased. She opened the car door. "*Danki* again for the ride."

As she strolled up to the door, she looked into the sky at the sun set squarely between the house and the silo, amid skies that were still a bluish gray, and positioned in such a way that Leah knew she was late for supper. She bit her bottom lip and picked up the pace, not realizing so much time had gone by. But Donna had wanted to stop for a root beer before heading home, and then they'd talked for a while, and now she was late . . . again.

She cautiously opened the screen door that led into the kitchen, expecting to find everyone seated for supper. The smell of Kathleen's beef stew filled the kitchen, but no one was in sight. Leah tiptoed to the stove, lifted the lid, and dipped the spoon into the dark brown sauce, making sure to pick up a chunk of beef. She blew on it, then opened her mouth.

"Leah!" Her father's abrupt tone caused her to drop the spoon. She scurried to pick it up, scooping the lost load into her trembling hand.

"*Ya, Daed.* How's Edna? Is everyone upstairs? I'm sorry I'm late. I had to catch a ride in town."

Daed's face was as red as Auntie Ruth's lipstick. He walked toward her, his hand raised in such a way that she actually thought he might strike her. He pointed his finger in her face.

"Your sister spent the day in the hospital. You were not even here to welcome her home, to make sure she's all right." He stood rigid, his eyes ablaze. "It is bad enough that you continue to test my will by being late to the meals and do not partake in your share of the chores around this *haus*." He pulled off his straw hat, raked a hand through his hair, and sighed. "There will be no more story writing. No more sneaking out for movies and fun times with your *Englisch* friends."

Leah's eyes widened. Who had told him?

"Your *mamm* and me are not *dumm*. Do you not think we know that you are sneaking out some nights? We have always looked the other way during our daughters' *rumschpringes*. But no more." He stomped his foot. "Edna will have to stay in bed for a while, and then she will be on a light chore schedule. You will do her sewing and mending. You will help Mary Carol with the garden. You will learn to cook from Kathleen. These things you will do to become a proper Amish woman."

"*Ya, Daed.*" Leah hung her head, and a tear ran down her cheek. She hated being such a disappointment to him, but she wasn't good at all these things he spoke of. *And no more writing?*

Her father drew in a deep breath and blew it out slowly. "*Mei maedel,* you are eighteen years old. A grown woman of marrying age. Do you want to live with your *mamm* and me forever?" He shook his head, then looked at Leah's tearstained face. "You are punished to the *haus* until I say otherwise."

"But for how long?" She stared into his cold eyes.

"Until I see fit." He pointed to the stairs. "Best go check on your sister. And dry your tears. Edna has had a hard day today."

Leah didn't say anything as she brushed past him. Then she turned slowly around. "*Daed?*"

He widened his eyes but didn't say anything.

"What about the Sunday singing that Aaron Lantz invited me to this weekend?"

"I will get word to Aaron that you will not be able to attend."

"But—"

"Leah!"

She turned and ran up the stairs, and despite her father's instructions, the tears fell full force.

Chapter Seven

MARIAN SCOOTED NEXT TO HER HUSBAND IN THE BED. She snuggled up close to him and laid her head on his shoulder. He wrapped an arm around her but kept reading his book—a book about raising daughters. Marian smiled.

"You do know that book is written by an *Englisch* man, no?"

James pulled his gold-rimmed reading glasses off and closed the book. "*Englisch* or Amish, I am finding that these daughters can be difficult to rear, no matter what. This man's words calm me. Makes me feel like I am not alone with our troubles."

"James, dear. We have four beautiful daughters, all in their *rumschpringes*. What did you expect when they reached this age? Do you not remember when I was in my running-around period?" She winked playfully at him. "Things will be challenging. But they are all *gut* girls." Then she nudged him with her shoulder. "Even Leah."

Her husband grunted. "I love all *mei* daughters. I just want Leah to do as she should."

"James, you cannot make Leah into someone she is not. As I've told you before, Leah will find her way."

He turned to face her and lifted his brows. "When?"

Marian chuckled. "Well, I don't know exactly when, but she will."

James settled himself atop the covers and pulled her close.

"Don't you think that maybe you were a bit hard on Leah? Punishing her to the *haus*—indefinitely."

"Maybe if she is here more, and not writing those silly stories and running with her *Englisch* friends, she will learn to do the things a *gut* Amish woman should. I am doing Leah a favor."

Marian cuddled closer to her husband. "It's such a shame that she won't be able to go with Aaron Lantz to the singing on Sunday." She paused. "He seems like such a nice boy."

"I'm not bending my rules." Her husband sat up taller in the bed.

Marian tenderly ran her finger down his arm. "Are you sure?"

James finally grinned. "I know what you are doing, my love. And it won't work." But he wrapped her in his arms just the same.

᪐

Later that evening, Leah sat down on the edge of Edna's bed and clutched her sister's hand. "I was so scared, Edna. I'm sorry I wasn't here when you got home."

"Leah," Edna said tenderly. "I told you when you brought me supper earlier, I have no worries about that." She paused. "How did *Daed* act during supper?"

"He didn't say much to me. He did ask me to hem his new pair of breeches."

"That's an easy task." Edna propped herself taller against her pillow and reached for the inhaler the doctor had given her.

"Does that help?"

"*Ya*, it does." Edna put the inhaler to her mouth and breathed in the medication, then said, "There's no need for all this fuss over me. I feel well enough to resume my chores tomorrow."

"Edna! You just got out of the hospital. At least give it a few days. I can handle your sewing and other chores." Leah released her sister's hand, then lowered the flame on the lantern that sat between them on the nightstand. She climbed into her own bed. "*Daed* said I'm not allowed to write my stories anymore."

Edna sighed. "I know you enjoy doing that, Leah, but is it really necessary?"

"To me it is." She kicked her quilt to the foot of the bed. "And I won't be able to go to the singing with Aaron on Sunday."

Edna twisted to face her. "*Ya*, Abner told me that the two of you were supposed to go together, and I must ask, why? You never seemed interested in Aaron."

Leah shrugged. "He's okay. I'm just not in the market for courting. I know you and Mary Carol are ready to get married, but I'm not yet."

Edna's face brightened. "It's a wonderful feeling to be in love, Leah. You'll see someday."

Leah thought for a moment. "I write about finding the Lord in my books, but I also write about finding love."

"Maybe when you fall in love, your writing will be even better." Edna smiled, then took another whiff from the inhaler. "I'm tired, Leah." She eased herself down in the bed. "But it won't bother me if you want to leave the lantern on and write."

"Actually, I'm tired too." Leah turned the knob on the lantern until the flame was extinguished, then lay down. Thankfully, there was a bit of a breeze blowing through the window screen, but it was still dreadfully hot.

"Leah."

"*Ya?*"

"Maybe if you are on best behavior for the next few days, *Daed* will rethink his decision and let you go to the singing."

"Do you think?"

"If you work really hard to please him, he might. For starters, don't be late for meals."

"How can I be late if I'm not allowed to go anywhere?"

Edna chuckled. "True. Good night, Leah."

"Good night."

Leah lay there for a few minutes, and despite how tired she felt, her thoughts were all over the place. "Edna, are you asleep?"

"Almost."

"Did you meet Abner and Aaron's Auntie Ruth?" Leah smiled as she recalled the high-speed car ride earlier in the afternoon.

Edna giggled. "*Ya*. I guess you met her too. I heard her say that she was going to go report to my sisters that I was doing fine. Isn't she a funny *Englisch* woman?"

"She seemed a bit odd, but I liked her." Leah recalled the way Auntie Ruth told her that perhaps her stories would touch someone someday. She couldn't imagine who at this point. She'd hoped that maybe Clare or Donna might be inspired by her stories to put more faith in God and His will, but she wasn't sure when she would even see her *Englisch* friends again. Surely her father would ease up on her.

They were quiet for a few minutes, then Edna started to cough badly. Leah bolted up in the bed. "Edna, are you okay?"

"Leah, I'm fine," she said in a hacking voice. "I just have to keep using this inhaler. I have an infection, and it worsened this asthma that I didn't even know I had."

Edna coughed, inhaled from the tube, and coughed some more. Leah recalled Edna's bluish color this morning. She closed her eyes. She felt like she couldn't pray enough for Edna, so she offered up yet another prayer for her sister before she dozed off.

⁓

The next morning, Leah made sure she got up extra early. Everyone seemed shocked, and almost afraid, when they walked into the kitchen to find Leah finishing breakfast. Nothing fancy. Scrambled eggs, sausage, and toast.

"*Ach*, I can take over from here," Kathleen said as she joined Leah by the stove and reached for the spatula.

Leah jerked it away. "It's almost ready. The sausage is keeping warm in the oven, and I'm almost done with these eggs."

"What's that smell?" Mary Carol entered the kitchen, pinching her nose.

Leah put one hand on her hip and stirred the eggs with the other. "I burned the toast, but only a little."

"It's black!" Mary Carol eyed the plate of toast on the kitchen table. "I'm not eating that."

"You will all eat what your sister cooked." *Daed* walked into the kitchen carrying a copy of the *Die Botschaft* tucked under his arm. He put the newspaper on the counter and sat down at the head of the table. "Your *mamm* is upstairs with Edna, and she said to begin without her. She will eat upstairs with Edna in a while."

Leah poured the eggs into a bowl, unsure why they looked different from usual. Then she took the bowl of eggs and the plate of sausage and placed both on the table. She took a seat beside Mary Carol and across from Kathleen.

"Let us pray," their father said. They all bowed their heads.

Since no one seemed particularly hungry this morning, Leah went first and spooned eggs onto her plate, snatched a piece of sausage, and helped herself to a piece of toast.

"Where're the jams and jellies?" Mary Carol scanned the table. "We're gonna need them," she added under her breath. She slowly reached for a piece of toast.

Leah cut her eyes at Mary Carol. "I'll get them." She rose from the table and returned with a jar of rhubarb jam and a jar of apple butter. Once she was seated again, she took a bite of the eggs. They weren't so bad. An odd texture, maybe.

She glanced around the table at the others.

"How long did you cook these eggs, Leah?" Mary Carol's mouth twisted with displeasure.

"The eggs are fine," *Daed* said with authority. He glanced at Leah with a slight smile.

That was all she needed from him. It was a start, and she was tired of being such a disappointment to him.

"May I be excused? I want to get started on Edna's sewing chores." Leah didn't think she could finish the meal. Her sisters would have to figure out their own way to avoid eating her cooking. *Maybe I'll be better at sewing.*

Daed nodded.

Leah left the kitchen, walked through the den, and headed up the stairs. She met her mother midway. "How's Edna?"

"She seems better this morning." Her mother paused. "What's that smell?"

Leah sighed. "I fixed breakfast."

Her mother's eyes widened. "*Ach*. That's nice, dear."

"I'm going to go hem *Daed*'s breeches. Maybe I'll be better at that." She scooted past her mother.

"Leah?"

She spun around and saw her mother coming back up the stairs. "*Ya?*"

"Keep making a *gut* effort, and I will try to convince your father to let you go to the singing on Sunday."

Leah smiled. "*Danki, Mamm.*" She knew she'd be more than ready to get out of the house by Sunday. And she was very eager to hear what Aaron thought about the rest of her story.

She headed upstairs to start on the sewing chores. First she'd hem her father's pants, then see what else was in the pile. She would plan on cooking for the next couple of days too. Surely that would win her some points.

Or maybe not.

Chapter Eight

JAMES EYED THE MENU AT PARADISO. HE DIDN'T TAKE Marian out to eat often, but a Saturday night in town, eating some fine Italian food, was just what he and Marian needed. Leah had insisted on cooking the meals all day on Friday, and he'd suffered through breakfast and lunch today. At Paradiso the food was always good.

"What's the occasion?" Marian grinned as she spread her napkin on her lap and picked up her menu.

"I reckon you know exactly what the occasion is."

"Yet you left Edna, Mary Carol, and Kathleen to fend for themselves, no?"

James decided on lasagna and closed his menu. "Kathleen made a batch of corn chowder while Leah was helping Mary Carol in the garden. She stashed it in the back of the refrigerator, in case Leah's meat loaf was not *gut*." He paused, tilted his head to one side. "How can you mess up meat loaf, though?"

"She's trying so *hatt* to please you, James. And I think her ham loaf last night would have been all right if she hadn't gotten her teaspoons and tablespoons mixed up." Marian sighed. "I failed with Leah, I reckon. I've tried to teach her everything she needs to know about being a *gut* Amish *fraa*, but I must have done something wrong."

"You didn't fail, Marian. Leah has never been interested in cooking, sewing, gardening, or cleaning. And now, at eighteen, she's trying to master these skills?" He shook his head. "She is only doing this so that I might change my mind and let her go to the singing."

Marian pressed her lips together, raised her chin, and opened her eyes wide. It was the look she wore when she was about to confront him about something. "Maybe you should let her go, James."

He knew she was right. A boy was interested in Leah, and he certainly didn't want to hinder progress. "I don't know . . ."

"I know the girls in the Lantz family. They have all been around Leah enough to know that she does not excel at certain things. I'm sure they've told Aaron that, and if he is still interested in her— perhaps you should reconsider her punishment, even if just for one night."

James nodded at the approaching waitress, then waited for Marian to order before he ordered his lasagna. Maybe Leah just needed the right boy to motivate her to learn the skills necessary to become a good wife. "I reckon one night would be all right."

Marian's face lit up, and James was suddenly anxious to get home. His wife still caused his heart to skip a beat when she looked at him a certain way. After twenty-one years of marriage, he was as in love with her as the first day he saw her on the playground at school. Her brown eyes still sparkled with youthful enthusiasm when she was pleased, the same way they did the day that James offered her a piece of chewing gum in the fourth grade.

"I think that is a *gut* decision," she said with a wink.

❧

Sunday morning, Leah wasn't surprised to see Kathleen, Mary Carol, *Mamm*, and even Edna making breakfast before she got downstairs. And they were up earlier than usual to do so.

"I know my cooking stinks." She sighed. "I'll get the jellies and such and put them on the table. Hard to mess that up." She shuffled toward the refrigerator, her head hanging low. She'd really tried. How hard could it be to scramble eggs?

"Leah," her mother said tenderly. "No worries. You will find something you excel at. And your cooking was fine."

"It is a sin to lie, *Mamm*." She placed the jams on the table, then thrust one hand on her hip. "I know that I got confused about the measurements with the ham loaf Friday night. And I know my meat loaf was heavy on the salt. But eggs? I should be able to do that." She stomped her foot a bit. "I put the oil in with the eggs just like I've seen Kathleen do a hundred times."

They all turned to face her, expressions blank.

Then Kathleen exclaimed, "That's for cakes, Leah! I mix the oil in with the eggs when I'm making cakes, not when I'm just scrambling the eggs." She shook her head and laughed.

"That explains it," Mary Carol said.

"Explains what?" *Daed* entered the kitchen.

But no one answered him. Instead, laughter erupted throughout the kitchen as all eyes landed on his pant hems. One leg was hemmed much higher than the other.

"Leah," Edna said, "is that the pair of pants you hemmed for *Daed*?"

Leah didn't answer. She glanced back and forth between her sisters. Even her mother was chuckling. Their laughter echoed in Leah's head as she ran out of the room.

She heard Edna calling after her, but she didn't turn around. Then she heard her mother say that no one was making fun of her. But they were. All of them. If they knew how hard she'd really tried, they wouldn't be laughing. She threw herself facedown on her bed.

❦

"We should all be ashamed of ourselves," Marian said. She dried her hands on her apron. "I'll go to her."

James cut in front of her path. "No. I will do it."

He wasn't even to the top of the stairs when he heard Leah crying. He slowly pushed open her bedroom door. She bolted upright and swiped at her tears.

"I'm sorry, *Daed*." She buried her face in her hands. "I tried. I really did. I even tried to help Mary Carol in the garden, but she said I wasn't picking the vegetables the right way. I'm not *gut* at any of this."

James didn't like to see Marian or any of the girls cry. And he was responsible for her pain. He sat down on Edna's bed, across from Leah. "Leah," he said tenderly, "the reason you are not *gut* with these skills is because you don't practice them enough. If you practice—"

"That's not true, *Daed*. I've tried on and off for years to be a better Amish woman. It just doesn't come naturally to me, and I don't know why."

I don't know why either. James stroked his beard and thought for a moment. "What do you want to do with your life, Leah? If these things that are necessary to become an Amish *fraa* don't interest you, what does?"

James knew the answer, but he'd been praying for some guidance where Leah was concerned. Maybe she could explain her writing to him in a way that he could understand, tell him why such a silly thing was so important to her and seemed to distract her from more important things. It would serve her no purpose in their community, especially as a woman doing so. Women had certain responsibilities within the district. His daughter knew this.

Leah sniffled. "I'm eighteen years old. I know that I need to work on my home skills, and I will continue to do so." She sat up taller.

James grimaced as he thought about more experimental meals, but he was the one who had forced this issue. *Why doesn't she mention her writing?* "Is there something else you'd rather do, Leah? If so, tell me about it. Help me to understand."

She looked at her feet. "No. Nothing. I will work harder to do better with my chores."

A sense of despair settled over James. This was what he'd always wanted to hear from her, but he knew that she was stifling her dreams to say what he wanted to hear.

"I know you have been working *hatt*, Leah. I have decided to allow you to attend the singing tonight at the Grabers'." He paused. "But your punishment is only on hold for tonight. Edna still needs to take things slowly until her infection is better, and I'd like to see you helping out more for the next couple weeks. No lunches with your *Englisch* friends or traveling to town. Then we will speak of this matter again."

"*Danki, Daed.*"

James left his daughter's room and knew he should feel victorious. Leah was finally coming around. But something just wasn't right in his heart.

Chapter Nine

AARON PUT LEAH'S THICK STACK OF PAPERS IN A PAPER bag and headed down the stairs. He slowed as he hit the den and listened for voices. Nothing. Maybe his sisters had already left for the singing. He wasn't eager for anyone to know he'd been reading Leah's book. He'd finished it last night and had to admit he was impressed.

His parents were in their room, and Abner was already on his way to the Petersheims' for a visit, since Edna didn't feel up to attending the singing. A clean getaway. Aaron tucked the bag under his arm and shuffled across the den to the front door. He'd already readied his horse and courting buggy earlier in the day. He pushed the screen door open and darted down the stairs.

"Where ya goin' in such a hurry?"

Auntie Ruth. He'd forgotten about her. Aaron spun around, "To pick up Leah and take her to the singing, and I'm running late." Which was true.

She stood up from the rocker on the porch, dressed in orange and red plaid breeches and a bright red blouse. Her toenails were painted a bright red and matched her long fingernails and the color on her lips.

You'd think that while she was here, she'd try to blend in just a little.

As she walked toward him, her eyes focused on his bag. "What's that? Aaron Lantz, you aren't trying to sneak alcohol into that singing, are ya?" She shook her head. "That stuff's bad for you."

Aaron glanced at the small glass in her hand half full of a dark liquid. "No, Auntie Ruth. It's not alcohol. It's—something of Leah's."

She toddled toward him. Aaron sighed, knowing he was going to be even later, and that was not a good way to start the evening. He loved Auntie Ruth, but he didn't have time for silly chitchat right now. She put one hand on her hip. "You read her book, huh?"

"What?"

"That's what's in that bag, isn't it?" Auntie Ruth took a sip from her glass, smudging it with red around the rim.

Aaron sighed.

"Don't worry. I won't tell. But was it any good?"

"Auntie Ruth, *ya*, it was *gut*. Now I have to go. I'm already late." Aaron started walking backward toward his buggy. "We'll talk later."

Ruth nodded, took another sip. Since she'd arrived, Aaron had seen her having an alcoholic drink every day, sometimes in the morning, sometimes in the evening. She'd never done that when she'd visited before, or when they visited her in Florida.

He turned around and hurried to the buggy. He set the bag down on the seat, then climbed in. He grabbed the reins and was getting ready to back his horse up, when he thought of something. Auntie Ruth was still standing barefoot in the front yard.

"Why did you tell Leah you have a secret?"

She raised her eyebrows. "Because I do." She took a few steps toward him. "Want me to tell you what it is?"

Aaron couldn't even begin to speculate what type of secret she might be keeping. This was the same woman who came to visit three years ago carting three baby ferrets with her. *Mamm* refused to let the "rats," as she called them, stay in the house. Another time, a few years before that, Ruth had shown up riding a big black motorcycle, wearing black leather pants and a matching jacket. There was just never any reckoning about what might be on Auntie Ruth's mind.

"If you want to tell me." Aaron began to back up the buggy as Ruth drew near. "But you don't have to," he added, hoping to be on his way.

But she kept walking until she was right beside the buggy, so Aaron stopped.

"I suppose it's best that you know." Ruth took a deep breath and let it out slowly. "I will be passin' on to the other side, to be with my heavenly Father soon." She raised her chin high. "Yes, Aaron. I'm going to drop dead shortly."

Aaron's mouth hung open. This was the most nonsense he'd ever heard from her, and he wondered why she'd make up such a thing. "Auntie Ruth," he finally said, "that's the craziest notion I've ever heard. What in the world would make you say somethin' like that? Are you sick?" He looked again at the glass in her hand.

"It's just my time, dear Aaron." She made the sign of the cross, took another sip of her drink, then pointed a crooked finger toward the sky. "I'll be goin' home soon."

He did not have time for her silliness. "Auntie Ruth, we'll talk about this later, but I reckon you ain't gonna drop dead any time soon."

"But I am, Aaron." She pressed her lips firmly together and blinked her eyes a few times. "I might drop dead right over there, amid the wildflowers in the pasture." She waved her free hand toward the wide-open field. "Wouldn't that be lovely? Taking my last breath in God's plush landscaping." Her eyes grew wide. "I think you best not tell anyone, though."

Aaron shook his head. He'd tell his mother about this as soon as possible.

⁊⁍

Leah was starting to think Aaron had changed his mind. Mary Carol and Kathleen had left fifteen minutes ago, and Abner arrived to visit Edna shortly after that. The singing started at eight o'clock and only lasted about an hour and a half.

Leah pushed the rocker on the porch into motion. She could hear

Edna and Abner talking and laughing with her parents in the kitchen. If Aaron was trying to be fashionably late, as Clare and Donna would say, he was bordering on making her mad.

Then she heard the shuffling of horse hooves and saw him pull into the driveway. She pushed herself up from the rocker and padded down the porch steps and into the yard, blocking her eyes from the setting sun.

She waited until he stopped beside her, then cupped her hands on her hips. "You're late, Aaron Lantz."

"Sorry. It was Auntie Ruth. She was telling me a crazy story, and her ramblin' held me up." He reached onto his seat and offered her a brown paper bag. "Here's your book. I read the whole thing."

Leah accepted it. "Did you like it?"

"*Ya*, I really did."

She could tell by the way he said it that he meant it. Leah couldn't wait to talk about it with him on the way to the singing. But first she wanted to put it safely away. "I'll be right back. I just want to go put this in the house." She held up her index finger. "One minute."

She skipped back into the house and entered through the den to avoid her family in the kitchen. Then she bolted upstairs. She set the bag on her bed and reached for her other completed story inside the drawer. Leah pounded the papers on her nightstand in an effort to straighten them somewhat. She pulled the first book from the bag and tucked it safely in the drawer, then put the other book inside the bag. She slammed the door shut and ran down the hall, taking the stairs two at a time, then dashed through the den.

༄༅

Aaron watched her coming toward him in her dark blue dress and smiled. Until he saw what she was carrying. *No, no, no.* He'd enjoyed Leah's story, but he needed sleep. He couldn't keep this up every night.

"Since you liked it, I thought you might want to read the second one I wrote." She pushed it toward him.

He forced a smile and accepted it, then stepped out of the buggy and offered her his hand. She latched on, and Aaron helped her into his courting buggy. He knew good and well that they weren't dating, yet he was about to have to read another book.

"I think it's better than the first, but it's much longer," she added.

Aaron slid in beside her, then took a peek inside the bag. He eyed the thick stack of paper but didn't say anything.

Leah waited until they pulled onto the two-lane road that wound through the back roads of Paradise. "So, what was your most favorite part?"

"The end." His meaning was twofold. When he had finished the last page, he'd assumed his sleep schedule would return to normal. But he decided to give her the other meaning within his answer. "Everyone is happy at the end of the book." *Particularly Rose and Jesse.*

Leah broke into a wide smile. "Wait until you read this next one!" She folded her hands in her lap and kept grinning.

Aaron eased his horse into a gentle gallop as he thought about all the sleepless nights ahead of him. "And when will we be talkin' about this next book? On the way to another singing?"

"Why, Aaron Lantz, you make this sound like a trade-off."

"I'm not the one who invited you to the singing. You invited me, no?"

"True. But I'm not sure when I will be able to go out again." She paused as her expression soured. "I have to help out more with the chores at home."

"Until Edna is better?" He was wondering how long that would be, and if she was just saying that as an excuse not to go anywhere with him.

Leah sighed. "I don't know. *Mei daed* said he would like to see me become a better cook, gardener, seamstress, and all the other things that go into making a *gut* . . ." She slanted her eyes in his direction, then turned and faced forward again. ". . . a *gut fraa*."

Aaron chuckled, then realized from the look on her face that he shouldn't have.

"What's so funny?" She'd twisted in her seat to face him.

"Nothing." He tried to sound convincing.

"Oh, I'm sure you've heard from your sisters that I'm not very *gut* at quilting. We've been at many quilting parties together. And I don't cook very well either. It's just that . . ." She pressed her lips together and frowned for a moment. "I could be happy eating a sandwich, and it doesn't really bother me if the house isn't all that clean. I'd rather be writing my stories. I really believe that they might help someone someday." She shrugged. "Maybe not, though."

Aaron was thinking about her story, the way she intertwined the Lord's goodness with her characters' quest for spiritual guidance. "Do all your books help someone find their way to God? And is there always a romance?" She must believe in true love or she wouldn't write about it.

Leah smiled. "Not always a romance, but always a happy ending."

They were quiet for a few moments. The sun was bearing down on the horizon, and Leah looked to her left at the old Bontrager place.

"It's a shame about that place." She nodded toward the run-down homestead. The front porch on the old home was tilted, the paint was peeling, and weeds had taken over the property. "I heard some man and his son used to live there, but they just up and left one day, and no one knows where they went or why."

"*Ya*. That's what I heard too." He paused, straining to see the house as the skies began to darken. "Maybe someone will buy the old place and fix it up."

Aaron could see the Grabers' farm up ahead, along with dozens of buggies parked out front.

"What else did you like about my story?" she asked, as if sensing she didn't have much time to pump him for information.

"It seemed like you were writing about—" Aaron wasn't sure if he should be this honest.

"About what?"

"About yourself." He guided his buggy onto the Grabers' driveway.

"What? Rose isn't anything like me. She's actually a *gut* cook, tends her garden, and even sews clothes for her niece."

Aaron slowed his horse with a "whoa." Once they were stopped, he turned toward her. "Rose is full of life, and she has a big heart. She wants to help others, and she's—she's beautiful, inside and out." He was so far out on a limb, he wanted to jump. But then Leah gave him a smile that sent his pulse racing.

"*Danki*, Aaron."

"Why, Leah Petersheim, I think you're blushing, no?" He stepped out of the buggy and offered Leah his hand, which she accepted as she stepped from the buggy.

Leah opened her mouth to say something, but the sound of feet shuffling across the yard caused them both to turn toward the movement.

Aaron recognized the person heading their way.

Oh no.

Chapter Ten

LEAH WATCHED HANNAH BEILER SWINGING HER HIPS toward them. In a world that discouraged vanity and pride, Hannah seemed to have a hardy abundance of both. Propane lights hung from the trees in the Grabers' front yard, and Leah could see several people gathered around a picnic table filled with food. But the closer Hannah got, all Leah could see was Hannah's pearly white, straight smile. Leah ran her tongue over her own teeth, and it wasn't a straight sweep.

"Hello, Aaron," Hannah said cheerfully. Then through those clenched straight teeth, she turned to Leah. "Hello, Leah."

"Hi, Hannah." Aaron gently touched Leah's arm and coaxed her to his side, nudging her to walk with him up the cobblestone steps that led to the Grabers' front yard. It was an obvious attempt to avoid Hannah, and Leah silently scorned herself for the wrongful and confusing feeling of pride that swept over her. This wasn't a date with Aaron, anyway. She'd made that quite clear.

She saw Rebecca Miller standing in the front yard with some other girls. Ben Weaver was standing off to one side with two young men, and Leah smiled. Everyone knew Ben was in love with Rebecca, and he was never far away from her. But ever since Rebecca's twin sister, Lizzie, died five years ago, Rebecca just hadn't been the same. She was a few years older then Leah, but Leah could remember when Rebecca was much more outgoing. Leah had always heard that twins shared a special bond.

"Hi, Rebecca." She eased from Aaron's side and walked toward Rebecca, who smiled slightly. They began to chitchat about the food spread out before them: a variety of dips and chips, several desserts—and Kathleen's Lazy Daisy Oatmeal Cake. After the events at breakfast that morning, Leah had lost herself outside, worked in the garden, brushed and fed the horses, and did anything that would keep her away from everyone. She'd forgotten that she'd asked Kathleen to help her make the oatmeal cake. *Probably best,* she thought, remembering the scrambled eggs.

As Leah chatted with Rebecca, she saw Hannah cozying up to Aaron, laughing and carrying on. *That's my date.* Two other girls joined the conversation, and Leah excused herself and walked toward Aaron and Hannah.

"*Ach,* Aaron, you're so nice to say that," Leah heard Hannah say. She turned toward Leah. "Aaron was just saying how much he always enjoys my tomato pies. It's his favorite kind of pie." She swiveled back to face Aaron and pointed toward the table. "You better get yourself a piece before it's all gone. What's your baking specialty, Leah?" Hannah raised an eyebrow and smiled.

Hannah Beiler knew good and well that Leah wasn't much of a baker. Leah recalled the quilting party last month where she showed up with a cheesecake, at her mother's insistence. It really didn't taste so bad, but her mother told her later that perhaps crushed pineapple was not the best choice for a topping. "Strawberries, cherries, or blueberries, Leah," *Mamm* had said.

"Too many to choose from," Leah responded with a shrug. Then she turned to Aaron. "I'm going to go in and say hello to Amanda and her mother."

"I'll come with you." Aaron eased to Leah's side once again, and before she turned to walk toward the house, Leah told Hannah, with a smile, "See you in a bit."

Hannah's face fell flat, and she forced a grin.

"*Danki* for saving me," Aaron whispered as they walked side by side to the front porch.

Leah glanced in his direction. "Saving you from what?"

"Hannah attaches herself to my hip every time I'm around her, and I have no interest in her in that way."

Leah faced forward again. "She's very pretty."

Aaron shrugged. "I hadn't noticed." Then he smiled at Leah in a way that caused her to instantly recall what he had said to her before they arrived, when he compared her to Rose in her story. Rose, he said, was beautiful on the inside and outside.

"Hmm," she mumbled.

Aaron opened the screen door for Leah and followed her into the Grabers' kitchen where Amanda was scurrying around with her mother. At twenty-four, Amanda was the oldest of seven brothers and sisters. She wasn't particularly social, and Leah didn't know her all that well. But Amanda had made a special point of taking a large helping of Leah's pineapple-topped cheesecake at the quilting party last month, then told everyone it was the best cheesecake she'd ever had.

It was an untruth, but Leah had found it so endearing that she longed to know Amanda better.

"Can I help you with anything?" Leah walked to Amanda's side while Aaron stood in the kitchen full of women, looking rather lost.

"Leah, hello." Amanda wiped her hands on her black apron and smiled. "No, you two go enjoy yourselves. We're just finishing up a few things in here, and we'll be right out."

Leah nodded and turned to go back outside. Aaron followed, but when the screen door closed behind them, he gently grabbed her arm. "Please don't lead me back over there to Hannah."

"But she makes your favorite kind of pie." She didn't try to hide her cynical tone.

"Very funny."

❦

After everyone stuffed themselves silly with food, they sang several songs in four-part harmony—something not allowed during worship service. Then some of the guests began to leave, while others started a late-night game of volleyball. The Grabers' outside lights lit the space well, and a full moon shone on the area. Aaron had joined some of the other young men near the barn, and Leah was outside watching the volleyball game and pretending to be interested in the conversation around her about an upcoming tea party. *Thank goodness I'm punished to the house and won't have to attend.*

Hannah, who was hosting the tea party, rattled on about the foods she would be preparing. Leah glanced at Rebecca, who was eyeing Ben on the volleyball court. She hoped a courtship could develop between those two. They'd arrived at the singing separately, but that didn't necessarily mean anything.

After all, she had arrived with Aaron, and there was certainly no courtship going on there. But she had to admit that it had bothered her when Hannah tried to get cozy with him earlier.

Leah saw Aaron walking toward them from the barn, and she wondered if he was ready to head home. Maybe if she got home early enough, she'd be able to do a little writing before she went to sleep.

⊶⊷

Aaron strolled across the yard toward Leah. He was ready to go and hoped Leah would be too. It was going to be another long night of reading. Another long *week*. He couldn't help but wonder what his reward would be for reading another book, since that seemed to be how Leah worked. For now, he'd take what he could get, in an attempt to spend more time with her and get to know her better.

"Hello, ladies," he said as he approached Leah, Rebecca, Hannah, and two of Amanda's sisters. He stopped near Leah. "I was wondering if you might be ready to go?"

Leah nodded with a yawn. "*Ya*, I think so."

There was no mistaking Hannah's disappointment. Hannah

had a striking appearance, and she was known in the community as a good catch for any young man. On several occasions, Aaron's mother had mentioned what a fine wife Hannah would make. And Aaron knew she was right. She just wasn't the person for him.

They said their good-byes, and Aaron offered Leah his hand and helped her into his buggy. The feel of her hand cradled in his sent a tingle up his spine. He looked up at the thick clusters of stars that dotted the clear skies above them and decided to take a chance.

"Why are we going this way?" Leah asked when Aaron turned left instead of right out of the Grabers' driveway.

"It's such a beautiful night, I thought we'd take the long way. Is that okay? I reckon we really didn't talk much about your book, and I know that was the *deal*." He smiled in her direction to let her know he was just fine with the arrangement.

"I—I had a *gut* time." She seemed hesitant with her comment, but her lips curved into a cautious smile. "So I guess it was a fine *deal*."

"So when would you like to get together again and hear my thoughts on this latest book?"

"Hmm. I don't know. There is the issue with *mei daed*." She turned to face him, and in the moonlight he could see a twinkle in her eye. "But maybe if I work really hard on my chores, and if Edna continues to feel better, then maybe he'll let me go do something. But, Aaron . . ."

"*Ya?*"

"I was thinkin' . . . I reckon it was *hatt* for you to read my book so fast, like you did. Probably too much to ask."

"Not at all. I enjoyed it." Aaron knew he was willing to read the other one equally as fast if it meant he'd get to see her again. "What about a picnic Saturday after I get off work, if your *daed* will allow it? I only work until eleven that morning." She seemed hesitant, so he added, "I'll have the book finished by then. We could talk about it and have some lunch."

Aaron knew that at some point he was going to need Leah to

want to spend time with him without having to bribe her. But for now, he'd take however much of her time he could get, and with whatever strings attached.

"I guess I could ask *Daed* if it would be all right."

Aaron smiled at the thought of sitting quietly with Leah somewhere and having a picnic. It seemed much more intimate than a Sunday singing. "That sounds *gut*. I'll have *mei mamm* make us a picnic lunch."

Leah giggled. "Aaron Lantz, do you think I'm not able to prepare us a lunch?"

"No, of course not," he immediately responded.

"I am quite capable of making chicken salad sandwiches and some side items for a picnic, and I wouldn't want your *mamm* to have to do that." She laughed again. "Unless you're scared?" Her mouth spread into a wide smile, and her eyes gleamed from the light of the moon.

"I'm a *little* scared," he teased back, loving the sound of her laughter. "But I'm willing to take the chance, I reckon."

"I'll have Edna get word to Abner by Saturday, whether or not I can go."

Aaron smiled. Then he kept up his end of the bargain for the rest of the way home, as he recalled some of his favorite parts of Leah's book.

Chapter Eleven

MARIAN STRIPPED THE SHEETS FROM THE BED AS JAMES fastened his suspenders. Monday was wash day, and she wanted to get the sheets downstairs and into the pile.

"I think it's lovely that you are letting Leah go on the picnic with Aaron on Saturday." She turned in his direction and winked. "Sometimes there is cause to bend the rules a bit, no?"

James sighed. "How can I not? A boy is actually interested in Leah, and it's for sure that he knows she is lacking in skills. I'm sure his sisters have told him of this."

"Maybe all that's not important to Aaron. Maybe he just likes Leah for the person she is." Marian scooped the sheets into her arms. "Besides, Leah has been trying harder lately, helping more around the house."

James sat down on the bare mattress pad. "But this trying harder cannot be just to gain her freedoms. It should be a way of life. Edna is much better, but I would still like to see Leah stay around the house and work on her skills. This exception is for Saturday only."

"Did you see the way Aaron looked at Leah during worship service yesterday? It was very sweet. He really seems to like her a lot."

James looked toward the ceiling and folded his hands together. "*Danki*, Lord." He turned toward Marian and smiled. "I was worrying the girl might live with us forever."

There was a knock at the bedroom door. "*Mamm?*"

"Come in, Leah." Marian bunched the sheets up and balanced them on her hip.

Leah pushed the door open and came in. "*Daed*, I made your lunch. It's in your pail on the kitchen counter."

Marian smiled at James. "Isn't that nice, James? That's a chore I won't have to do this morning." She turned to her daughter. "*Danki*, Leah."

Leah hesitated near the door. "*Daed*, I was wondering . . ."

"What is it, Leah?" James finished tying his shoes and stood up.

"I was wondering if I could meet Clare and Donna for lunch today in town? I haven't seen them in—"

"No." James folded his arms across his chest. "I am allowing you to go to your picnic on Saturday, but that is all for now. You are making great strides, Leah, with your household chores, and I would like to see continued improvement. I waited much too long to enforce these rules. Your sisters can't be expected to do more than their share."

"But I've been doing my share, plus more," Leah argued.

"Edna is not one hundred percent yet, and I'd like you to keep doing what you are doing."

"But, *Daed*—"

"Leah, that's enough," Marian said. "Be grateful that your *daed* is allowing you to go with Aaron on Saturday."

"Yes, ma'am."

When the door closed behind Leah, Marian asked her husband, "How long are you going to keep this up, James?"

"Until it becomes natural for Leah to pull her share of the load around here, instead of coming in late for every meal, not helping with preparations, laundry, gardening, and other chores. And until she realizes there is no place or time in her life for these fanciful stories of hers. I am pleased with what I see, and I would like to make sure these are habits she will keep up with."

Marian kissed her husband on the cheek. "I'm going to go take these to her. She said she would start up the wringer and get the clothes washed today." Marian grinned. "In the past, Leah has made herself scarce on Mondays. I know she dislikes doing the clothes, yet she offered this morning."

James twisted his mouth to one side. "It wonders me what the girl has prepared me for lunch. After I tend to the fields, I plan to touch up the red paint on both the barns in the far pasture. If it doesn't make wet later in the day, that's my plan." James scratched his forehead and sighed. "That's a lot of work for a man to do on an empty stomach."

Marian smiled. "I will have you an afternoon snack, as usual. So, James Petersheim, you won't starve today if it is something not of your liking."

Her husband grumbled as he walked out the door. Marian followed along behind him, toting the sheets, hopeful that Leah would stay on course.

⚬⚬

Aaron waited until he was able to catch his mother alone Monday morning.

"*Mamm?*"

"*Ya*, Aaron." She pulled a loaf of bread from the oven and placed it on a rack by the stove. "Your *daed* and Abner are already milking the cows."

"I'm heading out there, but there's something I wanted to talk to you about first."

Sarah Lantz pulled the kitchen mitt from her hand and placed it on the counter, then wiped a trail of sweat from her cheek. "I try to use this oven in the earliest part of the day, but yet this August heat is still unbearable." She looked up at Aaron. "What is it, dear?"

Aaron glanced over his shoulder and into the den. Seeing it was all clear, he asked, "Where's Auntie Ruth?"

"I imagine she's still sleeping. You know your aunt doesn't rise as early as we do."

Aaron didn't figure there was much he could tell his mother that would surprise her about Auntie Ruth, but Aaron had continued to be bothered about Auntie Ruth's comments.

"Did you know that Auntie Ruth thinks she is going to die soon?"

His mother scrunched her face. "What? Why would she think that? She's not sick, that I know of."

Aaron shrugged. "I don't know, *Mamm*. She said that she is going to drop dead soon." Aaron paused. "Do you think she's done gone crazy?"

Sarah patted her forehead with a napkin and took a deep breath. "I never know what to think about your Auntie Ruth." His mother took a seat at the kitchen table. "I remember when I was a girl, Auntie Ruth wasn't much different than she is now. Except she's slowed down with age." She smiled and shook her head. "Do you know that Auntie Ruth came for a visit once when I was twelve or fourteen, and she announced to the entire family that she was going to join a convent and become a nun?"

Aaron knew he needed to get out to the barn and help his *daed* and Abner, but he'd never heard this story. He sat down across from his mother. "A nun?"

Sarah laughed. "*Ya*. Of course, she changed her mind later, but I remember the look on everyone's face when she made the announcement." She paused. "Auntie Ruth is a spiritual person, but I reckon she is confused sometimes about her relationship with God. She often thinks God is *telling* her things."

"But doesn't God tell us all things—that little voice inside of us when we listen?"

"I suppose so. But, well . . . it's different with Auntie Ruth. Another time when I was young, she told me that God told her that He didn't approve of me dating a boy outside of our district." She smiled. "I don't think it was so much that God didn't approve, but that my parents and Auntie Ruth didn't approve." She shrugged. "That boy was your father, and all is *gut*."

"I'll go on to the barn. I just wanted you to know what she said."

"I wouldn't give it too much concern, Aaron. I love Auntie Ruth, but we all know she is a little—different."

⌒⊘

By Saturday, Leah was more than ready to go on a picnic—with anyone.

She packed the chicken salad sandwiches she'd made, along with some chips, sweet pickles, and two pieces of apple pie that Kathleen made the day before. She added two paper plates and some napkins, then closed the wooden lid on top.

"Leah?" Her mother walked to where Leah was standing at the kitchen counter, then placed a hand on her arm. "Your *daed* said that your chicken salad is quite *gut* and that he very much appreciates the way you have been making him lunch this week." She paused, grimacing a bit. "But he was wondering if, perhaps, you could make him something different next week."

Leah smiled. "I guess I finally mastered something in the kitchen, and I went a little overboard."

"Did you make chicken salad sandwiches for your picnic with Aaron today?"

"*Ya*, I did. I also made a tomato pie, *Mamm*, but it didn't come out right." Leah pointed to the pie on the kitchen counter, with one slice missing. "I tried it, and it doesn't taste anything like yours and Kathleen's. It tastes—grainy. So I snatched two pieces of apple pie that Kathleen made, instead."

Her mother picked up the pie and inspected it. "It looks fine, Leah."

"Taste it." Leah pulled a fork from the drawer and handed it to her mother. Then she watched her mother's face wince with displeasure. "See, I told you. It's not right at all."

"Leah, you are to *sprinkle* basil, parsley flakes, thyme leaves, oregano, onion powder, a little brown sugar, and some salt and pepper over the tomatoes. How much of the herbs did you sprinkle? Particularly, how much pepper?" Marian placed the pie back on the counter.

"Until it covered the tomatoes."

Her mother dismissed the subject with a wave of her hand. "We will work on this another time. For today, I'm sure Aaron will be very pleased with your chicken salad."

"Tomato pie is Aaron's favorite. I wish it had turned out." She stared at the pie and thought about the extra time she put in this morning to make it. *I could have been working on my story.*

"Are—are you and Aaron possibly starting a courtship?" Her mother's voice sounded hopeful but hesitant. Rightly so.

"No. We're just friends." Leah shrugged. "He's nice enough, I reckon."

Marian smiled. "He is certainly handsome."

"I miss Clare and Donna, *Mamm.* I hope *Daed* will let me have lunch with them soon."

"Your sister is much better, and you've been taking on your share of the household chores. I'm sure your father will come around soon." She paused. "But, Leah, he will expect you to continue doing your share of the work around here even after he releases you from your punishment."

Leah knew this to be true. And while she'd mastered chicken salad, she'd messed up everything else she'd tried to cook. Edna had resumed the sewing tasks, since Leah couldn't seem to sew a straight line or even hem a pair of breeches. Mary Carol practically forbade Leah to help her in the garden ever since she'd accidentally pulled up her sister's herbs, mistaking them for weeds. And Kathleen loved to do the cooking, so Leah didn't see why everyone was so insistent that she learn how.

"I just wish there was something for me to do that I'm more—

more suited to." She turned and faced her mother. "Like writing my stories, *Mamm*. I think that maybe someday they will touch someone, help them to find the Lord, or maybe——"

"Leah, these tales you weave . . . it is a fine hobby. But it does not prepare you to be a proper *fraa* some day. What will you feed your husband and children? Will you not have your own garden? Will your home not be clean and well tended? What about clothes for your husband and children? Have you thought about all these things and how important these skills are in our community?"

"*Ya, Mamm.* I guess so." Leah sighed. "But if I have to do all these things, I'd rather not get married."

"Leah. Now, don't say that. You know you don't mean it."

"*Ya*, I do! When I get married—a long time from now—my husband will have to allow me time to write my stories and live on chicken salad sandwiches."

Her mother hung her head, but when she looked up, she was smiling. "Leah, you will find your way."

Leah had heard her mother and Edna both say that before. Didn't they understand? *This is my way.*

"I think I hear Aaron pulling up," her mother said as she glanced out the open window in the kitchen. "Go, and have a *gut* time."

Leah picked up the picnic basket, kissed her mother on the cheek, and headed out the door.

Chapter Twelve

AARON RECALLED HIS CONVERSATION IN THE BARN WITH Abner that morning. "You better hope that Edna or one of the other girls prepared your picnic lunch." Then his brother had laughed.

He watched Leah toting the picnic basket out to his buggy, and he really didn't care what was in it. The sunlight danced across her angelic face, and there was, as always, a bounce in her step. When she smiled, Aaron could see her dimples, even from across the yard.

"I made chicken salad," she said proudly. She handed him the picnic basket. He placed it on the storage rack on the back of his courting buggy, then helped her in.

"I tried to make you a tomato pie, but . . ." She shrugged, then smoothed the wrinkles from her apron and folded her hands on her lap. "It just didn't taste like it was supposed to."

Aaron was touched that she would attempt to make him a tomato pie. He let his mind drift and pictured himself and Leah as a married couple. What would he eat? Even as the thought crossed his mind, Aaron knew he was going to do everything in his power to win her over. He gave his horse a flick of the reins.

"I love chicken salad." He smiled.

After a few moments of silence, she asked, "So what did you think about my second story? Did you like it as much as the first?"

Aaron had already pondered his situation. If he gave up all his sleep, finished the book, then met her today, they'd have no reason to meet again—unless she gave him yet another book to read, and he knew he couldn't keep this up. "I haven't finished it, Leah."

The disappointment registered on her face instantly.

"But I will." He smiled. *As soon as we spend enough time together for you to get to know me.*

"It's all right," she said as she turned toward him. "I know you probably need sleep. *Mei daed* has me doing all these chores I never used to do, and I am finding less and less time to write my books. I'm too tired at night." Her face twisted into a scowl. "And I don't like that."

"I guess you'll write your stories if it's important enough to you." Aaron carefully crossed Lincoln Highway. As they passed the Gordonville Bookstore, he said, "Maybe your books will be in that store someday."

"*Ach!* Wouldn't that be something?" Her dimples puckered inward. "So many *Englisch* tourists visit that store. They'd buy my book and maybe somehow find their way to the Lord. If I helped one person seek out God, wouldn't that be wonderful?"

Aaron couldn't understand why that was so important to her, especially since ministering was not their way. But the thought seemed to thrill her so much, he didn't want to spoil the moment. "*Ya*, I suppose it would be wonderful."

"How far did you get? In the book?"

"The fourth chapter. Amos and Annie are, uh . . ." Suddenly he felt awkward. "They're on the picnic."

It was her story, so obviously she knew that Amos and Annie shared their first kiss while they were at the picnic. Aaron found his eyes drawn instantly to Leah's lips. He quickly looked away.

"Oh." Her cheeks flushed as she stared straight ahead. "That's a very *gut* part of the story."

"Do they fall in *lieb*?" Now Aaron was blushing.

Leah turned toward him and pointed a finger in his direction. "No, no, no. I can't tell you."

Aaron chuckled. "Aw, come on . . ."

She folded her hands in her lap, then swiveled to face him. "What do you think?"

"I think that if all your stories have happy endings, then I reckon they fall in *lieb*." Aaron turned onto an unnamed dirt road that led to what he believed would be the perfect picnic spot. He'd spent his lunch hour this past week trying to find the ideal spot to take Leah. Somewhere shady, hidden away, and romantic. And he'd found that perfect place at his cousin's farm.

"Where are we going?" she asked, neither confirming nor denying that the characters in her book did indeed fall in love.

"My cousin's place. Leroy and his family are in Ohio, and I know he won't mind if we have a picnic by his pond."

The unpaved road narrowed, and trees arched overhead in a picturesque display, blocking the bright sun as they neared the long driveway that led to his cousin's farm. Aaron pulled into the gravel entrance and followed it almost up to the farmhouse, then veered to their left across the pasture.

"The wildflowers here are beautiful!" Leah eyed the stretch of meadow leading down to the pond.

Aaron knew this would be the perfect place. He pointed toward the water, surrounded by tall greenery, and toward a patch of trees off to the side of a wooden deck that stretched across the pond. "I was thinkin' that under those trees would be a *gut* spot. At least we'll have some shade." He ran his sleeve across his forehead. "Maybe it's too hot for a picnic. I'll be ready for some lemonade or tea." He pulled the buggy to a stop as close to one of the trees as he could, then jumped down and secured his horse. When he turned back to offer Leah a hand down, her face was puckered into a frown. He thought it was kind of cute the way her dimples showed even when she frowned. "What's wrong?"

She latched onto his hand and hopped down. "I forgot to bring anything to drink. And I didn't bring a blanket or anything to sit on."

Aaron recalled Abner telling him about the picnic he went on with Edna, complete with wet towels for cleanup afterward. He smiled. "It's no problem. I'll just walk up to the house and get us something to drink and something to sit on."

"Sorry." She shrugged.

"While I'm gone, would you fill this up and give ol' Pete a drink from the pond?" He handed her a metal bucket from the back. "It's so hot, I reckon he could use a drink."

"*Ya,* of course." She took the bucket and started to walk toward the pond.

"Don't fall in while I'm gone," he teased. "Back shortly."

Leah swung the small bucket all the way to the pond, leaned down, and dipped it into the water. Then she set it down, cupped her hands, and pooled some of the water up to her face. It wasn't cool water or fit for her to drink, but it was wet and felt good against her hot skin.

She carried the water back to the horse and offered it to him. "Pete, you're thirsty, no?"

After the horse emptied the bucket, Leah returned it to the storage rack behind the buggy, then eyed the wildflowers—orange, yellow, and pink buds nestled among towering green stems. She found a thick cluster of pink blooms in the middle of the meadow and lay down, thankful to God for the beauty that surrounded her. It felt good to be away from the house, out in the middle of the field, with only the cows voicing an occasional hello. She crossed her ankles and propped her hands behind her head. A breeze rustled through the flowers, and she thought about Rose in her story, how she loved the flowery meadows. Maybe Aaron was right. Maybe she did write some of her own personality into Rose's character.

She breathed in the moment. *Thank You, Lord, for this beautiful land You've given us, that calms us and nourishes us.* She propped herself up on her elbows, opened her eyes, and peered toward the house. She could see the front door still open, so she figured Aaron must be rounding up a blanket and something to drink. *I can't believe I forgot the lemonade.*

Leah glanced to her left. All was quiet, except for two brown cows grazing in the next pasture. Leah lay back down and closed her eyes.

≈∽

Aaron made his way across the front yard after locating a blanket and filling a thermos with lemonade, thankful his cousin didn't feel the need to lock his farmhouse door.

Aaron knew Leroy wouldn't mind the intrusion, especially if there was a young woman involved. He was always encouraging Aaron to find a wife and didn't understand his fascination with Leah. "She doesn't seem like the marrying kind to me," Leroy had said.

Aaron squinted and scanned the pond area, but he didn't see Leah. He draped the cumbersome brown blanket over his shoulder, got a good grip on the lemonade, and picked up his pace. *Where is she?*

Sunlight poured down from clear blue skies, and if it had been about twenty degrees cooler, it would have been a perfect day for a picnic. But he'd endure the heat for a chance to spend time with Leah. He tipped his straw hat back to have a better look across the meadow filled with colorful wildflowers, and as he left the yard and entered the pasture, he spotted her lying amid green leafy foliage topped with orange, yellow, and pink blooms. She looked like an angel, with her arms stretched high above her head, her dark blue dress in clear contrast against the colors around her.

Aaron smiled. *Only Leah would do something like this*, he thought as he neared her. He expected her to stand up at any moment, stretch her arms out, and gracefully waltz through the meadow, as Rose had done in her story. It was a perfect moment, watching her like this.

"I got the lemonade!" he hollered as he got within a few yards of her. "And a blanket."

No response. Aaron stopped a few feet away from her, his feet rooted to the ground.

"Leah!"

She didn't move, and suddenly Leah didn't look so angelic, and the soft swishing of the tall grass amid the flowers seemed eerie and sent a chill through him. He thought about Edna and how she'd been rushed to the hospital, barely able to breathe. Auntie Ruth's words had lingered in his mind all week too. *I might drop dead right over there, amidst the wildflowers in the pasture.*

Aaron dropped the blanket and the thermos, and his hat flew off as he dashed toward her, fell down in the grass beside her, and pulled her forcefully into his arms.

"Leah!"

She screamed, piercing his eardrum. "Aaron Lantz, let go of me! What in the world are you doing?"

Chapter Thirteen

LEAH FOUGHT TO WRIGGLE OUT OF AARON'S STRONG arms, pushing her hands into his chest and putting some distance between them, but one arm still cradled the small of her back, and an unfamiliar sensation swept over her. She stared into eyes wild with—with something.

"Aaron Lantz, what are you doing?" She shoved him back, stumbled to her feet, and brushed the powdery flower residue from her dress. "It wonders me if maybe you're not crazy!"

Aaron rose to his feet, put his hands on his hips, and stared into her eyes. "I thought you were . . ." He took a deep breath.

"Thought I was what?" She couldn't help but smile at how distraught he looked, for reasons she didn't understand. "I love this time of year, when all the wildflowers are in bloom. And I feel close to God when I lie on His precious earth. What in the world came over you?" She glanced over his shoulder. "Would that be our lemonade and blanket back there?" Leah was starting to question whether this picnic was a good idea.

Aaron pulled off his hat and wiped his forehead with his sleeve, something he did too much of. Didn't the man own a handkerchief? Then, without warning, he latched onto her hand and pulled her along beside him.

"I'll explain later. Let's go have our picnic."

His hand was strong, and although she was surprised by his aggressiveness, she didn't feel compelled to pull from his grasp. When they reached the blanket and the toppled thermos of lemonade, Aaron let go of her hand and picked up the thermos. He twisted off the attached cup and poured her a cup of lemonade.

"Here," he said, handing it to her. Then he chuckled.

Leah swigged the entire cupful and handed it back to him. "What's so funny?"

Aaron shook his head. "My crazy Auntie Ruth."

"Huh?"

He poured himself some lemonade and swigged it down in one gulp, then reattached the cup to the thermos. He picked up the blanket and swung it over his shoulder. "I'll explain later. Let's go spread this underneath the trees by the pond. I'm starving. What about you?"

"I reckon I'm a little hungry," she said as she cut her eyes in his direction. But as they walked toward the cluster of trees near the pond, Leah couldn't seem to shake the feel of his arms wrapped tightly around her earlier. She'd never been that close to a boy. And Aaron was hardly a boy. Discreetly, she allowed her eyes to dart in his direction and took in his tall stance, the way his blue shirt almost looked too small as his muscles rippled beneath it, the confident way he walked. Despite the scorching heat, a shiver ran down her spine. *What is happening to me?*

Aaron spread the blanket beneath the trees and motioned for her to sit. Then he walked to the buggy and retrieved the picnic basket. After he placed it on the blanket next to the thermos of lemonade, he sat down beside her.

"Do you want to tell me what all that nonsense was about?" Leah used her most demanding voice, even though she was secretly wishing they could replay the entire scene.

"Can we eat first?" Even his smile now sent a wave of something unfamiliar streaming through her veins.

She sat up taller, folded her hands in her lap. "I'm not sure I can eat until you tell me exactly what caused your strange behavior."

Aaron opened one of the wooden flaps on the top of the picnic basket, closed one eye, and playfully squinted into the basket. "Please, can't we eat first?"

Leah shook her head and shrugged. "I reckon so." She pushed his hand out of the way and pulled out two paper plates, then placed a sandwich on each plate, along with some chips and a sweet pickle. "I have apple pie too."

"I'm impressed." He grinned before taking a large bite of the chicken salad.

"Don't be. Kathleen made the pie." Leah picked up her sandwich, started to take a bite, then stopped, noticing that Aaron had already eaten half of his sandwich. "You've probably heard that I'm not exactly a very *gut* cook."

He swallowed, then grinned. "*Ya*, I've heard that." He paused. "Not much of a seamstress or gardener, either. That's what I'm told."

Leah slammed her sandwich down on the paper plate. "Then why did you even want to come here with me on this picnic? I'm sure *Hannah* could have prepared you a much better lunch." Leah regretted the statement the minute she said it.

Aaron ignored the comment. "I'm startin' to think that everyone's not been real truthful with me about your cooking. This is the best chicken salad I've ever had. And I mean that."

Leah took another bite of her sandwich, chewed, then swallowed. She smiled. "It really is good, isn't it?"

Aaron nodded.

When they'd finished, Leah pulled out the two pieces of apple pie and handed one to Aaron. "Compliments of Kathleen," she said. "Sorry my tomato pie didn't turn out."

"Not everyone can make tomato pie like Hannah." He grinned, then raised the piece of pie to his mouth and took a big bite.

Leah felt her face reddening. *Oh, you just wait. I will be making you a tomato pie—better than Hannah's.*

"I reckon not," she responded curtly. "Now, tell me why you assaulted me in the field."

Aaron held up one finger, indicating that she wait. He finished chewing, then slowly licked a pie crumb from his mouth. Leah watched his tongue slide across his bottom lip, and her pulse quickened. She put a hand to her chest, as if that might slow her heart rate.

"Let's finish eating first," he finally said.

When they were done and everything was loaded back into the picnic basket, Aaron stretched out on the blanket, leaned back on his elbows, and crossed his ankles. Leah sat Indian-style beside him, arms folded across her chest, facing him.

"Well?"

Aaron sighed, and his mouth twitched on one side. "I know it's gonna sound dumb, but I thought—well, I thought maybe something was wrong with you."

"What?"

He shook his head. "Auntie Ruth, who is a little nuts, told me a few days ago that she thinks she's gonna die soon, and that she hopes it's in a field full of wildflowers. And when I saw you there, you weren't moving, and I guess that was on my mind, and—and, I don't know. It just made me fearful for a minute."

Leah laughed out loud. "You thought I was *dead*?"

"I told you. It was dumb."

Then Leah gasped. "*Ach!* Is something wrong with Auntie Ruth?"

Aaron shook his head. "No, she ain't sick or nothing. She's just—just off in the head sometimes."

She smiled again. "You thought I was dead."

Tongue in cheek, Aaron sat there quietly for a moment. "*Ya.* As dumb as it sounds, I guess I did for a minute." Then his expression turned serious. "It ain't funny, Leah."

Leah stifled her grin, both amused and touched by his chivalry. "Okay," she said.

They were both quiet for a few moments.

"I like Auntie Ruth. Tell me all about her," Leah said after a while.

⸎

For the next hour, Aaron filled Leah in about Auntie Ruth— everything from the ferrets and motorcycle to her almost joining a convent. They'd both laughed, and eventually Leah had gotten comfortable on the blanket, resting her head on her hand as she lay on her side and faced him. Aaron wanted to hold her hand, but it had taken her this long just to seem relaxed and comfortable.

"Well, I just love her," she said, when Aaron took a break from telling stories. "She is an odd *Englisch* person, for sure. But I wish I could spend more time with her while she's here."

Aaron's mind began to work on ways to make that happen. It couldn't be a quilting, sisters' day, tea party, or other event for only the ladies. He wanted to assure himself another day in Leah's company.

"Auntie Ruth loves to go eat pizza at Paradiso. Maybe we can take her there for supper one night?"

Leah laughed. "Or maybe she can take us in that fancy car of hers?" Her eyes twinkled. "Even if her driving is a little scary."

Aaron chuckled, thrilled at the opportunity to spend more time with Leah. Even if it did mean they'd have Auntie Ruth in tow.

They decided on Wednesday night. Leah said she'd have to clear it with her father, since she'd been doing extra chores since Edna got sick, but Aaron was hopeful that James Petersheim would give his permission. They spent the next two hours talking about Leah's books, and Aaron loved the way her face glowed when she described her characters. He relished the warm sensation he had when he was in her presence.

Chapter Fourteen

JAMES WATCHED MARIAN STOMP ACROSS THE FRONT YARD and toward the barn, her expression familiar. Those beautiful lips of hers were pinched together and curved into a frown. She was about to scold him for something, and James strained his mind to think what he might have done to irritate her.

He finished washing his hands at the pump outside the barn, flung them a few times in the hot air, then wiped them on his pants. "And what brings *mei* lovely *fraa* out to the barn when it's nearly suppertime?" He raised his eyebrows and grinned, hoping to lighten her mood.

Marian stopped in front of him and planted her hands on her hips. "James Petersheim, you cannot punish Leah to the house when it suits you, then allow her to go out with Aaron. She just told me that you said she could go out with Aaron and his aunt tonight." She pulled off her black sunglasses and stared him down. "It ain't right to keep the girl from her other friends but agree to let her spend time with Aaron."

James tugged on his beard for a moment. "She likes to run with those *Englisch* girls, and when she ain't doin' that, she's writing those stories. I like it better when she's here working, like she's supposed to be. She's been slacking with her chores again, and you know that."

"Yet you allow her to go out with Aaron?"

James hung his head slightly, then looked back up at her. "That boy might be Leah's only chance for marriage. How can I say no?"

Her look softened, but not much. "James . . ." She shook her head. "Finish up out here. Kathleen has supper ready."

Screeching tires pulled their attention to the Cadillac turning onto the driveway, and they both watched the automobile come barreling down the drive as if there was some sort of emergency. The car pulled to a halt with a jerk.

"That looks like Aaron in the front seat," Marian said. "I reckon that big-haired woman driving is Ruth?"

James shrugged as he and Marian waited for their visitors to exit the vehicle.

"Hello, hello!" The woman was dressed most peculiarly, and James recognized her right away as she crossed the yard and came toward them, waving.

He cautiously waved a hand in her direction. She was wearing bright pink breeches that hit her about midcalf, and her blouse sported more colors than a full rainbow. She had on big gold fancy rings and loud dangly bracelets to match.

Ruth.

"James and Marian, how *gut* to see you both!" She thrust her hand at James, and he hesitantly took hold, thinking it just didn't sound right for her to be using the Dutch. "Been a long time. I didn't see you at the hospital. That nurse wouldn't let us in the back where you were with Edna. And I don't think I saw you during my last couple of visits. So *gut* to be here." She finally released his hand and offered Marian the same forceful handshake.

James saw Aaron shuffling up behind her, his face red as fire. *Poor boy.* He needn't be embarrassed for his aunt.

Aaron extended his hand to James. "Hello, sir."

James shook hands with the young man he hoped to be his future son-in-law. He was sure praying about it. "Leah's inside, Aaron. I reckon she'll be out any minute." He glanced at the car. "Pretty sure she heard ya comin'."

"Isn't it dandy that these two young people invited me to Paradiso for supper?" She nudged James, enough to cause him to lose his footing. "Not sure why they want me around." She chuckled.

Normally James might have found her comment offensive, but it was Ruth. He'd known Ruth since he was a boy. She had already converted to *Englisch* by the time James was born, but she was always at family gatherings and continued to make her trips to Lancaster County.

"I'm sure the three of you will have a lovely time," Marian said.

James could tell by his wife's expression that she was surprised to see Ruth accompanying the young people to supper, and so was he.

"Are you enjoyin' your visit, Ruth?" James glanced toward the house but saw no Leah. *Leave it to that girl to be late for her own funeral someday.*

Ruth puckered her red lips into a circle, sucked in an abnormal amount of air, and then blew it out extra slow. "For as much time as I have left," she said, her brows drawing together.

"What . . ." James scratched his forehead.

"There's Leah!" Aaron yelled over James. He grabbed his aunt by the arm. "Let's go, Auntie Ruth." He pulled her toward the car. "Nice to see you both." Aaron tipped his hat in James and Marian's direction.

James nodded as Aaron opened the car door for his aunt, then walked around to open the front door for Leah. "I'll sit in the back," he told Leah, who giggled.

"You think it's safer back there, no?" James heard his daughter say to Aaron, who smiled. They were clearly getting along, and James knew he'd made the right decision to allow Leah to spend time with Aaron, with or without his nutty aunt.

James and Marian watched Ruth maneuver the car down the driveway in the same fashion as she'd arrived, and James could see heads bobbing.

"Do you think they're all right in a car with her?" Marian clutched his arm. "That woman has never been quite right."

James smiled. "I think they'll be just fine."

Leah braced her hands against the dash when Auntie Ruth pulled into the parking spot at the restaurant. She twisted her head around and grinned at Aaron. This was great fun already, and they'd only just arrived. Not much was said on the short drive to the restaurant. Auntie Ruth mostly sang to the radio and danced in her seat.

Paradiso was her parents' favorite place to go on the rare occasion that they ventured to town for supper. Leah had only been here twice, so this was a treat on several levels. A good meal. Some time with Auntie Ruth. And she had to admit she was looking forward to being around Aaron. But the bonus was that she'd gotten word to Donna and Clare that she would be here.

Leah knew to clip a note to the mailbox when she needed a message to reach one of her *Englisch* friends, and Charles the mailman would deliver it. Usually it was just a note requesting a car ride, but the system worked just as well for something like this. She grabbed the plastic bag she'd brought with her and reached for the handle on the car door just as Aaron pulled it open for her.

"Whatcha got there?" He eyed the plastic bag, and his expression took on a hint of worry. "Leah, I haven't finished the second book yet."

Leah rolled her eyes but grinned. "It's not for *you*."

"I can smell manicotti!" Auntie Ruth slammed her car door, threw a big pink purse over her shoulder, and headed toward the entrance, where Leah and Aaron met up with her. "Do you eat manicotti, honey?" She clutched Leah's arm, and before Leah had a chance to respond, Ruth said, "You must. It's the best here."

Leah nodded, since the way Ruth advised her about the manicotti seemed a matter of life or death. The only Italian food Leah had ever heard of was pizza.

Aaron pulled the door open for the two of them. A Seat Yourself sign met them in the entrance, and Ruth made her way down the middle aisle of the restaurant, lined with booths on both sides and tables in the middle. It probably wouldn't be considered fancy to the *Englisch*, but Leah thought it was very nice. There were colorful placemats on the tables, and televisions in opposite corners of the room. The patrons were mostly *Englisch*, but Leah noticed two Amish families dining to her left.

They'd only taken a few steps when Leah saw Donna and Clare in a booth against the wall to her right. *You made it!* Ruth passed by the girls, but Leah stopped at the booth, whispering to Aaron that she would join them in a minute. Ruth chose a table for four in the middle aisle.

"We got your note!" Donna said. "Where've you been? I left a message on the phone in your barn, but I didn't hear back. Is everything okay?" Donna moved over to make room for Leah to sit beside her.

Leah put the plastic bag on the table and eased in beside her friend. "*Ya*, everything is all right. But *mei daed* has made me stay around the house since Edna got sick." Leah briefly filled them in about Edna's asthma.

"Who's the Amish hottie over there?" Clare nodded toward Aaron. "He's a babe. Are you two dating?"

"No. We're just friends. *Daed* allows me to go out with him because I think he's hoping we'll start to court, but you know how I feel about that. Too soon to be tied down."

Clare cocked her head to one side and gazed at Aaron. "I don't know, Leah. I think I'd have to give it a try. He's too cute not to."

Leah looked toward Aaron, who was chatting with Ruth. Then she turned her attention back to Clare, who was still mesmerized by Aaron. "I reckon he's not bad looking." The image of Aaron's arms around her waist in the pasture flashed in Leah's mind.

"Is he nice?" Donna sat up a little taller and eyed Aaron. "And who is that with you guys?"

"*Ya*, he's nice. We're friends. But that's all." She paused and pulled the stack of handwritten papers from the bag. "And that's his Aunt Ruth. She's visiting from Florida." She slid the story sideways until it was in front of Donna. "This is the book I was telling you about."

"Oh." Donna eyed the title. "*A Walk in My Shoes*. Sounds nice."

"It's about an Amish girl and her *Englisch* friend, and there's also a love story." Leah smiled. "But the best part is the way that the *Englisch* girl finds her way to the Lord, and how her life changes when that happens." Leah couldn't wait for her friends to read the book. "Aaron read it, and he seemed to really like it."

"*He* read it?" Clare's eyes grew wide.

"*Ya*, why do you look so shocked?" Leah rested her elbow on the table and supported her chin.

"Oh, I don't know. He just doesn't look like the reading type." Clare shrugged. "He just looks more—more the manly type."

"He said he loved the book. And I think both of you will too." She glanced back and forth between the two of them. "I can't wait for us to be able to talk about what you think after you read it. I think there are so many messages, messages that God wanted me to put in the book. It just felt so right to put the story into words, and—"

"Okay. Sure." Donna put the book back into the plastic bag and pushed it to the edge of the table, next to the wall. "I'll read it first."

"I better go to my table." Leah gently touched Donna's hand. "I've missed you both. Hopefully, it won't be long until *mei daed* will not be so strict with me. I'd love to meet you for a movie soon."

"Call us," Clare said. "We've missed you too."

Leah excused herself, stood up, and joined Aaron and Ruth. "I'm sorry. Those are two of my dear friends that I haven't seen in a while." She sat down in the chair in between Aaron and Ruth. Her eyes drifted in Aaron's direction, and she saw his mouth twitch a bit. *He's nervous.* Leah felt a little nervous herself, all of a sudden, as their eyes met and held for a moment.

"Manicotti for everyone!" Auntie Ruth bellowed when the waitress walked up.

"Auntie Ruth, don't you think we should give Leah time to look at the menu? She might not want manicotti." Aaron looked up at the waitress and smiled.

And Leah found it bothersome the way the *Englisch* waitress smiled back at Aaron, her light-colored hair draping down around her shoulders and framing her bright blue eyes. Leah suddenly felt even plainer than usual. *Stop looking at her.*

Leah silently scolded herself for allowing such feelings of jealousy into her mind. And it had been happening a lot lately.

"Mani—manicotti—is fine for me." She could feel a flush in her cheeks. "Did I say that right?" She turned toward Ruth, who was gathering up all their menus.

"Yep. You did. Here, hon." Ruth handed the menus to the pretty girl who couldn't seem to take her eyes off of Aaron. "Three teas too." Ruth leaned toward the waitress. "That's all, dear."

"Sorry," Aaron said to Leah. Then he turned to Ruth. "Auntie Ruth, you didn't even give Leah a chance to pick something."

Ruth puckered her red lips as her eyes widened. "Now, Aaron Lantz, why in the world would Leah want to order something else when the manicotti is the best thing on the menu?" She shook her head and turned toward Leah. "Honey, you wouldn't have wanted to do that, now would you?" She leaned back in her chair and folded her arms across her large chest. "I mean, think about it . . . Aaron and I would be having the manicotti, and you would have settled for something not nearly as good. Wouldn't have been right."

"I might have chosen something besides the manicotti too," Aaron mumbled.

Auntie Ruth didn't seem to hear him. She pulled her big pink bag from where it hung on the back of her chair and slammed it down on the table.

"Now, prepare yourselves, young people." Ruth leaned in closer and in a whisper said, "I have something to show you."

Chapter Fifteen

AARON BRACED HIMSELF FOR WHATEVER RUTH WAS ABOUT to show them, and wondered if using her as an excuse to see Leah was really going to be worth it. No telling what she might pull out of that bag of hers.

He glanced at Leah. Her smile stretched across her face, and somehow Aaron knew that whatever it was, Leah wouldn't be offended or embarrassed. She seemed in awe of Aaron's crazy aunt.

Ruth eased her hand into the bag and, as if to build tension, glanced back and forth between Aaron and Leah. "Are you ready?" She batted long black eyelashes at them. Then she took a deep breath and pulled her hand from the bag with a jerk.

Aaron thought he might fall out of his chair. He put a hand across his eyes and shook his head. But when he heard Leah giggle, he spread his fingers and viewed the object again.

"Ain't this the darnedest thing?" Ruth held up a stuffed pink cat as long as her arm. "I found this little critter at a shop in town. If you push this button, he sings and dances up a storm." Ruth fumbled around the back of the pink cat.

"Auntie Ruth, don't push that button." Aaron pulled his hand from his eyes and glared at her with enough of a warning that Ruth stopped her search for the switch.

"Well, all right." Ruth shrugged and stuffed the cat back into her oversized pink bag. "I'll show it to you later, Leah, when Mister Stuffy Pants isn't around."

Leah put one hand to her mouth, clearly holding back a giggle.

The manicotti arrived a few minutes later, and it was good, as

Ruth had predicted. For the next forty-five minutes, Leah hung on Ruth's every word as she detailed her travels and odd adventures. Aaron didn't think Leah had ever looked more beautiful. Twice she'd looked at him with a twinkle in her eye and smiled.

"Now, I reckon I best get to the ladies' room before we get back on the road." Ruth pushed her chair back.

"Me too," Leah said. "Be right back."

As Leah followed Ruth to the women's restroom, Aaron smiled. The two women were different in so many ways, but both had a spirited way of looking at life. He took a sip of his tea and thought about how he might be able to set up another date with Leah . . . without referring to it as a date, of course.

Paradiso was clearing out, but Leah's two friends were still in the booth nearby. He could hear them chatting quietly, and he didn't mean to eavesdrop, but when he heard Leah's name mentioned, he couldn't help but tune in. He smiled when he heard one of the girls say what a sweet person Leah was.

"But I wish she wouldn't force all this religious stuff on us," Aaron heard the other girl say. "I mean, she's fun to hang out with when she's not preaching. And now she wants us to read her Amish book? I don't think so."

But it's not an Amish book. It's about love, kindness, special friendships, and a relationship with the Lord.

"I agree. Leah is nice enough, but I'm not buying into all this religious junk."

Aaron cut his eyes briefly in their direction, long enough to see them stepping away from the booth and heading to the exit door. *Leah's book.*

They'd left it in the plastic bag, pushed up against the wall, as if it weren't anything special at all. *It's her only copy, and it's very special.*

Aaron acted quickly. He grabbed the bag filled with hand-written lined white pages—words Leah had toiled over until a perfect tale of love and God's blessings had spilled onto the pages. He scurried back to his seat, and he could hear Ruth's voice around the corner.

His urge to protect Leah overwhelmed him. *It's a good book.* He stood up, leaned over, and stuffed the plastic bag as far down in Ruth's giant bag as he could get it, amid items he was sure he didn't want to see. Aaron threw himself back into his chair right before the two women entered the room.

"I just love your aunt," Leah whispered when she sat down. "She's delightful."

"You're delightful." It just slipped out, and Aaron silently blasted himself for being so forward. But Leah's dimples shone with approval.

∽⌀

James peered out his bedroom window, straining to see into the darkness.

"Are you spying on our *maedel*?" Marian wrapped her arms around his waist and leaned her head around him to see. "They were gone for a good bit."

"*Ya.*" James watched Aaron walk Leah to the door, but once they hit the porch, James could no longer see them from the upstairs window. The car headlights lit up the front yard, and James thought about what an entertaining supper it must have been with Ruth.

"Perhaps they are becoming more than friends, no?" Marian pulled away from him and moved toward the bed. James followed her, rubbed his beard, and waited for his wife to pull back the covers.

He grinned. "I hope so."

James turned on the small battery-operated fan on his night table and sat down on the bed. He stretched his legs atop the covers, crossed his ankles, and yawned. Marian dimmed the lantern and snuggled up next to him, kissed him on the cheek, and then moved to her side of the bed. They both bowed their heads in silent prayer.

James thanked the Lord for the many blessings in his life, and once he was done with his usual prayers, he added a special request.

Please, dear Father, help Leah to master the skills necessary for her to be a gut fraa. *Help her to realize her place and to stop wasting her time with these silly stories she writes. Guide her, Lord, and help her to be a responsible young Amish woman. In Jesus' name, I pray.*

"Good night, my love." Marian extinguished the lantern.

James locked his hands behind his head and faced the small fan, the gentle breeze a small relief from the stifling heat. "Good night."

❧

Aaron climbed into the front seat with Ruth after he walked Leah to the door. There was an awkward but wonderful moment when Leah's eyes had fused with his in a way that made him think that they were becoming more than just friends.

"So did you ask her out again?" Ruth peeled down the driveway.

"*Ya*, I did. Worship service is at our *haus* this Sunday. I asked her if she'd like to take a buggy ride to Bird-in-Hand after the meal." He paused, checked his seat belt, and grabbed the dash as Ruth rounded the corner.

"She's a fine girl. Spunky." Ruth turned toward Aaron. He wished she'd keep her eyes on the road. "But Aaron, Leah isn't your ordinary Amish girl. As a matter of fact, I'm not seeing where you two have much in common." She stared straight ahead again. "You're rather boring compared to her."

"What?" Aaron twisted in his seat to face her. "How can you say that to me?"

Ruth shrugged. "I love ya, Aaron." She hesitated. "Actually, you're my favorite, but don't tell the others. Anyway, you just strike me as the kind of young man who is gonna want a woman to cook for ya, sew, tend to your house, and be, well—traditional." Ruth chuckled. "I didn't have to spend much time with Leah to realize that she ain't real traditional. And I've heard your sisters speak of her. When they heard we were all going out to supper, I heard Annie telling Mary that the two of you weren't a very good match."

How dare they? "Leah and I would make a fine match." Aaron sat taller and looped his thumbs in his suspenders. "And I'm not boring."

"Maybe that was a bad choice of words. But you ain't spunky like she is. And there's nothing wrong with that."

"It's one of the things I like about Leah, her free spirit."

Ruth pulled into the Lantz driveway. "From what she said tonight, I don't think that father of hers encourages that free spirit. And Leah don't strike me as someone who's gonna be tamed into something she's not."

Aaron thought about what Ruth was saying, surprised at how much sense his aunt was trying to make, even if she was wrong about him. "I wouldn't try to change her, Auntie Ruth."

Ruth turned the car off and grabbed her big pink bag, then Aaron remembered.

"*Ach*, Auntie Ruth. I stuffed something in your purse when you were in the bathroom with Leah."

She pushed open her car door, draped one foot out the door, but turned to look at him, her nose crinkling with displeasure. "Like the silverware, or what?"

Aaron grunted. "No." He pointed to her purse. "There's a plastic bag filled with papers. It's one of Leah's stories. Her *Englisch* friends left it on the table at Paradiso. I'll give it to her on Sunday, but I didn't want to make the night bad by telling her that her friends left something so important behind."

Ruth dug around to the bottom of the bag and pulled out the plastic bag. "I thought this purse felt heavier." She glanced at Aaron. "Have you read this?"

"*Ya*. It's *gut*."

They sat quietly in the dark for a moment. "Think Leah would mind if I read it?"

Aaron shrugged. "She seems to want people to read it. I reckon it'd be all right."

Ruth put the bag back in her purse, then groaned as she lifted herself to a standing position. Aaron eased out of his seat, and they both closed the car doors and began walking toward the house.

"I'll read it tonight. I might be dead tomorrow or the next day."

"Why do you keep saying things like that, Auntie Ruth?" Aaron shook his head, then latched onto her arm as she walked up the porch steps. He thought about Leah lying in the meadow and how ridiculously he'd acted.

He reached for the matches on the shelf inside the kitchen door, pulled the lantern from the same place, and lit it. He held it out so Auntie Ruth could see her way into the kitchen.

She dropped the big purse on the kitchen table, put her hands on her hips, and stared hard at Aaron. "I say it because it's the truth."

Chapter Sixteen

LEAH TIED THE STRINGS ON HER *KAPP* AND RUSHED DOWN-stairs for Sunday breakfast. She was late for the second time this week. Everyone was seated at the table, already eating, when she walked in. Her father didn't look up, but everyone else did.

"Why didn't you wake me up?" she whispered between clenched teeth when she slid onto the bench beside Edna.

"I shouldn't have to." Edna didn't whisper, and Leah cut her eyes at her sister.

"That's enough," their mother warned.

Leah was looking forward to spending time with Aaron after worship service, for reasons that surprised her. She wasn't sure what the point was. Aaron clearly wanted more than just friendship, and Leah wasn't ready for that. But every time Leah thought about him, a strange feeling overtook her.

"Daed?" Leah knew this wasn't the best time to approach her father about her plans with Aaron, but once breakfast was over, there would be morning chores, then they'd all be off to church service.

Her father looked up.

"Aaron asked me to go for a ride to Bird-in-Hand after worship service today. Would that be all right?"

Edna slammed her fork down on her plate, and Leah saw her draw in a breath and press her lips together. Leah watched her father warn Edna with his eyes. A first that she could recall.

Mary Carol and Kathleen glanced up but stayed quiet, as did their mother.

"I reckon it will be all right," *Daed* said as he reached for a piece of bacon.

Leah fought the urge to send grumpy Edna a smug grin. "*Danki, Daed.*"

Ever since she'd started spending time with Aaron, her father didn't seem to mind what she did or didn't do around the house. She didn't mean to be late for breakfast, she'd just stayed up too late working on her book. She thought about Donna and Clare, and she couldn't wait to see what her friends thought about her story, and whether it would help the girls have a better understanding of God and how a relationship with Him would change their lives.

∽

Ruth flipped open her big red suitcase, the one she'd purchased at the market in Tuscany. She recalled the big burly man trying to get her to pay the sticker price. *He didn't know who he was dealing with.*

It had been six months since she'd attended an Amish worship service, which was during her last visit to Paradise. She pulled out her favorite red dress with large white polka dots and glanced at her red straw hat hanging on the bedpost. *Perfect.*

As she dressed, she cursed herself for staying up almost all night to finish young Leah's story. The girl had a gift. That was for sure. But she couldn't help wonder how much this community would try to mold her into something she was not, and whether they would ever encourage her writing. Ruth thought about how difficult it was when she left the Old Order at eighteen, choosing not to seek baptism into the faith. She'd never let on to anyone, but many times she'd regretted her decision. She hoped Leah wouldn't make the same mistake. Ruth could tell that the girl had a spirit like a wild stallion, not to be harnessed. If her family would give her a little room outside the box within which they all lived, Ruth believed Leah could grow and thrive in this community. Back in Ruth's day there was no bending of the rules; an Amish girl was expected to perform a certain way, no questions asked.

But at this time in her life, so near to death, Ruth wanted to be in this peaceful place with family. *I'll be home soon, Lord.*

She pulled her hat over her gray hair, wound tightly atop her head, and covered her lips with a bright red color to match her ensemble. She looked in the small mirror hanging from a chain on the far wall. It was important to look her best each and every day. *When I go, I'm going out in style.*

She grabbed her big pink purse from the night before, dumped all the contents into an equally large red bag, then grabbed Leah's story from the dresser and stuffed it inside her purse.

❧

Aaron helped Abner take down the removable walls that separated the den and dining room to make room for the hundred or so people who would be attending worship service at the Lantz house this morning. Every eight to nine months, it was their turn to host worship. It was the only time the walls came down, unless they were hosting a Sunday singing, which they did about twice a year.

Aaron was anxious to see Leah, but something was chewing at his insides, and he couldn't seem to shake it. *I am not boring.*

Auntie Ruth's words kept ringing in his mind, and Aaron had thought about this for half the night, until sleep finally came at around midnight. He decided that he might be a tad set in his ways. He also appreciated a schedule and enjoyed the structure in his life. But boring? *I think not.*

Then why couldn't he get the comment out of his head?

"Hurry, boys. People are starting to arrive." His mother slammed her hands on her hips and glanced at the clock on the wall. "It's almost eight o'clock, and you still don't have those walls down." She turned to head back into the kitchen, and Aaron could hear her barking orders at

Annie and Mary. He shook his head. *Now there is a person who lives a structured life*, he thought. Sarah Lantz had everything organized to perfection all the time, and she was always on schedule—with everything.

Aaron listened to his mother's voice rise a little as she told Mary that the bread in the oven must be pulled out right when the timer dinged, not a minute afterward. All of a sudden, he wondered if his mother ever did anything just for fun. Even when his father took a break to read a book, *Mamm* was always tending to something on her schedule. She never seemed to do anything that wasn't preplanned. *Am I like that?*

Aaron searched his mind for some wild, adventurous thing he'd done lately—or ever. Failing that, he tried to recall the last time he'd done something out of the ordinary or veered from his schedule. *I read Leah's book.*

He saw Leah through the window then, walking across the front yard with her family, and he determined that today would be the day he was going to show Leah Petersheim that he was anything but boring, and he would prove his aunt was wrong.

❦

Worship service lasted three hours, as usual, with the men on one side of the room, the women on the other, and the bishop and deacons in the middle. Leah sat with her mother and sisters, and Ruth had chosen a seat next to her. She could hear Ruth's stomach growling—loudly.

"This is one thing I don't miss," Ruth whispered to Leah. "Three hours of worship on these backless benches every other Sunday."

Leah nodded, stifled a giggle. She felt sure that everyone around them heard Ruth's comment. Ruth sat a little taller in her red and white polka dot dress and matching hat and shoes. Leah had thought her mother's eyes were going to pop out of her head when she saw Ruth come downstairs earlier, making a proud grand entrance. Most everyone there knew Ruth, and it shouldn't have been a shock to anyone, but eyes bulged at the sight of her just the same.

"I hope we have ham loaf," Ruth whispered to Leah.

Leah nodded again, then looked across the room. She found Aaron, who was shaking his head but smiling. Perhaps Ruth's voice was carrying more than Leah thought.

She thought about the ride she'd be taking with Aaron after the Sunday meal and realized that she'd been looking forward to it ever since they'd all dined at Paradiso on Wednesday.

"Praise be to God!" Ruth stood up immediately after Bishop Ebersol closed the worship service in prayer.

Leah wasn't sure if Ruth meant the comment as actual praise to God in response to Bishop Ebersol's recitations or as relief that the service was over. Either way, the bishop glowered at Ruth.

She didn't seem to notice. "Let's eat," she said as she pushed ahead of the others toward the kitchen.

Following the meal, some of the older folks headed home, but a lot of the men gathered in the barn to tell jokes, and the women chatted in the kitchen and den. Rebecca Miller was organizing a volleyball game, and Leah smiled when she saw Ben standing nearby.

Leah was playing a game of croquet with a couple of the younger children when Aaron approached her from behind. She jumped when he poked her slightly in the back. "Ready to get out of here?"

She turned around. His lip was twitching, and she wondered what he was nervous about. But Leah was nervous, too, for some reason. Maybe it was the way his voice sounded when he asked her if she was ready to leave, or maybe it was the way he was looking at her. Something seemed different.

"Okay." She handed her croquet mallet to one of the children. "Let me go put my shoes on and tell *Mamm* I'm leaving."

A few minutes later Aaron flicked the reins and guided his horse down the driveway, and Leah was glad to be in the courting buggy, with no top, the wind in her face. She pushed back sweaty strands of hair that had fallen from beneath her prayer covering.

"I can't wait for fall. I know it's busy with the harvest and all.

But this heat is terrible." Leah jumped a bit when Aaron settled against his seat and dropped one hand right beside hers on the seat. As his finger brushed against hers, she wondered if he was trying to hold her hand. She lifted her hand, then folded both hands in her lap. She kept her head straight but cut her eyes downward to see his hand still sitting there, seeming even closer to her.

"*Ach*. I almost forgot." Aaron lifted his hand from the seat, reached behind him, and pulled out a bundle of roses wrapped in green tissue paper. He handed them to her and smiled. "These are for you. They're from Annie's garden. "

Leah felt the color rush to her cheeks. She'd never had a boy give her flowers before. She'd never been on an actual date before, and this was certainly a date if there were flowers involved. "*Danki*," she said sheepishly. She glanced up at him and forced a smile as she tried to decide how she felt about this.

Aaron kept the horse at a steady gait down the winding roads toward Bird-in-Hand, and Leah gazed at meadows covered with wildflowers that seemed to connect one Amish homestead to the next. Clapboard houses, mostly white. Outbuildings, roaming cattle, silos, and a sense of home. Leah had seen enough television in town to know that there was nowhere in the world she'd rather live. Some of her Amish friends talked of leaving as soon as they could gather enough money, choosing not to seek baptism into the community. It was a decision Leah didn't understand.

She glanced at Aaron. He sat tall in his seat, like a towering spruce, and his profile was sharp and confident as he flicked the reins and picked up the pace. This was not the quiet boy from their school days, but a man who caused her heart to flutter in an unexpected way.

When his eyes met with hers, Leah knew something was happening between them, whether it was a part of her plan or not.

Chapter Seventeen

JAMES WAITED ON THE FRONT PORCH FOR MARIAN AND the girls to gather up the dishes they'd brought to the Lantzes' for the Sunday meal. What a good day it was. A fine worship service, a wonderful meal, and plenty of good company. He waved as several buggies pulled out to head for home, as he was hoping to do soon. The heavy meal had settled on him, and he was ready to relax at his own home before bedtime, perhaps take in the sunset from the front porch. Tomorrow would be a busy day, but Sundays were a day of rest, and that was exactly how James planned to spend the remainder of this one.

The screen door slammed, and James turned to see Ruth joining him on the porch, toting a plastic bag. She'd shed her bright red shoes, and as she walked barefoot toward him, still dressed in the red polka dot dress, he couldn't help but smile. She didn't smile back.

"This is for you." She thrust the plastic bag at him, almost hitting him in the stomach. "Read it. Think about it. Pray about it."

"What?" James peeked into the bag. Dozens, or hundreds, of notebook-sized papers were bound with three rubber bands. "What is this?" He flipped through the pages for a moment, then looked up at Ruth.

"Leah has a gift from the Lord, James. Don't keep the girl from being who she really is by stifling her dreams." Ruth waved her hand in the air. "There's plenty of women around here who can cook, clean, tend gardens, and the like—but I don't know any who have the ability to touch another person through words on a page like your Leah. She is special, James. And someone is gonna read this book and be changed by it."

"This is Leah's?" He looked in the bag again. "Why are you giving it to me?"

Ruth grinned. "'Cause I think you're gonna be the first one to be changed by it." She slapped him on the arm. "Now, go store that in your buggy. No need to mention this to the others, but you take yourself home and you read that girl's story. Quit trying to mold her into something she ain't. She has a far greater purpose."

Then she actually gave James a little push on the shoulder. He just wanted her to go away, so he marched to the buggy, stashed the bag under the seat, and stalled a bit until he saw her go back inside. *Glad she's not my aunt.*

It wasn't long before Marian, Edna, Mary Carol, and Kathleen joined him, and they all squeezed into the buggy. Without Leah in between him and Marian, the ride was much more comfortable, even though his daughters were somewhat cramped in the back. But it was a short ride, and the entire way he thought about what Ruth said and about the bag under his seat.

∽◯

Leah flung her hands into the air and held her head back, the wind whipping her cheeks into a rosy shade of pink, and Aaron didn't think he'd ever seen a more beautiful vision. Her brown dress brought out the color of her eyes, which flickered like gold in the sunlight. He picked up the pace even more, until his horse was in a comfortable gallop.

"I love to go fast!" She dropped her hands and turned toward him, and Aaron smiled in her direction. "I hardly ever get to drive our buggy. We have two, the family-sized covered buggy and the spring buggy. But if *Mamm* and *Daed* aren't using one, Edna gets the first chance to travel in it. Since she's the oldest and all."

Aaron slowed the horse to a trot, glad that he was fortunate enough to own a topless buggy. Unlike a spring buggy, which wasn't enclosed and held four comfortably, his courting buggy only had one seat—just room enough for two. A cozy arrangement for those of dating age. "You wanna drive?"

"*Ya!*" She twisted toward him. "I sure do!"

"Whoa, boy," he said, bringing the buggy to a complete stop. "There aren't too many cars on this road, but watch that curve up ahead in front of the Miller place. Sometimes the *Englisch* come barreling around that corner in their cars."

"I will."

Aaron walked around to the other side of the buggy, and Leah slid over to his side and picked up the reins. He was just getting ready to give her some simple instructions when she whistled and slapped the horse into action. Aaron grabbed his hat just as it began to lift off his head. He pushed it down tighter around his forehead as Leah brought the horse to a faster run than he had a few moments ago.

I hope this wasn't a mistake. She seems fearless.

But as he watched her slow the horse and ease around the sharp corner, his heart rate returned to normal. Then she picked it up again, and they flew down a long stretch of wide-open road. Her smile was eager and alive, and Aaron slid an arm around her shoulder. She slowed down almost instantly, and the perk in her mood seemed to deflate. Aaron pulled his arm back, realizing he'd gone too far.

"That's enough for me," she said. She brought the buggy to a halt and wasted no time jumping from the seat. Aaron exited his side and met her up front where she was rubbing Pete's snout. "He's tired. We probably ran him too hard."

Aaron knew that wasn't what caused her to jump out of his buggy.

"Why are we going to Bird-in-Hand?" She tilted her head to one side, still stroking the horse. "It's mostly for tourists."

Aaron shrugged. "Just somethin' to do. We can go anywhere you want."

He saw her take a deep breath, and she avoided his eyes when she spoke. "Maybe back to your cousin's pond. It's pretty there."

And private. "Sure. We can go there." It wasn't in his plan. He'd wanted to buy her something at the market in Bird-in-Hand, sip root beer at the small stand on the way there, and make sure she knew he wasn't boring. But this was a far greater plan.

Less than five minutes later, Aaron parked the buggy, and he and Leah walked down to the water's edge. He followed her out onto the pier. She pulled off her black leather shoes and socks, sat down, and dangled her feet in the water below. Aaron followed her lead, careful not to sit too close to her.

"Remember when we were younger, how everyone used to go to the river? The girls would all sit on the bank and watch all you boys swim." She turned toward him with an expression of fond recollections.

"*Ya.*" Aaron remembered that he was always looking at Leah to see if she was watching him when he took his turn on the tire swing. "Those were fun times."

They sat quietly for a few moments.

"I can't wait to hear what Donna and Clare think of my book," she said out of the clear blue.

Aaron took a deep breath, knowing he was about to kill the mood and the moment.

"Leah, I need to tell you something about that."

"What?" She was still splashing her feet in the water, but she looked up.

"Your *Englisch* friends left the book on the table, and I picked it up, and—"

"What?" Her feet grew still in the water, and her eyes searched his.

"I'm sure they didn't mean to. I saw them leave, and they must have just—"

"But that's my only copy. What if you hadn't picked it up?"

Aaron didn't have the heart to tell her what he'd overheard the girls saying. He wanted so badly to take her in his arms, comfort her, and tell her that those girls were not the ones meant to read her book. They weren't ready.

She bolted upright. "Where's the book now?"

"I didn't want to upset you that night, so I stuffed it into Auntie Ruth's purse. I meant to bring it to you, but I forgot to get it back." He paused. "*Ach*, and I hope it's okay, but Auntie Ruth asked if she could read it."

This brightened her face. "Really?"

"*Ya*. Is that all right?"

"*Ya. Ya.* I can't wait to hear what she thinks of it."

"I'm sure that Donna and Clare want to read it too." It was a lie, and Aaron wished he hadn't said it, but he felt compelled to make her happy.

She shook her head, then turned to him and smiled. "Maybe they just aren't ready."

He smiled back at her, and then without warning, she cut her foot to the side and splashed water all over him. "You were sweating like our pig!" she said, laughing.

Aaron wiped the water from his face, cut his eyes in her direction, and then returned the gesture, covering her with water. "You looked pretty sweaty yourself!"

She screamed when the cool water doused her, and immediately kicked water back at him. "Take that, Aaron Lantz!"

Laughter erupted from way down deep. Aaron wasn't sure what came over him, but he suddenly grabbed her around the waist and threw her in.

Leah bobbed up, soaking wet, bobbed back under again, then bobbed up, gasped for air, and said, "I can't swim!"

Aaron's heart leaped from his chest as he jumped into the water to rescue her. He wrapped his arms around her, pulled her close to him, and then stood up in the four feet of water. Leah stood up then, too, laughing so hard she could hardly speak. "Gotcha!"

But Aaron still had his arms tightly around her waist. "Who's got who?"

She stopped laughing, and fear stretched across her face as her eyes met with his. He could feel her trembling. The honorable thing to do would have been to let her go and help her out of the water and back onto the pier. Instead he pulled her closer and kissed her gently on the lips. Then he kissed her again, and this time she closed her eyes and kissed him back.

"Leah," he whispered. He pushed a strand of wet hair from her cheek and attempted to tuck it back beneath her wet prayer covering. "I've wanted to do that for a long time."

"Aaron, I—I—" She pushed away from him. "I'd make a terrible choice for courtship." She crinkled her face as if she'd bitten into something sour.

He stepped closer to her in the water and gently put his hands on her waist and turned her so that her back was against the pier. She was still trembling. With ease, he lifted her up and onto the pier. He stayed in the water facing her. "Is this the part where you're gonna tell me what a terrible cook you are, and how you can't sew?"

She hung her head, then looked back up at him. "Not only is it true, it doesn't even bother me much that I can't do these things. I'd rather be writing and doing things that matter to me."

Aaron grabbed his straw hat, floating nearby. Then he lifted himself onto the pier. He set the wet hat down beside him, pushed back his soaked hair, and turned to face her. "Why don't we just see how it goes?"

Leah nodded. "Okay." Then she pointed a finger in his direction. "But don't say I didn't warn you. I'll never be one of those women who cooks and cleans and waits on a man constantly, without any other outside interests, and I also will not—"

Aaron kissed her again, and she stopped talking and fell willingly into his arms.

Chapter Eighteen

MARIAN CLIMBED INTO BED BESIDE JAMES, BUT HE DIDN'T even look up.

"Leah is home. She said she had a wonderful time with Aaron. *Gut* news, no?"

James nodded. "*Ya.*"

Marian reached for her lotion on the bedside table and lit her own lantern on her side of the bed. "Leah's clothes were damp and wrinkled, like maybe they'd been swimming, but I didn't ask."

Her husband still didn't look up.

"James, you've been reading all afternoon. Are you still trying to learn from the *Englisch* author how to rear daughters?"

James had Leah's note pages propped up against the book he'd been reading, so it was no wonder Marian thought he was reading the *Englisch* author. He veered the book in Marian's direction so that she could see the stack of notebook paper resting against it. "No, I am reading Leah's book."

Marian's eyes grew large. "Leah's book?" She scooted closer to him and pushed back his arm so she could see better. "Where did you get that? Does she know you're reading it?"

James pulled off his glasses and rubbed his eyes. "I don't know. Ruth gave it to me."

"Ruth? What was she doing with it?"

He raised his shoulders, dropped them slowly. "I reckon I don't know. She said she thought I should read it, though."

They sat quietly for a moment.

"Is it *gut*? The book," Marian finally asked.

James swallowed back the lump in his throat. "*Ya,*" he whispered. Then he wrapped an arm around his wife, pulled her closer. "Listen to this." James put his glasses on and read a page from Leah's book.

Rose thought about her relationship with God, and she couldn't imagine herself alone and without faith—like Lauren. She sat down beside her Englisch friend and prayed for guidance, for a way to open Lauren's heart to the Lord and His Son, Jesus. As she silently prayed, she thought about her father and what he might do in a situation such as this. Rose's father was the wisest man she knew, often strict with his daughters, but Rose had never doubted his love for her, or his faith in God. And he had a way of knowing what to do in a crisis.

Rose recalled the time when her father's brother died, Rose's only uncle. It was the only time she'd ever seen her father cry, and despite all of their grief, he'd reminded his daughters that God's will often causes us pain that we cannot understand, but that to question His will is to question all things in life and our purpose on this earth. "We each have a purpose," her father had said. "Mei brother's purpose has been fulfilled."

James took a deep breath, glanced at Marian.

"She's talking about you." Marian stroked his arm tenderly. "And David."

James thought back to when his brother's horse—an animal fresh off the track with no road experience—bolted out onto Lincoln Highway and into oncoming traffic. He nodded, then went on.

But this was a different kind of crisis. No one had died, yet a part of Lauren seemed to be dying on the inside. Her father was a loving man, but he thought Lauren should follow in his footsteps by running the family business. But Lauren had her own dreams, dreams her father couldn't understand.

"My father says my dreams are nonsense, and that playing music will never make me a fine living, like taking over his business will," Lauren said. *"How can I make my father understand that he can't make me into something I'm not?"* She looked at Rose. *"I want to make my father proud of me, but I also want to live my own life."*

James pulled off his glasses again and leaned his head against the headboard.

"James." Marian leaned her head on his shoulder, then kissed his cheek. "She is also talking about you here." Marian reached for the book on her husband's lap. "Here, let me."

James lifted his hand so Marian could take Leah's loose pages. He closed the *Englisch* book and placed it on his bedside table. Marian straightened Leah's pages, pulled her knees up, and propped their daughter's words in front of her. James kept his head resting against the headboard as his wife read.

Rose smiled at her friend, then latched onto her hand. "Let me tell you about Jesus. He is a personal friend of mine, and I'd like to introduce you to Him." Rose proceeded to tell Lauren about Jesus and His Father, and she prayed constantly that God's words would flow from her and into her friend's heart. When Lauren began to weep, Rose knew that the Holy Spirit was settling around her friend, and she thanked God continually. In the back of her mind, though, she kept wondering if her own father would be proud of her.

James felt a tear roll down his cheek.

His wife set Leah's book aside and kissed away his tear. "My darling James."

"I've been praying for the wrong things, Marian." He took a deep breath and gathered himself, embarrassed for Marian to see him like this. He'd only cried once in his entire life—when David died—and yet his daughter's words were having a profound effect on him. "I've prayed each night for God to rid Leah of these silly stories, not once considering that His will *is* being done." He turned toward Marian. "Perhaps this story of hers will change a life somehow."

Marian smiled. "Maybe it just did."

❦

When Aaron took Leah home, he kissed her yet again, and the feel of her lips against his stayed with him all the way home. What a wonderful day it had been. After their swim, they'd spent hours talking, and Aaron knew that someday he was going to make Leah his wife.

He wasn't surprised to see the Petersheim spring buggy at his house when he pulled up. When he dropped Leah at home, she'd commented that Edna had probably taken the buggy and gone back to see Abner. The closer it got to the wedding, the more inseparable Abner and Edna were.

Aaron tended to his horse, then walked up to the house, a new-found bounce in his step. He smiled. He might have to eat a lot of chicken salad for the rest of his life, but he was willing to do that to be with Leah.

When he hit the porch, he heard voices. Edna and Abner were evidently in the den. Aaron heard his name and paused.

"Leah is only using Aaron. You do know that, right?" Edna's voice coursed through him.

"What do you mean?" Abner asked.

Aaron inched closer to the door, careful to stay out of sight, then leaned his ear toward the door.

"*Daed* won't let her go out and do anything because she shirks all her responsibilities at home. She's late to meals all the time, and she just doesn't do her share," Edna said. "She helped a little bit when I got sick, but then she just slipped back to her old ways."

"How is that using Aaron?"

"*Daed* wants so badly for Leah to find a husband, he's not about to tell her she can't go out with him. She only goes because it's her ticket to freedom."

Aaron's chest tightened.

"She threw a fit that first night when I said Aaron was coming over. She's never had an interest in him. I think it's just wrong the way she is using him to get out of the house, because I think Aaron really likes her."

"*Ya*, he does," Abner said. "But are you sure about this?"

"Sure am." Edna paused again. "Remember the other night when Aaron and your aunt picked up Leah to go to Paradiso?"

"*Ya.*"

"Well, she'd already sent word by way of the postman for her *Englisch* friends to meet her there. *Daed* didn't want her spending time with them until she was doing her share around the house."

Aaron's stomach began to churn. *How stupid I've been.*

But then he thought about the afternoon they'd just shared, the kisses, the playfulness, the long talk. *No. This couldn't be true.*

"I don't want to see Aaron get hurt, that's all," Edna went on. "Leah has said over and over that she doesn't want to get married. At least, not any time soon. And Aaron seems ready to settle down."

Aaron had heard enough. He walked in the door, said hello, and marched up the stairs, but he did overhear Edna say one more thing before he hit the second floor.

"Uh-oh. Do you think he heard me?"

⌾⌾⌾

The next morning Leah beat everyone downstairs, started breakfast, and bounced around the kitchen, humming. And she had the strangest urge to attempt another tomato pie.

She busied herself all morning with the day's chores. After she finished the laundry, she worked on other things to help her sisters. She even took another stab at hemming a pair of pants for her father. She'd stayed up working on her latest story, but something was different. Leah didn't feel like she *had* to help out—she wanted to.

She wondered if this new attitude was what caused her tomato pie to turn out perfectly. She couldn't wait to take it to Aaron. Maybe he would kiss her again. Her stomach somersaulted at the thought.

"*Mamm*, can I take the buggy to town?" It was nearing two o'clock, and Aaron had mentioned yesterday that he would be leaving work at two o'clock to go home and start readying the fields for the fall harvest. She wanted to catch him at the furniture shop and give him the pie.

Her mother folded two kitchen towels and placed them in a drawer before turning around to face Leah. "I reckon it will be all right with your *daed*." Marian glanced at the pie. "Did you make this, Leah? Did it turn out this time?"

"I made it for Aaron, and it turned out perfectly," she said proudly.

"Hmm. I thought you didn't like to cook."

Leah shrugged. "I'm not good at it, but something about Aaron makes me want to try harder."

Her mother nodded. "Ah, I see."

"I'm going to go ready the buggy."

Chapter Nineteen

LEAH PULLED UP AT THE FURNITURE STORE AND PARKED the buggy in a designated space. She carefully retrieved the tomato pie. She'd never felt as proud of anything she'd done in the kitchen as she did this pie. Again she wondered if Aaron would kiss her. She wondered if Aaron's father and Abner were here or if they'd already left to tend to the fields.

The bell chimed when she walked in. She spotted Aaron right away. He was so tall, his head rose higher than the shelves on one side of the store; it looked like his hat was just bouncing along the aisle. When he rounded the corner, Aaron tipped his hat back, but he didn't look as happy to see her as she'd hoped.

"Hi. I brought you this." Leah handed him the pie, then bounced on her toes a few times, beaming from ear to ear. "I made this all by myself. Tomato pie."

"*Danki*." Aaron set the pie down on the counter next to a sales log and a cup full of pens. "You didn't have to do that."

"I—I wanted to," she said as he turned his back to her and walked around the counter to the other side. "Do you want to try a piece now?"

Aaron lowered his head and began writing numbers on the log. "I can't right now, Leah. I'm busy."

She glanced around the shop. "But there's no one here."

He looked up from the log he'd been focused on. "I still have things to do. I have responsibilities around here. *Daed* and Abner have already left to go work in the fields."

"So we're alone." It was much too bold a statement, and she wished right away that she hadn't spoken the words aloud.

"*Ya.*" Aaron picked up a box on the counter, walked to a shelf, and started unloading the items inside.

Leah's pulse quickened. What was going on? She walked to where he was squatting on the ground.

"Aaron, are you angry with me about something?"

He looked up at her, but his smile seemed hard, his eyes cold. "No. Why?"

"You—you just seem, I don't know . . . different."

"I'm just busy," he said with a shrug.

Leah waited a few moments to see if he'd finish what he was doing and resume the conversation, but he stayed quiet. She took a deep breath.

"Do you want to go on another picnic Saturday? I'm sure *mei daed* would let me, and—"

"I'm sure he would," Aaron grumbled.

"What?"

"Nothing, Leah." He stood, picked up the empty box, and walked back to the counter. "I'm sorry. I can't go on a picnic Saturday."

"Working in the fields?" Any bounce Leah had had in her step earlier was completely gone.

"Uh, *ya.* I have to work in the fields."

You're lying. "Well, Sunday there isn't any church service. Maybe we—"

"I'll let you know when I'm not busy anymore."

He turned and walked to the back of the building, and Leah wished she'd never allowed herself to feel anything at all for Aaron Lantz. She should have stayed focused on writing her stories, something that made her feel good.

As her bottom lip began to quiver, she ran out the door.

❧

Aaron walked to the front of the store and watched Leah through the large glass pane in the front of the shop. When she swiped at teary eyes, he whispered her name. He wanted to go to her, but what was the point? She probably forced herself to make the pie as an excuse to bring it to him, which got her out of the house for the day to go do whatever she really wanted to do.

He pulled his hat off and raked a hand through his hair, then blew out an exasperated sigh. He should have known better than to pursue Leah. He didn't want to live on chicken salad the rest of his life anyway. Aaron glanced at the pie. Or tomato pie.

But the ache in his heart defied his thoughts as he watched her drive her buggy out of the parking lot.

⚬⁓⊙

Leah allowed herself a good cry on the way home. Aaron's face kept flashing before her—his cold expression, the glassy stare. Not the same person as yesterday. She thought about how hard she'd worked to get the tomato pie just right and how good it felt to make the pie for him.

To make matters worse, she stopped at the bakery where Donna worked and asked her about leaving the book at Paradiso. She'd hoped her friend would apologize for being so careless, but Donna didn't seem to think it was of much importance. She just shrugged and said she didn't have time to read. Leah left the bakery with hurt feelings, wondering if her father had been right about the dangers of spending too much time with those unequally yoked.

Her thoughts drifted back to Aaron. If she hadn't allowed herself to get close to him, she wouldn't know what she was missing. In the stories she wrote, she could control every little detail and ensure a happy ending. Not the case in real life. She'd had a change of heart about her life and the possibility of something more with Aaron. What a mistake.

She crossed Lincoln Highway and headed toward home. On the way she passed Aaron's cousin's farm, and she could see the pond and the pier from the road. Memories of the playful time they'd had, their kisses, and their long talks swirled in her head, and anger began to build. Why would Aaron give her flowers and treat her with such kindness yesterday, only to turn on her today?

Leah pulled into her driveway, parked the buggy, then sat in a rocker on the front porch. She wasn't ready to see anyone just yet. She kicked off her shoes, pulled off her socks, then pushed the chair into motion. Her father was on the plow behind the mules, getting the fields ready for harvest, and she knew he'd be heading this way for supper soon. Leah could hear her mother and Kathleen scurrying around in the kitchen.

Sighing, she leaned her head back against the back of the rocker and fought the urge to cry again. She didn't even feel like writing. Anger tugged at her even more. Not only had Aaron played with her emotions, but now she wasn't even inclined to work on her stories. *Daed* would be happy about that.

❧

Supper was one of those meals where Edna and Mary Carol dominated the conversation with talk of their upcoming weddings, which only added to Leah's state of mind.

"Leah, I'd like to talk to you." *Daed* wiped his mouth with his napkin, and Leah's sisters all searched their father's face right along with Leah.

"Okay," she responded, then sighed. *What did I do now?* She finished off her tea, then rose from the table when her father did. She followed him onto the front porch, thinking it must be something really bad if he didn't want to scold her in front of everyone else.

"Let's take a walk." *Daed* walked down the porch steps, and Leah joined him.

"*Daed*, I got up extra early to do my chores. I didn't leave to go see Aaron until after everything was done. *Mamm* said she thought you wouldn't mind."

His face was solemn, his mouth drawn into a frown. "I know, Leah." He looped his thumbs in his suspenders and kept his eyes toward the ground in front of him.

Leah's heart was beating out of her chest. She couldn't recall her father ever asking her to take a walk with him before. They passed the barn and went to Mary Carol's garden, where there was a bench underneath a shade tree. Leah could smell the wisteria growing along the barbed wire fence off to her right, the sweet fragrance doing little to calm her nerves. A gentle breeze swept across her face.

This was one of her favorite places to write her stories. From this spot, she could see across the meadow to where the cows were grazing near the pond, and butterflies seemed to enjoy this place as much as she. She scanned the wide-open fields as the feel of the plush grass wrapped around her toes.

Daed sat down and motioned for Leah to do the same. He took a deep breath, then turned to face her. "I read your book."

"What?"

"The one with Rose and the girl Lauren."

"But how did you—"

"Ruth brought it to me. She said she'd read it, and she thought I should read it too." He raised his brows. "And I did."

Leah's chest hurt from the pressure. His expression was impossible to read, and while he didn't look angry, the wrinkles in his forehead had grown more defined as he spoke.

He pulled off his hat and set it on his lap, then wiped the sweat from his brow. "You have a gift, Leah," he began.

She felt the pressure in her chest lift just a little.

"And for me not to encourage you to use that gift as a way to reach those in search of the Lord . . ." He shook his head. "I reckon it would be wrong."

Leah tried to absorb what he was saying.

"It's not normally our way to minister to others, but after readin' your story, it seems to me that the Lord is working through you, and to keep you from doing His work would be a sin." He looked away from her and stared at the ground, twirling his hat in his hands. "You have my blessing to pen your tales, as long as you keep up with your share of the chores around the *haus*." He faced her again, sighed, and said, "I reckon everyone ain't meant to be a perfect cook, seamstress, and housekeeper. But if you plan to keep seeing that boy, you might want to at least work on those things just a little." He grinned.

Her father's words had lifted her up so much that she'd momentarily forgotten about Aaron. Afraid of crying, she just nodded.

He stood up, put his hat on, and started to walk away. Leah sat there. She needed to think.

"Leah?"

She looked up when she heard her name. Her father was looking back at her.

"I love you."

He turned around and hurried across the yard before Leah could say anything. James Petersheim was a man of few words, and he had never spoken those three words directly to Leah.

It was impossible to choke back the tears.

Chapter Twenty

ALMOST TWO WEEKS PASSED, AND NOT ONLY HAD LEAH not seen Aaron, but she hadn't worked on her latest story at all. Her father had given his blessing, so she didn't have to hide it anymore, and yet—her heart was filled with sadness and the words didn't seem to come. She chopped the weeds around the garden with the weed eater, and it sputtered a little. Probably running out of gas.

"Leah!" Mary Carol's snappy tone pulled her from her musings. She let the weed eater idle.

"What?"

Mary Carol threw her hands on her hips, scowled, then pointed to the ground. "Those are not weeds! Those are greens that *were* almost ready to pick. Move that machine away from my garden."

"Sorry." Leah rolled her eyes, moved to the bench under the tree, and whacked away at the weeds climbing up the legs of the seat.

How could he have kissed me? And more than once.

Leah wasn't sure whom she was angrier with, Aaron or herself, for stepping outside the safe pages of her books and into a real-life situation . . . one that had left her heartbroken.

She jumped when someone poked her on the back. This time she cut the motor on the weed eater.

"This was clipped to the mailbox." Kathleen pushed an envelope in Leah's direction.

Leah set the machine down, wiped her face with her apron, then accepted the envelope. "Who's it from?"

Kathleen shrugged. "How would I know?" She took off across the grass toward the house, and Leah plopped herself down on the bench, the shade a welcome relief from the glaring sun.

Edna used to do the weed eating, until she found out about her asthma, so they'd switched some chores around. Leah swiped her brow, thinking she'd gotten the bad end of the deal. Edna was inside, sitting at the table in front of the fan, chopping vegetables to make chow-chow.

Leah peeled back the flap on the envelope and pulled out a small sheet of red paper. In black ink it read:

Leah,

Please meet me at our place tomorrow at noon. There is much to be said, and I miss you.

Her heart fluttered.

Then she read the next sentence:

Can you please bring lunch?
Kindest regards, Aaron

Leah stared in disbelief at the letter. *Is he crazy?*

First of all, she didn't know that they had a *place*. Secondly, the nerve of him!

"Who's the note from?" Mary Carol was toting a garden hoe as she approached.

Leah stood up and stomped her foot. "It's from Aaron Lantz! And can you believe that he wrote me this note?" She showed the red piece of paper to Mary Carol. "The nerve of him to ask me to bring lunch. He barely talked to me the last time I saw him." Leah shrugged. "Well, I reckon I'm not going." She folded her arms across her chest.

Mary Carol burst out laughing.

"What's so funny?"

Her sister struggled to catch her breath. "I've just never seen you like this about a boy."

"Like what?"

Mary Carol handed the letter back to Leah and grinned. "So smitten. You really like Aaron."

"Well, I thought I did. Then he just turned very—cold. I can't imagine why he wants to meet." She scrunched her face up, but then couldn't help but grin. "Maybe he just loves my chicken salad and tomato pie."

"Somehow I doubt that's it." Mary Carol turned, walked back to her garden, and yelled over her shoulder, "I think you should go!"

"I'm not going!"

The next morning, Leah pulled her tomato pie from the oven, wrapped it in foil, and added it to the picnic basket, along with two chicken salad sandwiches and some chow-chow that Edna and Kathleen made the night before. She glanced at the clock hanging on the wall in the kitchen. Eleven thirty. She was going to have to ride her foot scooter to meet Aaron, since today was *Mamm*'s day to go to market. Leah didn't want to prepare the larger family buggy just to go down the road a mile.

As she toted the picnic basket outside, she felt torn about Aaron's note. As glad as she was that he wanted to see her, why the sudden change? And she couldn't get past how bold he was being about asking her to bring lunch. Irritation and a sense of excitement swirled together as she placed their lunch inside the metal basket on the front of the scooter.

She kicked herself into motion, and just as she was rounding the corner from her driveway to the road, she saw her father plowing the fields to her right. He waved, and Leah returned the gesture, balancing herself on the foot scooter with one hand. Things were different between them now, and Leah thanked God for that blessing each day. *Daed* seemed to see her in a new light, accepting her for the person she was as opposed to who he thought she should be.

Warm wind blew in her face as she scooted past the abandoned Bontrager place.

Leah slowed her pace on the scooter as she turned the corner and neared the Lapp farm. Aaron was already there. His courting buggy was parked near the house, and she could see him leaning against the buggy with his ankles crossed and—

Are those flowers he's holding?

She squinted against the sun's glare to have a better look. Sure enough, he was toting a bouquet of flowers in his right hand. She felt a tad guilty about balking over lunch.

As she pulled into the driveway, she could see that they were roses, again wrapped in green tissue. Her heart flipped as she neared him and slowed to a stop.

"These are for you." Aaron offered her the roses. "I've missed you, Leah."

Leah accepted the flowers but avoided his eyes. *"Danki."* She didn't move from the scooter, unsure what to say or do.

"I see you brought lunch." Aaron nodded toward the picnic basket. "That was nice."

You told me to. She tried to push back her bitterness about that, since he'd shown up with flowers and said he'd missed her. "Chicken salad and tomato pie." She lifted the basket out of the tray and gently set the flowers inside.

"I brought a blanket. Do you want to go back to our spot under the tree by the pond?"

"I reckon." Leah forced a smile. He seemed genuinely glad to see her, but she still wondered what had caused him to change his mind. They started walking toward the pond, and Aaron took the basket from her. He had the blanket draped across his shoulder and a thermos in one hand.

"I remembered to bring tea this time," she said as she eyed the silver thermos.

"We'll have plenty to drink then." He smiled.

BETH WISEMAN

Leah's head was filled with recollections of their last time here, especially of his tender kisses. But she was leery of him now. If he'd turned on her so suddenly before . . .

When they got to the pond, Aaron spread the blanket underneath the tree and set the picnic basket and thermos in a far corner. He motioned for her to sit down.

Leah folded her legs sideways beneath her and fingered the intricate stitching on the blue and yellow quilt, with weaving vines of greenery connecting the bright flowers. Aaron sat down beside her, too close. His leg brushed against hers and sent a ripple through her. She edged back and took a deep breath.

"I finished your second book," he said. "Like the first one, it was great."

She smiled. "*Danki.*"

"Auntie Ruth said she gave your first story to your *daed* and suggested he read it." Aaron scowled. "I told her I wasn't sure if that was such a *gut* idea."

"Actually, it turned out to be a very *gut* idea. *Daed* read it and decided that my stories were inspired by God, and he encouraged me to keep writing."

"Leah, that's great." Aaron reached for her hand, but she pulled away. She wasn't interested in talking about her book, her father, or anything else but why they were here.

"You said there were things to be said, Aaron. What things?" She sat up a little taller and held her head high.

"Huh? *I* said?" His mouth twitched slightly to one side, and he tilted his head.

"In your note to me, you said—"

"What? What note?"

Leah raised her brows. "The note you pinned to my mailbox, of course."

Aaron rubbed his chin. "Leah, I didn't pin any note to your mailbox."

Leah had on her working apron, and since she'd read the note again that morning, she realized it was still in her pocket. She pulled it out and shoved it in his direction.

She waited while he seemed to read the note over and over again, shaking his head. "Leah, I didn't write this." He looked up at her, his eyes filled with confusion.

"What? Of course you did!" She jumped up from the blanket, put her hands on her hips, and stared down at him. "Then what are you doing here?"

Aaron lifted himself up, reached into his own pocket, and retrieved a red piece of paper just like the one Leah had just handed him. "Because *you* pinned a note on my mailbox."

"I did no such thing!" She grabbed the note from his hand.

Aaron,

Please meet me at our place tomorrow at noon. There is much to be said, and I miss you.

It would be lovely if you could bring me flowers.

Kindest regards, Leah

Leah handed him the note back as if it were poison. "I can assure you, I did not write that." She brought her hand to her chest. "What *must* you have thought, to think that I would ask you to bring me flowers?"

Aaron shrugged, grinning. "I reckon it seemed strange, but . . ."

They both stood quietly for a few moments.

"I can think of only one person who would do this," Aaron said.

Leah snapped her finger. "And her favorite color is red!"

They grew quiet again, both lost in amused thought.

"I wasn't even sure what you meant by *our place*." Leah giggled.

"I wasn't sure either." Aaron looped his thumbs in his suspenders. "And just so you know, I wouldn't have asked you to bring lunch."

Leah's face soured, and she cut her eyes at him. "Because of my cooking?"

"No, no. Because it's just, well . . . rude."

"Looks like we have lunch, and I have flowers, and . . ." Leah folded her arms across her chest. "Why would Auntie Ruth do this?"

Aaron's mouth twitched slightly to one side, and he avoided her eyes. "I reckon it's because I've been mopin' around a bit lately. At least that's what Auntie Ruth said." He looked up at Leah. "She knew I missed you."

Leah didn't understand at all. "But you are the one who didn't want to spend time with me anymore." She turned away from him. "I feel silly even being here now."

Aaron walked up behind her, so close she could feel his breath against her neck. "I've always wanted to spend time with you, Leah. I just didn't want to be your excuse to get out of the house if you weren't feeling the same thing I was feeling."

She spun around, putting their faces only inches apart, and her recollections of shared kisses danced in her mind. "What? Why would you say that?"

"I overheard Edna telling Abner that the only reason you were spending time with me was because your *daed* wouldn't let you out of the house. I reckon it didn't seem right. I almost didn't come today."

Leah looked down. "Oh no. That's not true, Aaron." She glanced up again. "It must have seemed that way, but I love—love spending time with you."

"That's *gut* to know." Aaron backed away a little, his mouth twitching slightly. "Wanna eat?"

"I guess so."

He reached for her hand, and together they sat down on the blanket. Leah opened the picnic basket and handed Aaron a sandwich, but before they took their first bite, their attention was drawn to the road. Dirt flew from beneath the horse's hooves as Abner rounded the corner and came barreling onto the driveway, going much too fast and yelling Aaron's name.

They stood up, abandoning the picnic, and Leah followed Aaron across the field. His quick walk turned to a run, and Leah broke into a jog behind him.

"What's wrong?" Aaron tried to catch his breath.

Abner climbed out of the buggy and put his hand on his brother's shoulder. "It's Auntie Ruth." Abner's forehead creased with sorrow as he spoke. "She's gone, Aaron. Passed in her sleep while she was taking a nap. We need you at home."

Chapter Twenty-one

BISHOP EBERSOL GRANTED PERMISSION FOR AUNTIE RUTH to be buried in the Amish cemetery, even though she wasn't a member of the Old Order. Aaron's parents explained that Ruth didn't have any other family, and since Ruth was Amish by birth, the bishop had agreed. An autopsy was waived because Aaron's mother found Ruth's medical records in her suitcase, along with all of her affairs neatly in order. She'd had chronic heart disease.

Leah looked for Aaron amid the crowd of people in attendance at the funeral. She recalled the way his bottom lip had trembled when he drove her home after hearing the news three days ago. He'd hurriedly kissed her on the cheek when he dropped her off, and Leah suspected he was anxious to be away from her to experience his emotions. Leah had cried when Abner told them the news, but Aaron had clamped his lips tight and merely nodded. Leah hadn't seen him again until now.

She scanned the Lantzes' den, surprised at how many people in the community were in attendance to pay their respects to Ruth. But as she overheard various conversations going on around her, she realized that Ruth had touched a lot of people.

"Remember when the Miller family suffered such tragedy when young Lizzie died four years ago?" she heard Amanda Graber's mother say to her husband. "Ruth stood guard outside the gate and kept those pesky reporters away."

Katharine Graber paused. "She certainly had a good heart."

Leah walked across the room as people began to take their seats. Rebecca Miller was standing in a corner talking to Ben. Leah knew funerals were tough for Rebecca and her entire family. She was glad Ben was nearby, but Leah wondered if those two would ever become a couple. Rebecca seemed to be lost inside herself and kept most everyone at a distance. Particularly Ben. Leah reminded herself to say an extra prayer for Rebecca tonight.

"Did you know that Ruth helped to deliver you?" Leah's mother whispered to her as they took their seats.

Leah didn't know, and she turned toward her mother. "Really?"

"*Ya*. The midwife had taken ill, and Ruth filled in like she'd delivered a baby a hundred times." Her mother smiled. "Turned out, you were her first."

The room grew quiet, and Leah found Aaron sitting on the far side of the room with the men. Her heart hurt when she saw him hastily swipe at his eyes, and she wanted to run to him, hold him, comfort him.

During the two-hour funeral, many voiced their respect for Ruth, but the focus was on admonition for the living, as was the Old Order Amish way.

Following the service, they all made their way to the buggies, and the caravan accompanied Ruth to her final resting place where a hand-dug grave awaited. Her modest tombstone had been prepared, plain like the others in the cemetery.

When the bishop closed the outdoor part of the service, Leah knew that Aaron would stay behind to help close Ruth's grave, so she left with her family to go back to the Lantz house where a meal would be served.

༄

It was nearly two hours later when Aaron and Leah finally found some quiet time to talk, around the back side of the barn. Once they were alone and out of sight, Aaron wrapped his arms around Leah and kissed her tenderly on the cheek.

"I've been wanting to do that all day."

Leah burrowed her head against Aaron's shoulder and basked in the feel of his arms, a place that felt safe and somehow . . . right. He gently eased away from her and reached into his pocket. He pulled out a red piece of paper, just like the one their notes had been written on.

"*Mamm* gave me this when I got home from our picnic." Aaron handed Leah the note. "She was—she was writing us . . ." Aaron's voice broke. "Auntie Ruth was writing a letter to you and me just before she died."

Leah gasped. "What? Why?"

"Read it." Aaron swallowed hard.

Leah unfolded the crumpled red piece of paper, took a deep breath, and read silently.

My dear Aaron and Leah,

I'm getting ready to lie down for a nap this wonderful afternoon. The birds are chirping, and it's a beautiful day outside. But, Aaron, I ate your mother's peas, and you know what those do to me. Got a bellyache. Feels like I swallowed a watermelon. Do her peas do that to you?

Leah smiled. Auntie Ruth wrote just like she lived. A maze of thoughts that somehow made sense.

Anyways, Leah and Aaron, I have you two on my mind this fine day. I'm sure you done figured out that it's your old auntie who set the two of you up. Sneaky, ain't I? But you two kids belong together. And all this moping around is a waste of God's precious time that He allows us on this earth. Yes, Leah—I hear from Edna and Abner that you've been doing your share of moping around your house too.

Leah didn't look up, but she could feel herself blushing.

Do you know that right now there are two redbirds sitting on my windowsill? They're lovely. I think they're a couple. I can tell these things.

So I hope my little plan brought the two of you together, as that was my intention. I'm tired now. Very tired. So I'll close. Sending you both a big hug. Aaron, you're my favorite, but don't tell the others.

Love, Auntie Ruth

Leah folded the letter up and handed it back to Aaron. She blinked back tears as she gazed into his eyes. "Aaron . . . ," she whispered.

He kissed her again, this time on the lips, and Leah wanted nothing more than to stay in his arms forever.

⤲⤳

Marian walked toward her husband. Most of the funeral attendees had left, and James was sitting alone at a picnic table in the Lantzes' yard with his head in his hands. She sat down beside him.

"I saw you talking to Aaron earlier." She put her hand on his leg. "It looked like a serious talk."

"*Ya.* It was." James shook his head, turned toward Marian. "He wants to marry our Leah in the fall. *This* fall."

Marian jumped, then reached for James's hand. "*Ach!* James! That's wonderful! This is what we've been hoping, that Leah would find a *gut* mate and wed."

"*Ya, ya.* I know." James sighed. "But *three* weddings? We will have Edna's, Mary Carol's, and Leah's weddings all within two months of one another."

She squeezed her husband's hand. "It will be fine, James." Then she nudged him playfully. "Think how quiet it will be around our house."

He smiled. "*Ya*. I reckon so."

They sat quietly for a few moments. Marian was thankful for the slightly cooler temperatures, but the sun was bright as she raised her hand to her forehead and looked across the yard.

"Uh-oh," she said. Then she nudged James again and pointed toward a couple over by the barn.

"No, no, no." James shook his head as his face twisted in disbelief. "Not Kathleen too! Go over there and tell them not to be gettin' any notions in their heads!"

Marian laughed aloud. "Now, James," she warned, "you wouldn't want me to do that."

"She's only sixteen," he mumbled.

"*Ya*. It's young for marriage, but I was only sixteen when I married you." She laid her head on his shoulder, and they watched their youngest daughter grinning and talking with Mark Huyard.

Marian glanced to the porch where Mary Carol, Saul, Edna, and Abner were all sitting. Then she spotted Leah and Aaron chatting beneath an oak tree near the barn.

Marian wrapped her hands around James's arms and squeezed. "We're very blessed to have such wonderful daughters."

He twisted his head, kissed her lightly on the lips, and smiled. "*Ya*. We are."

Marian closed her eyes and silently thanked God for all she'd been blessed with. Not only for her four daughters, but for the wonderful man sitting next to her, whom she was just as in love with today as the day they married.

❧

Aaron latched onto Leah's hand and helped her up from their spot beneath the oak tree. "I have something else for you." He motioned toward the double doors that led into the barn.

"Yesterday I went to town for *Mamm* to run some errands, and this was in the window of a little shop off Lincoln Highway." Aaron pushed the barn door open with his shoulder and coaxed her inside. He pointed to a workbench against the wall.

Leah gasped. "That's for me?" She dropped his hand and hurried to the bench, toward the typewriter sitting on top of it.

"It's old. I think it's an antique. And not electric, of course. But you said you wanted one."

Leah caressed the black machine, surprised at what good shape it was in.

"It works too." Aaron rolled the piece of paper that was already inserted upward. He eased her aside and began to type. *I love you.*

Leah bit her bottom lip, blinked hard, and turned to face him.

He kissed her gently on the lips, lingering there for what seemed like an eternity. Then he pulled back, cupped her cheeks in his hands, and said, "Leah, you're never gonna be a traditional Amish *fraa*, and I'll probably have to live on chicken salad and tomato pie for the rest of my life . . . but I've loved you since I saw you the first day of school." He paused, took in a deep breath.

Leah could feel her heart pounding against her chest.

"I love your stories. I love the person you are. I just love—I just love you."

"Oh, Aaron." Leah wrapped her arms around him. Then she pulled away and looked deeply into his eyes. "I'll try to learn how to make something besides chicken salad and tomato pie."

"Love me, Leah." He kissed her again.

"I do."

WHEN WINTER COMES

By Barbara Cameron

Chapter One

REBECCA WRAPPED HER ARMS AROUND HERSELF AS SHE stood at the edge of the frozen pond. She felt drawn to it in spite of herself. It was here, one bitter cold day five years ago, that her life had changed so much.

She used to love rushing here after school and her chores. She'd quickly exchange her boots for skates and fly across the ice. No one understood her fascination with skating, not even her twin. Her parents thought it was a passing interest, but when it didn't fade as she got older, they bought her bigger skates as she needed them.

She wasn't trying to be special or stand out. That would be against everything she and her community believed in. *Demut*—humility—was valued above all among the Plain people.

It had been years now since she'd skated. The accident had changed everything. It had been her fault, and she'd had to pay for it. But as bad as she felt about losing a sister, she knew that it had to be worse for her parents, who had lost a daughter. Even if it appeared that they had been able to forgive her, Rebecca didn't believe it. She blamed herself so much . . . how could they not blame her too?

If she'd been a good daughter, Lizzie wouldn't be gone.

So she became the best daughter she could be, to make up for the missing one. She enjoyed cooking and helping out around the house when she wasn't working at the gift shop in town. And she watched and worried over her siblings like a mother hen, concerned that bad things might happen if she didn't.

It was so quiet here now she could hear the icicles tinkling like glass wind chimes as the chill breeze rustled the bare tree branches.

The fields lay dormant beneath the blanket of snow that also covered the nearby farmhouses and barns. Farmers who'd worked so hard harvesting their crops now studied seed catalogs and planned their spring plowing and planting. They repaired farm equipment, and even with the winter's shorter days, some of them enjoyed having a few hours to do some carpentry.

Families gathered indoors in front of the fireplace and played games. When friends came to visit, there was plenty of time for holding quilting circles and catching up on the latest news over cups of tea and cookies warm from the oven.

In quiet Paradise, Pennsylvania, things became even more peaceful in winter.

But Rebecca felt anything but peaceful. She'd come home from her job and found herself restless. So she donned her coat and bonnet again and went out for a walk in spite of the cold.

Stop being afraid!

Startled, Rebecca whipped her head around and scanned the field behind her. There was no one in sight. Hers were the only footsteps in the vast expanse of snow-covered fields that led to where she stood.

The voice was so familiar. She hadn't heard it for a while, but she'd never forget it.

Stop being afraid. It's time to stop being afraid.

"I'm not afraid!" she cried out.

But her words vanished in the wind that swept across the icy white surface of the frozen pond. She shivered and wrapped her arms around herself as the chill seeped into her feet, then her legs, then her body, and finally her heart. Still she stood and stared out at the pond.

She thought she saw something, there, at the far edge of the pond. Something—someone? Blinking, she looked again, but there was nothing. Her eyes were just watering a little in the cold, that was all. She should get home, help her *mamm* with *nachtesse*. On these cold winter evenings, it was so nice to sit at the big carved wooden table with her family and share a meal and try not to think about how she felt each year when winter came.

Her mind wandered. She felt herself moving, light as air, gracefully skimming across the icy surface of the pond, the wind a cold caress on her face. Flinging her arms out, she soared like a bird, her cape and long skirt rippling in the wind, the only sound her skates as they barely touched the ice. She leaped and spun and felt her heart lift and warm and beat harder and harder, faster and faster as the old excitement burst through her as she circled the pond.

Surely this was what it felt like in heaven, she thought, smiling.

Lost in her dreams, she didn't hear the crunch of steps on the snow behind her.

"I knew I'd find you here."

Startled, her eyes flew open, and she spun around at the sound of the deep male voice behind her. "Ben! What are you doing here?"

Her feet slipped on the snowy bank, and she started to fall. He reached out and caught her, but then his feet slid out from under him too. As he fell, he held tighter and tried to shield her from the worst of it, pulling her over as they landed on the snow.

Winded, Rebecca found herself staring down into the face of Ben Weaver. His brown eyes were full of concern. "Are you all right?"

"I asked you what you're doing here."

"You were skating."

"Skating?" She stared at him incredulously. "Look at my feet, Ben Weaver. Do they look like they have skates on them?"

"Skating," he repeated. "Flying across the ice like you used to."

"You're *ab im kopp*," she muttered. Shaking her head, she struggled to get to her feet.

But her long, dark blue *frack* had a mind of its own. It was tangled with Ben's trousers, and he didn't help her extricate herself. Instead, he just chuckled and watched her struggle. Finally, she yanked the material away and stood, her hands on her hips.

"What are you doing here?" she demanded again as she brushed at the snow on her skirt and coat.

"Your *mamm* sent me," he told her.

"Is something wrong?"

He held out his hand, seeking to reassure her. "Nothing's wrong."

"Then why would she send you?"

Ben got to his feet without effort, picked up his black felt hat, and brushed at the snow on his jacket and trousers. "She was worried about you," he said.

◦◦◦

The moment the words left his mouth, Ben regretted them.

Rebecca went still, and it was like a shutter came down over her face. "She has no reason to worry," she said. Turning, she started to climb the slope, slipping and sliding as she went.

Ben followed her, but even with his long strides it wasn't easy to keep up. "Rebecca, let me give you a ride home."

"I walked here. I can walk home." Then she bit her lip. "But thank you," she said.

"Stop it!"

She halted and stared at him. "Stop what?"

"You're just too polite."

"Too polite?" Her eyebrows rose higher, if that were possible.

"You don't have to pretend with me, Rebecca. I know you're upset."

"I'm fine. I need to get home."

"I thought we were friends."

His quiet words stopped her.

She turned. "We are. But no one needs to worry about me. I'm fine."

"No, you're still sad sometimes, especially this time of year." His eyes searched hers. "You're freezing, and I'm cold. Just get in the buggy and let me drive you home. Please."

Turning, he began walking to the buggy, not sure if she'd follow. He knew how stubborn she could be. But surely she wouldn't insist on walking home, as cold as she must be.

He heard her sigh of exasperation behind him and the stomp of her feet in the snow, and he couldn't hold back a chuckle.

"You think it's funny?" She hurried to catch up with him. Her breath huffed out in the cold wind.

"No, Rebecca."

As they walked, he cast her a worried glance. She was shivering even harder. "Here, let me give you my coat."

"You can't do that. You'll catch your death of cold without it."

"Better me than you."

She put out her hand to stop him. "I'll be fine. We're almost to your buggy. It'll be warmer there."

Something inside him relaxed. So at least she was going to let him drive her home.

What was it about her that attracted him so? There were other girls he could have pursued, but no . . . five years ago he'd realized how much he cared for Rebecca, and no one else would do.

He'd decided to ask if they could date, but before he could, her life had been forever changed. Nothing before the accident seemed to matter now. But it had been five years. Wasn't that long enough for her to heal?

And did she—could she—forgive him for what had happened to Lizzie?

Rebecca's steps were awkward by the time they were at the buggy, and getting in seemed to be an effort. He lifted her in his arms, startling her so that she whipped around and stared at him, her eyes wide.

"I can get in by myself."

His heart did a funny little flip in his chest as he realized how close their faces were. He settled her on the seat and reached for the blanket to tuck it around her.

"Really, there's no need to fuss——," she began, then sneezed.

He pulled out a handkerchief and handed it to her. "Do you want to worry your *eldre* if you get sick?" he asked quietly.

As what little color she had faded from her cheeks, he knew his words had hit home. He finished tucking the blanket around her legs, then walked around to his side of the vehicle and climbed inside.

She stared straight ahead as the buggy began moving, her black bonnet hiding her expression. "I thought you were at the Brownfield home today."

"I stopped by to see your father."

Ben worked for Amos, so Rebecca didn't question that. But business hadn't been the topic of their conversation today.

They passed their old schoolhouse, and he stopped the buggy for a moment. "We had some good times here, didn't we?"

"When you weren't annoying me, you mean?"

He grinned, unrepentant. "I was a young boy then. Besides, I was just teasing you."

"I looked it up in the dictionary. The word *tease*. It means 'to annoy in fun,'" she told him dryly.

He'd had fun, he reflected. Rebecca had always been so quiet, so composed, that he'd enjoyed getting a rise out of her. Then her cheeks would turn pink, her hazel eyes would flash, and she'd tell him in no uncertain terms to leave her alone.

From the time he was sixteen, he'd decided he wanted no other woman for his *fraa*. He told himself that all he had to do was wait until they were older. Then he'd ask if they could date.

That was before what he'd come to think of as *that day*.

She sneezed again, jerking him from his thoughts.

"Are you still cold?"

"I'm fine," she told him, using a tissue to blow her nose. "I'm sure it's allergies."

"To what? Snow?"

She rolled her eyes. "People can have allergies in the winter."

"You don't."

"Since when do you know everything about me?"

He opened his mouth and then shut it. How could he answer that question? They'd grown up together in the same small community and attended the same school. Everyone knew everyone else's business here in Paradise.

But sometimes her father confided his concern about his eldest daughter to Ben as they worked on a joint project. And her mother looked on him like another son and did the same.

He'd bided his time until he thought his suit would be successful with Rebecca.

And waited some more.

He glanced at her again and caught her looking at him. She quickly glanced away, but not before he caught the expression on her face. *Curiosity*, he mused. *Hmm*. Well, if she didn't yet look at him the way he wished, at least she was looking.

He'd take it.

❧

Rebecca felt herself blush when she realized Ben had caught her staring at him.

She looked away quickly, but not quickly enough. He'd been looking at her so seriously. Did he feel more for her than friendship? No, it was just that she wanted it to be so. But time couldn't be turned back, as much as she wished it possible.

Sometimes she felt he was about to say something, then he'd stop. She wished she had the courage to ask him about it.

Risking another glance, she saw that his attention was on the road now. She wondered why he hadn't yet gotten engaged or married as many of their classmates had. Girls had always liked him. She'd stood with them at recess and listened to them talk about how sweet, how sensitive he was. He might not say much, the girls said, but they saw that as a good thing. He wasn't trying to impress them or chase after them the way some boys did.

And then there was his appearance. He was tall, with impressive muscles from helping his father on the farm. He was square-jawed, his hair a dark russet, and his eyes were such a handsome brown color. According to the other girls.

"Like dark chocolate," one girl said with a sigh.

"And he's always making me laugh," another reported.

He didn't make Rebecca laugh. All he did was tease her and look at her with eyes that promised mischief. He didn't do that with other girls who flirted with him at singings. Mary Anne even confided that he'd kissed her once. Yes, Ben Weaver could have had—still could have—his pick of young women in the community.

So why wasn't he married?

"My mother didn't tell you where I was, did she?"

He glanced at her. "No."

"I wouldn't want her to think—well, you know, to . . . ," she trailed off, not knowing how to put it into words.

"To think that you were brooding by the pond?"

Rebecca frowned. "I wouldn't call it brooding."

"What would you call it, then?"

Her eyes flew to his, and in them she saw compassion. She looked away. "I can't help but think of Lizzie when winter comes."

"I know. Me too."

"Really?"

"Life changed for both of us the day Lizzie died, Rebecca."

The simple words struck at her heart. She nodded. "What made you look for me at the pond?"

He looked back at the road. "I've seen you there sometimes when I drive by."

She thought about that. It was the one place she'd thought she had privacy. How many others had driven past and wondered if she was—what was the word he'd used? *Brooding*. She sighed. Oh well. There were, after all, no secrets here in Paradise.

With a jerk of the reins, Ben let Ike know that he wanted to turn down the drive to Rebecca's house.

"Why did you say I was skating?" she asked suddenly.

He glanced at her. "You were moving and swaying, lifting your arms."

She studied him, looking into his eyes to see if he was teasing. But his expression was serious, his eyes kind. "Ben Weaver, I think you need to have your eyes examined," she said at last.

"I'm not crazy," he told her. "Weren't you wanting to be out on the ice, skating like you used to do?"

It felt like all the air in her left her body. "How can you ask me such a thing after what happened?" Her voice sounded strangled.

Ben stopped the buggy and reached out a hand to her. "I'm sorry. I didn't mean to upset you."

"How could I do it again?" she asked him, feeling tears rush into her eyes. "I got Lizzie to go with me that day. If I hadn't, if I'd been watching better, she wouldn't have died."

Rebecca saw a look of pain cross Ben's face. He reached out and took her hand, squeezing it so hard that it hurt.

"If you're going to blame anyone, blame me."

Chapter Two

THE FRONT DOOR OPENED, AND HER MOTHER APPEARED. "You found her!"

Rebecca pulled her hand from Ben's, feeling faintly guilty. "Thank you," she said, then quickly shoved aside the blanket that covered her legs and climbed out.

"I'm sorry I worried you," she told her mother. "I just went for a walk. I'll be down as soon as I change."

Mamm nodded as Rebecca rushed through the kitchen and up the stairs. In her room, Rebecca shed her damp things and put on another *frack*. Then she searched in her drawer for a fresh *kapp*.

She stood before a small mirror and stared at her reflection. Her cheeks were pale. She brushed her hair until it crackled with static electricity, parted it in the center, rebound it at the back of her head, and donned the *kapp*.

Her gaze returned to her reflection for just a moment. She didn't spend much time looking at herself in mirrors. Her looks were just average: hazel eyes, brown hair. Slender figure with barely any curves.

Her twin had gotten those.

And more. *Mamm* had always said the two were as different as night and day. From the time they were born, she always said that one chased after life and the other followed, worrying about the adventurer.

Everyone knew that while Rebecca was the oldest by six minutes, she was the follower, the worrier—never the dreamer or the adventurer.

She sighed. No, she'd never envied Lizzie. But sometimes she'd felt like she came in a pale second. Lizzie had been like a comet streaking across the sky. Rebecca was the homebody, lovingly taking care of the other *kinner*, helping her *mamm* with the house.

Except for when she was out on the ice, skating. There, everything was different. She felt like a bird—free, graceful, daring.

Sinking down on the bed, she thought about what Ben had said about her skating: that she was moving as she stood there in the snow, as if she were skating in her imagination. How ridiculous.

She missed skating so much, but she just couldn't face doing it again.

When she went downstairs, she found Ben leaning against a kitchen counter, laughing and talking with her *mamm*.

"I talked Ben into staying to eat," *Mamm* said. "After all, he went to find you for me."

Ben sneaked a cookie from the jar on the counter. Rebecca waited for her mother to chide him since it was so close to suppertime. But Naomi merely smiled fondly at him.

Rebecca moved to the counter and began slicing the loaves of homemade bread that sat on a wooden board.

"It smells wonderful," Ben said. "Nothing better than a good stew on a cold night."

"There's deep-dish apple pie too."

"My favorite."

Rebecca stopped slicing and looked over at him. "Everything's your favorite."

"Yes," he agreed, grinning. "I love everything your *mamm* makes."

"Everything's ready. Call the *kinner*," *Mamm* said.

Rebecca did as she was asked, hollering up the stairs. They came clattering down and seated themselves around the table. Rebecca frowned when she saw where Ben was sitting. Lizzie had always sat there . . .

He looked up at her, and she saw the light fade from his eyes. He started to move to a different chair.

"Sit, sit," Rebecca's father, Amos, said as he came into the room. "Glad you could join us, Ben."

Glancing uneasily at Rebecca, Ben nodded. "Me too."

Amos bent his head and the family followed, joining in prayer. Then noisy chatter filled the room as bowls and platters were passed and plates were filled.

Looking around the big carved wooden table that was the heart of a Plain kitchen, Rebecca felt a sense of quiet satisfaction. She was needed here. Her *mamm* often told her she didn't know what she'd do without her help. When her mother's last two pregnancies had been difficult, Rebecca had taken over running the house. She was good at it; she enjoyed cooking and baking and even cleaning, because that meant putting things back where they belonged, getting a sense of order.

And when she was going about taking care of their home, she didn't hear that voice in her head urging her to do something, to stop being afraid.

She'd been like other girls her age, thinking about boys, about dating, about getting married, before the accident. Now the boy she'd been interested in sat next to her as a friend and not as a husband.

She'd thought she'd be married, have her own *kinner* by now. This wasn't the life she'd imagined she'd lead by the age of twenty-two. But she could put aside her dreams, her desires, for the sake of her family . . .

Ben was saying something. Jerking to attention, Rebecca accepted the bowl of stew he passed her, then the basket of bread. Taking a slice, she passed the basket on and reached for the *budderhaffe*. Her hand collided with Ben's, and she pulled it back.

"Ladies first," he said, pushing the dish toward her.

With a slight smile, she nodded, scooped up some of the *budder*

BARBARA CAMERON

with her knife and spread it on the bread, then pushed the *budderhaffe* toward him.

"Rebecca, guess what I did at school today!"

Rebecca turned with a smile, but before she could respond to Esther, six-year-old Annie launched into a monologue about her day. Bright and eager to learn, she was thriving at her lessons, especially math.

Looking up, Rebecca caught Ben watching her, his expression thoughtful. What had he meant when he said if she was going to blame anyone, she should blame him? What did she have to blame him for? He'd been such a good friend, listening to her whenever she needed to talk about Lizzie. She didn't know what she'd have done without him since Lizzie died.

She wondered again why he hadn't yet married. He came from a large, happy family, just as she did. From what she'd observed, his parents had a happy marriage.

After leaving school he'd worked with her father, learning the carpentry trade, building and installing custom kitchen cabinets, built-ins, and bookcases in area homes, sometimes Amish, sometimes *Englisch*. He'd often been invited to stay for the evening meal at the Miller home—or charmingly found a way to invite himself, Rebecca noted—so he'd become a fixture in her home.

"So, Ben, I'm thinking that we're going to finish the White kitchen on Wednesday," *Daed* said, leaning back in his chair as he watched Naomi cut and serve slices of deep-dish apple pie.

"We can't go to the Anthony house early," Ben told him. "Remember, Mr. Anthony wants to take his wife off to a hotel while we work on the kitchen, get her away from all the noise and dust. They made arrangements to be out of their house for a week starting Friday, not Thursday."

"Don't you two spend enough time talking business during the day?" Naomi asked, but she smiled.

Amos nodded. "*Ya*. We'll figure it out tomorrow."

Mamm was passing slices of pie down the table and handed a plate to Marian. "This is for Rebecca."

"No, thanks."

"No dessert? You love apple pie."

Rebecca shrugged. "I'll have some later. I'm just not all that hungry right now." A headache was forming behind her eyes, and the stew was lying like a lump in her stomach.

She got up and collected stew bowls and put them into the sink. It had been a long day. She was looking forward to bed already, even though it was early. Her father smiled at her as she refilled his coffee cup, then her mother's.

"This is your piece, Ben," said Marian, the second oldest. She handed him the plate with a smile. Their fingers brushed, and a faint blush crept up her cheeks.

Rebecca stopped beside Ben and stared. Her sister was flirting with Ben!

≋

Ben realized that Rebecca was standing beside him, coffeepot in hand. Her expression was as cold as the ice cream topping the pie he'd just been handed. "More coffee?" she asked.

"*Danki*," he said and frowned as he watched her pour the hot liquid. Why did she look upset with him?

"Cream?" Marian asked. "I know you like it in your coffee."

"Yes, thanks," he told her, tearing his gaze from Rebecca, who seemed focused on her sister.

Confused, he glanced over at Marian as he accepted the pitcher of cream from her. She was looking at him from beneath her lashes, shy . . . flirty? No, it couldn't be, he told himself. She was what— sixteen? He searched his memory. Seventeen? Whatever she was, she was too young for him. And besides, he wanted her older sister.

He looked at Naomi. She was also watching Marian. Then her gaze moved to him.

"Ben, how is your pie?" she asked.

He took a bite. "Wonderful," he pronounced. He glanced at Rebecca, who had returned the coffeepot to the stove and sat back down. She was rubbing her forehead and looking down at her untouched cup of tea.

When Rebecca sneezed, her mother gazed at her daughter in concern. "Are you catching cold?"

"I'm fine, thanks."

"Maybe it's allergies," Ben said slyly.

If looks could hurt, he'd have been bleeding. He glanced around, but no one else noticed.

"Yes, I think it is," Rebecca responded, and she took a sip of her tea.

Ben sat back. He was pleasantly full from the meal and pleasantly tired from the day's work. Just plain pleasant, sitting here in the warm kitchen at the big kitchen table next to Rebecca. He wouldn't trade it for anything. Well, yes, he would. He'd trade it for a kitchen of their own, a family of their own. But he didn't think she was ready for that conversation.

"What kind of kitchen cabinets did you build for the Delaney family?" Marian asked Ben.

There was nothing Ben loved to talk about more than working with wood. With farmland becoming more expensive in Lancaster County, more men were turning to trades like carpentry. He'd worked with Amos for several years learning the trade, and while he could build just about anything, he found the most satisfaction helping to create kitchens. Maybe that was because he'd always considered it the heart of the home, the place where a family gathered to share God's abundance of food and talk about the events of the day.

He loved working with wood, all the varieties from maple to oak to birch—and, for some of the fancy *Englisch* kitchens, woods that came from faraway places like Brazil and Costa Rica.

But the more he talked, the more he realized that Rebecca was quiet. She looked even paler than before.

"Ben? Another slice of pie?" Naomi asked.

"No, thanks. I should be going. I'll see you in the morning, Amos."

Rebecca pulled out a handkerchief and wiped her nose. He started to say something, but she shook her head and glanced at her mother, who was supervising the clearing of the table. He got the message and nodded.

His going to find her this afternoon hadn't kept her from catching a chill. And it had only complicated things for him. He was going to remember for a long time how it felt to hold her and have her face so close to his. And he already regretted blurting out what he'd said about blaming him. He knew she'd be asking him about it the next time they were alone.

He pulled on his coat and watched as Naomi walked over to Rebecca and put the back of her hand against her daughter's forehead. Rebecca shook her head and said something too low for Ben to pick up, but Naomi put her hands on her hips and gave her the look, the one only mothers know how to give.

So, he thought, *Rebecca hasn't been able to hide her not feeling well from her mother.* It didn't surprise him. Parents could always sense such things. Especially mothers.

◦‿◦

"Rebecca, you go on to bed. I think you're coming down with a cold."

She turned and shook her head. "I'm fine." Taking several bowls from Annie, she put them into the hot soapy water in the sink.

"Annie, why don't you go ask Marian to read you a story before bed? I'll help Rebecca with the dishes."

Rebecca watched Annie, always a good helper, hesitate. Then she scampered off. Trying not to sigh, Rebecca turned back to the dishes. She sensed that her *mamm* wanted to talk, and she wasn't in the mood for it. All she wanted was to finish the chores and go to bed.

Picking up a clean dishcloth, Naomi came to stand next to the sink. "Is everything okay?"

Rebecca nodded. She handed her mother a bowl to dry.

"You were gone a long time."

"I just went for a walk."

"It was awfully cold for a walk."

Rebecca handed another bowl to her mother. "I know."

"Are things okay with you and Ben?"

She nodded. "Why do you ask?"

"I don't know. You were frowning at him when he went to sit down."

"He was going to sit in Lizzie's seat." She stared at the soapy water.

"It's not Lizzie's anymore," her *mamm* said gently.

"I know that!"

Naomi blinked at the sharpness in Rebecca's voice.

Rebecca bit her lip. "I'm sorry," she said stiffly.

"*Nee*, it's all right. You're not feeling well."

It wasn't all right to talk to her *mamm* that way no matter how she felt. Rebecca was ashamed. She cast about in her mind for something to say. "I thought I'd ask Anita for a morning off later this week so I can help take Abram and Annie for their checkups."

Naomi stopped drying a dish. "I'd rather you took some time for yourself, Rebecca. All you do is work here or at the shop."

"You need the help."

Setting down the dish, Naomi placed her hand on Rebecca's shoulder. "What I need more is to see you looking happier, *Dochder*."

"A daughter should—"

"You are a most dutiful daughter, but we want you to have your own life too. You don't go out enough with your friends, do the things a young woman does."

"I was just out with Ben," Rebecca told her with a slight smile.

"A ride home isn't out with a friend."

Rebecca took the dishcloth from her mother and began wiping down the counters. "I'm fine."

"Rebecca, I noticed that Marian—"

Amos walked into the kitchen. "There you are," he said to Naomi. "Would you look over a proposal for me?"

"Rebecca and I were—"

"It's all right," Rebecca said quickly. "I want to get to bed. I'll see you in the morning. *Gut nacht.*"

Looking away from the expression of disappointment on her mother's face, she kissed her cheek, then her *daed*'s, and walked quickly to the stairs.

Rebecca woke in the night, feverish, her head clogged and her body aching. Wrapping herself in a bathrobe, she went downstairs, found aspirin, and took two with a glass of water. When she climbed into her bed this time, she was warm—too warm—so she lay atop the covers. Several hours later she woke again, cold, and pulled the quilt back up to her chin.

When she woke next, Marian was shaking her shoulder. "Time to get up."

Muttering, Rebecca nodded. "*Minutt.*" She fell back asleep.

Her shoulder was being shaken again, this time by her mother. "Rebecca?" A hand touched her forehead. "Marian, Rebecca has a *fiewer*! Go get her some aspirin and some *wasser*."

"Some *wasser* would be good," Rebecca agreed as she sat up. "But I'm getting up. I have to go to work."

"No, you cannot go to work today," *Mamm* said firmly.

"It's just a cold," Rebecca said, hoping to convince herself. She was seldom ill, but this felt like the flu. She stood, and the room whirled about her. She sank back down on the bed. "Maybe in a minute."

Her mother shook her head. "Maybe tomorrow. I'll get Amos to go by the gift shop and let Anita know you won't be in today."

Marian returned with the aspirin and water.

Rebecca washed the pills down with the water, drinking every drop. "I'll lie down for a little while and see how I feel. I'm really not that sick. It's just a cold."

"I'll bring you breakfast after I get the *kinner* off to school."

"No, I'll come down," Rebecca muttered as she sank down onto the bed. "Don't want you to go to any trouble."

Her mother stroked her hot forehead. "It's no trouble, *liebschen.* You're no trouble. Ever. Rest, dear one. Let someone take care of you."

Rebecca watched her mother leave the room and felt guilty. How, she wondered, could *Mamm* still show her such love? She was supposed to watch out for her sister. She was supposed to keep her from harm.

The Bible talked about being your brother's keeper. She'd tried to be her sister's. She'd failed.

Chapter Three

Rebecca heard the whispering as she slowly came awake, her head throbbing and her throat tight and hot.

"Shh, be quiet!"

"*Ya, mauseschtill!*"

"Why do people say that? Are mice quiet?"

"I don't know. I don't like mice."

"Shh, if we wake her, *Mamm* will be mad at us!"

"She looks pretty sick."

"She's okay. She gets sick every winter. It's because she goes out there looking for Lizzie."

"No, she doesn't! She's not crazy!"

"Didn't say she was. But she stands out there in the snow looking at the pond. Marian says—"

Rebecca opened her eyes. "What does Marian say?"

Her brother Jonas, ten years old, slapped a hand to his chest. "You scared me to death!"

"You woke me up."

"I tolded him not to," said Abram, five years old.

"Told," Jonas corrected.

"Yeah, I tolded you."

Jonas sighed. "Anyway, are you feeling any better, Rebecca?"

She nodded and sat up. The room didn't whirl around her. "A little."

"Are you hungry? *Mamm* made you some chicken soup for supper."

Rebecca glanced at the window. Had she slept through the entire day?

Her mother walked into the room carrying a tray. "I wondered why it was so quiet up here. I should have figured someone was waking up Rebecca."

A chorus of "I didn't!" and finger pointing ensued.

Clutching her head, Rebecca shushed them. "*Ach, mei bruders*, not so loud! My head hurts!"

Immediately they were contrite. "Sorry," they chimed quietly. His eyes huge, Eli patted her hand.

"Jonas, maybe you could get your sister a wet washcloth for her hands."

He went for the cloth and returned with it dripping. Gingerly, Rebecca used it to wash her hands, trying not to get her quilt wet.

"I'll go help Marian set the table," he told their mother. "Come, *kinner*."

"*Mamm*, tell him to stop treating me like a *boppli*," complained Annie.

"You shouldn't be waiting on me," Rebecca said as her mother set a tray on her lap. She knew how hard her mother worked, and here she was waiting on her grown daughter.

"It's no trouble." Naomi put the back of her hand on her daughter's forehead. "Still warm. If you're not better tomorrow, maybe we should take you to the doctor."

"It's just a cold," Rebecca insisted. "I'm feeling better." But her voice came out sounding like a croak. She spooned up some of the chicken soup. "Mmm, this is good."

Looking up, she saw her mother frowning at her. "I'm better, *Mamm*, really. The nap helped. If you call sleeping all day a nap."

Her mother pursed her lips. "Are you sure? You've just been . . . delicate since you had pneumonia."

"That was five years ago."

"We nearly lost you too."

Rebecca saw that her mother was blinking back tears. "I'm sorry. *Mamm*, I'm sorry. You didn't need to have that happen after we lost Lizzie."

"It wasn't your fault you got sick."

But it was my fault that I stayed sick, thought Rebecca. "I got better. And I'm not going to get that sick again."

"A pneumonia shot," her mother said, nodding. "I feel better when I remember that you had the pneumonia shot. It seems there's a shot for everything these days. What will the *Englisch* come up with next?"

Both of them fell silent. Rebecca wondered if her mother was thinking, as she was, that no one had come up with a way to keep Lizzie from falling through the ice.

She set her spoon down on the tray. "Thank you for bringing me the soup. I'm sorry I'm so much trouble."

Mamm moved the tray to the dresser and returned to stroke her daughter's hair. "You are never any trouble. Drink your juice and try to get some more rest."

Rebecca nodded. "I'll be all better in the morning."

Bending, her mother kissed her on her forehead. "We'll see. For now, no worrying about your job and your chores, *allrecht*? Your father stopped by the gift shop, and Anita said to tell you to get well and come in when you're better."

Her energy gone, Rebecca lay back against her pillow. Before she could pull the covers up, her mother was tucking her in. It brought back memories of being tucked in when she was a child, and she smiled.

"Sleep now, *liebschen*. Things will be better in the morning."

❧

Ben pulled his buggy up to the familiar figure walking beside the road.

"So you're feeling better," he called out.

Rebecca stopped and looked up as the buggy pulled abreast of her. Ben leaned forward, the reins loose in his hands. His eyes were serious as he stared down at her.

"*Ya*, I'm well."

Her cheeks were pale, and she was breathing heavily. Each exhale produced a white puff in the cold air.

"Get in, I'll give you a ride home."

"I can walk. It isn't far."

"Your *daed* said your *mamm* was worried about you going into work."

Rebecca climbed into the buggy. "I'm fine. She worries too much."

"She worries because this time of the year you get sick a lot."

"I'm stronger than I look," she told him firmly.

Ben handed her the lap blanket, and she tucked it around her legs. They traveled without speaking for a few minutes, the only sound the clip-clop of the horse's hooves on the recently cleared road. There were few cars this time of year, so it was easy to imagine that only the Amish lived here. Tourists who clogged the roads and sometimes came dangerously near the buggies on the road were few and far between as winter lengthened.

The pond came into view. Children of varying ages, bundled up against the cold, skated on the icy surface. Ben noticed that, after an initial glance, Rebecca looked away.

"Rebecca, I've been meaning to talk to you . . ." He broke off as she began coughing. "Rebecca? Are you all right?"

She nodded but couldn't stop coughing. Ben pulled on the reins and stopped the buggy, tried patting her on the back. She pressed one hand to her mouth, the other to her chest, and spasms racked her. He stared at her. What if she stopped breathing? He focused on her mouth, trying to remember what he'd read about CPR. With his luck, he'd just do more damage, he decided. Or make Rebecca think that he was making improper advances.

Desperately, he looked around. What should he do? Then it came to him—there was a volunteer fire station just down the road. He turned the buggy in a U-turn and urged Ike into a run.

"What—what are you doing?" she gasped, grabbing at his arm to hold on. "Are you trying to kill us?"

She'd stopped coughing, although her face was still red and her breath was rasping in her chest.

"Are you okay?"

"I will be if you'll slow down!"

Ben brought the buggy to a halt and took a good look at her. Her color was returning to normal—well, at least her face was no longer bright red. And the coughing that had scared him to death had indeed stopped.

"You're sure?"

She nodded. "I'll be fine, really."

Leaning back in his seat, Ben hesitated as he studied her. What was it about this wisp of a woman that had made him want her as his *fraa* for so long? That made him wait for her and feel so protective of her?

"Where were you going?"

He made another U-turn and started for home. "To the volunteer fire station."

"Where's the fire?" she teased.

His eyes widened. She was always so serious. And after the past few minutes, he was surprised she could joke on the heels of such a coughing fit.

"I'm sorry if I scared you," she told him quietly. "I'm fine now."

"You shouldn't have worked today."

She bent her head and sighed. "Probably not. But if I'd stayed home, my *mamm* would have fussed over me like I was a *kind*." Her head snapped up then, as if she'd just thought of something.

"What?"

She shook her head. "Nothing."

In a few minutes they pulled up in front of her house. Jumping out of the buggy, Ben walked around to Rebecca's side and held out his hands to help her down. Judging from the surprise on her face, she hadn't expected such courtesy from him.

And why should she? he asked himself. He tried to keep their relationship strictly friendly. He didn't want to scare her off; he'd always felt that if he didn't approach her about a change in their relationship in just the right way, at just the right time, she might reject him.

Before she could say she could get down by herself, he clasped her around the waist and lifted her out of the buggy. They stared at each other for a long moment.

Ben set her on the ground.

She caught her breath. "Are you coming in for supper?"

He shook his head. "Not tonight. I told my family I'd be home."

Her hands fell to her sides. She nodded and started inside, turning at the door to look at him. "Thank you for giving me a ride."

He watched her as she went inside, then he turned to get into the buggy. He wished he hadn't promised he'd have supper at home tonight. Somehow, it felt as if their relationship was changing lately.

He hoped he wasn't imagining it.

❧

Rebecca's head was whirling as she climbed the steps to her room.

Ben turning the buggy around to get help wasn't so remarkable. Probably anyone would have done it. But the way he'd helped her from the buggy, like a gentleman, that's what had surprised her.

There was a different mood between them. And then, when he'd lifted her down, well, she didn't know what to think.

She walked to her dresser to brush her hair before going back downstairs and saw how wan she looked. *That was it,* she thought as she removed her *kapp* to redo her hair. He'd felt sorry for her because she still looked so ill.

She bound up her hair again, replaced her *kapp*, and, exhausted by her day, sank down onto her bed for a few minutes to get a second wind.

The bed on the other side of the room had been Lizzie's. But Marian, just thirteen then, began sleeping there to keep Rebecca company the first weeks after their sister died and Rebecca came home from the hospital. And then she'd just stayed instead of returning to the room she had shared with Esther.

Tired. Rebecca was so, so tired. She thought about what she'd said to Ben . . . If she'd stayed home, her *mamm* would have fussed over her like she was a *kind*.

Was it possible that this was why she'd stayed? Why she hadn't ventured outside the safe, loving circle of her family to create one of her own? Because here she could stay a *kind* her parents worried over, and she didn't need to assume responsibility for herself?

Stunned by the revelation, she didn't hear Marian calling her name until her sister came into the room.

Chapter Four

"Rebecca! Supper's ready." Marian stood at her bedside. "Do you want to come down and eat, or shall I bring you up a tray?"

"I'm coming down." She yawned. "I should have helped *Mamm*—"

"It's okay. I did."

"You are such a sweet sister," Rebecca told her, touching her arm. "Thank you."

Marian peered at her. "Are you feeling better? I heard you coughing last night."

"I'm sorry I woke you."

She smiled. "I'm sure I've woken you up sometimes."

"Yes. When you snore."

"Snore?" Her sister stared at her, aghast. "I don't snore!"

"Like a grizzly bear in hibernation," Rebecca said.

"I don't snore!"

Rebecca couldn't stop her lips from twitching.

"Oh, you!" Marian said. "You had me going there for a minute!"

The sisters walked downstairs to the kitchen, their arms entwined.

Naomi glanced up from where she stood at the stove and smiled. "I heard the two of you laughing. Did the nap help, Rebecca?"

Rebecca gave her mother a hug. "*Ya*, but you should have woken me up. I wanted to help you."

"It's better that you get well," her mother said. "And look, everything is almost done."

Abram was putting the silverware on the table, Esther was pouring glasses of water, and even little Annie was helping by putting a napkin on each plate. Rebecca washed her hands and set to work slicing the bread while Marian helped their mother set dishes of hot food on the table.

Daed entered the room and greeted Rebecca. "Feeling better?"

"*Ya,*" she said. "It was good to get back to work today."

He nodded. "Where's Jonas?" he asked as he took his seat at the table.

Naomi turned, frowning. "I thought he was out in the barn with you."

"I thought he was in here helping you."

Rebecca paused in the act of slicing the bread. She frowned as she caught the furtive glance two of her brothers exchanged.

"Abram? Where's Jonas?"

He hesitated.

"Abram?"

Naomi set down her spoon and crossed the room. "Tell us where Jonas is."

"He went sledding by the pond."

Rebecca heard *pond,* and her knife clattered to the counter. Fear clutched her heart, and for a moment she couldn't breathe. She rushed to grab her coat and bonnet from the peg by the door.

"I'll go," her father said, taking the outdoor things from her and hanging them back on the peg. He reached for his own coat and black felt hat. "I don't want you out in the cold."

The door opened at that moment, and Jonas walked in.

"Jonas, you did *not* have permission to go sledding," *Daed* told him sternly. "You know the rules. Your *mamm* here was worried, and you worried Rebecca as well."

"Me too," said Abram. "I was wordied too!"

Jonas hung his head. "I'm sorry."

"Go put on dry clothes and get your hands washed," Amos said sternly. "We'll talk about it after supper." He looked at Naomi, then at his oldest son. "My own *daed* would have sent me to bed without supper," he told him. "But your *mamm* here won't send a child to bed hungry."

"*Danki, Mamm*," Jonas said fervently. "I'm so very *hungerich*."

"Getting into mischief makes a youngster hungry, eh, Naomi?"

She nodded. "*Ya*, sometimes they return home because their stomach is helping them remember where they're supposed to be."

Jonas reddened and ran to change. When he returned and slipped into his chair, he wore a chastened expression. But Rebecca saw the sly look he sent Eli.

Sometimes Jonas reminded Rebecca of Lizzie. He was the Miller child who was always looking for adventure and not afraid to get into trouble to find it. The abraded skin on his cheek told Rebecca he'd taken a spill on the sled and encountered something harder than snow. She'd clean it and put some medicine on it before he had to face their father for his transgressions, she decided.

"Where's Ben tonight?" Marian wanted to know.

"He promised his family he'd eat at home tonight," Rebecca told her.

"Did he give you a ride home?" *Daed* asked.

"*Ya*."

He gave her a satisfied nod. "Ben always does what he says he will."

❧

Dinner at Ben's home was quieter than at Rebecca's. He was the youngest of the Weaver children, and all his brothers and sisters had their own families now.

Ben's mother, Emma, smiled at him. She was a tall, thin woman who had worked beside her husband in the fields. Years of being outside in the sun, years of smiling through joy and adversity, had etched lines around her eyes.

"It's good to have you home for supper, *Sohn*."

"Boy found out you made pot roast," his father muttered before putting a big forkful in his own mouth.

"You've never missed her pot roast either," Ben reminded him equably. "I remember the time you were lying in the emergency room having your broken arm set, and all you could talk about was how *Mamm* was making pot roast for supper and you were worried it would be all gone before you got home."

His father slapped him on the back, a little harder than affection usually merited. "You're right there." He shoveled in a forkful of oven-roasted potatoes and carrots. "Been spending a lot of time over at the Miller place. How long are you going to wait for her?"

"Samuel! It's not our way to pry into our children's lives in that area!"

"A man knows when he's found his *fraa*," he went on blithely. "You've been a little bit slow, haven't you, *Sohn*?"

Ben just looked at his father. "It's taking a little longer than I expected," he admitted.

"You sure she's not a lost cause?" Samuel Weaver asked bluntly.

"That's what he'd like best," his *mamm* said before Ben could answer. "He's never been one to do things the easy way."

Samuel nodded. "True. Aren't you worried that another man could come along and catch her eye, move faster?"

"Samuel!"

"It could happen," he asserted as he dragged a piece of bread through the gravy on his plate and put it into his mouth. "You know it, too, don't you?"

Ben nodded. "One day she could stop looking inward, blaming herself for her sister's death. She could look out and see someone else. Date him. But I can't rush her. It wouldn't be right."

"It's hard to know sometimes when to wait and when to press the issue," Emma said carefully.

His father thought about it and sighed. "Listen to your *mamm*," he told Ben. "Wisest woman I ever met."

His parents' eyes met, and Ben saw the love they shared. He wanted that kind of relationship, that warm glow of love after so many years of marriage. His *eldre* had weathered many challenging times together.

It was worth it to wait for the one you loved, wasn't it? Marriage was supposed to be forever.

"She's a lovely girl," his mother was saying. "I'm not saying this to sway you one way or the other. You've been a good friend to her."

Ben looked up and waited for her to gently say that perhaps he should move on, find someone else to marry him and give him children, and her, grandchildren. But she simply smiled.

"I know she took the death of her twin very hard," she went on. "There's no accounting for how long it takes for someone to accept the death of someone they love, to accept God's will."

"She still blames herself," Ben said, setting down his fork. "She hasn't said it in so many words, but . . ."

"But you know because you care."

He nodded. She understood him so well.

She touched his hand. "And I know that you blamed yourself for not being able to save Lizzie. The two of you have had much to deal with. Things will work out if they're meant to. In God's time."

"Sometimes it's hard for a man to accept God's time," his father said. "Maybe you should— Is that my favorite?"

Emma set the pan of baked apples fragrant with cinnamon in front of him on the table. "There's ice cream for on top if you want it."

Samuel jumped up to get it.

Emma winked at Ben as she handed him his own dessert. By the time his father returned to the table, Emma was talking about the upcoming quilting at the Millers'.

Rebecca walked into the barn a few days later and was startled to hear her father asking Ben to drive her to the doctor.

"Is she still sick?"

She stopped. Ben sounded concerned.

"No, no, she's fine," her father assured him quickly. "It's an appointment with one of those head docs, that's all."

Closing her eyes, Rebecca shook her head. *Great, just great,* she thought. *Now Ben's going to think I'm crazy.*

"It'll be on the clock," Amos said. "I need to stay here and work up a bid for the Brown kitchen."

"*Ya,* I'll be happy to do it."

"*Guder mariye, Daed,* Ben," Rebecca said as she strode forward.

"Rebecca. I was just asking Ben here to drive you to the appointment."

"I can drive myself."

"*Ya,* I know," her father said, handing Ben a list. "But I want Ben to pick up some supplies at the hardware store, so this will kill two birds, if you'll pardon the expression."

Rebecca rolled her eyes.

Her father grinned. "Ask your *mamm* if she needs anything in town."

"So we can kill three birds?" Rebecca shot back over her shoulder as she walked out of the barn.

"Smart mouth, that one," she heard her father say with a laugh.

She was still smiling when she entered the kitchen.

"You're in a good mood this morning," *Mamm* remarked as she looked up from her seat at the kitchen table. A steaming cup of tea sat before her.

"*Daed* said to see if you need anything in town. Ben's driving me and picking up some supplies from the hardware store."

"Is that why you were smiling?"

"I don't get excited about picking up supplies."

Her mother looked at her. "You know what I mean."

"Because Ben will be driving me? No."

But the last two times she'd seen him, it felt as if things were changing between them. There had been an awareness between them that couldn't be missed.

Her mother went to the refrigerator and pulled a list from under a magnet. "I'd appreciate it if you can pick up these things from Nellie's store. I'll need them for the quilting."

"Sure."

"Rebecca?"

"*Ya?*"

"Why do you think Ben stays for supper so often?"

"Because you're such a good cook?"

Naomi laughed and shook her head. "No. His mother is a better cook than me. Maybe if you think about it, you could come up with a reason."

Rebecca stood there for a moment. "Now why would I want to do that?"

Then she looked up and saw Ben striding toward the house. "I have to go." She kissed her mother's cheek. "See you later."

❧

The drive into town was silent.

Ben looked over several times and saw that Rebecca looked lost in thought.

"You okay?"

"Hmm? Yes, why?"

"You're being quiet."

"I'm not a chatterbox. You know that."

"There's quite a distance between quiet and a chatterbox."

"You're not exactly talking much yourself."

He nodded. "Feels strange not to be on the job on a weekday. Not that I mind, you understand. It's good to have a change."

Turning, she raised her eyebrows.

"What?"

"That's more than I've heard you say in a long time."

"I think you're teasing me."

She laughed. "I guess I am. Imagine that."

Ben wondered why she was going to the doctor. She didn't appear ill. There was no way that it was to see a "head doc" the way her father had teased. He knew of no one more levelheaded than Rebecca. Not that there was any shame in seeing a counselor if a person had emotional or psychological problems.

But the only thing Rebecca had, in his opinion, was a mantle of grief that was finally lifting.

Then it struck him: she could be going to see a doctor about a woman thing. The thought made the tips of his ears burn with embarrassment. He forced the thought aside and looked out at the passing scenery. "Nice day. You warm enough?"

"I'm fine. Thank you."

"Are you going to the singing on Sunday?"

"Thought I would."

"Shall I pick you up?"

She nodded. "That would be nice."

They talked about the last singing, the friends who'd attended, what couples were pairing up, Leah Petersheim and Aaron Lantz's recent marriage, an editor showing interest in publishing Leah's first story. They speculated on how the Petersheims had felt when three of their four daughters became engaged in such a short time.

A car came up behind them very quickly. Ben pulled over to the shoulder and it went speeding past, startling Ike. He reared, and Ben fought to steady him, to keep control.

His heart pounding, Ben turned to Rebecca and found her looking pale and shaken, clutching at the dash of the buggy.

"Someone should do something about drivers like that!" she muttered.

Nodding, Ben pulled the buggy back onto the road. Sharing the road with modern day horsepower could be dangerous. It was easy to get lulled into a false sense of security, listening to the clip-clop of the horse's hooves, talking and gazing at the scenery. When there were accidents, it was the buggy occupants who were hurt the worst.

Thank goodness nothing had happened. He couldn't stand it if something happened to Rebecca and he wasn't any more able to save her than he had been Lizzie.

Amos and Naomi didn't need another tragedy in their family.

Chapter Five

DR. PRATO HELD OUT HER ARMS. "REBECCA! IT'S SO GOOD to see you."

Rebecca hugged the woman who'd listened to her tears and fears after Lizzie died. She took a seat, and the older woman sat opposite her. The office was a comfortable place, filled with books and photos of Dr. Prato's children.

"So tell me how you've been," Dr. Prato invited. "I haven't seen you for, let's see here"—she consulted her file—"three years."

Her eyes were warm as she gazed at Rebecca over the rims of her poppy-red reading glasses. She'd once confessed that she was in her sixties, but she looked much younger with her streaky blonde hair and trendy *Englisch* outfits.

Bringing her up to date took a few minutes. Then Rebecca fell silent.

"So tell me why you wanted to come in today."

Rebecca stared at her hands.

"You don't need to choose the right words. Just say what's on your mind."

Looking up, Rebecca met her calm gaze. "I noticed my family sometimes still acts worried about me."

"They're responsible for their own behavior. You can't control that."

"I know." She twisted her hands in her lap.

"There's something else, isn't there?"

"I'm hearing voices. *A* voice," she corrected.

To her amazement, the other woman didn't blink. "And whose

voice is it? When we first started our sessions, I recall you thought you heard your sister's. I told you at the time that that wasn't unusual. Twins have quite a close bond."

"*Ya.* I remember."

"And your sister was quite—well, how would you describe her?"

"Dominant," Rebecca confessed. "Stronger, more outgoing. Definitely more adventurous."

"A risk taker."

Rebecca nodded.

"Which is why it wasn't surprising that she died that day."

"But I should have—" She stopped. "I know, you've been telling me for a long time that it wasn't my fault."

Dr. Prato smiled. "And one day you'll believe me. One day you'll forgive yourself. But you haven't yet, have you?"

Rebecca shook her head. "Not entirely. I'm supposed to believe it's God's will. That's what we learn from the time we're children, that everything is in order. That God is in charge. That it's His will—"

"If people live or die." Dr. Prato looked at Rebecca over her glasses. "From the way you're talking, I wonder if it isn't only yourself that you haven't forgiven. Maybe you haven't forgiven God?"

Rebecca bit her lip. "No, I don't think I have," she whispered. "I stopped being angry at Him. But how long is it supposed to take to stop missing her? To not feel bad that she's gone? To not remember the way that she died?"

"I wish I could tell you. Everyone's experience with grief is different."

"Some people tell me that it's time to be over Lizzie's death— not lately, you understand, but they've said so. Not *Mamm* and *Daed.* They never have. Or Marian."

Or Ben. He was around constantly, and though he'd seen her at her worst moments, he'd never suggested that she should be setting aside her grief. He just listened. And listened and listened.

"Something you want to say?"

Rebecca shook her head. She wanted to think about it for a while.

"So let's return to this voice you're hearing," Dr. Prato prompted.

"I heard it the other day when I stood by the pond."

"What did it say?"

"*Don't be afraid.*"

"Are you afraid, Rebecca?"

Rebecca started to shake her head, then stopped. "I could say that I'm not afraid, that it's simply that I haven't wanted to put on my skates since the accident. But that wouldn't be truthful."

"And you're always truthful."

There was no need to look at Dr. Prato to see if she was questioning or implying anything. She was simply stating the truth.

"You don't—you don't think I'm crazy?"

"Absolutely not."

"You don't think there's something wrong with someone hearing a voice?"

Dr. Prato smiled. "Do you?"

"Now you're answering a question with a question." Rebecca smiled in spite of herself. "No one else I know talks about hearing voices, so I have to think it's a little strange."

"Since I moved to this community, I've gotten to know a number of Plain people. I've never heard any of them having such experiences, no," Dr. Prato admitted. "But that doesn't mean that they don't." She leaned forward. "Sometimes, when others don't talk about deeply personal things, you can start to wonder if you're different, if something might even be wrong with you. Now, think about what the voice is saying."

"*Don't be afraid.*"

"Could it be you, talking to yourself? Is it possible that it's your inner voice? Maybe you didn't hear it a lot before, since you were around such a strong sibling. Maybe you're hearing your inner voice urging you to stop being afraid to live? To do things you haven't done since Lizzie died? You said you heard it when you were looking at the pond. That's where you loved to skate, where you did something that made you feel happy and free."

"And it's where Lizzie died."

"Yes. That voice could even be you telling yourself not to be afraid of going on without her, couldn't it? To not feel guilty any longer for not being able to save her?"

Rebecca stared at the doctor, her eyes wide. "I—I hadn't thought of that."

"Think about it. See if it makes sense to you." She sat back.

"I will."

"And maybe . . ." She hesitated.

"What?"

"Maybe it's God talking to you?"

Rebecca frowned. "I don't know. I doubt it. He knows I was so angry with Him for so long for taking Lizzie home."

"Was there anything else on your mind?" the older woman asked after a long moment.

"I was thinking on the way here that I'll always be grateful that you talked to my parents about me," Rebecca said quietly. "You really persisted."

"You were worth fighting for," Dr. Prato told her. "I can't tell you how gratifying it's been to see your community being more accepting of seeing a mental health professional when they need to." She smiled. "You've come a long way from the first time I met you."

Rebecca was ashamed to remember how she hadn't wanted to live after Lizzie died. She'd developed pneumonia and had been hospitalized for two weeks when Dr. Prato had stopped by her room at the request of the attending doctor.

Her parents were dubious at first about her talking with Rebecca.

Medical care was one thing, but Rebecca's *daed* had felt his daughter didn't need to speak to a psychologist. But something Dr. Prato had said convinced them. After Rebecca left the hospital, she visited Dr. Prato in her office in town a number of times.

"I know it was difficult for them to consider at first." Then she frowned. "That reminds me. I overheard my father calling you a 'head doc' today."

"It sounds like that bothered you."

Rebecca stared at her hands. "He was telling Ben, a friend of the family. Someone who works for him. I went to school with him; he's my friend. But I never told him that I've seen you. I'm not ashamed of it, but I live in a small community. I don't need people talking about me."

"Would Ben do that?"

"No," Rebecca said at last. "He's such a good friend to me."

Was it her imagination that the doctor was sitting up a little straighter, looking a little more attentive?

"Tell me about this Ben."

Rebecca shrugged. "He's just a friend." She picked at a thread on her skirt. "Well, he's just always . . . around, you know? People have asked me if he's a friend or more."

Dr. Prato's brows lifted. "And how do you feel about that?"

༄

Ben glanced at the clock in the hardware store. He'd dropped Rebecca off almost an hour and a half ago. She'd said she'd meet him here. But maybe she'd started feeling worse. Maybe she was waiting there for him to come get her.

He returned to the building where she'd asked him to drop her off and walked inside. He examined the building directory. Dr. Seaton, gerontologist. Hmm. No, that was a doctor for old people. An obesity clinic. No. Rebecca was slim.

There was a listing for a cancer specialist. His heart stopped for a moment, then beat again when he saw a little note attached that said they'd recently moved to a different location. Ben scanned the small list remaining. A pediatrician and a urologist specializing in male patients.

Then he saw the listing for a Dr. Hannah Prato, psychologist. Maybe Amos hadn't been joking about Rebecca seeing a "head doc." Maybe the thoughts Rebecca thought were dark, not insightful. Grief often did strange things to people. Sometimes they couldn't function anymore. Sometimes they even tried to hurt themselves.

Although . . . Amos hadn't been expressing worry about his daughter. He'd been almost jovial. And Rebecca had responded lightly, teasing him in return.

"Do you need some help, young man?"

Ben turned and took off his black felt hat in deference to the *Englisch* woman beside him. Her appearance was so different from that of the Amish women he knew: her hair was short, light brown with streaks of blonde that he didn't think came from being outside in the sun. She wore a very short dress that matched the bright red glasses perched on her nose. Instead of minding the way he stared at her, she gave him a direct and inquisitive smile as she waited for him to speak.

"No, I—uh—" He felt like a dolt standing there, unable to frame a reply. "I'm looking for a friend."

"Perhaps she's waiting outside."

He hadn't said *she*. He shook his head. "No, she wasn't outside."

Her eyes narrowed just a bit, as if she were sizing him up. "I see. Do you know which doctor she was seeing?"

Again he shook his head. "I don't think it was any of them."

The woman scanned the list. "No? Well, let's see if we can figure this out." She ran over the same list of specialists he had, and he shook his head at each one. "That leaves just Dr. Prato?"

He must have looked appalled, for she reached out and touched his arm. "It's okay, you know. Sometimes we all need someone to talk to."

"I don't know anyone who sees a head doctor," Ben told her. "Well, that's not exactly true. A friend of mine was diagnosed as bipolar last year, and he's been seeing one."

A man entered the building just then. The woman waited until he'd gotten into the elevator and the doors closed. "Sometimes a person needs to talk to someone other than their people or their God. It's okay, really. I've counseled Plain people." She stuck out her hand. "I'm Hannah Prato."

Ben took her small, smooth hand in his larger, work-roughened hand, feeling like a big, clumsy bear. "The head doctor."

She laughed. "Yes."

"I'm Ben Weaver." Was it his imagination, or did he see the faintest flicker of expression? "I think you know who I am," he said slowly.

Her smile never faltered. "I do?"

Ben tilted his head to look at her and nodded.

"Well, you know, whoever saw your friend wouldn't be able to tell you so," she said. "Doctors must maintain patient confidentiality."

"I know that. But I'm worried about her. She was supposed to meet me at the hardware store, and she didn't come. I started thinking—"

Dr. Prato's smile faded, and her eyes were sympathetic. "You're concerned that it could be something far worse than you imagined. I understand." She studied him. "This person you're worried about—she's very lucky to have a friend such as you. I can tell that you care about her very much. And what I can tell you is what I said before, that sometimes people see me because they need to talk to someone other than their people and their God. They need to say things and not feel judged. They need to feel that they can explore topics that are outside of the way they usually think." She paused. "You know what I mean, don't you?"

BARBARA CAMERON

"Ye-es," he said slowly.

"I thought you might." She gave him a nod of approval. Shifting her big shoulder purse and the files she carried, she fished in her pocket and then held out a business card. "If you'd ever like to talk to me, just let me know. When Plain people feel they need to see a doctor, they should feel they can see whatever kind of doctor they need."

"I'm glad my friend came to see you," he told her.

"I didn't say—"

"I know. And I'm glad I met you too."

Frowning, she searched his face. "Thanks. But I'm not sure I'd mention our conversation to your friend. I'm not saying to lie; that would be wrong."

"I agree. I wouldn't want her to think I tried to find out her business, even if it was because I cared. But I doubt the subject will ever come up."

The doctor's face cleared. "Let's hope not. Unless you ever find a good time to tell her, one when you know your looking for her will be understood and appreciated."

He let out a gusty sigh. "*I'm* not appreciated by her," he said, then his eyes widened at what he'd blurted out.

"Do you really think so?" she asked, and as she turned and walked away, he thought he heard her chuckle.

Tucking the card into his pocket, he began walking back to where he'd parked the buggy.

He was waiting there when Rebecca rushed up, carrying a bag from a popular sewing and craft shop. "Sorry I took so long. There was a line in the shop."

"Ready to go?"

"*Ya.*" She walked to her side of the buggy and looked surprised when he quickly appeared at her elbow to help her into it.

He frowned. He was always polite. Then he thought, *Maybe she's nervous since we got so physically close the last time I helped her into the buggy*. His face flaming, he rounded the buggy and got inside. With a jerk of the reins, he got the buggy moving. They traveled a few miles in silence, then Rebecca startled him by speaking.

"You're doing it again."

"Doing what?"

"Staring at me." She turned to him. "Are you wondering if I'm going to do something crazy?"

"I—why would I wonder that?"

"Because my father said I was going to a 'head doc.'"

Ben didn't know what to say. "I don't know much about them."

"Then ask. If I don't want to answer, I won't."

"*Allrecht*. Why did you go to one? Is something wrong with your head?"

"I met Dr. Prato in the hospital, when I had pneumonia. She helped me through the grief process."

"Then why see her today?"

She looked at him and hesitated. Shrugging, she looked out at the passing scenery. "I just wanted to talk with her." She smiled at him. "I'm glad I did. She thinks I'm doing really well."

"*Ya?*" He looked at her. There was a lightness to her mood that had been absent earlier that morning.

She nodded. "She says that grief's different for everyone, and there's no set time for people to come to terms with it."

Ben remembered how his mother had said something similar. "Sounds wise."

"And since Lizzie was my twin, there was more of a bond than I might have had with another sister."

"The two of you were always together," he recalled. "I hardly ever saw you apart." But he'd only been interested in her, not Lizzie.

She looked at him again. "You know, I thought about my *mamm* and *daed* and how they've never been impatient with me, never chided me about grieving for Lizzie for so long. It occurred to me that you hadn't either. I've never thanked you for it."

"You look surprised."

"I am." She stared straight ahead again. "Well, you don't make it easy to talk to you, you know."

"I—don't?"

Shaking her head, she turned to him again. "I mean, we've talked a lot about important things, like Lizzie dying. But then . . ."

When she closed her eyes and bent her head, he touched her hand. Her eyes flew open in surprise.

"Talk to me."

She lifted her shoulders, let them fall. "We've been friends for such a long time." She stopped, hesitated. "But something's felt different the last few days." Her eyes widened at what she'd said. It had never been in her to be so . . . bold.

He let that sink in. Maybe it was time to do some real talking. Ben pulled the buggy to the side of the road and turned to face her. "I don't always have the right words like some men." Now it was his turn to hesitate.

"I know. But when I was trying to say something to Dr. Prato earlier and I was searching for the right word, she said for me to just say what was on my mind."

He looked away, not sure what to say. While he'd waited until he felt she was over the death of her sister, while he worried that she blamed him for not being able to save Lizzie, he hadn't planned on what he'd say, what he'd do.

Looking back at her, he nodded. "Good advice." He hesitated, wary of blurting out his feelings and being rejected. "Five years ago I had started thinking about whether we could be more than friends," he said carefully. "Then Lizzie died."

"And everything changed," she whispered. "But why didn't you say something before this?"

"When? How? I felt it would be selfish of me. And you weren't ready."

"No," she said, sighing. "I wasn't. Still might not be. Oh, Ben.

So many years you wasted. You waited when you should have been looking at someone who could be there for you."

He touched her hand. "I wanted to be there for you, Rebecca."

"This is a lot to think about," she told him, pressing the tips of her fingers to her temples. "When I was talking to Dr. Prato, she kept asking me questions about you."

"About me? Why? She doesn't know me."

Rebecca smiled. "I was telling her how patient *Mamm* and *Daed* had been with me about grieving for Lizzie. And my sisters and brothers, of course, especially Marian. Then I said you had been, too, and suddenly Dr. Prato was asking all these questions about you, asking me why I thought you were hanging around so much. She said that was a lot of effort on your part, even for *mei mamm*'s meals. Told me maybe I needed to take another look at you and think about things."

Ben let out the breath he hadn't realized he'd been holding. "Well, I guess I'm glad your father asked me to drive you to your appointment today."

"Me too."

A car drove by, and a passenger looked out to gawk at them. Ben glanced at the darkening sky and picked up the reins to urge Ike back onto the road and toward home.

"So where does this leave us?" he asked as silence stretched between them.

Rebecca turned to him and took a deep breath. She didn't think he was going to like her answer, but she needed to say it.

Chapter Six

REBECCA MADE TINY STITCHES IN THE SECTION OF QUILT before her. Outside it was cold, and snow was predicted for later in the day. But inside the Miller home there was a roaring fire in the fireplace, and it was time for talking and sewing. They drank cup after cup of tea and coffee and ate cookies while discussing everything from speculation about who was dating whom to when spring would arrive.

Quilting was such good therapy, Rebecca thought, feeling content. There was something so reassuring about sitting around talking with friends and family, sewing patterns that had been passed down for generations, here in a home that had been in her family for more than a hundred years.

She looked around the circle at her friends and family. Marian was helping her and *Mamm* to host the quilting frolic. The three of them had worked hard at *redding-up* the house and putting chairs in place. Little Annie wasn't happy about having to go to school today instead of being here, but one day she'd be old enough to sit with the womenfolk in the circle.

The Petersheim sisters were here today—well, they'd been Petersheims before three of them had gotten married this past fall. Rebecca couldn't help thinking that they all glowed with happiness. New *fraa* Edna, expert seamstress, had laid out the design of the quilt they were working on today. Mary Carol had brought thumbprint cookies filled with the jam made from mouthwatering strawberries she'd grown in her garden and Kathleen had preserved.

And Leah. Rebecca smiled as she watched Leah struggle with

making tiny stitches and then laughingly give up and retreat to a corner to write in the notebook she carried as a constant companion. Leah wasn't talented in the typical skills of an Amish woman—she'd nearly set the *kich* on fire more than once when she tried to cook. But Aaron, Leah's new *mann*, insisted that she was the only *fraa* for him. Those who loved saw with different eyes than others, Rebecca thought.

Amanda Graber was chatting with Leah. Amanda reminded Rebecca of Lizzie with her exuberance. But Amanda bustled around taking care of others, not worrying them with her risk taking.

Sisters Lydia King and Miriam Fisher worked well together cutting pieces of fabric for the quilt. Rebecca watched them and reflected on how they both had married men they'd known years before. Circumstances had separated the couples, but God's will had drawn them together again for great happiness.

As she sewed, Rebecca thought about her conversation with Ben on the drive home from her appointment with Dr. Prato. Now she knew how he felt about her. Had felt about her for years. But after she'd admitted she had feelings for him as well, she'd told him that she needed a little more time.

"I know it's a lot to ask, considering how long you've been waiting. But this is the first time I've had a chance to really think about it. The part of me that dreamed about the future, about how I felt about you, has been in cold storage," Rebecca told Ben.

When he glanced over, she took a deep breath and smiled at him.

"Okay. I understand." Ben had returned her smile, and the mood had been lighter, happier on the drive home.

She pricked her finger and quickly glanced about to see if anyone had noticed her daydreaming.

How could she have missed seeing how Ben felt about her? Even as lost in grief as she'd been at first, she should have known that his frequent appearance at the Miller kitchen table wasn't due only to her mother's cooking.

Sometimes she'd wondered if Ben hung around so much because

he felt guilty. He hadn't been able to save Lizzie when she fell through the ice. No one had, not the other boys who'd tried to help, not the paramedics who'd arrived so quickly and tried to make her breathe. Not the doctors at the hospital.

She still had to ask him what he'd meant when he said if she was going to blame anyone for Lizzie's death, she should blame him. Even if she had trouble accepting Lizzie's death as God's will, it was time to stop reliving what she couldn't change. It was time for Ben to stop blaming himself, too, if he was doing that.

The door opened, and her father came in, stamping his feet on the mat. He took off his black felt hat and shook the snow from it before hanging it and his coat on a peg. *Mamm* rose and walked to the stove to pour him a cup of coffee. They spoke quietly for a moment and then he looked over and caught Rebecca's eye. With a tilt of the head, he silently asked to speak to her.

She got up and followed him into the hallway, wondering what was going on. When she stopped before him and he wouldn't meet her eyes, her breath caught. Visions of tools running amuck, saws biting into flesh, blood spurting from arteries flashed before her eyes.

"Ben? Did something happen to Ben?"

"Whoa, nothing's happened to Ben," he said quickly.

He glanced over at Naomi. "Rebecca, your mother told me I need to apologize to you."

"Apologize? For what?"

"For telling Ben that you needed to go to your 'head doc,'" he said. "It's a family matter, and I shouldn't have said that."

"I'm not ashamed of seeing Dr. Prato."

"No, I know you're not. And your mother and I will always be indebted to her for helping you so much."

She looked up at him, at this man who had been such a rock for her, and she nodded. "I knew you were just teasing. I know you don't think I'm crazy."

He hugged her. "Of course you're not. You're the most level-headed young woman I know."

Rebecca hugged him back. "I don't know about that. But I love you, and I'm not upset."

"Well, I guess I'd better be getting back to work. Now that we've talked."

"Amos? Is everything all right?" Naomi came to stand next to him.

"It's fine," Rebecca assured her. "*Daed* apologized like he said you wanted him to."

"I didn't mean you had to do it right now, while we're having the quilting!"

Amos shrugged. "Best to apologize as soon as you know you've done wrong," he said. "Besides, I think I was doing a little . . . interfering."

"Interfering?"

Amos cleared his throat. "I—uh, well, I think I was trying to find out how Ben felt about Rebecca. If it bothered him that she was seeing Dr. Prato, he wasn't the kind of *mann* that I wanted around our daughter."

"Amos!" Naomi stared at him, shocked. "I don't think we should interfere—"

"*Ya.*" He looked at Rebecca. "Sorry."

These things were supposed to take place in privacy. Some couples only told their parents of their engagement after they'd arranged for the banns to be read in church.

But Rebecca could tell they were concerned, and she wanted to reassure them. "Ben just told me how he felt on the way home after I saw Dr. Prato," she told them carefully.

"What about you? How do you feel?" her mother wanted to know.

"What, is Rebecca sick again?" Marian asked as she stepped into the hallway. She peered at her sister. "You didn't say you weren't feeling well."

Rebecca threw up her hands. "Enough!" she said, laughing. "This has gotten completely out of hand."

Standing on tiptoe, she kissed her father's cheek, then her mother's and her sister's. "I love you all, and I'm going back to the quilting. Everyone must be wondering what kind of hosts we are!"

When she returned to the living room, Rebecca found needles poised in midair and everyone looking curiously at her.

"*Daed* needed something," she told them.

Rebecca picked up her needle and began making small, meticulous stitches. There was silence for a long moment, then the other women went back to stitching. Sarah Fisher began talking about Katie Ann, her toddler, and asking advice about teething problems, and suddenly there was chattering around the quilt frame as the mothers in the group gave advice.

Rebecca glanced over and gave Sarah a grateful smile. Sarah smiled back. *She knows what it's like to be the object of concern because of a loss.*

Yes, Rebecca thought, it was good to sit here sewing on familiar patterns while she thought about the change that had suddenly presented itself in the pattern of her own life. She had much to think about, but nothing had to be decided in a day. She'd take things slowly and carefully to make sure that Ben was as right for her as he thought she was for him.

❧

"Something wrong?"

Amos looked over. "What?"

Ben planted his hands on his hips and looked at his boss. "You've been watching me all morning."

Shaking his head, Rebecca's father ran his measuring tape along a wall in the Greenstein kitchen. "You must be imagining it."

Ben watched Amos jot some numbers down on a pad of paper. "No, I'm not. Is there something you don't like about the way I'm doing the job today?"

"'Course not."

"Then it's about Rebecca and me."

Amos looked up. "*Is* there a Rebecca and you?"

"That should be between us at this point, don't you think?" Ben said it respectfully, but he felt his heart beating hard in his chest while Amos regarded him, his bushy black eyebrows drawn together in a frown.

"You're right," the other man conceded after a long moment.

When he muttered something beneath his breath as he turned back to his measuring tape, Ben's ears perked up. "What did you say?"

"You'd think you'd be grateful to me," Amos told him, sounding a little irritable. He let the metal measuring tape snap back into its container. "After all I've done to put the two of you together."

Ben leaned against the counter behind him. "Are you saying you've been playing matchmaker?"

"Why do you think you get invited for supper so often? I do have enough mouths to feed."

But although he sounded like he was growling, Ben saw the corners of the other man's mouth quirk up into a grin. "Why, you're as bad as my *daed*, trying to push us together," he said at last.

"Even sent you to town with her that day when she could have driven herself. Girl knows how to drive a buggy better than you."

Letting the joking insult slide—at least, he thought Amos was joking; he didn't think anyone knew he'd had that little accident with the chicken last year—Ben thought about what he'd said. "So you didn't really need those supplies at the hardware store?"

Amos shrugged. "They could have delivered them."

"Why, you—I don't know what to say."

"Well, I shouldn't have said what I did that day. About Rebecca seeing a 'head doc.' Naomi made me apologize to Rebecca for that. But I knew it'd get your curiosity up. Thought you'd either stick with her, or it'd finally make you run."

Ben stood straighter. "I don't run," he said quietly. "If I did, I'd have decided not to wait like I have."

"And now?"

"I don't know what's going to happen, but she knows how I feel now. I'm giving her a little time to think things over."

"Don't let her take too long," Amos said gruffly. "Enough water under the bridge."

"She's not the kind of person who'd treat my feelings lightly."

Amos gave Ben a long, measuring look and nodded, then he turned back to his work.

Ben didn't need reminding. He knew how long he'd been waiting. Even this space they were standing in was a reminder. It had gone on the market just last year, and Ben had thought about buying it. He knew he would get married eventually, even if Rebecca didn't want him, and the place had been a good price because it needed a lot of repair—just the kind he and his friends and family could do in the evenings and on Saturdays.

But he'd waited, and the house had sold. Well, there'd be another. And if things went the way he hoped with Rebecca, they'd find it—or build it—together.

He and Amos worked together companionably, talking little for the rest of the afternoon. When quitting time came, they loaded their tools in the buggy and climbed inside.

"Staying for supper?" Amos asked casually.

"Not tonight," Ben told him. "I'm giving Rebecca a little time to think. A *little* time," he repeated before the other man could speak. "And, Amos, you'll have one less mouth to feed tonight."

Amos chuckled as he lifted the reins and got the buggy moving.

෴

Rebecca was about to enter the kitchen when she heard her parents talking. Thinking it might be a private conversation, she hesitated.

"Ben's not staying for supper? You didn't scare him away, did you?" Naomi asked.

"Of course not. He says he's giving Rebecca a little time to think." He caught her look. "I told him not to give her too long."

Rebecca's eyebrows went up. *Well, that's interesting*, she thought. She knew her parents liked Ben, that he was the kind of person *Daed* wanted working for him. But interfering in Ben's relationship with her?

She stepped into the room. "Are you taking sides?"

"Eavesdropping?" her mother asked mildly.

"No, I was just walking in and I heard my name."

Her father reddened. He glanced at his wife, then back at Rebecca. "What I meant was, your mother and I know that Ben has been interested in you for a long time. If he sees you're not feeling the same way, he shouldn't keep waiting."

"But I didn't know that he was interested until now. I thought he just looked at me as a friend."

"She took Lizzie's death hard, Amos," Naomi reminded him. "She wasn't thinking about boys. Unlike another young woman in the house," she muttered.

Rebecca tried not to smile. She'd noticed Marian was already showing interest in the opposite sex—and not just Ben. She walked over to the stove and looked into the simmering pot. "Mmm, tomato soup. Perfect on a cold night. How can I help?"

"Amos, here's your coffee," Naomi said, handing him the mug she'd just poured.

"I've got some paperwork to do. Call me when supper's ready," he said and left the room.

Rebecca could have sworn she saw the two of them exchange a look. In her opinion, there was suddenly too much interest in what was going on—or not going on—between her and Ben.

"Why don't you slice some bread so we can make grilled cheese sandwiches to go with the soup? I baked brownies for dessert. That should be plenty."

Nodding, Rebecca began slicing bread, then turned to slicing cheese. Her mother spread butter on the bread, stacked slices with cheese, and set several sandwiches sizzling on the grill pan on the gas stove.

Naomi gave the sandwiches her attention. "I don't want you to feel pressured by what your father said," she offered, breaking the silence and looking up at Rebecca. "Ben chose not to reveal his feelings to you before this, but that doesn't mean you're obliged to suddenly conform to his plans for a life together."

"He's not pressuring me."

"Good. *I've* seen how he feels about you, but the fact that you haven't tells me that you weren't ready . . . or that you don't see him as the man you want to marry someday."

"I think marrying him would make *Daed* happy."

"And that should be the least of your concerns," her mother told her tartly. "You're the one who'll live with him for a very long time." She glanced in the direction of the den where Amos had retreated to do his paperwork. "I want you to be as happy with your marriage as I've been."

Rebecca hugged her mother, and they stood there for a long moment. "I love you, *Mamm*."

"I love you, too, *liebchen*."

"What's burning?" Marian asked as she walked into the kitchen.

Naomi spun around. Tsk-tsking, she used a spatula to lift the sandwiches from the grill onto a plate.

"The pigs will have these for breakfast," she said with a rueful laugh. "Rebecca, cut some more bread and cheese, please."

Marian sidled up to her sister at the counter. "So, Rebecca," she said, "is Ben joining us tonight?"

Chapter Seven

NO ONE EXPECTED REBECCA TO ATTEND ANY FUNERALS in the community for several years after Lizzie's death. But the Lantzes' flamboyant Auntie Ruth had died last summer, and a few days ago, a beloved *onkel* had died, so Rebecca went to the services. She was grateful that both had been elderly and lived good, long lives. But she couldn't help it; going to *Onkel* John's funeral made her think about Lizzie's.

Now she wanted a connection with her sister, a more cheerful one. She pulled Lizzie's journal from under her pillow and climbed onto her bed. Somehow, reading her words almost made her feel as if Lizzie were in the room with her—even in the same bed. She smiled as she remembered how, when they were little girls, her parents would find them sleeping together, as if they still wanted the closeness of the womb.

After Lizzie died, Rebecca felt she was invading Lizzie's privacy when she read her journal. But she justified it by telling herself that she missed her sister so much, she just wanted the closeness. Besides, she and Lizzie had always shared everything.

Well, she'd thought they shared everything. The first time she opened the journal and read an entry, she'd been shocked. She turned to that page again.

I've known my twin sister, Rebecca, all my life, Lizzie had written in the journal, in the quick, careless scrawl that would have made their teacher wince. *It still surprises me that we're so different. She's almost timid compared to me. And she's always watching me and worrying over what I do, almost like she's my mother, not my sister. I love her, but I wish she'd stop that. She tells me that she's the oldest and it's her job to look out for all of us. She was born six minutes before me. Six minutes! Should that really mean she's the oldest? Maybe she crowded me when it came time to be born. No, I don't really mean that. Rebecca would never put herself first. She never does.*

Rebecca winced. Lizzie sounded . . . annoyed that she'd simply cared enough to look out for her. Imagine!

She heard footsteps on the wooden stairs and quickly thrust the journal behind her. Marian walked into the room. "You okay?"

"Sure, why?"

Marian shrugged. "I just thought maybe you were upset after going to the funeral."

Rebecca studied her sister. Marian's forehead was drawn in concern. It was an expression she saw often on her sister's face.

Marian was becoming her! She was worrying over Rebecca the way Rebecca had worried over Lizzie. Guilt swamped her. "I'm fine. Really. I was just reading. It was a long morning."

Her sister nodded. "I'm going to have some hot chocolate with *Mamm*. Want some?"

"No, thanks."

Marian walked out and Rebecca stared after her. When she heard her sister's footsteps descend the stairs, she got up and walked over to her chest of drawers. Reaching back behind a stack of underwear, she pulled out a leather-bound journal and took it to her bed. She leafed through the pages and frowned. The last entry was a year to the date from Lizzie's death.

The handwriting was large and dark, slashing across the page, not her usual neat writing. Here and there the words were marked by patches where her tears had fallen.

It's not fair! she'd written. *God, why did You take my sister from us?* It was written over and over again, a litany of anger. She glanced heavenward. Thank goodness her God wasn't an angry God, or He'd have struck her down.

She leafed through the pages and found more of the same, until she reached the page where she'd written about the awful day at the pond. Taking a deep breath, she moved on and found the entries before that.

I wonder what will happen one day when one of us finds that special man, the one we want to spend the rest of our lives with. I'll be happy, of course, to be with him. But it will be strange to be so completely separate from this sister I've lived so close to from the moment our hearts started beating in the womb. We share thoughts without speaking, have shared memories. Mamm *always talks about how we had our own language no one else understood until we started talking with others in the family.*

My husband will have to understand that Lizzie will be a frequent visitor, of course. We'll visit often. Maybe we'll get married at the same time . . . find our special men and have a double wedding? And wouldn't it be so wunderbaar *to have our* kinner *play together and grow up close cousins?*

Maybe one of us will even have twins. I know God determines these things, but I think Lizzie should have them. I know she thinks of me as a little mudder, *always watching over her. But she has a sense of adventure I admire.* Kinner *need that, not just the mothering.*

I wonder if it'll be Ben I marry. He's so cute. And he's been paying attention to me, not the other girls. Well, teasing me, but he doesn't do it with them. I think he likes me, and I know I like him. A lot.

Rebecca smiled as she closed the book and slid the two journals under her pillow. That's where Lizzie had kept hers—under her pillow. She hadn't made any secret of it to Rebecca, pulling it out and writing in it each night before bed. But no one else had known about it. Rebecca felt a little guilty that she hadn't shared it with her mother, but the time had never been right. Maybe one day. There were entries in there about *Mamm* and *Daed*. Some of the things that Lizzie had written would make them smile, even when she complained about their being too strict. There were lots of those entries because Lizzie frequently wanted to do things that she shouldn't. But she had written just as often of her love for her parents and for her sisters and brothers.

Her entries about Rebecca had made her smile and made her frown. But Rebecca didn't want to think about those now. So what did *she* want to do now? Rebecca found herself thinking about Ben, how he'd looked at her that day. How it had felt to be held in his strong arms when he picked her up to put her in the buggy. How they'd looked at each other, breath held, their faces inches apart. How it had felt when his hand touched hers.

She wanted to see him again. Be with him.

So what was she waiting for?

She jumped up, freshened up, and then went clattering down the stairs. Her *mamm* and Marian looked up in surprise.

"Are *Daed* and Ben still out in the barn?"

Naomi nodded.

Rebecca threw on her coat and slipped out the door. As she went to shut it, she heard Marian saying, "Bet it's Ben she wants to see, not *Daed*," then her mother's answering laugh.

❧

Ben and Amos looked up in surprise when Rebecca entered the barn.

"*Daed*, could I talk to Ben for a minute?"

Amos put down the sandpaper he'd been using on a cabinet and nodded. "I think I'll get a cup of coffee," he said as he strolled out.

As he passed Ben, out of sight of Rebecca, he turned and winked at him.

"*Guder mariye.*"

Ben nodded as he searched her face. "*Guder mariye.*" He hesitated and then plunged ahead. "I'm glad you went to your *onkel*'s funeral. It meant a lot to your *Aenti* Esther. I wasn't sure you'd go."

"I'm fine." She smiled. "People don't need to baby me, Ben. Not anymore."

He found himself smiling back. Weak sunlight came filtering in through the half-open barn door, bringing out the golden flecks in her hazel eyes. He could stand and look into them for hours. Then he realized she was talking to him. "What?"

"I wondered if you'd like to go on a picnic tomorrow?"

"Tomorrow?"

"*Ya*, it's Saturday, remember? I have this Saturday off."

"I was just thinking it's cold out."

She laughed and shook her head at him, and he thought how he loved her laugh. He hadn't heard it much these past few years.

"I know. So we'll wear coats and sit in the buggy if it's too cold to sit at a picnic table somewhere. I thought I'd pack us a basket lunch, and we could go for a ride."

Ben swallowed. This was more than he'd expected when he'd first tentatively talked with her about their seeing each other.

"That'd be great."

"Good. I'll make some of your favorites." She started for the door, then turned and glanced over her shoulder. "That would be food and food and food, right?"

Laughing, he nodded. "Right. Noon?"

"Noon." She looked back at him for a long moment. "'Bye."

Ben stood there for a long time after she left. What a surprise.

He didn't know how long he might have stood there thinking about what had happened. The barn door opened, and he quickly picked up a hammer just in case it was Amos.

"Did I give you enough time?" Amos asked politely.

"Yes." Ben gave him a level stare, then followed the older man's gaze to the hammer in his hand.

Before Rebecca came, he'd been sanding the wooden cabinet in front of him. Setting down the hammer, he picked up the sandpaper and began running it over the wood.

Amos just chuckled.

⌒⌒⌒

Rebecca shut the barn doors and grinned. Well, that had been easier than she'd thought it would be.

And Ben had looked surprised. Well, it wasn't something she'd ever thought she'd do—ask a *mann* out. But Ben wasn't just any *mann*. He was—Ben, her best friend.

She was humming when she walked back into the house. Taking off her coat, she turned around and found her mother and Marian staring at her.

"What?"

"Something in the barn make you happy?" *Mamm* asked.

"More likely some*one*," Marian said.

Rebecca clapped a hand to her mouth. She'd meant to talk to her sister about how she felt about Ben. "Oh, Marian, I hope—"

"*Nee*, it's all right!" Marian said, laughing. "I'm not interested in Ben. I was just practicing."

"Practicing?" Rebecca and *Mamm* said at the same time.

She batted her eyelashes at them. "Yes, practicing." Then she giggled and jumped up to hug Rebecca. "It's always been you and Ben. Always."

Rebecca smiled. "*Ya*."

⌒⌒⌒

"I should have taken you somewhere." Ben gestured at the spot beside the road where he'd pulled the buggy. "A restaurant or something. We haven't been anyplace like that for a long time. Remember when we went to a movie?"

"That was a long time ago. During our *rumschpringe*." She looked around, enjoying the quiet. "You never ran with the boys who wanted to see more of the *Englisch* world."

He shrugged. "I had everything I wanted here. Family. Church." He paused. "You."

A blush crept up her cheeks. She'd felt the same. This was her world, so aptly named Paradise, full of friends and family. And a man who had waited for her.

"You warm enough?"

Nodding, Rebecca poured hot chocolate into a cup and handed it to Ben. "*Ya.* You?"

"That chili you made for us should be melting the snow from the roof of the buggy," he told her with a laugh. "I can't believe I ate two bowls."

As they'd expected, it had been too cold to sit outside, so Ben had taken them for a drive and found a place where they could pull the buggy off the road and park for a quiet picnic.

"It wasn't so hot it kept you from eating it."

"I'm stronger than I look."

"Guess you had to be, to be around me the past five years," she said with a rueful smile.

He touched her hand. "Don't say that. I cared about you. I care about you."

Rebecca looked down at his hand and turned hers over so that she could clasp it. A gust of wind shook the buggy, and cold crept in with icy fingers. She shivered.

"We should go."

"Not yet." She stared out at the landscape. "I'm ready for winter to be over."

"Rebecca?"

Turning, she saw that he was watching her with those serious eyes of his. "Does this mean you want us to be more than friends?"

"Yes," she said simply and was warmed by the look in his eyes.

∽◦∽

BARBARA CAMERON

They went for drives and to singings. Ben often stayed for dinner with her family. On the surface, nothing appeared different to the casual observer.

But the way they looked at each other was different. Rebecca had the sense that Ben was being careful, that he knew this was important and wanted to take the time for them both to be comfortable with their changing relationship.

They held hands under the table as they ate dinner at her parents' table and when she walked outside to talk to him privately, quietly, before he left for home.

And one night, when Rebecca went to bed, she pulled out her journal again. Instead of the angry, slashing words demanding to know why God had taken her sister, she wrote: *Forgive me, God, for being angry with You. I still don't understand why You took Lizzie home. But I trust You.*

Then, as if the pen had a mind of its own, she wrote: *God, is this the man You have set aside for me?*

Chapter Eight

REBECCA LOOKED STARTLED TO SEE HIM WALK INTO THE gift shop in the middle of the day. She hurried to his side.

"Ben! What are you doing here? Is something wrong with *Daed* or *Mamm?*"

"No, nothing's wrong," he reassured her. "I came into town for supplies and such. I thought I'd stop in and see if you'd like to have lunch."

She glanced at the clock. "I'm not due for lunch break for another fifteen minutes."

"That's fine." He glanced around and saw a woman he assumed was her boss looking over curiously. "I'll wait outside."

Even on a cold day—maybe because it *was* a cold day—there were some people out shopping, walking briskly along the sidewalks, going in and out of shops, eager for after-Christmas bargains.

Ben felt odd being in town in the middle of the day during the workweek. Even odder was thinking about having his midday meal at a restaurant instead of eating at home or with Amos and Naomi and sometimes Rebecca, if she were home. Or, if they were on a job site, sometimes he and Amos ate a packed lunch to save time.

A female tourist walked past, eyeing Ben's Plain clothing. Her hand moved to the camera that hung by a strap around her neck. He frowned, and she apparently thought better of it. She smiled apologetically and hurried on.

Ben sat down on a nearby bench and idly watched people passing. Now that he'd decided to move forward, he wondered why he was feeling a little anxious. Maybe it was because it was unaccustomed territory. Once a man decided he wanted a woman for his *fraa* and he was assured that she was indeed interested in a serious relationship, there was no uncertainty. They got to know each other better in the months before their marriage and that was that. Occasionally a couple might decide not to proceed to marriage, but it didn't happen often.

He didn't know why things had to be so complicated with him and Rebecca. He knew how he felt about her, and he knew she was attracted to him. They'd been friends for years, and that was the best foundation for a marriage, wasn't it? Long after that initial passion for each other faded to a warm glow, the love they'd shared, the friendship they'd nurtured, their strong faith in God guiding them . . . well, that would be what kept them together. He'd seen this in the many enduring marriages around him in the community.

As a practical man, he didn't rush into things. But from the way his parents and his friends, even Rebecca's *daed*, talked, he'd been dragging his feet. While he wasn't going to allow someone else to influence him, he was tired of watching other men he knew marrying and starting families.

He knew family was important to Rebecca. But did she want a *mann* of her own? *Kinner* of her own? Or was she content to stay with her parents and her siblings?

What if he'd hung around all this time only to find out she didn't want what he wanted? What if his steadfast belief that it was God's will that they be together was just his own stubborn determination to get what he wanted? He wiped suddenly damp palms on his pants. *Enough of this.* He didn't need to feel nervous. This was Rebecca.

Then she walked up to him. He saw the anxiety in her eyes even though she smiled.

"My boss let me go a little early. I think she was surprised that someone came in for me."

"I haven't been to town to eat in a long time. Why don't you show me where the food is good and the service is fast. You have just a half hour, *ya?*"

"She said that I could take an hour today if I wanted to. It gets slow this time of day when people stop to eat." She gestured toward a small restaurant down the block. "They have good food, and the prices are reasonable. This time of year there won't be a lot of tourists."

They walked down the sidewalk, and when another couple approached, Ben reached out and took Rebecca's hand to draw her closer, to keep her from getting bumped. She glanced at him, and he saw surprise but also shy pleasure in her eyes. After the need passed for them to touch, she didn't pull away and he didn't let go. He was sorry when they reached the restaurant and he had to take back his hand to open the door and remove his hat.

The restaurant was quaint, decorated to look like a big, comfortable Amish kitchen, and the food was good, familiar country fare. A waitress came and took their orders, then they were left alone.

Rebecca fiddled with the silverware. He watched her take a deep breath and then look up at him.

"So, Ben, why are you here?"

Ben started to talk, but the waitress interrupted to set their drinks on the table. "Your order will be right out," she told him with a bright smile.

His throat was suddenly dry. He took a sip of iced tea, then set the glass down. *Don't rush things,* he told himself. *This is too important. And what were you thinking, doing this at a meal? If you ask now and she says no, how are you going to sit here and force your sandwich down?* So he made small talk, asked her about her job, got her talking. Their food came, and he found himself eating quickly.

Rebecca ate more slowly, as she usually did. Both of them declined dessert—Ben because the sandwich he'd eaten lay like lead in the pit of his stomach. Their plates were removed, and they were left to finish their drinks.

Ben cleared the frog from his throat and wished he'd spent more time hanging out with young men he knew who were smoother with the ladies. He'd been too serious, too focused on apprenticing with Rebecca's father, and then too focused on Rebecca.

"I wanted to talk to you about something," he began.

She smiled slightly. "*Ya*, I figured you did. You've never asked me to have a meal out."

"We've known each other for a long time. Been friends for a long time."

"I couldn't have gotten through these past years without you."

He sat back, a little surprised. "You've never said that before."

She dropped her gaze to her silverware again. "I'm coming to realize that for some time now I've been a little . . . self-centered."

Ben reached to touch her hand. "That's not true."

She stared at his hand covering hers, then raised her eyes to look at him.

His hand curled around hers. "Rebecca, I want us to be married."

It was a good thing she was sitting down, he realized. She paled, then blushed, and her eyes widened.

"I—this is sudden—" she began.

"I think we'd suit," he said, and the minute the words were out, he knew he'd made a mistake.

She straightened, and her expression became blank. "Suit?"

"We get along so well, enjoy the same things. That's more important than being madly in love, isn't it?"

She pulled her hand back and placed it in her lap. "I suppose so, for some people." She took a deep breath, then her eyes met his. "I'm sorry, but I don't think we want the same things, Ben."

"Well, we haven't talked about having *kinner*, but you want to, don't you?"

"Yes, but that wasn't what I was talking about," she said softly.

"I don't understand."

"I'm sorry," she said again. She pushed back her chair, and it scraped the floor and jarred his nerves. "I have to get back to the shop."

She fled before he could even get to his feet.

Stunned, Ben sat there staring after her. "Nice job, Ben Weaver," he muttered. "Real smooth."

Rebecca found herself out on the sidewalk, in the midst of people who parted and moved around her like water around a stone in its path. She blinked at the tears that threatened. *Don't cry*, she told herself firmly. There was no way she could go back to the shop all upset. A quick glance at a clock hanging outside a shop showed that she still had some time, since her boss had been so generous about a longer lunch break.

Glancing back, she saw Ben emerging from the restaurant. He looked to his left. Before he could look in her direction, she ducked into a shop. She couldn't endure talking to him right now. He walked past the shop a few minutes later, and when she drew closer to the front window, she saw that he stood outside the one where she worked. His hand went to the doorknob, then it fell to his side. Shaking his head, he walked away.

Rebecca bit her lip. Wasn't it bad enough that she'd started to feel like an old maid without having the least romantic proposal in history? And she wasn't even the kind of woman who harbored silly, girlish dreams of a man sweeping her off her feet. She'd been raised to be a practical woman, concerned with what was really important— faith, work, dedication to family.

But was it so wrong to want a man to want her because he *loved* her, because he felt something so powerful that he could envision spending the rest of his life with her? Did he have to say they'd "suit"?

"Can I help you with anything?" a salesclerk asked.

The voice sounded familiar. Rebecca's heart sank. With a sigh, she turned.

"Oh, Rebecca, hi. I didn't realize it was you."

"Hi, Mary Anne." The woman was several years younger than her, small and sharp-featured. Rebecca gestured at the rack of embroidery thread. "I had a few minutes left of my break. I thought I'd pick up a few things for my *mamm*."

Mary Anne's eyes narrowed. "Are you okay?"

"*Ya.*"

"Your eyes look red, like you've been crying."

"The cold wind made my eyes burn."

The other young woman glanced outside, then back at Rebecca. "Did I see you go past with Ben Weaver a little while ago?"

"Yes. He was in town picking up supplies."

"You didn't come in with him?"

Rebecca busied herself picking out colors of thread. None would be wasted, and it was a good way to stay casual and not give Mary Anne something to gossip about.

"No, I'm working today. He just decided since he was here we could have lunch. He has meals at our house a lot, since he works with *Daed*."

"So you think he wouldn't want to do it if he didn't have to," Mary Anne said, her small eyes scanning Rebecca for a reaction.

"Yes, wouldn't you?" Rebecca responded with a nonchalance she didn't feel.

"I always wondered if the two of you would get married."

"Really? We're just friends." She moved away, and Mary Anne moved with her, standing too close. "I think I'll get *Mamm* a new thimble too. The one she has is so old and worn, you can nearly see through the metal."

"Not to discourage you from buying it," Mary Anne said, "but sometimes a woman gets attached to such things and won't use a new one."

Rebecca nodded and put the thimble down. "You're right. Lizzie bought her that thimble that last Christmas."

Glancing at the clock, she moved to the counter with the cash register. "Can you ring these up for me? I need to get back to work."

Her package in hand, Rebecca left the shop. She didn't want to go back to work, but she had no choice. There was no way she'd let her employer down, even if Anita had said things were slow today. Fortunately, when she returned, the other woman looked up in relief.

"Thank goodness you're back," she exclaimed. "It started getting busy a few minutes ago."

The distraction was just what Rebecca needed. She put the package away and turned to help a customer choose some stationery with photographs of Paradise printed on it. The hours passed quickly, and when it was time to turn the Open sign around and lock the door, Rebecca realized she'd gotten through the afternoon without thinking about Ben and his disappointing proposal.

"We were so busy I forgot to ask how your lunch with your young man went."

"He's not my young man," Rebecca told her politely. "He's just a good friend."

"Really?" Anita glanced up from counting money. "Hmm . . ." She stopped and shrugged. "Well, I probably shouldn't be so nosy. After living here in Lancaster County for twenty years, I've learned that Plain people don't talk about such things, especially to the *Englisch.*"

"It's all right," Rebecca assured her. "I meant to tell you that I did appreciate your letting me have the extra time. Ben doesn't come to town often."

Anita nodded and slipped the money into a bank deposit bag, then filled out a deposit slip. She looked at Rebecca and sighed. "You're such a sweet girl, and I know you've had some real tragedy in your young life. I'd just like to see you find a young man, get married, and be happy. Even if it meant that one day I'd lose the best employee I've had since I opened the shop."

"That's really sweet," Rebecca managed. "But I don't have to be married to be happy."

"No, of course not. Blame my romantic heart." She retrieved her purse from a locked drawer under the cash register. "I had thirty-four wonderful years with my Phil."

She gave the shop a quick look over, nodded, then turned to Rebecca. "Ready to go home? I'm looking forward to having a nice supper and putting my feet up."

Rebecca was too. Then her eyes widened. What if Ben came to supper at her house? What would she do if she had to sit next to him and pretend nothing was different? Because everything was different now. Everything about her relationship with Ben had changed in just a few minutes. And she didn't know what she was going to do about it.

With the workday finally over, Rebecca was glad to be home. That is, until she shed her coat and bonnet and walked into the kitchen.

Ben was sitting in his usual place at the table, having a cup of coffee. He looked up, then away as she stopped and stared at him.

Her mother smiled. "Did you have a good day?"

"It was fine. Hello, Ben."

"Hello."

"Ben's staying for supper." *Mamm* opened the oven door and peered inside.

What's new? Rebecca wondered, trying not to look at him as she went to wash her hands.

But what was he thinking? He wasn't going to act like nothing had happened today, go on the same way he had for years, was he?

"Your mother insisted I stay because it's Abram's *Gebottsdaag*," he told Rebecca quietly as Naomi pulled a big casserole from the oven.

As was family tradition, the meal consisted of the birthday child's favorites. The chicken and noodle casserole was one of Rebecca's favorites, too, but her stomach was in knots. She took just a small portion and pushed it around on her plate.

"Ben, you're not eating much," Naomi said.

"Sorry, I had a big lunch in town today while I was picking up supplies."

Rebecca casually placed her napkin over part of her plate and jumped up to collect them so dessert could be served.

"Well, you must have a slice of birthday cake, right, Abram?"

"He doesn't have to. I could eat his piece for him." But Abram, just turned five, grinned to show he was joking.

Ben accepted a plate with cake and ice cream and passed it to Rebecca. There was a look in his eyes, she thought, a silent accusation, as if he wondered how she could eat. Why should he care when he'd been so casual and unemotional with his proposal?

She knew she wasn't as attractive as her twin sister, and she didn't have as interesting a personality. But even if she'd been looking at him with different eyes lately, that didn't mean that she was willing to give up the right to a life with a man who loved her. She'd lost enough in her life. Did she have to lose the dream most young girls dreamed too?

Rebecca stabbed at a bite of cake with her fork and shoved it into her mouth. It tasted too sweet, and the frosting stuck to the roof of her mouth. Food just wasn't agreeing with her tonight.

And it didn't appear Ben was doing much better. He shoveled in a couple of mouthfuls and then, quietly taking her cue, covered the rest with his napkin. When she glanced over and saw what he'd done, he gave her a look that was a silent challenge. She shrugged, not interested in making him look bad to her family.

She just wanted him gone.

Finally the meal was over and she could turn her back— politely—on Ben. Get the dishes done and escape to her room.

Six-year-old Annie got up on a step stool and held out her hands for a dish towel. She smiled as Rebecca handed her a dish to dry and worked on the task with great concentration.

She looked up. "Becca?"

"Yes?"

"Are there birthdays in heaven?"

Rebecca nearly dropped the dish she was washing. "I don't know. I guess so. I mean, birthdays are good and heaven's good, right?"

"So Lizzie gets to have birthdays?"

Tears threatened. Rebecca nodded. "With lots of cake and ice cream."

"And Jesus sings the 'Happy Birthday' song to her?"

"Yes, *liebschdi*." Wiping her hands on a towel, Rebecca turned and bent to hug her little sister.

"I think she's having a wonderful time in heaven," Ben said.

Startled, Rebecca turned at the deep timbre of his voice. She hadn't realized he'd come up behind them with an empty coffee mug.

"You do?" Annie asked him, staring up at him with big eyes.

"I do," he told her, stroking her hair with his big, work-roughened hand.

"We're all done. Why don't you go ask *Mamm* if she needs any help?" Rebecca suggested.

"Okay. Bye, Ben."

"Bye." He turned to Rebecca. "I'll wash this since you're already done."

"Don't be silly. You're a guest." She tried to take it, but he resisted for a moment, then released it. She turned back to the sink.

"I'm sorry. I tried not to stay," he said in a low voice.

"I'm sure you did."

"What's that supposed to mean?"

Glancing over her shoulder to make sure no one was in hearing range, Rebecca met his eyes. She sighed. "I'm sorry. That was rude. I don't want to fight with you."

"I don't understand what happened today."

He stopped as Amos came into the room to get himself a cup of coffee, then left.

"You acted like I did something wrong. What did I do?"

Quivering with emotion, Rebecca put the last dried mug in the cabinet and slammed the door. "If you don't know, Ben Weaver, I'm not going to tell you." And she turned and left the room.

Chapter Nine

REBECCA NEARLY RAN INTO HER MOTHER IN HER RUSH out of the kitchen.

"I heard raised voices. What's going on?" When Rebecca didn't answer, *Mamm* looked past her. "Ben? What's the matter?"

"Ask her," he said shortly and started to walk past her. Then he stopped. "I'm sorry, Naomi. I don't know. You'll have to ask Rebecca. Tell Amos I'll see him in the morning."

Then he left.

"Did the two of you have an argument?"

Rebecca avoided looking at her mother. "Not exactly."

Naomi touched her daughter's cheek and frowned. "It's obvious you're upset about something. Tell me what's wrong."

"It's—personal."

Naomi took her daughter's hand and drew her down to sit. "You would tell me if Ben . . . touched you or said anything inappropriate."

"Ben would never do that."

"But you're angry at him. Can't you tell me why?"

"It's complicated," Rebecca said finally. She was tired, so tired of holding in how hurt she felt. How could she tell her mother that Ben had asked to marry her in just about the most passionless way that a man could?

He'd been a good friend to her, knew her better than anybody except her family. But even when she'd been grieving, when she'd been depressed, when she'd been in emotional deep freeze, she was still a person who wanted someone to think she was pretty, to want her for a better reason than that they would "suit"—whatever that meant.

It sounded like they'd be like two passionless people walking together through decades.

She couldn't tell her mother that. She could barely wrap her mind around it herself.

Naomi squeezed her hand. "Love doesn't always run smoothly." Her voice was gentle, her eyes warm and compassionate.

If only she could have heard Ben, Rebecca thought.

"It's a mother's wish that you find a *mann* who'll love you and who you'll love," Naomi said gently. "If it's God's will, you'll find him and experience the joy of married love, grow together spiritually as a couple, as parents."

Annie came running in. "*Mamm*, Abram says his tummy hurts."

"Tell him I'll be right there." She turned back to Rebecca with a smile. "I shouldn't have let him have that second slice of cake."

"Do you want me to go?"

Naomi got to her feet and bent down to kiss Rebecca on the cheek. "No, you've had a long day."

Rebecca looked around the kitchen, found it spotless, and then went into the den to say *gut nacht* to her father. It took a few minutes to look in on each of her brothers and sisters and wish them sweet dreams.

Then, dressed in her nightgown, snug in her bed, she pulled out her journal and wrote about her day, pouring out her disappointment in the pages. When she thought she'd written all that she could, she started to slide it back under her pillow. Her fingers touched Lizzie's journal, and she brought it out to stare at it for a moment. Sweet Annie had asked if Lizzie got to have birthdays in heaven. When she thought of her twin, Rebecca thought of Lizzie at the age of seventeen when she'd left the earth.

She'd been feeling sorry for herself earlier, when she'd let what Ben had asked make her unhappy. But Lizzie wasn't going to have the chance to marry a man she loved or have children with him or grow

BARBARA CAMERON

old with him. Guilt swamped her for a moment. Then she shook her head. She needed to make peace with God's will.

Ben had been there for her so many times when she'd been grieving for Lizzie. Maybe their friendship was all that they were supposed to have, maybe he just wanted someone safe—something safe. When he'd approached her at the sink in the kitchen, he'd sounded like he truly didn't know what he'd done wrong.

Maybe Ben was as lonely as she was sometimes. After all, it was written in the Scriptures that a man should not be alone. Perhaps he was simply trying to find someone to walk down life's path with. She had to find it in her heart to forgive him, to give up this hurt and anger she was feeling. Otherwise it was going to be too hard to bump into him at church services, at frolics, at so many events and in so many places in their community.

Even though she felt tears of hurt well up in her eyes again, she blinked them away. A verse from the Psalms came to her: *"Tears may endure for a night, but joy comes in the morning."* Tomorrow would be better.

◌∕◌

Even though it was cold in the barn, Ben was grateful that he was able to work here this morning instead of within the close confines of someone's kitchen. It felt good to be doing manual labor, pounding out his frustrations with his hammer.

Why had he thought that the only answer that he could get from Rebecca would be yes? Why had he been so assured that Rebecca was the one God planned for him that he hadn't considered that he would be going home with his heart discouraged and colder and lonelier than ever?

All these years he'd waited for her, and now he wondered if he'd wasted his time. Had he stubbornly been insisting on what God's will was for his life instead of listening for God to tell him?

He rubbed at his chest, feeling as if his heart hurt, physically hurt, this morning as the monotony of his work gave him the time to reflect.

How did he go within hours from being someone's friend and confidant to a person to be avoided, even treated with hurt and anger?

His eyes filmed, and his sight wavered. When he swung his hammer, he missed the nail and hit his thumb instead. With a cry of pain he jumped back, stuck his injured finger in his mouth, and sucked on it to relieve the pain.

"Ben? You okay? *Sohn?*"

He felt a hand on his shoulder and turned to stare into the face of Amos. Nodding, he pulled his hand from his mouth. "Just hit my thumb."

"Looks like you really hurt yourself there. Your eyes are watering something fierce." Amos pulled a bandanna out of his back pocket and handed it to Ben.

Ben nodded his thanks, too miserable to speak.

"Let's go inside, get some ice on this."

"No need. It'll be okay."

But Amos shepherded him inside the house and nudged him into a chair in the kitchen. Naomi was working there, preparing the noon meal. Two-year-old Ruth was coloring at the table.

"Naomi, we need some ice. Ben hit his thumb."

She rushed to get the ice. Ruth crowded closer to Ben and investigated his hand with wide eyes. "Ben got boo-boo?"

He laughed. "Yes."

"Kiss it make it better," she said, and she pressed her lips to his thumb.

Ben stroked her hair with his other hand. "Thank you, Ruth."

"Here, this should help," Naomi said as she handed him a kitchen towel filled with ice.

"Thanks." He watched her fill a plastic cup with juice and give it to Ruth. Although he knew she was in her late forties and the mother of eight *kinner*, Naomi didn't look much older than Rebecca. This was what Rebecca would look like when she was older: an attractive woman who was strong and capable, a woman who was the heart of her home.

He swallowed hard.

"Want some coffee?"

"I can get it; you're busy."

She pressed a hand to his shoulder. "It's no trouble. I'm going to get you some aspirin too. You're in pain."

His heart hurt more than his finger. Then he shook his head. He was being melodramatic. Two years ago, a childhood friend of his had asked a young woman if he could see her, and she'd turned him down. His friend had been disappointed and moped around for a few months, then met someone else, fallen in love, and married her. They'd just had their first child last month. Life had moved on.

Naomi went to get some supplies from the pantry, and Ben drank his coffee. When she returned, she placed a pan with two roasting chickens in the oven.

"Will you stay for supper?" she asked as she did every day.

"*Danki*, but not tonight. I'll be eating with my parents."

He glanced at the kitchen clock. It was nearly time to stop work for the day. He wanted to be gone by the time Rebecca came home.

Just then he heard the door open, then close, and she walked into the room.

"Rebecca! You're home already?" Naomi exclaimed.

"Anita decided to close a little early." Taking off her bonnet and coat, Rebecca hung them on pegs. "We're doing inventory later in the week. Hello, Ben." She walked over and looked down at his hand wrapped in the towel. "What happened?"

"Hit it with the hammer." Getting up, he dumped the melting ice from the dish towel into the sink. He folded the towel and left it on the counter.

"That's not like you."

Shrugging, Ben reached for his coat. "Wasn't paying attention, I guess. Thanks for the ice, Naomi. *Gut nacht*."

He found Amos in the barn and said good-bye, then hitched up his horse to his buggy. As he pulled out of the drive onto the road, something made him glance back. Rebecca stood at the window, watching him.

Turning back to face the road, Ben rode along, the clip-clop of his horse's hooves on the road a soothing cadence to his thoughts. He passed by the Bontrager property. The old house stood abandoned, paint peeling, windows broken. He'd thought about buying it and fixing it up. The house was in sad shape, but he knew its construction was solid. Windows could easily be replaced, the outside of the house scraped and repainted, the interior cleaned and fixed up. It wouldn't be hard. He was, after all, a carpenter, and many of his friends were tradesmen who could help him with the necessary repairs.

The Bontrager property was only a mile or so away from Rebecca's family home, and he'd thought she'd like that. It would make it handy for him to work with her father as well. He'd wanted to talk to Rebecca about it first, but a man couldn't talk about a future home until he was assured he was talking to his future wife. So he'd waited.

And now everything had changed.

Dragging his gaze away from the lost promise of the house, he stared straight ahead. That was how he'd gotten through the day— doing the first thing on his list, then the next, then the next, without thinking. The first time he'd lost his concentration, he'd hit his thumb. He wouldn't make that mistake again, and not just because his thumb was still throbbing. He was a practical man, and he had his work to keep him busy.

A few days from now, maybe a few weeks, maybe he'd do what some of his friends had urged him to do for some time now: he'd open his eyes and look around at other young women in the community.

❧

Inventory was a welcome distraction.

As much as Rebecca enjoyed helping customers and ringing up sales and answering the dozens of questions from tourists about her community, doing some mindless counting and tallying was just what she needed.

Ben had been avoiding her. He hadn't stayed for supper since Abram's birthday and was usually gone by the time she got home from work. Her parents eyed her curiously but kept their questions to themselves. Even Marian hadn't said anything, although Rebecca often caught her watching her. Occasionally, one of the *kinner* would ask if Ben was going to stay to eat with them, but the younger ones saw him at midday dinner or after school.

"Hungry?" Anita interrupted her thoughts.

"*Ya.*"

They went into the break room in the back of the store to eat sandwiches Anita had slipped out earlier to buy. As she peeled back the paper from the sandwich, Rebecca hesitated, remembering.

"Did I get the wrong kind?"

Rebecca shook her head. "No, it's fine, thanks. I was just thinking of the last time I went to this restaurant, that's all."

"The day that young man surprised you by coming to take you to lunch?"

Nodding, Rebecca took a bite of her sandwich. She didn't really feel like eating now that she'd remembered, but she didn't want to hurt Anita's feelings. "I remember how you said you have a romantic heart," she said. "Do you think all women have one?"

"I think many do. Most, maybe."

"Do you think any men are romantic?"

Anita smiled and wiped her lips with a paper napkin. She regarded Rebecca sympathetically. "Am I to assume by your question that the young man isn't romantic?"

"Not very." Rebecca drained the last of her lemonade and tossed the paper cup into the trash can. "I'm going to put the rest of this sandwich in the refrigerator for tomorrow's lunch."

"What about other young men in your community? Are they different from—I hate to keep saying 'that young man.' What's his name?"

"Ben. I don't know if he's different from the others. I mean, I think they're more practical than *Englisch* young men because so many of them work in trades or farm or whatever, but I still hear they can be romantic. I see my father being very sweet and romantic with my *mamm* sometimes."

"My Phil was that way. He brought home a dozen roses each week, and he left notes for me when he had to leave the house early and I wasn't up yet." She stood. "Ready to finish up?"

They worked on inventory some more, occasionally exchanging comments about what stock had been popular, what they should order more of, what should be eliminated.

"You've been such an asset," Anita told her as they finished up. "You're good with the customers, you sense what they want before they ask, and you're unflappable."

Rebecca laughed and shook her head. "I assure you, I'm flappable."

Anita handed Rebecca her coat and bonnet. "Your young man really hurt you, didn't he?"

"I don't think he meant to," Rebecca said slowly. "He's been a good friend, gotten me through some bad times since my sister died. But I want . . ."

"You want some romance. You want to believe you're loved."

"Yes," Rebecca said at last. "Yes."

They were silent on the way home and then, just before she

BARBARA CAMERON

pulled into the drive of Rebecca's house, Anita spoke. "You know, I believe that the right young man is out there for you. You're a sweet, religious young woman with a lot to offer. When it's time, God will send along the right man."

Surprised, Rebecca glanced over at Anita. Although the woman was very nice to her, they didn't often talk so personally. Rebecca was glad she'd offered to stay and help Anita with inventory.

"I hope you're right."

Anita smiled and took her hand from the steering wheel to pat Rebecca's. "I am."

The front door opened, and *Mamm* stepped outside and waved.

"Tell your mother I said hello."

"I will." Rebecca started to open the car door, then turned back. "Thank you, Anita."

"You know I'm always happy to give you a lift home."

Rebecca shook her head. "No, that's not what I meant. Thank you for caring."

Anita smiled. "You make it easy. See you in the morning."

Chapter Ten

BEN WAS CLIMBING INTO HIS BUGGY WHEN, OUT OF THE corner of his eye, he saw Rebecca. He heard her call his name.

"Ben!" She appeared at the driver's side of the buggy, sounding out of breath. "I was calling you!"

"Sorry. Did you need something?" He kept his tone brisk and impersonal.

"Yes, Ben." She tugged at his sleeve. "I need to talk to you."

"There's nothing to say." He picked up the reins, not caring if he was being rude.

To his utter surprise, Rebecca grasped the reins and made him look at her. "I'm sorry, Ben. I'm sorry if I hurt your feelings. But can't we still be friends?"

He stared at her hand over his for a long moment, then shook his head. "I don't think so, Rebecca. I'm sorry, but I have to go."

It felt like something was pressing against his chest; he had to get away.

There was that expression of hurt in her eyes again. But she'd rejected *him*. He steeled himself against it. "I have to go."

When she stepped back, he set the buggy in motion. This time, he didn't look back. He couldn't look back. She'd told him no, and so he had to move on.

He went to a singing the next night, and after he was there for only a few minutes, Mary Anne walked over.

"I don't see Rebecca."

Ben shrugged. "Maybe she'll come with someone else."

Mary Anne's eyebrows arched. "Oh, so that's the way it is."

When the singing began there wasn't another opportunity to talk. But Mary Anne looked over often and smiled at him, and when the food was served, she appeared at his elbow.

"I baked these cookies," she told him. "Try one."

He did and found it delicious. Mary Anne was something to look at, too, with her sparkling green eyes and saucy smile. She had this habit of leaning close to talk to him in a low, intimate tone. She was so diminutive and girlish, he felt tall and very male next to her. She was so different from Rebecca, who was nearly as tall as he was and so independent. Mary Anne made a man feel he needed to take care of her. Rebecca let him know that she could take care of herself.

Rebecca came in with Marian a little while later. Ben was aware that people near him were watching as he and Rebecca carefully ignored each other.

"What's going on?" his brother John came over to ask. "And don't tell me you don't know what I'm talking about."

"Keep your voice down."

"It doesn't matter," John said, but he lowered his voice. "If everyone else didn't know, they wouldn't be watching the two of you and trying to figure out what's going on."

"People need to mind their own business."

John just laughed and slapped his shoulder.

Ben had always considered himself to be an average-looking guy. But suddenly he was getting lots of attention, and not just from Mary Anne. He wondered if the other young women had ignored him because he was always with Rebecca.

So when Mary Anne asked him if he'd give her a ride home, he was happy to oblige. She held his arm to keep from sliding on the ice as they walked to his buggy and gave him an openly flirtatious smile as he helped her inside.

As the buggy rolled away from the singing, he told himself he was glad he'd taken some action and not sat around being miserable.

But remembering how he'd seen Rebecca talking with Jacob Stolzfus at the food table made him wonder if he was just kidding himself.

He wasn't a shallow man. Forgetting how Rebecca had been such a big part of his life wasn't going to happen quickly just because someone like Mary Anne—or a half dozen other young women—flirted with him.

⧼⧽

"Well, he certainly didn't let any grass grow beneath his feet," Rebecca muttered as she and Marian rode home later.

"Huh?"

Rebecca realized that she'd talked out loud. "Nothing."

"Who hasn't let any grass grow beneath his feet? Ben?"

Rebecca sighed. "Yes, Ben."

Marian just laughed. "Everyone was watching the two of you."

"Everyone was watching Mary Anne throw herself at him."

"That too," Marian said matter-of-factly. "What did you expect? How long did you think he'd hang around?"

Rebecca blinked. "He wasn't 'hanging around,'" she said, stung. "He was always at the house because he works with *Daed*."

"Right."

"I never said he wasn't a friend. That's hardly 'hanging around.'"

Marian shook her head. "Rebecca, if you want him, I'm sure all you have to do is let him know."

Rebecca laughed until tears ran down her cheeks.

"Whoa, Brownie, whoa," Marian told their horse, and she brought him to a stop. "Are you all right?"

Rebecca nodded, then she shook her head. "It's not true, what you said. I wish life was that simple. The fact is that he let me know he wants me. *Wanted* me," she corrected.

"Oh, how wonderful."

"*Wanted*, Marian." She told her sister what had happened and watched the joy fade from her face.

"I'm so sorry." Reaching over, Marian hugged Rebecca. "But if you're interested, maybe you can talk to him about it."

"He didn't say he loved me," Rebecca said flatly.

"No, he didn't," Marian said slowly. She called to the horse, and the buggy began rolling again.

"Listen, I haven't told *Mamm* and *Daed* about this," Rebecca said. "I don't want to talk against Ben. They think of him as a son. I wouldn't want anything to get in the way of his relationship with *Daed* about work, either. I'm trying to forgive Ben, and I hope he'll forgive me for not agreeing to what he wanted."

But when she remembered how he'd acted when she tried to apologize, she thought his forgiveness might be a long time coming.

"Sometimes life is a mystery, isn't it?" Marian mused. "We're taught that it's God's will that this or that happened, that God has plans for us. But I still don't understand why Lizzie had to die. And I don't understand why someone like Ben isn't the man God prepared for you."

Rebecca sighed. "Remember Hebrews 11? 'Now faith is the substance of things hoped for . . .'"

"'The evidence of things not seen,'" Marian finished. "I just wish you didn't have to see Mary Anne flirting with Ben. It can't feel very good."

Rebecca bit her lip. "It doesn't. I'm still ashamed of how jealous I was when *you* flirted with Ben."

Marian laughed. "Like I told you before, I was just practicing!"

∾∶

Her chatter was driving him nuts.

Comparisons weren't fair, but Ben couldn't help thinking how much he preferred being with Rebecca instead of Mary Anne.

Rebecca didn't have to be talking every minute. Sometimes he felt like he couldn't think, his brain was so filled with the sound of Mary Anne's voice.

And what she talked about—well, it was all about Mary Anne. She chattered about every little aspect of her day, and oh, how she loved gossip. She never wanted to talk about something deeper, like faith, the way Rebecca did. He wondered if it was because she hadn't had to deal with something big, something beyond what she'd expected life to deal her, as Rebecca had when Lizzie died. But he was beginning to suspect that Mary Anne didn't ever think about things beyond surface, everyday happenings.

Mary Anne wound down as the buggy turned into the drive to her house. "Thank you so much for giving me a ride home from services," she said, turning to him and smiling flirtatiously.

"You're welcome," he said politely, waiting for her to climb out.

She started to open her mouth to say something else. Clearly, she wasn't ready to leave him yet.

"Let me help you."

"You're such a gentleman," she told him.

Was she batting her eyelashes at him? Yes, she was batting her eyelashes at him. He didn't think a girl had ever done that to him. He didn't think he liked it.

As he rounded the buggy, he saw her bend down to pick up something from the floorboard. She was holding it in her hand when he stepped to her side.

"What is it?" he asked as she studied whatever it was in her left palm.

"Nothing, just a hairpin I dropped." Her fingers curled around it. She gave him her right hand and he helped her step down from the buggy.

But even after there was no need, she continued to hold his hand as they stood there beside the buggy.

Of course, it was at that exact moment that Rebecca had to drive by with Marian.

"*Wie geht!*" Marian called.

Rebecca's eyes met Ben's, then she looked at him holding hands with Mary Anne.

Great, Ben thought. *Just great.* He tried to pull his hand back and was surprised to feel it held tightly by Mary Anne. Dragging his gaze away from Rebecca, he was startled to see Mary Anne's smile as she looked at Rebecca.

Using more force, he retrieved his hand and backed away. But the damage was done. Rebecca was looking straight ahead as the buggy moved on.

"Well, you'd better get inside. It's cold out here."

"See you later!" she called loudly, as if she wanted the occupants of the other buggy to hear.

Ben climbed into his buggy and continued on home. *What a mess,* he told himself. How he wished he could go back and undo what he'd said that day in town. Then he sighed. No, he'd felt it was time to speak to Rebecca as he had, and now at least he knew he needed to move on.

But he didn't think Mary Anne was the one he wanted to move on with.

⁓✧⁓

Ben's mother was cooking supper when he walked into the kitchen after work the next day.

"You're home early. Again."

He stopped and stared at her. "*Ya.* Is that a problem?"

She laughed and shook her head. "Of course not. Sit down, I'll get you a cup of coffee."

He sat and watched her reach for two mugs and pour the coffee.

She moved a little stiffly—her arthritis acted up sometimes in the winter—but she never complained. Her hair was salt and pepper but her face was smooth, the only lines were those around her eyes when she smiled. *Mamm* was in her sixties. From what she'd told him, he was a surprise gift from God long after she thought she'd borne her last child.

She served him his coffee and surprised him by kissing the top of his head before she joined him at the table with her own cup. "This is the only way I can be on the same level with you, since you've grown so tall."

He smiled at her, then his smile faded as he stared into his cup of coffee. "Guess you never thought you'd have me hanging around the house so long, did you?"

"Now you're being a *bensel*!" she said fondly.

"I'm hardly a silly child," he told her. "I'm twenty-two. Most of my friends have married. Some of them even have *kinner*."

"You're hardly an old man. It just hasn't been your time yet."

He traced the grain of wood on the table with his forefinger and avoided looking at her.

"*Sohn*, do you want to tell me what's troubling you? I think it must have something to do with Rebecca."

His head shot up. "Why do you say that?"

She smiled gently. "You've been home for dinner every night lately."

"Maybe I missed your cooking."

Laughing, Emma shook her head. "I don't think so. But I think you're missing Rebecca."

"I'm seeing someone else. Mary Anne. You know her."

"You're missing Rebecca," she repeated. "Otherwise you would not look so miserable, *mei sohn*."

She put her hand over his. "I do not wish to pry if you've decided to see Mary Anne instead." She paused. "But I think something has happened, something that hurts you so much you would stay away from a young woman you've cared about for years. She was your friend, if she was nothing more."

"She turned me down." Ben looked up. "I asked if she would marry me, and she turned me down."

His *mamm* stared at him, clearly shocked. "Did she say why?"

"She said if I didn't know why, she wasn't going to tell me."

"*Ach!* She didn't!"

"She did."

Leaning back in her chair, she studied Ben. "Tell me what you said to her."

He shrugged. "I just—you know—asked her if she would marry me."

"Exact words, please."

He relayed the conversation as precisely as he could remember. His mother listened without expression or comment until he was finished, but he thought he saw her wince once. Maybe it was his imagination.

His father came in then, stamping his boots on the mat by the door.

"Why, look who's home." Samuel took off his coat and hat and joined them in the kitchen.

"I found out why," Emma said, getting up to pull a meat loaf from the oven and set it on top of the stove to rest.

Samuel took the mug of coffee she poured him and joined Ben at the table. "Figured you would." He turned to Ben. "Good day at work?"

"*Ya*," Ben said, relieved at the change in subject.

"Aren't you going to ask me why?" Emma asked, putting her hands on her hips.

"Emma, you know it's not our way to pry into how our young people court."

Ben's head snapped up. "Court?"

"I didn't tell him," his mother assured him. "How could I? You and I were just talking now."

"I've got eyes. And ears," his father said. "I see things. Hear things. If Ben wants to tell me, he will." He glanced pointedly at the meat loaf.

His mother let out a gusty sigh. Going to the stove, she transferred the meat loaf to a platter and set it on the table. "Well, I don't want to get in between a man and his stomach."

"*Gut*," Samuel said with a grin. "That's why we've been happily married for so many years, *mei fraa*."

If Ben hadn't been watching his mother, he might not have seen the gleam come into her eyes. She finished putting the food on the table, bringing a plate of sliced bread and a crock of *budder*. They bent their heads for the blessing, then it was silent at the table for a few minutes while they filled their plates and ate the savory meat, carrots, potatoes, celery, and parsnips.

Emma cleared the empty plates, brought a *snitz* pie to the table, cut two large slices, and served them to her men. She picked up her mug of coffee. "I think I'll let you two men talk over dessert," she announced.

"You're not feeling well?" Ben asked her.

She shook her head and stroked his hair the way she'd done when he was a boy. "I'll have some later. I think I'll go put my feet up for a few minutes. I was on them quite a bit this afternoon helping a friend with some cleaning."

"You're sure you're feeling okay?" his *daed* asked.

Emma smiled at her husband. "I'm fine." She kissed his cheek. "Maybe you can tell Ben how you asked me to marry you."

Daed tilted his head and studied her. "I could do that, if he wanted to know."

Ben watched his father's eyes follow his *fraa* as she left the kitchen. Then he began eating the pie.

It was quiet in the room, with just the scrape of fork on plate and an occasional slurping of coffee by his father. Ben could hear the ticking of the kitchen clock.

BARBARA CAMERON

Ben was used to his father's stoic ways, but finally he could stand it no longer. "Well, are you going to tell me?"

Samuel looked at him. "*Ya*, sure, if you want to know."

More silence filled the room, as Samuel cut another piece of pie and poured himself more coffee.

Ben rolled his eyes. "*Ya*, I want to know."

❧

He was ready for winter to be over. As he hunched inside his coat, riding to Rebecca's house, he looked for signs of spring.

Each year, when winter came, Ben saw a sadness come over Rebecca. Then, this year, he'd seen a change in her, a moving past the tragedy of Lizzie's death. She was growing, changing, even laughing. Oh, how he loved her laugh!

Perhaps he hadn't waited long enough for her to really look out at the world around her—and at the man looking at her. He'd thought only of his own wants and needs. He'd convinced himself that it was God's will that they should be together. Now.

She'd tried to apologize to him for saying she didn't want to be courted, and he'd been angry and turned her away.

It wasn't one of his shining moments.

He needed to tell her he wasn't angry with her. She had a right to say no. Maybe she'd grown so used to seeing him in her home that she'd begun to think of him as a brother. He shuddered at the thought. He certainly didn't think of her as a sister.

But just because she wasn't interested in him as a future husband, was he really willing to throw away the years of friendship with her, the memories? The answer was no.

But he didn't know what to do with the love he felt for her.

Ben jerked on the reins, and Ike stopped abruptly, then turned to look at him as if to say, "What?"

Glancing around, Ben was grateful there were no cars behind

him. He could have caused an accident. Pulling over to the side of the road, he stared at the frozen pond in the distance. What he'd said that day in town came rushing back.

He hadn't said anything about love.

No, he'd been so nervous, rushed at things as if it were a job to be completed quickly instead of a foundation to build a future on. He had talked about how they "suited" each other.

As if they were socks and boots pairing up to stay warm for the winter, he thought, instead of two souls who loved each other and would merge in God's presence to form a loving union.

What a fool he'd been!

Even his father, whom he didn't think of as an articulate or romantic man, had done better than him. The comparison had made him wince.

He needed to talk to her and make things right between them. Even if he wasn't as gifted with words as other young men, surely he could find a way to tell her that he was sorry for his anger, sorry for the way he'd asked to court her.

It was one of her workdays at the shop. Ben decided to drive to her house and meet her there when she arrived, ask to speak to her. Surely she wouldn't refuse him that.

❧

Rebecca's day had been stressful. Customers had been standing at the door when she arrived. A tourist had pointedly remarked that she was five minutes late opening.

Since one of the reasons people came here to visit was because they wanted to experience a slower, more peaceful way of life, Rebecca had been surprised at the comment. She was going to tell the tourist that Brownie had not been feeling well that morning and she'd had to arrange for a ride to work, but changed her mind when the woman quickly pounced on their most expensive quilt and proclaimed she had to have it.

Anita called in to say she had a plumbing emergency at her condo and would get in as quickly as she could. The whole day was hectic, and Anita finally arrived the last half hour the shop was open, apologizing profusely.

But that wasn't the end of their bad day.

On the way home, they had a flat tire. Grumbling, Anita pulled onto the side of the road. Anita rooted around in the trunk and brought out a spare tire and a jack.

She looked at Rebecca. "I've never changed a tire. You?" Then, realizing what she'd asked, she started laughing.

Rebecca laughed too. What else could they do?

"Wait a minute, what am I thinking?" Anita said suddenly. She pulled out her cell phone. "I have roadside service."

But before she could dial, a buggy stopped beside them. "Rebecca! Do you need help?" a man called.

"Jacob! *Ya*, we have a flat tire. Do you know how to change it?"

"Of course." He pulled his buggy over and joined them beside the car. After touching the brim of his hat and introducing himself to Anita, he set to work. In no time, the tire was changed, and the flat one and the jack were in the trunk.

"Well, I hope your mother isn't worried that you're late getting home," Anita said.

"I just went by there, looking for you," Jacob told Rebecca. "She said she expected you soon."

"Jacob, would you mind taking Rebecca home? I'd like to take this tire by my garage before they close."

"Of course."

"Thanks for everything. See you, Rebecca." Anita winked at her when Jacob started toward his buggy.

Rebecca didn't feel at her best after the long day at work, but she was grateful for the ride home. Her back and feet were aching, and she was afraid her stomach was going to growl at any moment. She'd been too rushed to stop for lunch.

All she wanted to do was eat her supper and put her feet up and relax. But Jacob was being charming and acted so interested in talking to her.

Obviously, Ben had decided to do what she'd heard the *Englisch* call "moving on"; maybe it was time for her to start looking at someone new too. She'd gone to school with Jacob, and he'd always been nice to her.

When they pulled into the drive, Rebecca saw Ben sitting there in his buggy.

Jacob glanced at Rebecca and raised his eyebrows.

"He's probably here to see my father," Rebecca said. Why else would Ben visit? "They work together."

"*Ya*, I know."

"Thank you for the ride and for changing Anita's tire."

"I was happy to help. Rebecca, I came by because I thought I'd see if you'd like to go for a drive sometime?"

"I'd like that."

They set a day and time. She climbed out of the buggy and waved as he drove off. Then she turned and found Ben alighting from his buggy.

"What was he doing giving you a ride?"

When she stared coolly at him, he shook his head.

"I'm sorry, that was none of my business," he said.

"Did you come to see *Daed*? You could have gone inside. It's cold out here."

"I came to see you. Can we take a drive and talk?"

Rebecca rubbed at her aching forehead. "The other day you didn't want to talk. Now you do?"

"I was wrong," he said simply. "I came to apologize."

The memory of how he'd hurt her was as sharp as the cold winter wind. "Apology accepted." But her lips were stiff as she spoke the words. "I—Thank you for coming by." And she rushed inside.

Chapter Eleven

SUNDAY WAS HER FAVORITE DAY OF THE WEEK.

Rebecca loved gathering with friends and family to attend services and sing God's praises. And every other week, when there were no services in a member's home, she loved gathering with friends and family just to enjoy the day.

Today, services had been in the home of Ben's parents. She had to admit that she was a little apprehensive about seeing them for the first time since she'd turned Ben down. She didn't think Ben's mother would be rude to her—that wasn't her way. But she'd been nervous about how much he might have said to her about what had happened between them two weeks ago.

She told herself that chances were good that he hadn't even told them.

"So good to see you again, Rebecca." Emma's hug was warm and welcoming.

If Emma knew anything, she wasn't going to let it affect how she treated Rebecca. Rebecca felt herself relax.

Other women bustled about them in the kitchen after services, chattering as they prepared the light meal that would be served before everyone departed.

Mary Anne sidled over, holding out a plate of butterscotch cookies. "Emma, I made Ben's favorite cookies." She gave Rebecca a superior look.

"Very nice. Why don't you put them over there on the counter?" Emma said.

Was it Rebecca's imagination that Emma wasn't as welcoming to

Mary Anne as she'd been to her? Then she heard Emma sigh as she watched Mary Anne smile smugly as she showed off the cookies to a friend standing on the other side of the kitchen.

The older woman turned to look at Rebecca. "I haven't seen you for a long time. How is the family? Work?"

"The family's fine. Work is busy like always." Rebecca glanced around. She had arrived right on time and had missed seeing Ben.

"He's out in the barn."

"Who?"

There was a distinct gleam of mischief in Emma's faded blue eyes. "You know who. My youngest son."

"I—wasn't looking for him."

The gleam of mischief faded, and Emma took Rebecca's hand and drew her into the hallway for what privacy they could manage.

"You've known my son for a long time. You know words don't always come easy to him. He's like his father in that respect—he's a good man, but a quiet one. Some women might not recognize that."

Rebecca glanced down at the work-worn hand that held hers, then looked up at the older woman. "I do. But . . ." She struggled for words. "Emma, Ben doesn't feel about me the way you think he does."

"Really?" Emma looked disbelieving.

Mary Anne took that moment to walk slowly past them. Rebecca noticed that she took her time and swept the two of them with an assessing look.

"Ben is . . . looking in another direction." Her gaze followed Mary Anne as she found Ben and stopped him to talk.

"Promise me you won't do anything quickly," Emma said.

Puzzled, Rebecca stared at her. "Like what?"

"Like look elsewhere yourself."

She thought about Jacob. But one drive to have lunch was hardly looking. *Jacob is nice, but he's not . . . Ben.* "I'm not, Emma. I'm busy with my job and helping out at home. And it's not like there are a herd of suitors chasing after me," she admitted ruefully.

To her surprise, Emma touched her chin with her hand, and Rebecca was forced to look up at her. "I know you must have felt you lived in Lizzie's shadow," she told her quietly. "She was so exuberant people couldn't help noticing her. But there's an expression I always thought fit you: 'still waters run deep.' You have a sweet, thoughtful nature, and you look out for others before yourself." She smiled. "Now, I probably shouldn't have spoken at all, but my heart prompted me to. Give it some time, *liebschen*." She walked slowly back into the kitchen.

Rebecca was relieved to watch her sink into a chair. It was obvious that her arthritis, which was worse in winter, was making movement difficult for her today. Yet Emma hadn't been willing to cancel services or stay in bed while others were guests in her home.

Time. How could time resolve the differences between herself and Ben?

"Why are you frowning?" Sarah Fisher stopped to ask. The rosy-cheeked toddler she balanced on one hip held out her chubby hands.

Rebecca smiled and took Katie Ann and held her high. "I can't have been frowning, not when this sweet *kind* is anywhere near." She held her close and inhaled the special clean baby scent. "Oh, whenever I see this one, I am so very happy for you and David."

Sarah nodded. "I prayed for a long time for God to send me David. And to send me a *boppli*."

"David?" Rebecca stared at Sarah. "He was always yours, from the day he saved you from that stray dog that was chasing you. What were you, twelve?"

Laughing, Sarah grasped Katie Ann's hand as she tried to pull one of the strings on Rebecca's *kapp*.

"Sometimes other people see what we cannot," Sarah murmured obliquely. "He never lacked for the attention of the other girls at singings and such." She stroked her child's cheek. "But he was so worth waiting for. He got me through the pain of my miscarriage and the waiting for Katie Ann here. It was God's will if we had children, if we received this precious gift, he kept telling me, and if we didn't, we would be a family, the two of us."

Rebecca bounced Katie Ann, and she gurgled.

"Could you watch her for a moment for me?" Sarah asked. "I need to use the bathroom. I've had to run to it three times already this morning." She laughed when Rebecca's eyes widened. Glancing around, she leaned in and with her eyes sparkling admitted, "Yes, I'm wondering if I'm pregnant again."

Swaying and bouncing Katie Ann, loving the way the toddler giggled and giggled, Rebecca walked around the room.

When Katie Ann squealed with delight, Rebecca turned to see David approaching and handed her over.

After greeting Rebecca, he looked at his daughter. "So what did you think of the services today, Katie Ann?" He listened with a thoughtful expression as she babbled baby talk. "*Ya*, the singing was my favorite part too."

"She's quite a talker."

David nodded. "Takes after her *mamm*." When Rebecca looked over his shoulder and smiled, he rolled his eyes. "She's standing behind me, isn't she?"

"*Ya*," Rebecca said, and she laughed.

David turned, and his grin faded. "Sarah, are you all right? You look a little pale."

"I'm fine, but do you think we could leave now and eat at home?"

"*Ya*, sure. I'll go get the buggy and meet you out front. Be sure to bundle up."

He put Katie Ann in her arms, then turned to Rebecca. "Sarah and I are feeling a little tired. Katie Ann had a tooth coming in this week and kept us up."

Sarah and Rebecca exchanged glances.

"What?" David looked from one to the other.

"I'll tell you later," Sarah said.

Rebecca helped Sarah put Katie Ann's coat on. It took two of them because Katie Ann was laughing and pinwheeling her arms. Sarah got her own coat on, and then Rebecca hugged her. "I'll be praying for you," she whispered to Sarah.

"I said I'd be happy if God sent me one child," Sarah whispered back. "But now, if He sent another . . ." She stopped, as if she couldn't even envision such happiness.

Rebecca nodded. "I know."

She was standing at the kitchen window, watching the buggy leave, when Amanda joined her.

"Are you coming to the singing tonight?"

"I'm not sure." As if drawn by magnets, her gaze locked with Ben's on the other side of the room.

Amanda's gaze followed hers. "You care for him, don't you?"

"Shh!" Rebecca glanced around to see if anyone had heard.

Ben was opening the oven door for his mother, but she was talking to him, and there was so much chatter and noise with others moving about in the room, she realized no one could have heard.

"Besides, it doesn't matter."

"It *does* matter!" Amanda insisted in a lowered voice. "Go after him if you want him." She gave Rebecca a not-so-gentle push.

"Not now," she told Amanda.

"Then when?" Amanda demanded. "When?"

Don't be afraid!

"What is it?"

Rebecca blinked. "What is what?"

"You just looked funny—kind of startled. What is it?"

Don't be afraid!

Although she realized that Amanda was staring at her, waiting for an answer, Rebecca wasn't about to explain.

Ben used potholders to pull a heavy casserole from the oven and set it on top of the stove. He closed the oven door and turned to her. "Anything else you need?"

"No, thank you, *Sohn*."

He saw Rebecca standing, looking out the window near the front door with Amanda and wondered what they were talking about. When Rebecca looked over and saw him, then glanced away quickly as Amanda did the same, he suspected they were talking about him.

He wondered if that was a *gut* thing or bad.

Then something Amanda said to Rebecca upset her. Amanda walked away and Rebecca stood staring after her, her forehead creased in thought. Ben started to walk over to her but found his way blocked by women hurrying around in the kitchen. By the time he could move forward, Jacob was standing there talking to Rebecca, and he lost his chance.

Ben knew that women found Jacob attractive. He was fair-haired, with blue eyes and dimples. He was several years older, and his farm was one of the most prosperous in the county.

An unaccustomed jealousy flared up in Ben as he watched the two talking. It was so immediate, so strong, that he felt his steps propelling him toward the door and outside into the chilly day.

It took several minutes for him to become aware that he'd left his jacket and hat inside. Feeling a little foolish, he debated going back inside for them. He heard the door behind him open, then shut.

"Forget something?"

His *daed* held his coat and hat in his hands.

Looking sheepish, Ben took the coat and pulled it on, then accepted the hat, settling it on his head. "*Danki*."

They stood staring at the fields surrounding the house. "I saw you come out here after Jacob began talking to Rebecca."

Ben gave him a sideways glance but said nothing.

"You know, I'd always been taught to turn to God, to pray to Him as my Father," Samuel said after long moments had passed. "After I had children, I started thinking about what it must be like to be God watching over His children. You know, He sees them happy, and He sees them sad or hurting."

He paused and glanced over at Ben. "The happy part would be easy. But I wondered how He felt watching them when they're having difficult times. It's hard for a father not to jump in and try to fix things, like you fix an engine that's not working or repair a broken fence. I asked myself if our heavenly Father had trouble not jumping in to fix things for His children."

He turned as a couple emerged from the house and said good-bye to them. After they were out of earshot, he turned back to Ben and laid a hand on his shoulder. "It's been a long winter."

Ben nodded. "For years it's been a sad time for Rebecca. But she's finally more at peace about Lizzie and looking happier."

"And maybe becoming interested in someone?" his father asked quietly.

"Yes, it seems so," he said finally.

"Just like you and Mary Anne."

Ben's head shot up. "Not because I wanted to."

"Don't see any harness on you," Samuel said, and with that, he ambled back inside.

Laughing ruefully, Ben stared after him. No, Mary Anne had no harness on him.

But there was sure something tying him to Rebecca. Always had been.

Amanda came out of the house. She stopped and looked at Ben. "Are you going to stand out here forever?"

"Just getting some air."

"Awfully cold air."

Turning, he looked at her. "Is there something you want to say, Amanda?"

Her hazel eyes sparkled with mischief. "I think you should come to the singing."

"Because?"

"*Ya*, because." With that she fairly danced down the steps.

Ben wondered what was going on. He'd known Amanda all his life. While she was sweet, she was always nosing about in someone's business—not for bad reasons, but because she cared.

He guessed he'd be going to the singing tonight. Then he stopped and laughed at himself. He'd been so upset, he'd forgotten—his family was hosting it because they'd had services here earlier and the benches and hymnals were already present. It was obvious God's hand was at work.

❧

Rebecca knew the minute Ben walked into the singing.

If she hadn't, Amanda's sharp elbow in her ribs apprised her of the fact. "Go over there and talk to him," Amanda hissed in her ear.

"He just came in."

"Are you going to let Mary Ann fawn all over him? Or are you going to do something before she gets her claws into him?"

The image made her laugh. She saw Ben's head come up, and he stared at her from across the room. And then Mary Ann walked up and put her hand on his arm.

Rebecca took a deep breath and let it out. After the services, she'd returned to her house and gone to her room to read for a while. Instead, she'd lain there and found herself thinking about what had happened earlier, when she'd been talking with Amanda and heard that inner voice urging her not to be afraid.

It was time to be brave, to approach Ben and tell him she was sorry about what had happened between them. Maybe she couldn't get their relationship back to what it had been, but she didn't want this rift, this distance between them.

As much as she fought it, Ben mattered to her. Each day that passed made her miss him more. She missed talking with him, missed him listening to her with that quiet, intense way of his. Missed doing things with him and being with him and seeing the way he showed what a big, generous heart he had every time he was around her family or his.

She hadn't appreciated what she had when she had it, she thought. It was as simple as that.

"You're looking *lieblich* tonight," Jacob said, his voice low and intimate in her ear. "That color is very pretty on you. Brings out the green in your eyes."

Rebecca stared down at her dark green *frack*, then up into his eyes. There was frank interest in them. But while it was flattering to have him tell her she looked lovely, she noticed that he was looking around the room, assessing not just her but other females there as if he were in a candy store.

"Why don't I get us something to drink?"

When she nodded agreement, he sauntered off.

Ben wanted to marry her. She knew what kind of husband he'd be, since they'd spent so much time together. And she knew he had the qualities to make someone a good *mann*. Other young women might not mind that he didn't have the right words, and maybe she wouldn't have minded either. She'd just needed more than to be told they'd "suit."

It wasn't often that Rebecca acted on the spur of the moment, but the last time she had, when she'd asked Ben to a picnic, well, that had turned out well, hadn't it?

She found her steps carrying her across the room to Ben. As if he were attuned to her thoughts, Ben looked up and saw her. He started walking toward her.

"Rebecca? Rebecca?"

Blinking, she stopped. Jacob stood before her, holding out her soft drink.

"Where were you going?" he asked.

And then he saw Ben.

"She's with me," Jacob said bluntly, even a little belligerently.

"Rebecca says who she's with," Ben told him in his quiet voice. "No one owns her."

"*Ya*, you had your chance." Jacob moved possessively, positioning himself to block off Ben.

Rebecca held up her hand. "Jacob, I just need to talk to Ben for a moment."

Jacob glowered at Ben for a long moment, then he nodded and walked off.

The moment he was gone, Rebecca and Ben turned to each other.

"I—"

"I—"

They stopped and laughed.

"Ladies first," said Ben.

"I'm sorry for what happened between us," she began.

"Me too," he said, moving closer. "I've been wanting to talk to you about it. Could we maybe go for a ride?"

Rebecca glanced around. "I should tell Jacob—" She broke off.

Mary Ann was standing with a group of her friends, showing them what looked to Rebecca like a small card in her hand.

"What is it?" Ben asked her.

There was a buzz of conversation, and several people looked over at Rebecca. Mary Ann was walking toward her, a gleam in her eyes.

"Is this why he hangs around with you?" she asked Rebecca, holding out the card. "Does he feel sorry for you because you've got . . . emotional problems?"

Rebecca stared at it blankly for a moment. It was one of Dr. Prato's business cards. "What's this about?" she asked, lifting her eyes. "Where did you get this?"

"Why don't you ask Ben? I found it in his buggy." With that, Mary Ann strolled back to her friends.

Feeling as if someone had pulled the rug out from under her feet, Rebecca looked at Ben. "I don't understand. Ben? What was this doing in your buggy?"

"I can explain."

She looked around and saw that Mary Ann and her friends were staring at them. "Did you go talk to Dr. Prato about me?"

"I talked to her, but she didn't tell me anything confidential."

Rebecca shook her head. This was like a nightmare. "And you shared it with Mary Anne?"

"No. You heard her. She found the card in my buggy. I guess I dropped it. She must have figured one of us went to visit the doctor and decided it was you."

"Lucky guess." Rebecca crossed her arms over her chest. "And now she's really enjoying herself, isn't she?" she said as she watched the other woman talking with her friends.

"I'll go talk to her."

"No." She put a hand on his arm to stop him. "I will."

She marched over to Mary Ann, and all talk stopped.

"I'm not ashamed of going to see Dr. Prato. I don't have 'emotional problems.' But even if I did, I'd be proud of myself for going to someone to help myself. I hope that you never go through what I went through," she said in a steady voice. "I didn't want to live after Lizzie died. Dr. Prato helped me through my grief."

"You should have gone to God about it," Mary Ann told her in a superior tone.

"'Judge not, that ye not be judged,'" Rebecca replied. With that, she turned and walked away.

"Rebecca!" Marian caught up with her. "What's going on?"

"Mary Anne's just trying to cause trouble."

"How? Why?"

People were still staring.

"I don't want to talk about it now."

"Do you want to go home? We can go home."

Rebecca shook her head. "I don't want to spoil your time."

"I can take you home," Ben said quietly from behind her. "Please let me."

"No. I don't want to talk to you now," Rebecca told him without looking at him.

"Fine. Then I'm coming over tomorrow, after I finish work."

Rebecca turned to tell him not to, but he was already striding away.

Chapter Twelve

Rebecca laced up her ice skates and stood.

There was no voice this time urging her not to be afraid. Maybe that was because she was facing her fears. At least, facing one of them.

It had taken her five years.

She wobbled, and her arms shot out and flapped as she fought for balance. Finally, relieved that she wasn't going to fall on her bottom, she cautiously pushed out onto the ice. She wobbled again for a moment and then, to her utter amazement, it came back to her—the balance, then the miracle of skimming along on the ice, free as a bird.

It was so quiet here, just the scrape of ice beneath her feet, the cold wind against her cheeks. Freedom, such freedom. A sense of being outside herself, of doing what she couldn't do when she was walking on the ground.

She stayed in the area where everyone skated, mindful of the fact that it was late in the season. There was no way she would risk what had happened to Lizzie.

She'd gotten home early that afternoon and felt restless. She knew Ben was coming and they'd have to talk. But she couldn't sit still.

So she'd started out for a walk and then turned back, impulsively running upstairs to get her skates.

Around and around the pond she skated; then, after a time, she experimented with a small twirl, a jump, a backward circle. Oh, it was nothing compared to the way she had skated before, but the joy was there. The joy was there.

She'd seen an ice skating movie once, during her *rumschpringe*, with Lizzie and other girls at a nearby theater. Of course, Rebecca was the first to admit that she was in no way as good as the skaters in the movie, not back then and certainly not now since she was out of practice. But she'd always enjoyed it and spent every free moment on the ice on the pond in the winter, so she became more skilled than the others.

Not that she drew any pride from it. *Hochmut* was sinful. She simply skated because of how calm, how free it made her feel. All else faded away.

A little out of breath, she skated over to the edge of the pond and sat down on a log someone had put there. Maybe she'd take a rest and then skate just a little more before heading home. She'd promised Ben she'd talk to him after work. No doubt he'd come find her if she wasn't there.

"Rebecca!"

Looking up from lacing her skates, she saw that Lizzie was already streaking across the ice. It was just Lizzie's way—it wasn't that there was a competition and she wanted to be first. She simply couldn't wait for anyone else when she was ready to dive into her next adventure.

Lizzie wasn't as good a skater as Rebecca. She was enthusiastic, but she wasn't willing to practice. If it didn't come easily and wasn't enough fun, Lizzie moved on to something else.

As Rebecca stepped onto the ice, she watched her sister zoom by.

"About time, slowpoke!" Lizzie called, laughing as she executed a sloppy twirl.

There were two other skaters on the pond, boys she and Lizzie had gone to school with. While Rebecca skated by herself, Lizzie and the others played tag and generally whooped it up.

Rebecca felt her skate boot wobble and skated over to the log to retie her laces.

"Hi."

Looking up, Rebecca saw Ben. "Hi. What are you doing here? You don't have any skates."

He shrugged. "I was on my way home. Thought I'd stop and watch for a few minutes." He gazed out at the ice. "Lizzie's sure having fun."

Rebecca felt herself withdraw. Yes, people usually noticed Lizzie with her vibrant personality. Bending, she retied her skate.

"You looked like you were enjoying yourself out there," he said. "I don't think I've ever seen anyone skate as well as you."

"You should have seen the movie Lizzie and I saw. The skaters were amazing." She remembered the costumes the skaters had worn. They were short and colorful and so formfitting, like nothing she'd ever imagined. Looking down at her own long dress, she wondered how it would feel to move without the restriction of a long skirt.

There was loud laughter out on the ice. Rebecca looked up to see that the two boys and Lizzie had joined hands and were doing the whip, with Lizzie at the end. Faster and faster they skated, and Lizzie was laughing, her skirts flowing out behind her.

"Faster!" she shrieked. "Faster, faster!"

Then she lost her grip, and she was hurtling toward the farthest edge of the pond. Her shriek was cut off as her foot must have hit a rough patch and she went sprawling.

And then they heard it—an awful crack! and the splash of water as Lizzie vanished from sight.

Ben was the first to move, running and slipping toward the hole in the ice. Rebecca jumped to her feet and raced over on her skates.

"Get back!" Ben cried as he stopped near the edge of the hole. "It's not safe!"

"Lizzie!" Rebecca screamed. "Lizzie!"

Ben lay down on his stomach and edged toward the hole. Turning his head, he called to the boys to hold his legs as he inched forward, calling Lizzie's name.

Lizzie popped to the surface, gasping, and Ben grasped one arm, then *the other, and dragged her toward him. But she slipped from his grasp once, twice, before he was able to grab the neck of her dress and pull her toward him.*

Rebecca and the boys inched back and back until Lizzie had been pulled from the water and they were all safely away from the edge of the hole. Then one of the boys ran for help.

Her face was so white, her body so still. Rebecca felt for a pulse. "She's not breathing!"

Ben pushed Rebecca aside and turned Lizzie to her side, pressing on her back. Water flowed from Lizzie's mouth, but her chest didn't move. He began pushing on her chest and then breathing into her mouth. Rebecca had never seen anyone do such.

"Breathe, Lizzie!" she cried hoarsely. "Please, God, make her breathe!"

A siren blared down the road, getting louder and louder as it approached. An ambulance screeched to a halt, and men came running.

Tears ran down Rebecca's cheeks as she remembered that day.

"Oh, Lizzie, I miss you so much."

She wiped her tears away from her cheeks with her hands. Looking upward, she shook her head. "*Mamm* always said you'd get to heaven first if you weren't more careful."

There was a splash of color on the bank of the pond near her, a purple crocus struggling up through the snow. It was a tiny reminder that spring was coming. Reaching over, she plucked it up.

Rising, she skated over to the center of the pond. "'To every thing there is a season, and a time to every purpose under the heaven,'" she recited. "'A time to be born, and a time to die; a time to plant, and a time to pluck up that which is planted' . . . and a time to heal. Goodbye, Lizzie," she whispered, and she threw the flower over to the place where Lizzie had fallen through the ice.

She heard something behind her. Turning, she saw a buggy pull to the side of the road and a man get out, waving his arms frantically. Frowning, she squinted to see better.

It was Ben.

What was she doing?

Ben couldn't believe his eyes as he drove his buggy down the road to the Millers' house. That was Rebecca, skating out in the middle of the pond.

Didn't she know that no one had skated there since last week, that the pond was showing signs of an early thaw? A sign had been posted, but he didn't see it now.

As soon as he could get his horse to stop, he jumped from the buggy and began yelling and waving his arms. She must have heard him because she turned.

He didn't hear the car coming until he heard the screech of brakes. Turning, he saw the driver fighting for control as the car slid on the thin ice covering the road. Ben threw himself toward the side of the road, but he felt the bumper hit his hip and toss him high in the air. His breath rushed out as he slammed down in the snow and his head hit something hard.

He woke. His head hurt, and someone was screaming his name.

Rebecca came into view and knelt by his side. She was praying as she put her hands on his face.

He reached up his hand and touched her cheek. "I'm okay." To prove it, he tried to sit up, but he fell back and passed out.

❧

The driver of the car, a middle-aged woman, came running over with a blanket to cover Ben.

"I called 911 on my cell phone. They'll be here any minute." She wrung her hands. "He ran right in front of my car. I tried to stop, but the car slid on the road."

"I know. I saw." Rebecca took the blanket and tucked it around

Ben. She didn't know how much good it was going to do. He was lying in the snow.

The woman looked up and down the road. "Why aren't they here yet?" She wrung her hands as she turned to Rebecca. "What else can we do?"

"There's another blanket in the buggy."

The woman ran for it, then glanced at Rebecca's feet. "You're wearing skates," she said. "I'll go get your shoes."

Rebecca put the second blanket on Ben and tried not to think about how the wait for the ambulance for him felt even longer than the one for Lizzie had. She busied herself with unlacing her skates and pulling on her boots.

As she waited, Rebecca wondered why Ben had been making such a commotion, yelling and waving his arms at her instead of walking to the pond to talk to her. It wasn't like him.

She was so absorbed in watching for the faintest movement from him, a flicker of his eyes opening or his hand stirring under hers, that she didn't realize at first that the woman had knelt in the snow beside her. "What is it?"

"I'm so sorry . . ."

Rebecca patted her hand. "I saw what happened. I don't know why Ben didn't watch what he was doing."

"You know him?"

Nodding, Rebecca touched his face with hands that shook. His face was so cold.

The woman gave her an impulsive hug. "This must be so hard for you. Thank you for not blaming me."

Rebecca took a deep breath, lifted her shoulders, then let them fall. "It wasn't your fault. But even if it had been, it's not our way."

The police and paramedics arrived, and within minutes Ben was carefully loaded up into the ambulance and Rebecca was allowed to climb in with him for the ride to the hospital. They seemed to assume she was his wife, and she didn't bother to tell them any different.

After all, if she hadn't been such an idiot, she'd be engaged to him by now.

At the hospital she was separated from him. She filled out the paperwork as best as she could and went to sit in the waiting room.

She felt so guilty. This was what she got for not being afraid and skating, she thought. Ben had been driving to her house to talk to her, and he'd seen her and become upset enough to walk into the path of the car.

The antiseptic smell of the hospital was bringing back awful memories. To distract herself, Rebecca looked at the program on the television. A man was reading some news stories, and then there was a woman standing before an animated map of the state. She talked about spring coming early.

Engulfed in worry and guilt over Ben, Rebecca realized why Ben might have been creating a commotion—had he worried that the ice wasn't frozen enough to skate on?

Samuel and Emma came rushing in at that moment, looking frantic, and a nurse took them back to Ben. *They are family and I'm not*, Rebecca thought, sinking down into her chair. If things had gone differently, she would have been regarded as family; she would be able to go see him.

All she could do now was sit here and think the worst. No, she told herself. That was *not* all she could do. She could pray. Bending her head, she asked God to please heal Ben, to make him well.

When she opened her eyes, Emma was taking a seat next to her. "He hasn't regained consciousness yet. They're doing some tests." She traced the rose design on the wooden cane in her hands. "Ben made it for me. Rose is my middle name." Tears welled up in her eyes and ran down her cheeks.

Ben had made a thing of beauty out of a simple piece of wood to help ease her steps, Rebecca thought. He didn't always have the words. But it was obvious that he had the heart.

Grabbing some tissues from a box near her, she pressed them

into Emma's hands. Then she put her arms around the older woman. "He's going to be okay. He's got to be."

"Rebecca!"

"Mamm! Daed!" She threw herself into their arms. "I'm so glad to see you."

Amos turned to Emma. "How is he?"

"They're doing tests. Samuel is back there with him." She paused, her lips trembling. "They don't think he's in a coma, but he hasn't woken up yet."

They all looked up as a nurse came approached. "Would you come back with me?" she asked Emma.

Rebecca was able to wait until Emma had left the room, but then her tears started. "I can't go back. I'm not family."

Naomi urged her down into her chair and sank into the chair that Emma had vacated. "I know, *liebschen*. I know."

"God wouldn't take Ben, would He? It's not fair! I lost Lizzie. I shouldn't have to lose Ben too."

She looked up to see her parents exchange a look.

"I know, I was so foolish. I should have told him how I felt. I was going to, today. He was coming to see me." With tears hitching her breath, she told them what had happened.

"You were skating?" her *daed* asked, his voice sounding funny.

"*Ya.*" She watched the color drain from his face.

"Signs were posted on the pond last week. The ice is melting early. No one's supposed to be skating on it."

"There was no sign," she whispered, staring at them in shock. "Someone must have taken it." A strange feeling swept over her. So that was why Ben had been so upset, why he hadn't watched out for his own safety. He was trying to warn her.

"I decided I didn't want to be afraid anymore." She swallowed hard. If not for Ben, her parents might at this moment be mourning the loss of a second daughter. "I was saying good-bye to Lizzie," she said. The tears started again. "I can't say good-bye to him too."

　　　　　BARBARA CAMERON

Her *mamm* patted her back. "Don't think that way. I'm sure he'll be all right."

The nurse came out again. "Rebecca? Would you come back with me?"

It had to be good news, she thought as she jumped to her feet. She glanced at her parents, and they gave her reassuring smiles.

"We'll pray for him," they promised.

⟋⟋⟍

He saw her skating like a graceful bird on the pond, and for a long moment, he just stood and enjoyed the sight of her gliding across the ice. He didn't know anyone else who could do such twirls and turns and leaps on the ice. She was a beautiful bird that soared.

Then he saw the ice opening and Rebecca—no, it was Lizzie—no, it was Rebecca—screaming and falling into the icy water. He tried running to save her, but his feet were sliding on the snowy road and he couldn't get to her. Something hit him, and he flew into the air, but not like a bird, for he fell hard and hit his head.

Everything was so mixed up. His head and his hip hurt and he was so cold. And there was a funny smell to the air. He told himself he needed to get up and make sure Rebecca was safe. He had to get up before she was lost forever.

"Rebecca!" he called urgently. "Rebecca!"

⟋⟋⟍

"Shh, I'm here. I'm here."

He opened his eyes and saw Rebecca sitting beside his bed.

"I'm here," she whispered. Tears were sliding down her cheeks. "You scared me to death."

"You're okay? I'm not dreaming?"

"I'm okay."

"You scared *me*," he told her. "No one was supposed to be skating on the pond."

"I didn't know." She bit her lip and shook her head. "But you're the one who got hurt." Brushing at her tears, she got up.

"Don't go!"

"I'm not. I promised the nurse and your parents that I'd let them know when you woke up. I'll be right back."

If he woke up had been on the minds of all of them, even though the doctor had assured them that while Ben had a concussion, he didn't think he was in a coma.

Rebecca went just a few steps out of the room and caught the attention of a passing nurse.

"I'll get the doctor," the woman assured her.

"And his parents?"

The nurse nodded and rushed away.

Rebecca returned to Ben's room and stood by the side of his bed. He held out his hand, and she took it. "I want to explain about Dr. Prato," he said.

"Not now," she told him, squeezing his hand. "It's not important. I need to tell you something before everyone comes in." She paused, took a deep breath. "Before I lose my nerve."

Don't be afraid!

"Ask me again, Ben Weaver. Ask me to marry you."

His expression was a little wary. "You're not feeling sorry for me?"

"No. If you don't want me, I imagine that Mary Ann will be around very shortly."

"Don't you dare!" he said, some of the old sparkle showing in his eyes. He tried to sit up, but it felt like his head would fall off. "Come here."

She moved closer.

"I fumbled when I asked if you'd marry me before," he said quietly. "But I know how I feel. I love you, Rebecca. I should have told you that when I asked you to be *mei fraa*."

Those were the best words, she thought, and her eyes filled. "And I love you!"

He pulled her toward him for a kiss.

The door opened. Rebecca jumped back guiltily and spun around to stare into the faces of both sets of parents.

"Uh, Ben's awake," she told them.

"*Ya*," Samuel said dryly.

"She was attacking me," Ben joked.

"Stop that!" she hissed and felt herself blushing.

"Does this mean what I think it means?" Emma asked, smiling as she walked toward them.

Grinning, Ben nodded. "*Ya*, Rebecca asked me to marry her."

"Ben!"

His grin faded, and he looked at her with such love in his eyes. "I told her what I should have weeks ago. I love her."

Rebecca was so relieved he was all right, so glad they had a life ahead of them, she bent and kissed him in front of all the parents and the doctor who'd come into the room.

"Congratulate us," she said with a smile. "Ben and I are engaged."

A Place of
His Own

By Kathleen Fuller

Chapter One

"AMANDA, THOMAS PINCHED ME!"

"I don't wike peas."

"Waaaah!"

Amanda Graber surveyed the chaos swirling in the kitchen as she tried to get supper on the table and corral her six much younger brothers and sisters. None of them were cooperating.

"Thomas, leave Andrew alone." She set down a warm loaf of freshly baked bread in the center of the long oak table. "Christopher, you only have to eat four peas. You can manage that." She bent down and picked up her youngest sibling, Jacob, kissing the small red mark where he had bumped his forehead when he fell on the kitchen floor. "All better?"

He nodded, then sniffed.

Amanda wiped two big teardrops from underneath his large blue eyes, then handed him to Rachel. "Put Jacob in his high chair," she said, giving the tot a quick tap on his chubby cheek. She leaned against the counter and wiped her damp forehead with the back of her hand despite the cool fall breeze wafting through the open window.

The clip-clop of their father's horse and buggy reached her ears. Turning to Andrew and Thomas, she said, *"Daed's* home. Please go outside and help him with the horse. And, Thomas, no more pinching!"

Twenty minutes later everyone, including *Mamm,* settled down to eat. Amanda placed a bowl of steaming mashed and buttered potatoes on the table, then took her place next to her sister Hannah.

Daed cleared his throat, the signal for everyone to quiet down and bow their heads.

Amanda listened and prayed along as her father blessed the meal. After saying amen, she sat back and watched her family pile their plates with the food she'd prepared for supper. Thick slices of meat loaf and the vegetables, along with bread and butter, quickly disappeared from the serving dishes.

"Amanda?"

She turned at the sound of her mother's voice. *"Ya, Mamm?"*

"Aren't you going to eat?" Dark shadows underscored Katharine Graber's brown eyes.

"*Ya*, I'll have something in a minute." She regarded her mother for a moment. "Are you feeling all right?"

"I'm feeling fine. Just a little tired."

Amanda glanced at her mother again before looking at the empty white plate in front of her. Lately her mother had seemed more than a little tired, and she couldn't help but worry about her. As she neared the end of her pregnancy, her *mamm* seemed to be having a more difficult time with this baby than she'd had with the other ones. Amanda silently prayed for both her mother and the unborn child's safety.

Mamm gave her a weary smile. "Everything looks and smells delicious, Mandy. *Danki* for making supper tonight. I don't know what I'd do without you."

Amanda smiled back. She enjoyed cooking, just as she enjoyed taking care of her brothers and sisters. Sure, they were a handful, but they were also a lot of fun and brought tremendous joy to her life. Some of her friends complained about having to care for younger siblings, but not Amanda. As an only child until the age of fourteen, she had always longed for a brother or sister. Now that she had them, she counted them as blessings. She was twenty-four, plenty old enough to be thinking about a family of her own. And while she stood only five-foot-three and possessed a thin frame, she hoped she would follow in her mother's footsteps and have a large brood of her own, God willing.

Although a couple of young men had shown interest in her, Amanda had yet to meet the one she wanted to marry. One man in particular, Peter Yoder, didn't seem to get the message. Each time he asked her to a singing or expressed an interest in courting her, Amanda firmly told him no. Still he doggedly pursued her.

God would bring the right man into her life. Until then, she kept her focus on helping her mother with the younger children.

"*Sehr gut, Dochder.*" David Graber shoveled a forkful of mashed potato and meat loaf into his mouth, then wiped his brown beard with a napkin. Threads of gray were starting to show through, but her father still looked several years younger than forty-four, and acted at least a decade younger than that.

"Yuck." Christopher picked up a green pea and made a face.

"Christopher." *Daed* gave the boy one of his infrequent stern looks. "Mandy went to a lot of trouble to make us a *wunderbaar* supper. Eat your peas without complaint."

Frowning, Christopher nodded, then put the pea in his mouth and chewed, wrinkling his nose.

Daed remarked that business was booming at Yoder's Lumber, where he worked as a sawyer and foreman. Being in charge of the first shift of workers, he made very good pay. "God has blessed me, Katharine," he said, looking at his wife, then panning his gaze over his family before returning to her. "He has blessed us all."

Taking in the tender look her parents exchanged, Amanda sent up another silent prayer of thanks for her father's job and for being a part of such a wonderful family. Even though they sometimes fought among each other and life didn't always run smoothly, they were all satisfied and happy.

"Rachel, please clear the table," *Mamm* said after everyone finished eating. "Hannah, it's your turn to wash the dishes. Andrew can help you dry."

"Aww." Andrew scowled. "That's women's work."

"*Nee,* it's not just women's work." *Daed* shoved away from the table. "And for that remark, *mei sohn,* you can dry the dishes for the rest of the week." He rose from the table, tapped Andrew lightly on his sandy blond head with his fingertips, then ruffled Christopher's dark brown hair. "I'm sure the animals are hungry by now. Thomas, come with me."

They left the kitchen to go to the barnyard and feed the family's six pigs and three cows, which would be slaughtered in a couple weeks to provide the family with more than enough meat for the following year. They would share the extra with other families in the community.

Andrew continued to scowl, but he scampered from his chair and headed to the sink to do his assigned chore.

Mamm rose from her chair, picked up a napkin, and wiped mashed potatoes from Jacob's face. "*Danki* again, Amanda. You may be excused."

With a nod Amanda rose and headed upstairs to her room. Her mother and father would put the younger children to bed with Rachel and Hannah's help, leaving Amanda free to do whatever she wanted. Usually in the evening she worked on her sewing, making Amish dresses, lightweight spring coats, and shawls to sell at Eli's Country Store and Dry Goods just outside Paradise. Sometimes she read, and during the warm spring and summer evenings, she liked to go outside to walk, pray, and be alone. After a busy afternoon watching her siblings and making dinner, she definitely needed to spend some time with the Lord.

She paused and looked out the window of her bedroom, her reflection obscuring the view outside. Noticing the awkward tilt of her white *kapp,* she straightened it, then adjusted one of the bobby pins holding it in place against her light brown hair. She pushed open the window, allowing the fresh evening air into her stuffy room.

As she looked around her family's property, she again thanked the Lord for His abundant blessings. Her parents had purchased the house and its attached five acres when Amanda was two years old. Their barn sat to the left of the house, set back about two hundred yards. There they kept the pigs and cows and their two horses. A wooden play set, complete with a slide and three swings, was situated closer to the house. Three acres beyond that were woods, where Amanda and her friend and only neighbor, Josiah, used to play when they were young.

She sighed as Josiah's image came to her mind. She had thought of him often over the years, since he'd moved away a decade ago at the age of fourteen. He'd been an only child, as she was for so long, and the two of them had spent nearly all of their time together, hiking in the woods, building forts, and sometimes, to Josiah's great misery, playing house. Amanda smiled at the memory. Josiah had been a nice boy, and even though she knew he hated pretending they were married, he went along with it every once in a while.

Then when he turned thirteen, his *mamm* had died. What a horrible day, not only for him but for the community. Emma Bontrager had been a sweet woman, beloved by many. After her death things had changed. Amanda didn't see Josiah as much, and when she did there was an underlying sadness in his green eyes that never completely disappeared.

Then one day he was gone. There had been no explanation, no good-bye. She had waited for him at their special place in the woods, a small clearing where they had often played. He never showed up. That evening, when her parents told her Josiah and his father had moved away, she had burst into tears. How could he leave without telling her? Without even saying good-bye? It had taken her a long time to get over his leaving.

She often thought about him. Was he married? Did he have any children? Had he even stayed in the Amish faith? She prayed that wherever he was, he had found the happiness he deserved.

"Amanda? Would you read me a story?"

She turned around to see Christopher standing in the doorway, clutching his favorite book to his chest with both hands. From the way he kept looking over his shoulder, she had a feeling he had sneaked upstairs without their mother's knowing. If she had, she would have called him back down to the family room and told him to leave Amanda alone for the evening.

Smiling, she went and knelt in front of him. She plucked the book out of his hands and turned it over, glancing at the orange and green cover. "Aren't you tired of hearing this one?"

He shook his head. "'I do not like green eggs and ham,'" he quoted. "'I do not like them, Sam I am.' You know, Mandy, I don't like green eggs and ham neither. They look yucky."

"You don't like any food that's green, Christopher." Laughing, she grasped his hand and led him downstairs to the bedroom he shared with Andrew and Thomas. "You know what," she whispered to him a few moments later as she sat on the edge of his bed and settled him on her lap. "I don't think I'd like them either."

⁓

Josiah Bontrager gripped the horse's reins until his knuckles turned white. He fought an onslaught of memories as he stared at the decrepit house before him, a house he hadn't seen since he'd left Paradise ten years earlier. Long curls of white paint stuck out from the siding and littered the surrounding tall, brownish grass. A crack ran down the middle of one window, and he spied a couple of missing panes. The porch that spanned the front of the house tilted, and he suspected there were more problems with it than splintered boards. A decade of neglect loomed before him.

He loosened his grip on the reins and guided the used buggy—new to him, along with the horse—onto the rut-ridden dirt driveway. When he glimpsed the barn behind the house, he groaned. It was in even worse shape than the house. He took off his hat and ran his

KATHLEEN FULLER

fingers through his sweat-dampened hair. Why had he bothered to come back here?

But he already knew the answer. He'd returned to Paradise because he'd had no choice. Even now he wanted to turn around, take what little money he had, and head for Holmes County, Ohio. No one knew him there. A perfect place for him to start over, to leave this mess and the pain of the past behind. But he couldn't do that just yet. He couldn't ignore this place any longer, although God knew he'd tried many times over the years.

The horse whinnied, signaling her hunger to Josiah. He steered the mare toward the entrance of the barn. After he jumped out of the buggy, he stroked the horse's brown nose, then dragged the sliding door open. The musty, stale scent of old hay and decaying manure hit him full force. He walked into the dim, cool barn, autumn sunlight spilling through the open slats and holes in the weathered wood. Everything remained as he remembered, though covered with cobwebs and dust.

He spied the back corner of the barn, his gut tightening. Unwilling to fully contemplate the memories of what had happened there, he scanned the rest of the structure, focusing on the list of things he would have to do to get the barn and the house back in shape. Anything to keep his mind off the past.

The horse whinnied again, and he moved to take care of her. He went to one of the three stalls and found an upended, rusty metal tub. Not the most sanitary water container, but it would have to do until he bought a new one. Flipping the tub over, he set about preparing the stall so the horse would have a fairly decent place to spend the night.

Thirty minutes later he had filled the tub with fresh water from the pump. The water had been rust-colored at first, but once he'd let it run awhile, it had turned clear. He also turned over the matted-down hay and poured a small bag of feed into the trough. Tomorrow he would pick up fresh hay, paint, and a few other things he needed to get started on the repairs. The sooner he finished, the sooner he could leave.

He watched the good-natured mare as she munched on her feed, apparently indifferent to her less-than-ideal surroundings. "You're a *gut* girl," he said, though he missed his old horse, Patches. He wished he could have brought the gelding with him, but he had no way to transport the animal. Everything about coming back to Paradise had been hard. He'd been a fool to think it could be otherwise.

The sun had already set, and he needed to get things set up in the house. Making his way through nearly waist-high grass, he reached the two concrete steps leading to the back door. He yanked on the screen door and nearly stumbled backward when the rusted metal frame immediately separated from its hinges. Grimacing, he tossed the door to the side, and it hit the side of the house with a dull clang. Tomorrow morning he would fix it. He pushed open the solid wood door, not surprised to find it unlocked, and stepped inside the dark kitchen. As his eyes adjusted to the darkness, he saw the shadow of the old battery-operated lamp his mother had always kept on the counter. No use turning it on; he knew the batteries would be dead by now. He'd put new ones in the lamp in the morning.

Using his flashlight, Josiah guided himself to his old bedroom upstairs. All he wanted was a decent night's rest. He was too tired to do much else.

But as he continued to inhale the stale yet familiar smell of his childhood home, he wished he were too tired to feel.

❧

Amanda finished reading to Christopher and tucked him into bed. Then she ran back upstairs to her room and grabbed a flashlight before leaving the house, prepared to enjoy the pleasant October evening. The sun had just dipped past the horizon, bathing the sky with pale swaths of color. Taking a deep breath as she stood on the back stoop, she inhaled the sweet scents of grass and freshly cut hay and the pungent odor of livestock.

Something soft and furry brushed against her legs. She glanced down to see Lucy, their pregnant calico cat, weaving around her ankles. "How are you, sweetheart?" she said, bending down to scratch behind the cat's ears. Lucy started to purr, but another sound interrupted the cat's contentment, making her perk up her ears.

Amanda stilled her hand and listened. "I hear it too." The sound recurred. A horse's whinny. Soft, and sounding far away. "Probably Jack," Amanda said, rising to a standing position. She pulled her plain navy blue sweater closer to her body. Sometimes her father's horse had trouble settling in for the night, so she decided to go check on him.

She went to the barn and slid open the door. The pigs jumped up immediately, all snorting at the same time, even though her father had fed them little more than an hour ago. The cows lowed but didn't move toward her, content to chew their cuds.

"*Nee*, I have nothing for you," she said, laughing at their eagerness. She walked over to the horse stalls. Nelly and Jack both seemed all right. As she nuzzled Jack's gray nose, the pigs settled down and stopped their grunting. She had just turned to give Nelly some attention when she heard it again.

Another whinny. Louder and more urgent. Confused, Amanda walked out of the barn and listened again. By this time the sky had darkened considerably. She flicked on her flashlight and listened again. A third whinny broke through the silence. Turning, she realized it came from the Bontragers' barn. Her brow furrowed. The old building had been abandoned for a decade. How did a horse get inside?

She looked in the direction of Josiah's barn, and a wave of sadness washed over her, as it normally did when she saw the poor state of both barn and house. Theirs and the Bontragers' were the only two homes on their small road, and for a while after Josiah and his *daed* moved away, her father tried to keep the place up. He mowed the lawn, fixed a shutter when it blew off during a particularly strong thunderstorm, and generally tried to maintain the property. But the demands of his own growing family made it difficult for him to work on both properties. No one knew where the Bontragers had gone, and no one had heard from them after they left. They had just disappeared.

Amanda walked to the barn, determined to find the horse. The tall grass whipped against her bare calves and ankles, both tickling and scratching her skin. When she reached the shabby building, she hesitated for a moment, waiting to hear the whinny again. The only thing she heard was the faint sound of crickets chirping. With fall in full swing, their night music would soon fade away during the cooler evenings.

Maybe she was hearing things. She was about to turn around when she heard a rustling movement coming from the inside. Her curiosity getting the best of her, Amanda grabbed the rusty handle of the door and pulled. The door slid open with surprising ease, considering it hadn't been used for such a long time. The cloying odor of moldy hay hit her immediately.

She shined her flashlight around the nearly pitch dark barn. Cobwebs covered the corners and walls, and in the right corner she saw a short wooden stool lying on its side and the black outline of a horse whip resting next to it. Shifting the light over to the other side of the barn, she saw the stall. Sure enough, a horse stood inside it. Puzzled, she took a few steps forward.

Then someone grabbed her shoulder.

She screamed and spun around.

Chapter Two

JOSIAH NEARLY JUMPED OUT OF HIS SKIN AS THE WOMAN'S shriek pierced the air. He dropped his hand from her shoulder, then shielded his face when she pointed the flashlight directly in his eyes.

"Who are you?" she asked, sounding breathless.

He shut his eyes against the blinding light. "I should ask you the same thing. What are you doing in my barn?"

"*Your* barn? Listen, I don't know who you are, but this property belongs to the Bontragers. You're trespassing."

"Look, can you put down the light?"

She complied, and Josiah dropped his hands.

"*Danki.*" Green and yellow spots danced in front of him, rendering him sightless for a moment. But his relief was short-lived when she shined the light in his face again.

"Josiah?"

It was a soft, familiar voice. His heart tripped as he groped for the flashlight and plucked it from her hand.

"Hey, that's mine! What are you doing?"

"Keeping you from blinding me, that's what." He shined the light on her, although not directly in her face. When he got a good look at the woman standing in front of him, he nearly lost his breath. "Mandy? Is that you?"

"*Ya.*" Her full lips slanted upward in a smile that lit up her entire face. "Oh, Josiah! I can't believe you're here!"

He almost lost his footing when she threw her arms around him. The top of her head brushed against his stubbly chin, and he inhaled the sweet scent of her hair, neatly secured beneath a white prayer *kapp*. When her cheek touched his chest, all the air pushed out of his lungs. He wasn't prepared for this or for his reaction to her nearness. He hadn't thought he'd see her so soon after his arrival. He wished he didn't have to see her at all. Yet his body betrayed his thoughts, and his arms automatically started to go around her slight frame until she stepped away and slapped his arm.

"Hey!" he said. She had just hugged him, after all. "What was that for?"

"Scaring me to death. You shouldn't sneak up on people like that."

"And you shouldn't be snooping around someone else's property." He held the flashlight at an angle so he could see her face without aiming the light directly on her.

"I heard a noise. I wanted to see what was going on."

"That wasn't very smart of you. You don't know who could have been hiding in here."

"Well, I certainly wasn't expecting *you*." She crossed her arms. "I thought you'd disappeared completely."

He only wished that were true. "*Nee*. I came back."

"I see that." She tilted her head in the direction of the mare's stall. "I heard your horse whinnying. Is he all right?"

"*She* should be fine." He shined the light toward the stall. Everything seemed in order. "Probably getting used to her surroundings." He could certainly relate. He looked back at Amanda. "She's okay."

"*Gut*."

They stood there for a moment in the dark barn as he held her small flashlight between them. The light cast her face in shadows, but he could still make out her features. She had changed a lot since he'd last seen her, when they were both fourteen. Even then she had been pretty, a fact that had struck him full force the year he turned twelve. But the word hardly did her justice now. Her eyes were large and round, her nose small and pert, and her lips full and lovely. Unable to help himself, he took in the rest of her slender frame, immediately noticing she had become a beautiful woman.

He turned away, not liking one bit the unstoppable attraction flowing through him. Despite his efforts, he'd never gotten over his boyhood crush, one he had kept a secret from everyone, especially her. Even at that time he knew he was tainted.

"Josiah?" she said, stepping toward him. She put her hand on his arm. "Please don't be upset with me. I'm sorry. You're right, I shouldn't have been snooping. I didn't mean to make you mad."

Now that was the Amanda he remembered. A people pleaser through and through, always worried about other people's feelings, never wanting them to be uncomfortable or, God forbid, angry.

He looked at her, eager to give reassurance. "It's all right, Mandy. I reckon I should have let your parents know I was here. Didn't mean to scare you, either."

She grinned, and his heart skipped several beats. *Not a good sign.*

Slipping her arm through his, she guided him away from the stall. "You must come over and see them right now. I know they'll be happy to see you, just as I am. Your father can come too."

"He's not here."

"Oh. Is he coming later?"

"*Nee.*"

"Okay. Well, then you can tell us where you've been all these years." She looked up at him. "I'm dying to know."

But he wasn't dying to tell her. In fact, he didn't want to explain anything to her or her parents or anyone else in Paradise. But that wasn't realistic. People would have questions, and they would want answers. He would tell them a few things, enough to satisfy their curiosity, but no more than that. Better to let the past stay buried.

He glanced down at her arm in his. Amanda had always been demonstrative, a stark contrast to many of the Amish, who were much more reserved. Her walking arm in arm with him seemed so natural, just as it had when they were kids. His life in Paradise up until the day his mother died had been carefree and happy, and Amanda Graber had a lot to do with that.

"I made chocolate chip cookies yesterday," she said as they exited the barn. "We can have some cookies and milk and catch up on old times."

Reluctantly he stepped away from her. "*Nee*, I can't. Not tonight."

Disappointment seeped into her eyes. "Then maybe tomorrow. I'll let *daed* know you're here. I'm sure he'll want to talk to you."

He nodded, remaining noncommittal. "It's been a long day, and I just got here a couple hours ago."

"Of course. I'm sure you had a long trip from . . ." She hesitated. When he didn't respond, she simply shrugged and smiled. "Josiah, I'm so glad you came back home." Whirling around, she started to walk away, then called over her shoulder, "See you tomorrow!"

He watched as she headed for her house, a house nearly as familiar to him as his own. The glow of gas lamps burned like welcome beacons through several of the windows on the bottom floor. He'd spent many hours inside, sharing lunches and dinners with Amanda and her parents, who treated him like their own child.

For the first time since he'd stepped back in Paradise, his mind opened to the pleasant memories from his childhood. His life hadn't always been a living nightmare.

Only after Amanda had gone inside did he glance down and realize he still held her flashlight. He thought about returning it. He could imagine her inviting him inside and his being enveloped by the warmth of a family who cared about each other and also cared about him. His soul ached for that, yet he knew he would never have it. He couldn't. Just like he couldn't walk the hundred yards or so to Amanda's house. Not tonight.

Because if he did, he would never want to leave.

∽◌∾

Amanda practically floated up the stairs to her bedroom. She couldn't believe Josiah Bontrager had come back to Paradise! She also couldn't believe how much he had changed. Her last memories of Josiah were of a scrawny boy who had a crackly voice and was at least three inches shorter than she.

He certainly wasn't that scrawny boy anymore. Josiah had grown into a tall, fit man with a deep, smooth voice she could listen to all day. Even in the low light of her flashlight, she could see how handsome he'd become.

Her flashlight. She had forgotten to get it back from him. For a brief moment she considered walking back to retrieve it, but she decided not to. He seemed eager to go inside his house. He looked tired, weary even, and she didn't want to bother him again. Besides, she would see him tomorrow. Then she'd not only get her flashlight back but find out where he had been all these years.

Slipping the bobby pins out of her *kapp*, she removed it and laid it on her dresser, then opened the drawer and pulled out her nightgown. She had her own room, another added benefit to being so much older than her siblings. Small, but the perfect size. She didn't need much space.

After she put on her nightgown, she knelt beside her bed and said her evening prayers. Once she finished, she slipped between the cool sheets and pulled the green-and-white basket-patterned quilt over her body. Despite the fatigue from putting in a long day of work, helping her *mamm* with the children and chores, she still couldn't get Josiah out of her mind.

Obviously he had changed physically, but she sensed something else different about him, something intangible and mysterious. She smiled in the darkness. Tomorrow she would find out exactly what that was. She rolled on her side and hugged the extra pillow she couldn't sleep without, Josiah Bontrager still filling her mind.

⁂

"Josiah Bontrager's back," Amanda announced as she bounced into the kitchen the next morning.

Her *mamm* paused as she pulled nine white plates out of the cabinet, a surprised expression on her face. "He is?"

"*Ya.*" Amanda took the plates from her *mamm* and started setting the table. "Last night while I was outside, I heard a sound coming from the Bontragers' barn. When I went inside, I saw a horse in one of the stalls."

"Really?"

"*Ya.* Then Josiah came up behind me. Practically scared me to death at first, but I was so happy to see him I didn't care."

"You shouldn't be nosing around someone else's property, Amanda. Especially by yourself." *Mamm* gave her a somber look as she cracked an egg into a skillet on top of the propane stove.

Amanda smirked. "He said the same thing."

Rachel yawned as she entered the room with Hannah. "Who's 'he'?"

"Josiah." At that point the kitchen filled with children, some wide awake and full of energy, others still dragging. Amanda scooped up Jacob in her arms before Thomas accidentally trampled him.

"Who's Josiah?" Hannah asked.

"The young man who used to live next door."

"You mean someone actually lived there?" Andrew said. "In that dump?"

"Thomas, come butter the toast," *Mamm* said, scooping the fried eggs onto a platter. "Andrew, that's not nice. Josiah and his *daed* moved away nine years ago."

"Ten," Amanda corrected, helping her younger siblings get settled at the table. "Josiah moved away ten years ago, *Mamm.*"

Just as she went to pick up the platter of cooked eggs, her father walked into the room, pulling his black suspenders over his shoulders. "Did I hear you mention Josiah?"

Amanda grinned. "*Ya, Daed.* He's back. Came in sometime yesterday."

Daed looked at her. "How do you know that?"

"I saw him last night. For just a few minutes."

"Was he alone?"

"David," *Mamm* said in a low voice.

Amanda didn't miss the look that passed between her parents, but she thought she should answer her father's question. "I think so. He didn't say anything about his *daed*."

Daed nodded and sat down at the table.

When everyone finished eating and her father left for work, Amanda picked up Jacob out of his high chair. "I invited Josiah over, *Mamm*. I thought you would like to see him again."

"Hannah, it's your turn to clear the table." *Mamm* looked up at Amanda as Hannah began to remove the dirty dishes. "Of course I want to see him. So would *Daed*. He was like a *sohn* to us, and a brother to you."

Amanda's face reddened. What would her mother say if she knew that last night her thoughts about Josiah Bontrager had been anything but sisterly?

"When is he coming over?" *Mamm* asked, slowly rising from the chair. She laid her hand over her swollen belly.

"I don't know."

Jacob squirmed in Amanda's grasp, and she set him down, watching him as he toddled over to the living room to the large toy box in the corner. Flipping open the lid, he bent over, his head disappearing inside the box as he searched for his toys.

"Josiah didn't say. We didn't talk very much. He seemed pretty tired. I thought I might take some lunch over to him, if we don't see him before then."

"I'm sure he would appreciate it. Now, if you could start the wash for me, Amanda . . . It's such a nice, breezy day. The clothes should dry quickly on the line. Get Rachel to help you."

Amanda nodded and searched for Rachel. She found her sister swinging outside while Andrew and Thomas chased each other into the woods. As she breathed in the fresh spring air and let the warmth

of the sun seep into her skin, she agreed with her *mamm*. The Lord
had blessed them with a beautiful day. Before long autumn would
end and winter would set in, and days like this would be a memory.

An hour later she and Rachel were putting the second load of
laundry on the line that stretched between the house and the barn,
when she saw Josiah emerge from his house. He stood on the back
stoop and leaned backward, stretching. She couldn't help but stare at
him. Even though he stood some distance away, she could see him
clearly enough, more clearly than she had in the dim light of the barn
last night. He didn't have his hat on, and she took in his hair—thick,
brown, and wavy, with coppery, sun-streaked highlights. A little long
for the traditional Amish hairstyle, but she didn't mind. In fact, she
liked it that way, noticing how the ends brushed a little past the top
of his shirt collar.

A light breeze rustled the colorful leaves of the oak trees surrounding Josiah's property, causing a few to release and flutter to the
ground. The movement lifted a couple of locks of his hair. Amanda
squeezed the light blue dress she held in her hands.

"Mandy, are you gonna hang up that dress or what?"

Amanda looked at her sister, who held up a damp pair of
Christopher's small trousers. Quickly she clipped the dress to the line
and took the trousers, all the while unable to keep her gaze off Josiah.
They had been the best of friends, and now he'd come back into her
life after all this time. No wonder she couldn't get enough of looking
at him.

As she finished hanging the wash, she peered over the line of
clothes and watched Josiah heading for the barn. Disappointment
threaded through her when he didn't even look in the direction of
their house. Hadn't he heard Rachel and her talking? If he had, he
must be purposely ignoring them, and she didn't know what to make
of that. He had never ignored her before.

Josiah disappeared into the barn and emerged with his horse a
few moments later. He led the horse to the buggy parked next to the

barn and hitched it up. As Amanda hung the last item of clothing, he jumped into the buggy and steered it down the dirt driveway.

"Is that Josiah?" Rachel asked, turning around to see the buggy turn onto the road and disappear in the distance.

Amanda ducked underneath the line. "*Ya*, that's Josiah."

"Were you two friends?"

"We were *sehr gut* friends," Amanda said, remembering that her sister was just days old when Josiah left.

"Are you still?"

She looked at Rachel. Doubt pressed at her, but she shoved it away. Their encounter in the barn had been awkward. Maybe it would take time for Josiah to pick up where their friendship had left off. While she had several good friends and many acquaintances, no one had ever taken Josiah's place.

"*Ya*," she said, grabbing the laundry basket and motioning for Rachel to follow her. "We're still friends."

Chapter Three

"As I live and breathe," Josiah's Aunt Vera said, slowly rising from her kneeling position at the back edge of her almost completely harvested garden. She wiped her hands on her apron and walked toward him, then placed a soft, wrinkled hand on each side of his face. "Josiah." Tears filled her brown eyes. "I didn't think I'd ever see you again, *kind*."

He smiled, and the knot that had formed in his stomach as he drove to his aunt and uncle's house loosened a tiny bit. After finishing up in town and making a stop at his mother's gravesite, he'd decided at the last minute to stop by Vera and John Yoder's home on his way back from town. He had spent a lot of his childhood here.

"You look like your *mamm*," Aunt Vera said, swiping a thick finger underneath her lower lashes. "Heavens, I miss my sister. It's *gut* to have you back, Josiah." She drew him to her and enveloped him in her fleshy arms, then released him. "John's in the shop. I'm sure he'll be just as excited to see you. *Geh*, and I'll bring you some fresh iced tea."

"*Danki*," Josiah said, then left the expansive front porch and walked around the back of the house to his uncle's buggy and harness shop. Glancing around at the well-kept property with its large white house, barn, huge storage shed, and attached shop, he realized not much had changed here. The Yoders' property remained in its usual pristine condition. Not a single leaf or twig could be found on the black asphalt driveway that connected all three buildings, which were surrounded by perfectly manicured grass. A stab of envy went through him. Even when things hadn't been so bad at home, his family's property had never looked like this.

The knot in his stomach re-formed as he approached the door to the shop. He hoped his uncle would react with the same welcoming attitude as his aunt, but he couldn't be sure.

As he pulled open the door, the familiar tinkle of the bell above the door frame rang out. He scanned the room, which, like everything else he'd seen since his return, seemed to stand still in time. The shop had two sections. He stood in the front "office" where his uncle and cousin dealt with customers and showed them pictures of buggies and samples of paint, leather, and upholstery fabric. In the larger back room, secluded from the public, the buggies and harnesses were made.

The office was empty, and Josiah assumed they were all working in the back. He walked over to a small counter and ran his hand over the binder that held the pictures of his uncle's handiwork. Flipping it over, he glanced at the photos of a variety of Amish buggies, memories once again flooding over him. He recalled the times he had been allowed to help his uncle in the shop.

"Can I help you?"

Josiah looked up to see a tall, broad-shouldered young man walk into the office, wiping black grease off his hands with an old rag. The man's blue eyes narrowed. Josiah stood face-to-face with his cousin Peter, the one person in Paradise he knew for sure wouldn't welcome him back.

Peter's expression reflected the wariness Josiah felt. "What are you doing here?" Peter asked, tossing the rag on the counter. "We all thought you were gone for *gut*."

"Nice to see you too." Josiah held his temper, not an easy thing to do since there was no love lost between the two cousins. As far back as he could remember, Peter had seemed to resent him. Apparently time hadn't softened those feelings.

"Peter, do you need some—"

Josiah focused his attention on the man who entered the room. The short, stocky Amish man held his gaze for a moment before his face broke into a wide grin. "Josiah!" He crossed the room and wrapped his nephew in a big hug.

The knot of tension completely released as he embraced his uncle.

Uncle John stepped away, his gaze taking in Josiah from head to toe. His smile remained in place, causing deep crinkles to form around his light blue eyes, eyes that were identical to Peter's. "I've missed you, *sohn.*"

Josiah thought he saw tears behind the man's large, wire-framed glasses. "I missed you too."

"Peter, watch the shop for me." Without looking at his son, John clapped an arm around Josiah's shoulders. "Your cousin and I have a lot of catching up to do."

Josiah didn't miss the resentment in Peter's eyes. But to his cousin's credit, he simply nodded and said, "*Ya, Daed.*"

John led Josiah to the main house. Once inside they went to the kitchen and found Aunt Vera placing amber-colored glasses of iced tea on a wicker tray. "We can talk here," John said, gesturing to one of the wooden chairs at the polished kitchen table.

Josiah sat down, and Aunt Vera placed a glass of tea in front of him. She put her hand on Josiah's shoulder and squeezed. He glanced up and met her soft gaze. "*Danki, Aenti* Vera."

She smiled. "Are you hungry, Josiah? I can whip you up something for breakfast. Or since it's close to lunch, perhaps you'd like a sandwich. I have some honey-roasted ham in the icebox, and the most delicious Swiss cheese you've tasted in your life. We picked it up at the Stoltzfuses' when we were there last week."

Although Josiah had skipped breakfast, he shook his head. "*Nee.* The tea will be enough, *danki.*"

She nodded and handed her husband his drink. After giving Josiah one last smile, she left the room.

Josiah took a long swallow of the perfectly sweetened tea, letting the cold liquid slide down his throat. John leaned forward, his eyes filled with intensity. "I guess you got my letter?"

"*Ya*. It came a couple weeks ago."

"When did you get back?"

"Last night."

"Took me awhile to find you, Josiah. We haven't heard from you since you left. I suppose there's a *gut* reason for that."

Josiah nodded but didn't say anything. He had his reasons for not contacting anyone after leaving Paradise, reasons he wouldn't share with anyone, not even his uncle.

"There's been a couple people interested in the property. David Graber mentioned a real estate agent snooping around a few months back, asking questions about it. As I'm sure you know already, it's a sight. David tried to keep up with it, but it became too much for him after a while. He has his own family and property to mind first, and I haven't had much of a chance to go over there like I wanted."

"I appreciate David's help," Josiah said. "And I'm glad you contacted me. To be honest, I hadn't thought about the house in a long time."

John removed his straw hat and placed it on the table, revealing his salt-and-pepper hair, molded in the shape of the crown of his hat. "What did your *daed* say about you coming back here?"

"He passed away two years ago."

"*Ach*, Josiah." John sounded distressed. "I had no idea. I'm so sorry for your loss."

Josiah stared at his hands cupping the glass. "*Danki*," he said, his voice barely audible.

"What happened?"

"Got sick. How do I get in touch with the folks interested in the house?"

John hesitated, then finally said, "David might know the name of the realty company. You could ask him. You could probably sell it as is, but I thought you might want the opportunity to get what the house and land are worth. If it's your intent to sell."

"It is."

"All right. If you need any help, let me know. If I can't be there, I'll send Peter."

"I'm fine. I'm not afraid of a little work."

"A little?" John shook his head, letting out a chuckle. "I'd say a little is a huge understatement. But then again, you always were a hard worker. Dependable, always did a *gut* job for me when you helped out here in the shop."

Josiah warmed at the compliment. It had been so long since someone in his family had given him one. "I appreciated the opportunities you gave me to work here."

John nodded. "Do you need any money, Josiah? To help pay for materials?"

"I'm *gut*. I have all the money I need."

"How about a place to stay, then? We have plenty of room here. Can't imagine that place is fit to sleep in."

"It's not that bad," Josiah said. "Really, I'm fine."

"Well, if you need anything, let me know." He clapped Josiah on the shoulder. "We're family, *sohn*. Sometimes that's the only thing you can depend on."

Josiah nodded, but he didn't share his uncle's view. If anything, family was the last thing he could depend on.

⁓

Amanda sprinkled powdered sugar over the pan of brownies she had baked earlier that day. She slid a sharp knife through the soft, chocolatey dessert, cutting it into even portions. Putting four pieces on a plate, she covered them with plastic wrap and placed the dish on the counter, then she walked over to the kitchen window and peered outside. From here she had a good view of Josiah's house. Dusk had arrived, and he still hadn't returned.

Through the window screen she could hear her family laughing and playing outside. Her *daed* had come home from work early and was outside with the rest of the children, playing a game of catch with the boys while the girls played on the swing set. Her *mamm* sat on a chair and watched the ruckus while she knitted a small, pale yellow cap for the baby. Taking advantage of the evening, the entire family had enjoyed a simple picnic outside with turkey sandwiches, homemade sweet pickles, and potato salad.

Taking one more glance at Josiah's house, she stepped away from the window. After covering the rest of the brownies, she quickly washed the dishes. She had hoped Josiah would be back by now. All day she had looked forward to his coming home so they could talk. They had ten years of conversation to catch up on. But as the hours passed, her disappointment and frustration grew. To be honest, her pride was a bit pricked as well. Maybe he wasn't as eager to catch up on things as she was.

After she dried the last dish and put it away, she wiped down the counters, intending to join her family outside. It was a beautiful evening, although slightly cool. She slipped on her sweater but decided not to wear shoes, anticipating the feel of the soft earth and cool grass between her toes.

Suddenly she heard the sound of a buggy approaching. Peering out the window again, her grin grew to full size. Josiah. He'd finally come home. She picked up the plate of four brownies and walked outside toward his house.

"Amanda!" From her seat in a white plastic lawn chair, Katharine motioned for her daughter to come toward her. When Amanda reached her, she asked, "Where are you going?"

"To take Josiah some of the brownies I made earlier." She held up the plate.

"But he just got home. Maybe you should wait until tomorrow?"

Amanda frowned. "I won't be gone long, *Mamm*. I'm sure he would appreciate the treat."

"Is that the only reason you're going over there?"

"What other reason would there be?"

Mamm tilted her head. "To be nosy?"

Amanda sighed at her mother's knowing look. "Aren't you the least bit curious as to what he's been doing all this time? Where he moved to? How his father is doing?"

Her mother's expression grew serious. "Sometimes it's best to let things be, Amanda. If Josiah wants you to know those things, he'll tell you. On his own."

"What do you mean?"

"I know you, Amanda Marie. And while you mean well, sometimes you can push too hard."

"*Mamm*, I'm just going to take him some brownies, not give him the third degree."

Katharine gave her a weary smile. "All right. Then you'd better get on over there, if you're going to go."

Amanda nodded and turned. This wasn't the first time she'd been told she could be too pushy. It was a flaw she worked to correct, with varying degrees of success.

She strode over to the Bontragers' barn, the small rocks and dirt clods on the driveway poking into the bare soles of her feet. Josiah had his back to her as he unhitched his horse, the sleeves of his pale blue shirt rolled up a few inches above his elbows. His movements were efficient, and she could hear him speaking in low tones to the horse as he took a moment to stroke her nose. She approached him quietly so as not to disturb the horse, then tapped him on the shoulder.

He jumped and spun around, nearly dropping the horse's reins. "Amanda! Don't sneak up on me like that!"

Amanda opened her mouth to speak, but the words fled her lips. She had thought him good-looking in the dim light of the barn last night and at a distance this morning, but now that she stood close to him, in the full light of evening, he was twice as handsome. His yellow straw hat was positioned low over his forehead, the brim shading his eyes but not obscuring them. She didn't remember their being that bright shade of green, a lighter shade than the grass tickling her toes. His tan face had a dark shadow of whiskers above his lip and on his jaw.

"Did you need something, Amanda?"

His impatient tone startled her. She looked up into his eyes again, which were flat, almost lifeless. An ache appeared in her chest. She had never seen anyone look so . . . empty.

"Here," she said, holding out the plate of brownies, struggling to keep her tone steady. "I remembered how much you liked my brownies, so I made a pan today. Of course, I had to save most of them for my brothers and sisters, but I was able to spare a few." She smiled, hoping to lighten his somber mood.

Instead, he frowned. "Brothers and sisters? I thought you only had one sister. She was born right before we left, I think. What was her name?"

"Hannah," she said, a little hurt he didn't remember. "After you left, *Mamm* and *Daed* had five more children, and *Mamm*'s expecting another one soon."

His flat expression softened, but only a bit. "Seems they've been busy."

She blushed. "*Ya*."

He took the plate from her hand. "*Danki*, Amanda. That was mighty kind of you."

"Don't mention it. I like to cook. Have you had supper yet?"

"*Nee*, but I'm not really hungry."

"Josiah, you can't go without dinner. Tell you what, while you take care of the horse, I'll go inside and fix you something to eat." Her anxiety lessened. The kitchen had always been her comfort zone.

"You don't have to do that—"

"It's no bother at all," she said over her shoulder, already heading to the house. When he called out her name again, she ignored him, determined not to let him turn down her offer. He'd been out all day, and he shouldn't have to fix his own supper. Not when she could easily do it for him.

Tall weeds and grass tickled her bare legs as she made the way to the back door. She skipped up the two concrete steps and noticed the screen door missing. Glancing around, she saw it lying on the ground next to the house. She picked it up and leaned it against the house before going inside.

She hadn't been in the Bontragers' home since they had moved away. Although her *daed* had tried to take care of the outside, no one had ventured in as far as she knew. The dank, stuffy smell confirmed her suspicion. Stepping inside the small mudroom, she opened another door, which led into the kitchen. She couldn't see much more than shadows in the darkened space, so she searched for a battery-operated lamp or gaslight. Finally, she found a small battery lamp next to the metal sink and flipped on the light. The glow illuminated a thick layer of dust on the counter.

Cobwebs decorated every corner, from the ceiling to the wood-planked floor. Some of the nails had come loose, and the planks themselves were rough and dirty. Grime covered the stove, and two of the cabinets were missing doors.

"Not much to look at, is it?"

She turned around at the sound of Josiah's voice. He stood in the doorway, his expression shadowed from her view, his tone expressing his displeasure. Not that she could blame him. The kitchen, and probably the entire house, was a mess.

Still, there was a stove—and running water, she hoped. She started opening cabinets, looking for any kind of ingredients to prepare what would surely be a simple meal. The first two cabinets revealed only more cobwebs.

The thud of his shoes sounded against the floor as he came up behind her. He put his hand on one of the cabinet doors, his arm hovering over her shoulder. "Don't."

Twirling around, she looked up at him, their faces only inches from each other. Her breath hung in her throat at his nearness, and her heartbeat accelerated. But not out of fear or even anxiety. Attraction crackled between them, pure and simple.

Her reaction to him didn't make sense. This was Josiah, her best friend from childhood. Yet the person standing before her wasn't a child anymore, but a man.

Licking her suddenly dry lips, she asked, "Um, do you keep your food somewhere else?"

"I don't want you making me anything."

His words were low, with a tinge of anger in them. Hurt pricked at her. When did he develop such a short fuse?

They stared at each other for a moment. His hand didn't move, and suddenly her confusion at his tone melted into something else. The last remnants of sunlight shone through the kitchen window, blending with the stark light of the lamp. She could see his face clearly now, saw the darkening of his eyes as he continued to hold her gaze. Then he suddenly dropped his arm and stepped away.

"Best if you go home now, Amanda." His voice sounded slightly hoarse, and a shiver passed through her at his raspy tone.

"But—"

"*Geh!*"

She shrank back. "All right." Spinning around on the balls of her bare feet, she turned to leave. She'd taken no more than three steps when she felt something sharp pierce the bottom of her foot. "Ow!" Lifting up her foot, she spied a dark streak of blood on the bottom of her heel.

"What?" Josiah said, striding toward her. His harsh tone had softened into concern.

"*Nix.* I just cut my foot." As the stinging pain traveled through the bottom of her heel, a drop of blood landed on the floor.

He hesitated, then sighed. "Let me see." He pulled out a chair from the kitchen table and gestured for her to sit.

"It's nothing, Josiah." Her voice held more of an edge than she meant it to. "Just a little cut. I'll go home and put a bandage on it." She didn't want to stay here any longer, especially when he didn't want her to, something he'd made very clear. But when she put her foot down to walk out, she couldn't hide her wince.

He grabbed the lamp from the counter and set it on the table. "Sit down, Amanda."

His sharp tone brooked no argument, and neither did the resolute expression on his face. She sat.

Chapter Four

"GIVE ME YOUR FOOT," JOSIAH SAID, CROUCHING IN FRONT of her.

"Josiah, it's not that bad. You don't have to—"

He grabbed her ankle, effectively cutting her off. Gentling his grip, he balanced the back edge of her heel on his knee and examined the wound. "Cut's about an inch wide. Not bleeding too much."

"See, I told you."

"But you have a big splinter stuck in it." He put her foot down and left the kitchen.

"Josiah?" She frowned when he didn't answer her. Josiah hadn't only changed physically. He had a completely different personality than she remembered. He'd never behaved like he didn't want to be around her, or that she was in his way.

Disappointment threaded through her. She'd been so excited to have her best friend back. Now she wondered if they would ever be friends again.

She looked up as he entered the room carrying a bandage, tweezers, and a brown bottle of peroxide. At her questioning look he said, "I always keep a first aid kit around. Never know when you might need it."

Setting the supplies on the table, he knelt in front of her again and took her foot. He hesitated for a moment, and a wave of embarrassment flowed through her. She'd never been too concerned about her feet before. But with him crouched in front of her, holding her foot in a surprisingly gentle grip, she suddenly became self-conscious.

Silently he took the tweezers and yanked out the splinter so quickly she barely felt it. He unscrewed the white cap of the peroxide and poured it over her heel, apparently not caring that the antiseptic dripped on his pants. A glimmer of hope sparked inside her. Maybe he hadn't changed completely after all.

Her heel still damp, they stayed motionless for a few seconds. Her foot twitched, and he grabbed it, as if worried it would fall off his knee. But instead of letting go, his thumb brushed the instep. An accidental movement, yet so featherlight she shivered.

Clearing his throat, he let go of her foot, snatched the bandage off the kitchen table and used his teeth to open the wrapper. He quickly affixed the bandage on the bottom of her heel, smoothing out the adhesive. "Done," he said, his voice brusque.

"*Danki.*" She put her foot down.

The moment she moved, he jumped up and took several steps backward, not looking at her, erecting a noticeable wall between them.

Inwardly she sighed. He really didn't want her here. She stood and turned around, being more mindful of the splintery floor, and walked toward the door, ready to be gone. But instead of leaving, she hesitated at the doorway. Facing him, she asked, "What did I do wrong, Josiah? Why are you so upset with me?"

❧

Josiah couldn't answer right away. He had fully expected her to leave, and a part of him had wanted her to. But another, stronger part wanted her to stay. Confusion and hurt were displayed on her lovely face. He had no idea how to soothe them away.

Over the years since he'd left Paradise, Josiah had thought of Amanda often. They'd had more than a close friendship, at least from his standpoint. At the tender age of twelve, he had decided to marry her, but of course he didn't tell her that. There would be time for that, he had thought. Plenty of time for him to make her fall in love with him.

Then his mother died, and everything changed. Amanda had been there for him during that dark time, more than she realized. And after he left Paradise, he had dreamed of the day he would see her again. But as time passed, he realized how impossible that would be. So he tried to push her out of his mind. He'd even tried dating a couple of girls, hoping to quash his feelings for Amanda, but the idea of courting anyone else felt like a betrayal. Then his life had gotten so out of control he refused to allow himself to have feelings for anyone. Even so, Amanda had never been all that far from his thoughts, or his heart.

And now he was back in Paradise, and Amanda was back in his life. Before leaving his house that morning, he had seen her putting out the wash, and it had taken everything he had to keep from staring at her. He'd had to dig deeper still when he tended to her foot. He couldn't let her leave with a bleeding foot, especially since she had injured it on his pathetic excuse for a floor. When he knelt in front of her, trying to ignore her small, delicate foot, he had to fight for the resolve to keep his feelings from breaking the surface.

Then he had stroked her instep. The movement had been instinctive, and it was done before he could stop himself. At that point he knew he couldn't be that close to her again. He'd spent more than a decade smothering any feelings and tightly controlling his reactions. Yet in the span of a few minutes, Amanda Graber had threatened to undo all of that, without even knowing it. He couldn't afford to let that happen.

"Josiah?" Her steps were tentative, and not only because of the sad state of his kitchen floor. He'd been so cold to her, no wonder she was skittish. "Josiah, I don't understand. I thought after all these years you would be happy to see me."

"I am." The words were out before he knew it. Clamping down his lips, he didn't say anything else. Then she smiled, and his knees almost buckled.

"I'm so glad to hear that," she said as she moved toward him. She sighed, a light, pleasing sound that sent a ripple down his spine. "I thought maybe I'd somehow made you mad without knowing it."

He shook his head, unable to let her believe she was at fault for his keeping his distance. "It's just that . . . I'm tired, I guess. It was a long trip here, and as you can see"—he held out his arms wide—"I have a lot of work to do on the house and barn."

"I can help you."

She was now standing only a few feet away from him. Close enough that he could see flecks of green in her hazel eyes, which were rimmed by thick lashes. Another detail he either had forgotten or had been too young to pay attention to. But now he couldn't stop staring at her. "I appreciate the offer, Amanda, but I won't be needing help. It'll take me awhile, but I'll get it done."

"Well, that doesn't make any sense to me." She put her hands on her hips. "I'm as able-bodied as you, and you said yourself you have a lot of work to do. You know what my *grossmammi* used to say when I was little?"

He crossed his arms over his chest. "Many hands make light work?"

"*Nee,* although that's true too. She used to say that only a fool refuses a neighbor's outstretched hand. I remember a lot of things about you, Josiah Bontrager. But I don't remember you being a fool."

His father would have begged to differ, but he didn't say that out loud. "I don't think it's foolish to not want to put you to any trouble."

"It's no trouble. Besides, my sisters and brothers can help. They're out of school on the weekends. Actually, they're out of school for the rest of the week because their teacher has the flu, so we can start right away."

"How many brothers and sisters did you say you had?"

"Six." She ticked their names and ages off on her fingertips. "Hannah is ten; Rachel, nine; Andrew turned eight last month;

Thomas is six, although he'll insist he's six and a half; Christopher is four; and Jacob is eighteen months. *Mamm*'s expecting number eight in July."

Josiah's eyes widened. "That's incredible."

"I know. They really thought I would be the only one, especially after trying for so long, but then once she got pregnant with Hannah, the babies kept coming."

"So what's it like having all those brothers and sisters underfoot?" He couldn't hold back his fascination or his wonder at Amanda's enthusiasm as she talked about her brothers and sisters. When he'd left Paradise, he and Amanda had been only children. He couldn't fathom having so many younger siblings.

"*Wunderbaar!*" She clasped her hands together for emphasis. "Sure, it's a lot of work, especially since *Mamm* doesn't feel well right now. She usually gets extremely tired in the last trimester. But I help out as much as I can, and I really love taking care of them. I hope to have a large family someday."

Josiah bit the inside of his cheek. He remembered playing house with Amanda when they were kids, at her insistence, of course. A stupid game, he'd thought at the time, but he gave in because she would always agree to climb trees with him afterward. So it didn't come as a surprise that she would want a large family. And while as a boy he'd felt dumb playing house, now he longed to have a wife and children of his own. No, scratch that. He had longed to have a family of his own with Amanda. But as he did with every other yearning, he suffocated it. Marrying Amanda wasn't in his future. Not out of choice, but out of necessity.

"I know Andrew and Thomas are young, but they're hard workers," Amanda said. "They've been helping *Daed* around the house since they were small. And I'm sure Hannah and Rachel won't mind working in here with me." She strolled around the kitchen, ideas obviously rolling around in her mind. She ran her fingertips over the dusty countertops. "First we'll need to scrub everything down. Then we can fill the pantry with food and figure out a place to put the cooler so you can keep ice and the cold stuff. And you'll need some sort of stove." She opened up the rusty gas oven and peered inside, then coughed. "We'll clean this out too." Standing, she looked at him, her mouth curved in a lovely smile. "Before long you'll smell the sweet aroma of apple pies baking."

"I don't bake." This was getting out of hand. He had merely wanted her not to feel bad; he hadn't meant to open the door for her to do all this for him.

"Silly, I know that. Remember the time we made cookies together at my house?"

He nodded, his mind transported to the past. They had been ten years old, and although he'd followed the recipe and done everything Amanda's mother had said, his cookies were hard and tasteless, while Amanda's had been delicious. He had never baked before—his father believed only women should cook and would get angry when he'd catch Josiah helping his mother in the kitchen—and after that failure he never attempted it again.

"I'll make the pies," she volunteered. "Is apple still your favorite?"

He hesitated before answering. The idea of coming into this desolate house and having a fresh-baked pie waiting greatly appealed to him, wearing down his already thinning resolve. Perhaps one pie wouldn't hurt. "*Ya.*"

"Then it's settled." She brushed past him, giving him another one of her wonderful smiles, the kind that not only brightened her face but lit up the entire room. "The kids and I will be here tomorrow morning," she said over her shoulder as she headed for the door.

"Amanda, wait."

She turned around.

He almost told her no. He could repair the house and barn by himself. He had the tools, the skills, and—after selling his horse and the tiny mobile home he and his father had shared in Indiana—he had enough money for materials. But it would take him twice as long to complete the renovations if he did them alone. That would make it twice as long before he could sell the house and leave Paradise for good. If he had Amanda and her siblings' help, he would finish much sooner and finally be on the road to Ohio.

"Did you want to tell me something, Josiah?" Amanda asked.

"*Ya*," he said, finally making up his mind. "I . . . I'll see you in the morning."

With another smile and a wave of her hand, she disappeared outside.

He leaned against the countertop and blew out a breath. Deep down he appreciated the help. If only it hadn't come in the form of Amanda Graber. At least she would be inside most of the time while he worked on the exterior of the house. The less contact they had with each other, the better off they both would be.

༄

The next morning Amanda awoke well before sunrise. She had to get all her chores done before she went to Josiah's and got started on the kitchen. What a mess! She had assumed there would be some problems with the outside of the house after ten years of neglect, but she hadn't thought the inside would be so bad. It made her wonder if the interior had been in bad shape before Josiah and his father had moved away.

But that didn't matter anymore. She had discussed her plan to help Josiah with her *mamm* and *daed* the night before, and they both agreed it would be a good idea. Not only was it the neighborly thing to do, but it would be good for Andrew and Thomas to learn a little about repairing a house—not to mention that it would keep them out of trouble. Hannah would stay home and help with Christopher and Jacob, but Rachel would be allowed to assist Amanda, who had spent the rest of the night creating a long list of what needed to be done.

Amanda put on her *kapp* before retrieving her shoes from the closet. She'd learned her lesson about going barefoot at Josiah's, and she would make sure her siblings also protected their feet when they went over there. As she slipped on her black shoes, she felt a tiny stab of pain on the bottom of her heel, reminding her of Josiah's tender care of her foot. While she didn't completely understand why he behaved so strangely toward her, she was glad he had agreed to let her help. She didn't think she could stand seeing him working so hard by himself when he didn't have to.

She dashed down the stairs, careful not to trip in the dark. When she reached the kitchen she turned on the lamp and started breakfast. Before long everyone in the house had awakened and settled down for a morning meal of flaky biscuits, flavorful sausage gravy, and lightly scrambled eggs.

After everyone had finished eating, and Hannah and Rachel had cleaned the kitchen, Amanda drew Rachel, Andrew, and Thomas to the side. "We're going over to Josiah's house today," she said, bending down in front of them so she could meet their gazes.

"We are?" Andrew asked, tugging on one of his black suspenders. "Why?"

"To help him fix his house. He has a lot of repairs to do, and it would be hard for him to do them on his own."

"Will I get to use a hammer?" Thomas asked, his eyes filling with excitement.

"As long as you don't hit his thumb with it like you did *Daed*'s, then I'm sure you can."

"That was an accident," Thomas said, guilt crossing his cherubic features.

"I know, honey. And *Daed* did too. Just be careful, and do what Josiah tells you to." She eyed her brothers directly. "Without argument."

"We will," they said in unison.

"What am I supposed to do?" Rachel asked.

"You and I will be cleaning the kitchen. It needs a lot of work."

Rachel nodded. "Are we going over there now?"

"As soon as you get your shoes on."

"Aww, I don't wanna wear shoes," Thomas said.

"You have to." She pointed to her foot. "I have them on, and with good reason. Yesterday I got a splinter in my heel. There's also rusted nails and broken glass in the yard. You don't want to cut open your feet, do you?"

Thomas and Andrew both ran to get their shoes.

She waited for her siblings to get ready and watched Hannah take Jacob out of his high chair, knowing her sister was probably glad she didn't have to help Josiah. Hannah had never been keen on doing chores, but she didn't mind watching her baby brothers.

"We're ready." Andrew and Thomas ran from the living room to the back door of the kitchen, skidding to a stop in front of her. Rachel, more mature at age nine, ambled a bit more slowly.

"Okay, let's go!" As Amanda trailed behind her sister and brothers, carrying a blue bucket filled with rags and cleaning supplies, a strange feeling formed in the pit of her stomach. She couldn't shake the feeling that Josiah had agreed to this reluctantly. What if he had changed his mind overnight? The boys would be disappointed . . . and so would she.

Andrew and Thomas chased each other in the tall grass while she and Rachel went to the back entrance. The rusted screen door still leaned against the house, and in the early morning light she noticed a fist-sized hole in the screen. She knocked on the wooden door. Once, then twice. After the third time she turned the knob, finding it unlocked.

"Stay out here for a minute," she instructed Rachel, then tilted her head in the direction of her brothers. "Keep an eye on them, make sure they don't go into the barn. We shouldn't disturb Josiah's horse."

Rachel nodded and walked toward Andrew and Thomas, who were now playfully pushing each other.

Amanda opened the door and stepped inside, once again greeted by the musty, dank smell. None of the lights were on, and she didn't see any sign that Josiah had been in the kitchen since she'd left last night. She turned on the lamp, then went to the window over the kitchen sink. With a few strong pushes she opened it, breathing in the welcome fresh air.

Aided by the steady stream of sunlight through the window and by the lamp, she could see that she had underestimated the amount of work she and Rachel would have to do. The light blue paint on the walls underneath the wood cabinets had peeled off in spots, and dust and cobwebs coated everything. Further examination showed several piles of small black pellets, a clear indication that mice had taken up residence. Rodents and bugs outdoors had never bothered her, but vermin had no place in a house, especially the kitchen. A good scrubbing down of everything would help, but she suspected Josiah would have to set out a few traps to get rid of them completely.

The squeak of a floorboard sounded, and she whirled around to see Josiah entering the kitchen. His streaked hair stood up in tufts all over his head, his suspenders were dangling around his waist and legs, and his shirt was buttoned partway. Clearly he had just woken up.

He rubbed his eyes and looked at her. "Amanda?"

"*Guder mariye!*" she said. "I knocked a few times, but no one answered, so I decided to go ahead and get started."

"Guess I was more tired than I thought." He looked at her for a moment, then he quickly buttoned up the rest of his shirt and slid on his suspenders.

"Andrew, Thomas, and Rachel are outside," she said. "The boys are excited to help."

Josiah ran a hand through his hair, trying unsuccessfully to tame the tufts. His wavy hair looked so thick and soft. As he continued to thread his fingers through the unruly locks, she wondered what the texture felt like.

She blushed and looked away. She had no business thinking about touching Josiah's hair. Still, she had difficulty getting the temptation out of her mind. Hoping the flaming color on her cheeks had ebbed, she looked at Josiah. "I thought I'd start by wiping down the counters."

He shrugged. "Whatever you want to do."

Her shoulders sagged. Back to treating her like a stranger. In fact, now he wouldn't even look at her. Instead he went to the back door and grabbed the pair of work boots that had been placed nearby. He sat down on one of the wooden kitchen chairs and pulled them on. "You say your brothers are outside?"

"*Ya*," she said, trying to hide her disenchantment at his mood.

"I'll send your sister in to see you." He grabbed the yellow straw hat hanging on the peg near the door and walked outside.

Amanda frowned, crossing her arms over her chest. Not a thank-you or a good-bye or even a see-you-later. He could at least show a little appreciation. She was half tempted to walk out of the kitchen and take her siblings back home.

But that wouldn't be right. She had told him they would help, and she would keep her word. Closing her eyes, she prayed aloud, as she often did when she as frustrated. "Dear heavenly Father, I don't know what's going on with Josiah, but You do. He's changed so much, and I don't know why. I have no idea where he's been all these years, and for some reason he doesn't want to tell me. Help me to help him with whatever he needs and to do it with a selfless heart."

Chapter Five

FOR MOST OF THE MORNING JOSIAH FELT LIKE HE HAD two little shadows. Andrew and Thomas were more than eager to help. Whatever task he gave them, no matter how mundane, they did without complaint. So far they had picked up all the sticks in the backyard and put them in a pile a few feet from the house. They also collected as much small debris as they could and put it in a glass mason jar. Surprisingly, there weren't too many rusty nails or shards of glass, and those were mostly near the house where a window had been broken and a couple of shutters had fallen off. Undoubtedly there had been a few storms over the years, and heavy winds could do a lot of damage. He should be grateful the house wasn't in worse shape. But when he took a look at all the work he needed to do, gratitude was far from his mind.

"Here, Mr. Josiah." Andrew held the half-filled quart jar out to him. "What else you want us to do?"

He glanced around the yard, pushing back the brim of his hat and letting the air dry his damp forehead. Most of the morning had been spent cleaning the front and back yards enough so he could use the push mower on the overgrown grass. He sized Andrew up. For eight, the boy seemed tall, reminding him of Amanda's father. He also seemed to possess his *daed*'s work ethic, something Josiah had appreciated in David Graber even as a boy. "Ever use a push mower?"

Andrew nodded. "For a long time. Since I was seven."

Josiah hid a smile. "Sounds like you have some experience, then."

"*Ya*, I do. Lots. And your lawn needs mowing bad, Mr. Josiah."

He let out a deep breath, maintaining the serious tone of the conversation. "I think you're the man for the job. I bought a brand-new push mower yesterday. Want to break it in for me?"

Showing a grin that featured two gaping holes, one on the top and one on the bottom, Andrew bobbed his head up and down. "I sure would."

"It's in the barn. Wait here and I'll bring it out to you."

"What about me, Mr. Josiah?" Thomas wiped his nose with the back of his hand.

Josiah squatted down in front of him. "What would you like to do?"

"Use a hammer," Thomas said matter-of-factly.

Rubbing his chin, Josiah said, "All right. I've got some rotted boards on the front porch that need replacing. You can pull the nails out for me. How does that sound?"

Thomas nodded. "Sounds *gut*, Mr. Josiah."

Josiah chucked the boy under the chin and stood, his mood lighter than it had been in days. Something about being around these boys, with their earnest and genuine eagerness to help, combined with the beautiful, crisp fall weather, elevated his spirits. "Be right back," he said and went to get the mower. A few moments later Andrew went to work on the lawn while Josiah and Thomas tackled the front porch.

Josiah held up the hammer and pointed to the claw. "Have you ever used this end before?"

The boy shook his head. Unlike Andrew, Thomas said few words, something Josiah could relate to.

"See that nail sticking up over there?" Josiah pointed the hammer at the flat head of a bent, rusty nail poking through the end of a long plank of wood. A soft breeze kicked up, and a few brown leaves danced across the porch. "You get it out like this." He demonstrated how to use the hammer to remove the nail, then handed the tool to Thomas. "Now, find another one and try it yourself."

Thomas searched the porch until he found a second protruding nail. He squatted down and tilted back his small yellow straw hat. After a few attempts he slid the claw around the nail. With a couple of tugs, the nail slid free, due more to the softness of the rotted wood than to Thomas's natural strength.

"*Sehr gut*," Josiah said, happy to see the surprise in the boy's blue eyes when the nail gave way. "Ready to do some more?"

Thomas grinned. Unlike his older brother, he still had all his baby teeth. "*Ya*. This is *schpass*."

For the next hour or so Josiah and Thomas removed nails while Josiah kept one ear out for Andrew and the mower. He wasn't used to being responsible for anyone but himself.

When he'd removed the last nail, the front door opened with a loud squeak. He turned to see Amanda standing in the doorway behind the screen door. Hopping to his feet, he opened it himself, in case it fell loose from its hinges like the back door had.

"You *buwe* hungry?"

When Thomas nodded enthusiastically, Josiah inwardly cringed. He had nothing to eat in the house. Most times he ate fast food or sandwiches and chips, and he hadn't even planned for either of those today. He stepped forward and looked at Amanda. "Give me a minute to hook up the buggy, and I'll go into town and get us something."

She waved him off. A damp lock of light brown hair had escaped from beneath her *kapp*, and she tucked it behind her left ear. That and the rosy glow of her cheeks were a testament to how hard she'd been working. "Don't bother. I already have lunch prepared."

"You do?"

"*Ya*. Rachel ran home and brought over a few things. It's nothing fancy, but it's food."

Thomas dashed past Amanda, not waiting for an invitation to go inside. She turned around and called, "Wait on the rest of us, Thomas. And don't forget to wash your hands!"

"I'll need to go to the pump," Josiah said, moving to leave. "I haven't had the water hooked up to the house yet. *Daed* had it disconnected when we left."

"Took care of that too. There's a bucket with clean water by the sink, along with some bar soap." She glanced down at his hands. "Don't forget to clean yours too." She winked at him, then turned around and went inside.

This time Josiah couldn't stop his smile as he followed her inside the house. When he reached the kitchen, he blinked. How she had managed to do so much in such a short period of time amazed him. All the cobwebs were gone. The table and chairs were wiped clean, along with the countertops and cabinet doors. He glanced down at the uneven wood floor. Despite looking in desperate need of repair, he couldn't detect a speck of dirt on it.

"Thomas, I know you're a big boy, but let me help you anyway."

He glanced at Amanda, who was helping Thomas rinse his soapy hands. A blue bucket—not one of his, he noticed—sat next to the metal double-basin sink, which had been polished to a brilliant shine. A bar of gold-colored soap lay next to the faucet.

Amanda lifted the bucket and poured water over Thomas's sudsy hands, then handed him a towel. "Now, go remind Andrew that he said he'd be in here five minutes ago. I think he's having way too much fun with the lawn mower."

Josiah chuckled, and Amanda turned around and looked at him, her expression soft. "Nice to hear you laugh, Josiah."

Actually, it felt good to laugh. He hadn't laughed in such a long time, longer than he cared to remember. There hadn't been much to be happy about in his life over the past few years.

"Your turn," she said, pointing to the bucket. "Hands. Now."

He smirked. "I'm not twelve, Amanda. You don't have to remind me. Twice," he added.

A flush came over her face. "Sorry. I guess I get carried away sometimes."

"Sometimes?" a female voice said.

Josiah turned to see Rachel placing plastic forks beside the white paper plates on the table. She was several inches shorter than Amanda, with darker brown hair and a more olive tone to her skin. In some ways she reminded him of Amanda at the same age.

"Very funny, Rachel." But Amanda didn't seem to mind her sister's good-natured teasing.

The boys bounded inside as Josiah finished washing his hands. He helped Andrew with the almost-empty bucket. He would take it out after lunch and refill it for Amanda. No need for her to fetch more water, not after everything she'd already done.

They crowded around the small, circular kitchen table. As a family of three, the Bontragers hadn't needed a large table, but it was a tight fit for five. Amanda sat across from Josiah, with Thomas to her left and Rachel to her right. Andrew was sandwiched between him and Rachel.

"Let's pray." Amanda held out her hands, and Rachel and Thomas quickly entwined their fingers with hers.

Josiah swallowed. When had he last prayed, much less said grace before a meal? Since his mother's death, his father had given up on praying, and on God altogether. Josiah hadn't taken his grief that far, but he had come close over the years. And while he had joined the church when he turned twenty, it had been more out of a desire to fulfill his mother's wishes than to become closer to the Lord.

"Mr. Josiah?"

He looked down at Andrew's outstretched hand.

"Aren't you gonna pray with us?"

Josiah glanced at Amanda, who gave him an expectant look. He noticed something else behind her eyes. Curiosity . . . and compassion. He averted his gaze and grasped Andrew's small hand, then Thomas's even smaller one. Regardless of his standing with the Lord right now, he didn't want to keep the children waiting on their food.

"Josiah, will you pray, please?"

He looked at Amanda again, then glanced at the children. Shifting in his seat, he slowly bowed his head, wondering what he would say.

Suddenly a prayer from childhood came to mind. "God is great God is *gut* let us thank Him for our food amen," he said all in one breath, then released the boys' hands.

"We say that prayer at home sometimes, Mr. Josiah," Thomas remarked. "Although we don't say it that fast."

Everyone laughed, and he felt the tension drain from his body. Surveying the food on the table, his mouth started to water. Diagonal wedges of tuna fish sandwiches were piled high on one plate, a bowl of small sweet pickles situated beside it. A bag of potato chips lay open near Rachel, and in the center of the table was a pitcher half filled with lemonade. Either she or Rachel had already poured the drink into everyone's red plastic cup.

Amanda handed him the plate of sandwiches. "Tuna fish. Hope you still like it."

Nodding, he took two halves. "My favorite sandwich."

"I remember."

He met her gaze. Sweet heavens, she was so pretty. And so capable. Another quality he hadn't been old enough to appreciate fully when they were younger. But then again, she had always approached everything with confidence, whether it had been baking cookies, climbing trees, or fishing in the stream two miles down the road. He couldn't remember her ever failing at anything.

He passed the sandwiches to Andrew, who only took one half. Clearly the young boy didn't care too much for tuna fish.

Soon everyone had what they wanted and started eating. Josiah tried to keep his attention focused on his food and not on the woman across the table who kept bringing out so many emotions in him.

But he was finding that impossible to do.

⁓

Josiah continued to confound Amanda. One moment she would see a glimpse of the Josiah she used to know—his deep-throated chuckle, his crooked smile, his kindness as he dealt with her brothers. She had watched him and Thomas through the front window in the living room as they had removed the nails, and the gentle yet respectful way he dealt with her six-year-old brother tugged at her heart. A natural with children, something he probably wasn't even aware of. Although she had warned her brothers not to give Josiah a hard time, she knew their compliance had been due more to his treatment of them than to her directive.

With Rachel's help they had made quick work of surface cleaning in the kitchen, which had given her enough time to put together a decent lunch. Remembering how much Josiah had loved tuna fish sandwiches—which she didn't particularly care for—she had asked Rachel to go home and bring her the ingredients for lunch.

Taking tiny bites of her half sandwich, she thought about his discomfort with praying. She had never noticed it before, at least that she could remember. But when they were kids, they said rote prayers, repeating what their parents said at the supper table and what they had heard during church. His rapid-fire prayer had tickled her brothers' funny bones, but it made her curious. Had he joined the church? He dressed and lived as an Amish man, but that didn't necessarily mean he had been baptized. More questions. She wondered if she would ever discover the answers.

Josiah, who had kept his head lowered during most of the meal, pushed the last bite of sandwich into his mouth. After washing it down with a gulp of lemonade from his cup, he looked at her. "*Danki* for the lunch. It was *sehr gut*."

"You're welcome." She left her mostly uneaten sandwich on her plate, planning to throw it in the pig trough before she went home so it wouldn't go to waste.

He pushed back from the table and stood. "I better get back to work." Glancing at the boys, he added, "Andrew and Thomas have put in a full day already. They don't have to help any more if they don't want to."

Seeing the disappointment on their faces, Amanda said, "I think they have enough energy to work a little while longer. Right, *buwe*?"

"*Ya*," Andrew said, standing. "I still need to mow on the other side of the house."

Thomas nodded his agreement.

Josiah stroked his chin, something she noticed he did when deep in thought. She surmised he was still reluctant to accept their assistance. But surely he saw how quickly they completed the work with all of them helping out.

"Okay," he finally said. "Andrew, finish up the lawn. But then you're done for the day. A *bu*'s got to have time to play. Thomas, you can come with me to the barn. I've got to feed the horse."

"Does she have a name?" Thomas asked.

Josiah shook his head. "Not yet. Having trouble coming up with one. Maybe you can help me out with that too."

Thomas smiled, his chubby cheeks puffing up.

Amanda's heart warmed as she watched Josiah and her little brother leave the kitchen together. Josiah had said exactly the right thing to Thomas. Instead of dismissing him, he had included him, making him feel important and needed. Wasn't that what everyone wanted?

She and Rachel cleared the table, which had been easy to do since they had used mostly paper products. "Why don't we work on the pantry and cabinets next?" she said to Rachel. "Tomorrow I'll tackle the stove."

The rest of the afternoon went quickly. By late afternoon Andrew and Thomas had already gone home, presumably to grab a snack and play outside. Amanda planned to finish scrubbing down the inside of the cabinet under the sink before calling it a day.

She climbed practically halfway inside the deep cabinet, trying to reach the very back, when she felt something touch her shoulder. Jerking up, she hit her head. "Ow!" As she backed out of the cabinet, she said, "Rachel, don't scare me like that!"

"Are you all right?"

Looking over her shoulder, she saw it wasn't Rachel who had tapped her, but Josiah. Rubbing the top of her head, she nodded. "I'm fine." Then she chuckled. "We seem to be in the habit of startling each other."

He didn't share her humor. "I'm really sorry." He peered down at her, examining the sore spot. "Are you sure you're all right? Sounded like you smacked your head pretty *gut*."

"No worries. I've got a hard head." She grinned. "Or so I've been told."

His lips twitched, and she thought for a moment he might smile.

She started to rise, and his hand came under her arm to assist her. When she stood, she realized how close they were to each other. That funny tickle in her stomach that seemed to always appear when they were near each other returned. She met his gaze for a moment, unable to pull away. Once again she reminded herself that this was Josiah Bontrager. She had no business having these crazy feelings about him. And once again her heart refused to listen.

He pulled away first. Averting his eyes, he stepped back. "Glad you're not hurt."

"You could never hurt me, Josiah."

His head shot up, and he stared at her again. And in that moment she saw something in the depths of his eyes. Pain. Stark and raw, it disappeared when he deadened his expression again. "You should be getting home. It's near suppertime, and I'm sure your *mamm* and *daed* will want you there."

"*Ya*, they're probably expecting me," Amanda said, still concerned about what he had unwittingly revealed. What could have happened to cause him such pain? Did he still grieve his mother's death so deeply after all these years? Possibly, but she suspected that wasn't all.

He pushed his straw hat farther back on his head. "Then I don't want to keep you."

"Why don't you join us? I don't know what we're having, but *Mamm*'s cooking tonight, and I'm sure it will be delicious."

"I wouldn't want to impose."

"You wouldn't be imposing, Josiah. Even though you've been gone for a long time, you're still a part of our family." She stepped toward him. "That hasn't changed, and it never will."

Chapter Six

JOSIAH FOUGHT AGAINST THE REGRET AND LONGING coursing through him. More than anything he wanted to say yes to Amanda, to take her up on her invitation and have supper with her and her family. Especially with her. No matter how hard he tried to look at her through the filter of childhood innocence, he couldn't do it. He didn't see his friend standing in front of him, or even the object of a schoolboy crush. He saw a woman. A beautiful, kind, caring woman who was everything he wanted . . . and needed.

He never should have agreed to let her help him with the house. Getting the renovations done quickly wasn't worth the pain her presence in his life caused. And spending the evening with the Grabers was the last thing he needed to do. He had gotten a taste of how wonderful being with a real family could be at lunch earlier that day. He didn't want to put himself through that again, being on the outside looking in, knowing they had something he desperately wanted but couldn't have.

"*Danki* for the invitation, but I planned to get something in town," he said, turning his back to her. He couldn't look at those beautiful hazel eyes anymore—eyes filled with invitation and promise. He doubted she realized how she looked at him, how her feelings were revealed so clearly to him. He hadn't imagined the spark that had ignited when they stood so close together in the kitchen.

"You're going to eat fast food? You'd prefer that over a home-cooked meal?"

No, he didn't prefer that at all. But he had no other choice. "I have a couple more things to pick up in town," he said, coming up with the excuse on the fly. And because he couldn't stand there in his kitchen, wanting more than anything to say yes to any request she made of him, he headed toward the door. "*Danki* for everything." Unable to help himself, he glanced over his shoulder.

Her bright expression faltered. "You're welcome, Josiah. But you don't have to keep thanking me. It's a pleasure to help out a . . . neighbor."

He turned and looked at her. The emotion in her eyes was anything but neighborly, and it tugged at his heart. He had to get out of there, fast. "Shops will be closing soon. I need to get to town before five." He stood near the back door of the kitchen, gesturing with his outstretched hand for her to go.

"Oh. Okay." She looked at him with uncertainty one more time before sliding past him and walking out the door.

Her arm brushed his, and he closed his eyes. He had faced challenges in his life—a lot of difficult challenges— but keeping his feelings for Amanda securely wrapped was by far the hardest.

A moment later he followed her outside and surveyed his backyard. Andrew had done an excellent job mowing. The shorn grass was already turning brown, and tomorrow it would need to be raked up. But the boy had done the hard work. Pushing that mower through grass that had in some places reached his waist couldn't have been an easy task.

Amanda faced him, the afternoon sun shining through the rustling branches of the oak trees behind her. He couldn't help but breathe in the sweet scent of the freshly mown grass as he gazed at her. For a fleeting moment he forgot everything, concentrating on nature's beauty as well as the natural beauty in front of him.

"So I'll see you tomorrow morning," she said. "Same time?"

Her words broke the spell. "I don't—"

"Josiah Bontrager, if you tell me *nee* again, I'll . . . I'll . . . well, I don't know what I'll do, but you won't like it! You're making me *ab im kopp*, you know that?" Striding toward him, she stopped barely a foot away. "You never used to be like this, Josiah. Stubborn. Bullheaded. Cold. And above all, frustrating."

He looked away, not liking her description of him even though it was accurate. "People change, Amanda."

"*Ya*, but they don't change into completely different people. Not unless . . ." Her tone softened. "Not unless something happened to them." She moved closer. "What happened to you, Josiah?"

His jaw jerked, and he couldn't face her.

She laid her hand on his shoulder. "Josiah, we're friends. Whatever you went through, you can tell me. I want to help."

The warmth of her hand seeped through the cotton cloth of his shirt. Stepping back, he forced her to drop her hand. "You can't help me, Amanda. You can't change the past."

She sighed. "*Nee*, I can't. But you don't have to live in the past either."

The soft sigh she expelled covered him like a warm blanket on a cold winter's night. He looked at her. So sweet, so innocent. She had no idea what she had asked of him. He had made a vow to himself not to reveal those deep secrets, and he wasn't about to break that promise.

She moved toward him, placing her hand back on his arm. "Talk to me, Josiah. You never had trouble doing that before. Remember how much time we spent just talking? Lying on a soft bed of grass on a summer night, looking at millions of stars, sharing our hopes and—"

"Stop." He grabbed her hand, a little harder than he meant to. But he couldn't help it. Every word she spoke dug into him.

Shock registered on her face, and she tried to twist out of his grip. "Josiah, you're hurting me."

He glanced down at his hand locked around her wrist. Stricken, he released her, not missing the red ring circling her pale skin. He staggered backward. "Amanda, I'm . . ." Unable to finish, he turned and ran to the barn. Only when he reached the inside, away from her view, did he allow himself to breathe.

She had said he would never hurt her. Just now, he had proven what he always knew—he could.

Amanda rubbed her wrist as she watched Josiah flee. It didn't hurt that much, only tingled, and she had been surprised more than anything. Why had he grabbed her like that? She was tempted to follow him but thought better of it. In the old days she would have chased him down and demanded that he talk to her. But his reaction gave her pause, and she remembered her mother's warning about being too nosy. Instead she headed for the house, trying to figure out what to do.

As she passed through the backyard, she barely noticed her siblings running around and playing by the swing set. She had to find a way to help Josiah. But how, when she had no idea what was wrong?

Still thinking, she walked into the kitchen, where the scent of fried chicken filled the air. Her mother stood next to the stove, a hot pot of oil bubbling over the gas burner. She dipped a chicken leg into a shallow dish holding beaten eggs, then rolled it in a separate dish of flour. Grease spattered as the floured piece hit the hot oil. Katharine wiped her forehead with the back of her hand, looking less tired than she had been lately.

Her mother turned her head, apparently noticing her for the first time. "Amanda. I'm glad you're home. I could use some help. I know you've been over at Josiah's all day, but if you could fix the corn, I would appreciate it."

Amanda nodded and walked to the pantry to retrieve two quart jars of home-canned corn. As she dumped the vegetables into a large pot, she continued to consider her dilemma.

"Andrew and Thomas seem to have had a *gut* time today," Katharine remarked, flouring another piece of chicken. "They couldn't stop talking about *Mr*. Josiah. I've never heard them get that tickled from doing a day's hard work."

"He's *sehr gut* with them." Amanda added a soft pat of butter to the corn and stirred. "And they worked really hard. So did Rachel. We got a lot accomplished in the kitchen."

"There's much satisfaction in a job well done." Katharine cast Amanda a sidelong glance. "You always do a *gut* job, *Dochder*."

"*Danki, Mamm*." She set the pot on top of the stove and turned on the burner, staring at the small yellow kernels as if they held the answers she needed.

"Amanda?"

Her mother's voice jerked her out of her thoughts. "*Ya?*"

"Is everything okay? You haven't said much since you got home." Using a small wire mesh basket with a long wooden handle attached, she fished out three pieces of golden brown chicken and put them on a platter covered with two layers of paper towel. "That's not like you."

"I just have a lot on my mind." Amanda stirred the corn again, which had started to bubble.

"I suspect Josiah's on your mind."

Amanda looked at her mother and sighed. "*Ya*, he is. He's different, *Mamm*. A lot different than he used to be."

"Of course he is, Amanda. You are too. The last time you saw each other you were barely teenagers. Now you're both adults. You can't expect him to be the same *bu* he was back then."

"I don't. But I don't expect him to be a stranger, either."

Katharine dropped two more chicken pieces into the large pot. The cooking oil bubbled and splattered. When she didn't say anything, Amanda took the opportunity to explain.

"I've missed him, *Mamm*. A lot. I didn't realize how much until he came back." She turned the heat down under the corn and faced her mother. "He never said good-bye, you know. I want to know why he left so suddenly. And what he's been doing over the past ten years." She frowned. "But he's built this shell around himself. Like a turtle. And just when I think we're to the point where we can have a real conversation, he ducks inside."

"Maybe he feels threatened."

"But why?" Amanda held up her hands. "How can he feel threatened by his best friend?"

"*Former* best friend. Don't forget that." Katharine checked on the chicken, then placed one hand behind her on the small of her back.

"Here, *Mamm*. Let me finish the chicken. You sit down." Amanda led her to a chair by the kitchen table.

Her mother plopped down. "*Danki*, Amanda. Really, I'm fine. Just a twinge in my back."

"All the more reason for me to finish supper. There're only a few pieces left anyway. You go ahead and rest."

Amanda returned to the stove and dredged the last three chicken legs in flour and dropped them in the oil. Wiping her floured hands on a towel, she turned to her mother, picking up the thread of their conversation. She couldn't let it go just yet. "Do you know why Josiah and his *daed* left so abruptly?"

"Even if I did, it's not my place to say, Amanda. I don't indulge in gossip, and neither should you."

"But this isn't idle gossip, *Mamm*. I can tell there's something really wrong with Josiah, but he won't talk to me."

"Did you stop to think he has his reasons?" *Mamm* looked at her again. "Amanda, I know you care for him. You two were so close when you were young, so it makes sense that you would be curious. But even though you shared that closeness at one time, a lot has happened, in both your lives. Maybe you weren't meant to be friends beyond your childhood."

Amanda shook her head. "I don't believe that. I can't." She

paused. "I think God brought him back to Paradise for a reason, and not just to fix up his house."

Katharine looked skeptical. "Do you really believe that? Or is it wishful thinking?" She rose from her chair and walked over to Amanda, putting her hand on her shoulder. "You have such a beautiful heart, *kind*. You want to solve everyone's problems because you care so much. But there are some things in this world you can't fix. You might have to accept that this is one of them."

A couple of hours later, after they finished eating supper and washing the dishes, the rest of the family gathered in the living room to listen to *Daed* read from the Bible, something they did at least one night a week. Although Amanda usually joined them, she didn't this time, and instead grabbed her jacket from the peg by the back door and slipped outside to the swing set.

The sun had dipped beneath the horizon, cloaking the sky in dusky gray. She sat down on a swing. Stretching her legs in front of her, she dug her toe into the cold dirt and gently pushed the swing back and forth as she stared out at Josiah's house. She didn't see his buggy near the barn.

She thought about her mother's words. Normally she followed her counsel, but she couldn't shake the niggling thought that her *mamm* might be wrong in this case. Somehow she'd find out the truth on her own.

No, she wasn't completely on her own. She had God on her side, just as Josiah did. And while she didn't think she would get him to open up about his past right away, she could do her best to remind him that whatever he had been through, he hadn't been alone. Not then, not now. From the discomfort he had displayed praying over the meal, she had a feeling he had forgotten that.

Chapter Seven

JOSIAH AWOKE TO THE SOUND OF TWO BOYS ARGUING outside. Although the night had been cool, he had slept with the window open to dispel the mustiness in his room. He could hear Thomas and Andrew's voices clearly.

"But you got to help him yesterday," Andrew said. "It's my turn to work with Mr. Josiah."

"But I don't wanna go home," Thomas countered.

"You don't have to. I'm sure there's other stuff you can do around here. Like help Amanda in the house."

"I wanna use a hammer again."

"It's my turn. I just tole you that."

Josiah rubbed a hand across his face. Apparently Amanda hadn't listened to him when he said he didn't need any help today. Throwing back the ratty quilt he had used as a covering, he got out of bed and went to the window. The boys were pushing each other now, and Josiah knew soon they would be rolling around on the ground, half fighting and half playing, as boys were wont to do.

He heard a door slam, and a moment later Amanda stood at her brothers' sides. He couldn't hear her words, but the way she placed her hands on her slim hips expressed her displeasure. Today she wore a black apron over a dark green dress that reached her calves. He forgot about Andrew and Thomas as he watched her, mesmerized. After a few moments, he regained his senses. He clenched his fists and turned away.

He didn't want to deal with this today. Last evening, he'd gone to Paradise, slowly riding down the side roads until long past dark, not wanting to go back home. Even though he hadn't lost his temper with Amanda, he had caused her pain, and he could hardly stand that. Gripping her wrist enough to make a mark served to solidify what he already knew—he couldn't be trusted to keep himself in control.

He pulled on his trousers, then picked up a blue shirt from his duffel bag and slid it over his shoulders. He hadn't bothered to unpack everything, and he didn't intend to. Having to pull everything out of a duffel bag every day served as a reminder that he wouldn't be here any longer than necessary.

It took him only a few minutes to get dressed. He scrubbed his hand over his face one more time. He hadn't shaved in two days, and he couldn't let his beard or mustache grow out any more. For a short time he had tried to live like the *Englisch*, but during that part of his life, he felt that he was turning his back on his mother somehow. Despite his inner struggles, he found a tiny measure of peace living Plain and following the *Ordnung*, even if he wasn't sure about his relationship with God.

He scrambled downstairs and went into the bathroom. Ten minutes later he emerged, clean shaven, but no more ready to face Amanda. How could he look her in the eye after he'd physically hurt her yesterday?

"Josiah? Is that you?"

Her lilting voice filtered from the kitchen to the other side of the modest house. Steeling himself, he headed toward her. He would put a stop to her coming over once and for all.

But then he saw her standing in front of the stove, as if she had always belonged there, in his kitchen, in his house. Once he smelled the tantalizing aroma of bacon cooking, he lost his resolve.

Turning, she told him good morning with a bright smile.

The thought of seeing her beautiful face every morning meandered through his mind, making his breath catch. How long had it been since he'd had someone make him breakfast, other than a cook in a restaurant? Years, since his *mamm* died. He swallowed as more memories overcame him, thoughts of his mother's buckwheat pancakes and homemade maple syrup so sweet and rich he would eat until almost bursting. His favorite breakfast, one she made for him often. What he wouldn't do to taste those pancakes now.

"I hope you're hungry. I'm used to cooking for a crowd, and I think I made too much." The oven door squeaked painfully as she opened it. Reaching inside, she pulled out a platter piled high with— he couldn't believe it—pancakes.

She lightly touched the top one. "The oven's not working yet, but the pancakes are still warm. Can you yell for Andrew and Thomas to come in?"

He hesitated. The scene seemed so strange, like he had gone back in time to when he and Amanda used to play that silly game of house. Only now it seemed almost real.

"Josiah?" She looked at him as she set the pancakes on the table. "If we wait much longer, they'll be cold."

He nodded and walked out the back door. Obviously the boys had made up with each other, because they were both climbing the old oak tree about twenty yards from the house. He cupped his hands around his mouth and yelled. "Andrew! Thomas! Breakfast, *nau!*"

The boys scrambled down the tree and broke into a sprint. He could tell they were racing, and the sight brought a smile to his face. A couple of inches shorter than his older brother, Thomas had a more natural stride. But Andrew had a superior kick, which he employed when they were a few feet from the house. They finished even.

"I . . . won!" Andrew said, gasping for air.

"*Nee*," Thomas said, not sounding quite as winded. "I won." He looked up at Josiah. "Didn't I, Mr. Josiah?"

Josiah cleared his throat, trying to maintain a serious tone. "It was a tie."

"Naw," Andrew said. "I beat him by a mile."

"Mr. Josiah said it was a tie, so it was a tie." Thomas gazed up at him again.

A mix of pride and possessiveness filtered through Josiah as he took in the young boy's admiring gaze. To be considered with such unabashed regard was humbling. Unable to stop himself, he reached out and ruffled Thomas's hair.

"What's taking you so long?" Amanda appeared on the back stoop. She looked at her brothers. "Wash up now. I fixed your favorite—pancakes and bacon."

"Awesome!" Andrew and Thomas gave each other a high five, then ran inside the house.

Josiah turned around and faced Amanda. "You didn't have to make breakfast, you know."

Instead of protesting as he expected, she simply smiled, winked at him, then went back inside the house.

He let out a sigh. Pancakes and a beautiful woman. How could he resist that? Somehow he had to try. But not until *after* breakfast.

∽

Andrew and Thomas inhaled their food, and Amanda sent them outside to play again until she and Josiah were finished eating. Then they could all get started on the work of the day.

She cut her pancake in half, then in quarters before pouring a small amount of syrup over the pieces. Glancing up, she noticed Josiah had his head down again, eating nearly as fast as the boys had. "Is my cooking that bad?"

He glanced up, one protruding cheek stuffed with food. "What?"

"The food. Is it so bad you can't slow down and taste it?"

A sheepish expression crossed his features. He chewed, slowly, and swallowed. "Just the opposite. It's very tasty."

She smiled. "I'm glad you enjoy it. I think you'll enjoy it more if you don't stuff it down your throat."

"Are you telling me how to eat my breakfast?"

"I suppose I am. Seems to me you need some tutoring in that area."

"Is that so?" Moving in slow motion, he picked up a piece of bacon and brought it to his mouth, then chewed with exaggerated movements. "Is that better?"

She giggled. "Much." Finally. This was the Josiah she remembered. Playful. Funny. Not sullen and somber. She held out the almost-empty platter of pancakes to him. "Do you want any more?"

"Best not." He patted his flat stomach. "I've eaten more than enough."

Clearly it was a compliment on her cooking, and she took it. Rising from her chair, she started clearing the table. She was surprised and pleased when he helped out. After putting the dishes in the sink, she turned around and looked at him. "Rachel was going to come today, but she and Hannah are helping *Mamm* repair a few of the boys' pants. They go through clothes like you wouldn't believe. I thought I'd work in the living room today. That shouldn't take that long. Unless the bathroom needs cleaning first? After seeing the kitchen, I can only imagine what it looks li—"

"Amanda."

The soft way he said her name made her shut her mouth.

He glanced down at his feet, then shifted from one to the other before looking up, all traces of his earlier playfulness gone. "I know I've said this before, and I really, really appreciate your help, but you can't keep doing this."

She tilted her head. "And as *I've* said before, I don't mind. I have *Mamm*'s blessing, and as long as my chores are done at home, it's no problem to give you a hand."

He shook his head. "You're not understanding me. I don't *want* you to help me." His gaze hardened. "I don't want you here."

Leaning against the sink, she crossed her arms over her chest, hurt. "Why not?"

"Does it matter why?"

"*Ya*, Josiah, it does. You can't just say you don't want me here and then not explain."

He threaded his fingers through his hair. "Okay, you want an explanation, here it is. I came back to Paradise for one reason—to fix this house up enough so that it will sell. Once I've done that, I'm putting it on the market. And when it sells, I'm taking the money and going to Ohio."

"You're not staying?"

"*Nee*. I never planned to. So as you can see, there's no point in your being here."

"But our friendship—"

"Look, Amanda. After I'm gone, we'll never see each other again. That's the way it has to be. That's the way I *want* it to be. I'll pay you for the food you brought yesterday and this morning, but after that I don't want you to bother coming over here."

Awareness dawned, and she felt like a fool. He had a girlfriend waiting for him in Ohio. How could she be so stupid? He was already spoken for, and it wouldn't do for him to be spending so much time with another woman, even though they were only friends.

Meeting his gaze, she realized that her mother had been right all along. Nothing was the same between them. Too much time had passed, and too much distance had separated them. Josiah seemed like a stranger to her because he truly was. And he seemed content to keep things that way.

"I understand," she said, turning her back to him. She blinked back tears, unwilling to let him see her mourn as he pounded the last nail in the coffin of their friendship. "I'll finish up the dishes," she said, distressed at the thickness in her voice. "Then the boys and I will *geh*. You don't have to worry, Josiah. We won't bother you again."

Silence surrounded her, and she knew he hadn't moved. After a long moment, she heard him walk out the kitchen door. Only then did she let the tears fall.

"Mr. Josiah!"

Clenching his jaw, Josiah stalked past Andrew and Thomas, ignoring their calling out his name. Bile clawed up his throat as the image of Amanda's stricken expression rewound itself in his mind. He had finally gotten through to her, although it had nearly killed him to do it.

"Mr. Josiah, wait up!"

He continued to walk toward the barn. He had hurt her once again. Not physically, as he had yesterday, but deeply nevertheless. He had seen it on her face, heard it in the tone of her voice. Seen it in the tears she tried to keep from him.

For a split second he had thought to put his arms around her, to apologize for being so harsh. But he stopped himself. She said she'd leave him alone, and that was what he had wanted all along.

"Mr. Josiah!"

He spun around in front of the barn entrance. "What do you want?"

Both Andrew and Thomas shrank back. "We just wanted to know how we could help you today."

"You can help by going home."

"But—"

"*Geh!* Get out of here!"

Andrew turned around and ran back to the house like he had flames licking at his heels. But Thomas didn't move. His lower lip quivered, and his hazel eyes, the same color as Amanda's, filled with tears.

Perfect. He'd made two innocent people cry today.

Thomas looked at him for a long moment, his shoulders slumped. He turned around, but unlike his brother, he didn't run. Instead he walked slowly, each trudging step driving a knife deeper into Josiah's heart.

"How dare you treat them that way!"

He looked up to see Amanda storming toward him. The sorrow he'd seen in her expression had been replaced with anger. Her fists pressed against her sides, she stopped short a few feet in front of him.

"All they wanted to do was help, Josiah. They look up to you, especially Thomas."

"They shouldn't."

"You're right. Not if you're going to treat him like that." She pressed her fingertips to her brow. "If you're mad at me, fine, but they don't deserve your taking it out on them."

The sound of a horse's hooves reached his ears. He looked down the length of his driveway to see a buggy approaching Amanda's house. A superbly constructed buggy, outfitted with as much reflective tape as the *Ordnung* would allow. He knew whose it was.

Josiah had thought this day couldn't get any worse. He had thought wrong.

Chapter Eight

"YOU GOT COMPANY," JOSIAH SAID.

Amanda glared at him, then turned around to glance at the buggy pulling into her driveway. "I'm not expecting anyone. Maybe one of *Mamm*'s friends is dropping by." She faced Josiah, looking as if she wanted to lay into him again. Instead, she frowned. "You look like you know who that is."

"Don't you?"

She turned again. A tall, slender man exited the buggy and tied his horse to the hitching post at the top of the Grabers' driveway. Cousin Peter.

"Oh no," Amanda groaned.

Well, he hadn't expected that reaction from her. "What's wrong?"

Her angry expression had been replaced by one of irritation. "He's been trying to court me for the past year. I've tried to be nice about it and let him know I'm not interested, but he's not getting the message." She glanced over her shoulder. "I wonder what he wants now."

Their argument apparently over, or at least postponed, Josiah moved to stand next to Amanda. "He shouldn't be bothering you like this."

"Maybe he's just dropping off something at the house."

"Has he ever done that before?"

She shook her head. "*Nee*. He's never even visited before."

Josiah wasn't in any hurry for her to leave now, not with Peter walking inside her house. He had a small measure of satisfaction knowing Amanda wasn't interested in his cousin. She'd always had good taste.

Within minutes Peter walked out the door, and Josiah hoped he would get in his buggy and take off. But instead he walked right past the buggy and across the yard, straight toward his house. Great. Just what he needed.

"*Wunderbaar*," Amanda said, lowering her voice and echoing his own thoughts. "He's coming over here."

"I can see that."

"What should I say to him?"

He looked at her incredulously. "You're asking me?"

"He's your cousin." She leaned closer to him. "How do I get him to leave me alone?"

Josiah could think of several ways of convincing Peter to leave her alone, but none of them were appropriate for Amanda to use, or even remotely Christian. He tried to think of a useful response as Peter came toward them with his hat perched low on his head the way he normally wore it, obscuring his eyes.

"Hello, Amanda," Peter said as he reached them. He stopped right in front of her, completely ignoring Josiah. "Your *mamm* said I could find you here."

"Hello, Peter."

Josiah could tell that she was struggling to be cordial, which was unusual for Amanda. He was surprised to find another person in Paradise who disliked his cousin. As the son of one of the most successful businessmen in the area, Peter didn't have to worry about the future. He made good money working beside his father in the buggy and harness shop, and when his father retired someday, the business would be his. He had a lot to offer a woman—a steady job and good stream of income, a nice house, and a secure future. Why wouldn't Amanda want that?

Then Peter opened his mouth, and Josiah realized why.

"I took a break from work to *personally* ask you to the singing at my house two weeks from this Sunday. Even though we're very busy at the shop, I made the extra trip. We've got over a dozen customers on a waiting list, and we're busting our tails to get all the work done." He leaned forward and put his face close to Amanda's, closer than he had the right to. "But you're worth it," he drawled.

Amanda took a step back, clearly unnerved. "Um, *danki*, Peter. You didn't have to go to so much trouble."

"I know." He gave her a haughty smile.

Josiah moved closer to Amanda, his guard up. He didn't like the way his cousin was looking at Amanda, as if he already possessed her. Amanda, for her part, appeared both frustrated and confused.

"I'll come by and pick you up at five," Peter said. He turned to go, still not saying a word to Josiah.

"Peter, wait." Amanda bit her lower lip. "I'm sorry. I can't go with you."

A spark flashed in his eyes. "Why not?"

"Because . . . because . . ." She looked up at Josiah, helplessness in her eyes.

Peter put his hands on his hips. "I'm getting tired of you putting me off, Amanda. There're plenty of *maed* who would jump at the chance to go out with me."

Josiah took a step forward. "Then maybe you should go find all those *maed* you're talking about and leave Amanda alone."

For the first time, Peter acknowledged him. "Stay out of this, Josiah. Better yet, why don't you stay out of Paradise?"

"Peter, how could you say something so terrible?" Amanda said. "And about your own cousin?"

Peter looked down the length of his nose. "He's no cousin of mine."

"Blood says otherwise," Josiah retorted.

"I'm having a private conversation. Do you mind?"

Josiah crossed his arms over his chest. "Since you're on my property, I do mind."

Peter shook his head, then turned his back on Josiah. "Come on, Amanda. We'll continue this at your house."

"There's nothing to talk about." She took a deep breath. "Peter, I already said I can't go with you."

"But you didn't tell me why." He put his arm around her shoulders and guided her away from Josiah. He was at least six inches taller than she was and twice her size in bulk. The gesture seemed innocent enough, but Josiah kept his guard up. When they were a few feet away and in Amanda's front yard, Peter dropped his arm and faced her.

⤫

Amanda glanced over her shoulder at Josiah, who remained on his side of the property line. Disappointment washed through her when he didn't follow her. Not that she should have expected him to. Peter Yoder was her problem, and Josiah had made it perfectly clear that he didn't want to get involved in her life.

Fine. She would deal with Peter. She didn't need Josiah's help anyway.

"I'm really sorry, Peter," she said, looking up at him. Well, she wasn't all that sorry, but she didn't want to be outright rude to him. "I can't go with you to the singing."

"Amanda, I drove all the way out here to ask you. I took time off from work."

"I know, Peter, but—"

"I don't understand why you keep refusing me. It's not like you've had any other offers. And face it, you're getting old. It's not like you can afford to be picky."

His words stung. "I'd appreciate it if you'd leave, Peter." She moved toward the house, fighting the irritation rising inside her. She wasn't that old. He made her sound like she needed to be put out to pasture.

"Wait—Amanda." He grabbed her upper arm, preventing her from moving any farther. "I'm sorry. It's just that I've liked you for so long." He pulled her toward him. "I don't understand why you don't like me too."

"Peter, let me go." The desperation she saw in his eyes stunned her.

"If you'd only give me a chance . . . please." His head tilted toward hers, and suddenly she realized he intended to kiss her. "You'd see how much I want you—"

"Let her *geh*!"

At the sound of Josiah's booming voice, Peter dropped his grip. Amanda immediately stepped back in shock. Peter had tried to kiss her. Right in front of her house. Had he lost his mind?

Josiah stormed toward Peter. "You touch her one more time and I'll—"

"You'll what?" Peter smirked. "Hit me? Go ahead. I'm sure the bishop will be happy to hear about how you beat up a member of the church, not to mention a member of your own family."

Amanda's gaze darted to Josiah, who remained in place. His fists were clenched at his sides, and his mouth was pressed in a flat line. For a brief moment she thought he might cave in to his cousin's taunt. Then his posture relaxed, but only slightly. "I suggest you leave, Peter. Now."

"Not until Amanda tells me why she can't go to the singing with me."

"I'll tell you why. Because she's going with me."

Amanda's mouth dropped open. Josiah couldn't have surprised her more if he had sprouted wings and started flying around the yard. She should have done a better job at hiding her shock, but she couldn't, not when only moments ago he had made it abundantly clear that he wanted her to leave him alone.

"You're taking her?" Peter scoffed as he looked at Amanda. "Seems to me she had no idea about that."

She met Josiah's gaze. The slightly confused look in her eyes spoke volumes.

"Just as I thought." Peter crossed his arms over his chest. "She's not going with you."

"*Ya*, I am." The words came out before she could stop them. Turning to Josiah, she said, "I'd be happy to go with you. Extremely happy."

Still looking at Peter, he said, "*Gut*. It's a date."

A *date*? Her mouth suddenly went dry. His words were obviously aimed to irk Peter, and from the way the other man's face reddened, it had worked. Still, to proclaim aloud and to his cousin that he had asked her out on a date seemed unreal.

"Fine," Peter said, backing away from them both. "If you want to be with this loser, go ahead. Just remember what you're giving up." He looked past them, gesturing with an upward tilt of his chin at the run-down barn behind them. "He's as worthless as that barn. You'll see." Spinning around, he stalked back to his buggy.

Amanda didn't breathe until Peter and his buggy were well out of sight.

"Are you all right?" Josiah asked.

Her cheeks reddened. "*Ya*. I'm sorry about that."

"Not your fault he's a jerk. He always has been. Comes from being spoiled, if you ask me." He gave her another look. The horse suddenly whinnied from inside the barn. "I've got to feed her. 'Scuse me." He turned and went inside.

Amanda followed him into the barn, squinting as her vision adjusted to the dark interior. She glanced around, seeing the horse in her stall waiting patiently to be fed. There was room enough for three more horses, but she didn't remember the Bontragers ever having more than one at any time.

She watched as Josiah dragged a bale of fresh hay from the other side of the barn closer to the horse's stall. He pulled a small knife out of his pocket, flipped it open, and cut the rough twine securing the square bale. He loosened the hay with his hands, then grabbed what looked like a brand-new pitchfork and tossed fresh hay over the stall door into the horse's trough.

"Josiah."

He didn't stop, nor did he look at her. *"Ya?"*

He wasn't going to make this easy for her. But she wasn't about to walk away. "I appreciate your helping me out with Peter."

"No problem." He shoved the pitchfork into another pile of hay.

"I'm sorry you had to be dragged into it. I wish he would just leave me alone. He's right about one thing: there are plenty of *maed* in the community who would love his attention. Plenty of them that are more his age."

"He's only two years younger than you."

"Two and a half. Besides, twenty-one is too young. For me anyway." She winced, remembering his words about her being old.

Flipping the hay into the stall, Josiah didn't comment.

She clasped her hands together. How could he be so unaffected by what had just happened? She had thought he would at least say something. Instead, he seemed content to ignore the incident entirely.

Stepping forward, she moved until she was almost right beside him, but clear enough away that she wouldn't get the in the way of his work. "Look, Josiah, I know you don't want to take me to the singing. I won't hold you to it." She looked away, suddenly feeling embarrassed and more than a little insecure. "I know you only said that so he would leave me alone."

He moved to grab more hay, but before sliding the pitchfork underneath a large clump, he halted. Turning, he looked at her, his expression resolute. "I said I'd take you, and I'll keep my word."

He didn't have to sound so enthusiastic about it. Also, it wasn't right, not when he was already spoken for. "What about your girlfriend in Ohio?"

His eyes grew wide. "What girlfriend?"

"The one you're going back to once you sell the house." How

painful it was to say that aloud. Why should she be bothered that he had someone waiting for him? She should be more surprised that he hadn't married by now. They were both twenty-four, and most of her friends were already starting families. Even her mother had expressed concern recently about Amanda's lack of a beau.

He resumed working, sliding the pitchfork underneath the last remnants of hay and dropping them in the trough. The crunching sound of hay being mashed between the animal's teeth filled the barn. Slowly Josiah leaned the pitchfork against the wall, then faced her. "There's no one waiting for me in Ohio."

"Oh. She's still in Indiana?" She frowned, confused. If his girl-friend lived in Indiana, why was he going to Ohio?

"Amanda," he said, looking directly at her. "I don't have a girlfriend."

She nearly let out a sigh of relief, but stopped just in time. "Then why are you going there? Why not just stay here in Paradise?"

He kicked at a dirt clod on the barn floor. Dust particles rose and danced in the beams of light streaming through the open gaps in the barn wall slats. "I can't. Not in this house."

"Well, of course not, not with things the way they are. But once you get everything fixed up, this will be a great place to live. Just the way it used to be."

"*Ya* . . . maybe."

She didn't miss the doubt in his voice, and figured he must be tired and overwhelmed. "It will. I promise you that."

Josiah walked to the other side of the barn and leaned against the wall. "Doesn't matter. I'm selling."

Fighting her rising disappointment, she said, "I hate to see you do all this work for nothing, Josiah."

"It's not for nothing. This is a great piece of property and a fairly large house. And look at the barn." He gestured to it with his hands. "Four stalls, a loft, another place to store hay on the ground floor. You can't find barns this nice anymore. Well, it will be nice once I'm done with it. In the backyard there's a place for a large garden, and when I finish with the front porch, it will be a *gut* place to relax at the end of the day."

Amanda could hear a tinge of excitement in his voice as he spoke, and she warmed to it. "In other words, a great place for *you* to live."

He didn't answer her for a long moment as he stared at the horse finishing her meal. Finally he said, "What time did Peter say he was gonna pick you up for the singing?"

His change of subject had been severe, and she had to respect that, even though it frustrated her to do so. "Five. It starts at five thirty. I think we have a problem, though. Peter thinks you and I will be on a date."

"Oh, that." He shrugged, but she noticed he kept his gaze from hers. "I said that for his benefit. I didn't want him to get any ideas that he had a chance with you."

"I see." She hid the disappointment from her voice. "But what if he tells everyone that we're courting?"

Josiah looked up at her. "He won't. The last thing Peter would do is admit he had lost you to me."

"Oh." She didn't know how to respond to that.

He came toward her, his handsome features softening a bit. "Amanda, about this morning. I'm sorry. You're right, I shouldn't have yelled at your brothers that way. They didn't deserve it. I'll make it up to them, I promise."

The sincerity in his eyes touched her. "I know you will."

"And if you still want to help, I can use it. Although I don't understand why you'd want to spend your time working here."

"Because that's what friends are for, Josiah."

"I figured you'd have lots of other things you'd rather do."

She stepped toward him, her heart squeezing at the self-deprecating tone in his voice. Somehow she had to convince him he was worth it. "Remember when we were ten, Josiah? How we promised each other we would always be friends?"

He nodded slowly.

"I intended on keeping that promise. I'm going to keep it now. Nothing you can do or say is going to change that."

The corner of his mouth lifted. "You're stubborn, you know that?"

"I prefer 'persistent.'"

He chuckled. "At least that part of you hasn't changed."

"And what part of me has?"

As soon as she asked the question, she wanted to take it back. It might have been okay to ask such a thing when they were kids, but wholly inappropriate now that they were adults. Still, she held her breath as she waited for him to answer.

"Mandy . . ." His voice, barely above a whisper, sent pleasant waves through her body.

"Amanda! Amanda!"

She whirled around at the sound of Rachel's panicked calls. "In here!" She dashed out of the barn, barely aware of Josiah following closely behind.

Rachel ran to Amanda, the black strings of her *kapp* flying behind her. "It's *Mamm*," she said, taking a big gulp of air, her eyes filled with fright. "There's something . . . wrong." She burst into tears.

Amanda put her arms around her sister's shoulders, fighting the alarm rising inside her. "Let's *geh*," she said, and they rushed to the house. When they burst through the kitchen door, Amanda put a hand to her mouth, her resolve to keep calm abandoning her.

Her mother lay on the floor, unmoving.

Chapter Nine

JOSIAH BLANCHED AS HE ENTERED THE KITCHEN AND SAW Katharine Graber lying on the floor, apparently unconscious. From the large size of her swollen belly, she looked far into her pregnancy. A very young boy sat next to her, confusion on his round face.

Amanda ran to Katharine's side and knelt down near her head. "*Mamm! Mamm*, can you hear me?"

"What's wrong with *Mammi*?" Rachel asked, her voice heavy with tears.

At this point several more children came into the kitchen and started hovering over their mother. They crowded closer to Amanda and peppered her with questions.

"Rachel, Hannah," Amanda said as she looked up, her voice barely controlled. "Take the *kinder* upstairs until I tell you to come back down."

The girls nodded and rounded everyone up. Amid the younger children's protests, they departed the kitchen, leaving Amanda and Josiah alone with her mother.

"*Mamm*," Amanda said, taking her mother's hand. "Please, *Mamm*. Wake up."

Josiah came around the other side. Just as he started to kneel down, Katharine opened her eyes.

"Amanda?" Her eyelids fluttered.

Amanda's shoulders slumped with relief. "How do you feel?" she asked, still holding her hand.

"Okay," Katharine replied, trying to sit up. She looked pale, but otherwise fine. "I guess I must have fainted. One minute I was standing near the stove, the next I'm looking at you."

Amanda put her other arm around Katharine's shoulders and tried to assist her. "You need to lie down on the couch."

Seeing Amanda struggle to help her mother spurred Josiah into action. He crouched down and assisted Katharine to her feet.

"*Danki*, Josiah."

He nodded and put a supporting arm lightly around Katharine's shoulders as Amanda left the room. By the time he and Katharine reached the couch, she had returned with a damp white washcloth.

"Honestly, I'm fine." Katharine waved off Amanda's offer of a cold cloth and sat down. She shifted awkwardly on the couch until she settled in a lying down position, smoothing out the skirt of her plum-colored dress. "I just got a little light-headed, that's all. I don't think I drank enough water today, and it's warm in the kitchen."

Standing next to Amanda in the Grabers' living room, Josiah was sent back into the past. The interior of the house hadn't changed much over the years, and he clearly remembered the light blue, rosebud-covered couch Katharine lay on now. He looked down at her, glad to see some color return to her cheeks.

When he'd entered the kitchen with Amanda and Rachel and seen her lying motionless, a stab of terror had gone through him. His own *mamm* had passed away in a hospital, and that had been traumatic enough. He imagined how frightened the young children were to see their mother lying on the floor.

"*Mamm*, please, just put this on your head for a minute." Amanda placed the washcloth on Katharine's forehead. "You might have gotten overheated too. This will help cool you off."

"All right." Katharine leaned back and closed her eyes, holding the cloth against her forehead. "Where are the *kinder*?"

"I sent them upstairs with Hannah and Rachel."

Katharine opened her eyes, revealing her regret and concern. "I bet they're scared to death. Tell them to come downstairs so I can tell them I'm all right."

"But I don't want to leave you. I'm sure Rachel and Hannah are letting them know everything's okay."

"Amanda, nothing is more reassuring than hearing a mother's voice, especially to a young *kind*. Now, I told you I'm fine. I don't feel dizzy anymore, and certainly nothing is going to happen to me on this couch if I'm alone for five seconds."

"But—"

"I'll get them," Josiah said. "You stay with your *mamm*."

"*Danki,*" Amanda said, giving him a grateful glance.

As a child Josiah had visited the Grabers so many times he knew their house as well as his own. He went down the short hallway to the staircase, then took the stairs two at a time. He'd made it halfway up when he heard the children's murmurs, although he couldn't make out what they were saying.

There were three bedrooms upstairs. He followed their voices to the room at the end of the hall, the heels of his shoes clomping against the wooden floor. The door was partially open, but he knocked anyway.

A girl answered the door, one he hadn't met before. Hannah, he assumed. Like Amanda and Thomas, she had bright hazel eyes and light brown hair. Right now those eyes were filled with anxiety, even though he could tell she was trying valiantly to keep her composure.

"Did *Mamm* say we could come downstairs now?" she asked. Hannah wore a prayer *kapp*, black in color to symbolize that she was under age sixteen. She tugged on one of the ribbons as she spoke.

"*Ya*, your *mamm* wants to see you." Josiah peeked inside the small room, taking in the two single beds on opposite walls, which were painted a light green color. A faceless Amish doll lay on one bed, while the other was covered with a brightly patterned quilt in pinks and blues.

Rachel sat on one bed, holding a young boy in her lap. The child was sucking his thumb and trying to squirm out of his sister's arms, but he wore a playful expression. Fortunately he seemed unaware of what had happened to his mother. Another boy, the one Josiah had seen by Katharine when she fainted, sat on the floor moving a small wooden train engine back and forth over the circular rag area rug. He looked to be a couple of years older than the toddler but younger than Thomas. He, too, appeared oblivious of the worry shared by his siblings.

Andrew and Thomas sat on the other bed, the one with the colorful quilt. Andrew wouldn't look at Josiah, and he didn't blame him. Somehow he had to make it up to the boy. But Thomas caught his gaze, scooted off the bed, and walked over to him.

"Is *Mamm* gonna die, Mr. Josiah?"

Pain lanced him. He had been only a few years older when he'd asked his father that same question, after seeing his mother at the hospital for the last time. His *daed* had refused to answer him, just stared straight ahead, his face blank. From that day forward his father only had two expressions: blankness and fury.

Josiah shook his head, clearing his mind of the memory. Kneeling down in front of him, Josiah said, "*Nee*, Thomas. Your *mamm* is gonna be fine. She wants all of you to come downstairs so she can tell you that she's all right."

The anxiety melted from Thomas's face. "*Danki*, Mr. Josiah. I was really scared."

"We all were," Rachel added, letting the toddler down from her lap.

What did Amanda say his name was? Jacob, that's right. As Josiah stood, Jacob came over to him with arms outstretched. Josiah stared at him, unsure what to do.

"He wants you to hold him," Hannah said, smiling. As with Thomas, the tension seemed to have drained from her body. "That's a *gut* thing, as he normally doesn't take to strangers."

Josiah lifted the boy, who couldn't have weighed more than

thirty pounds. He looked at his face for a moment, noticing a small smear of something above his lip. Chocolate, maybe. He didn't know much about kids, and even less about babies and toddlers. Was this child even old enough to eat chocolate?

"Christopher," Hannah said, holding out her hand to the young boy playing on the rug. "Let's go see *Mamm*. She's feeling better now."

Without a word Christopher stood up, his train engine clutched to his chest. They all filed past Josiah, including Andrew, who still didn't look at him.

Josiah turned and followed the children, carrying Jacob downstairs.

"*Mammi!*" He heard Christopher's high-pitched voice as he rounded the corner. By the time he reached the living room with Jacob, the children were seated on the floor in front of Katharine. Amanda knelt beside the couch, near her mother's head. She removed the rag as Katharine moved to sit up.

"You should lie back down," Amanda said, sounding more like Katharine's mother than her daughter.

"*Nee*, I don't need to." She looked at Amanda, her blue eyes reassuring. "The same thing happened to me when I was pregnant with you, Mandy. It was on a Saturday, and your *daed* was here at the time, which was a *gut* thing. I about scared him to death, too, but it never happened again. Not until today." She smiled. "I promise, I'm all right." She looked at the children, her gaze landing on each of them briefly, individually reassuring them that she was fine. Then she glanced around. "Where's Jacob?"

"He's right here." Josiah walked farther into the room. But when he tried to hand Jacob to his mother, the little boy grabbed hold of Josiah's suspenders. Gently Josiah extracted the child's small hand from the black strap and set him on the ground. The boy immediately toddled to his mother, putting the index finger of his right hand into his mouth.

Amanda intercepted him and set him on her lap. "*Mamm* needs her rest, Jacob," she said, her voice low and soft. "She can hold you later."

Josiah stood in the middle of the room, watching the scene before him, feeling like an interloper. His arms felt empty after he had released Jacob, and jealousy stabbed at him as he surveyed the family gathered together. The love they all had for each other flowed throughout the room.

Fortunately the children all seemed all right. A little shaken up, but they appeared to take Katharine's reassurances to heart and had already started getting fidgety.

"Can we go outside now, *Mamm*?" Andrew asked, rocking back and forth on his knees. Josiah could relate to his desire to be outside.

"Sure," Katharine said with a laugh. "Why don't you all go outside and play a bit. It would be shameful to waste the fresh air. Hannah, do you mind taking Jacob?"

Hannah picked up her youngest brother from Amanda's lap and led him out of the living room. The rest of the children all scrambled off the floor and headed outside, leaving Josiah and Amanda with Katharine.

"I'll have lunch ready in about an hour," Katharine called out after them.

"I'll prepare lunch, *Mamm*." Amanda rose from her seated position on the floor. "You'll stay here and rest."

Katharine nodded, leaning back against one of the small pillows that matched the pattern of the couch. "I'm not going to argue with you. I do feel tired." At Amanda's look of alarm, she added, "But I'm *fine*. I will admit, though, that this *boppli* is taking more out of me than the other *kinder* did." She let out a chuckle. "Guess that's what happens when you get old."

"You're not old, *Mamm*."

"You're sweet to say that. But I'm getting there, that's for sure."

Not wanting to eavesdrop on the conversation more than he

already had, Josiah turned to leave, grimacing when the floorboard squeaked beneath the heel of his shoe.

"Josiah?"

He turned at the sound of Katharine's voice. *"Ya?"*

"Danki for your help. You don't have to leave just yet. Please join us for lunch."

"I'm sorry, but I can't. I have a lot of work to do at the house. But I appreciate the offer."

"All right. Just know, Josiah, that you're always welcome here. Anytime. We're glad you've come back."

Josiah nodded as he met her gaze, then left the room.

"I know you're in a hurry to get back to work," Amanda said to him as they entered the kitchen. "But I want you to know how thankful I am that you were here to help me with *Mamm.* I don't know what I would have done . . . I couldn't have lifted her . . ." Her lower lip trembled.

Something broke inside of Josiah as he saw tears form in Amanda's eyes. Only now did she reveal how truly scared she had been for her mother. Then he remembered her encounter with Peter, and his heart went out to her. She'd had a rough morning. As one tear slid out of the corner of her eye, he couldn't resist wiping it from her cheek with the side of his thumb. At the sound of her soft sigh, he snatched his hand back, regaining his senses.

He cleared his throat, thrusting his hands into his pockets. "Glad I was here. I'll see you later." He paused, remembering he had to take care of something first. "I need to set things right with your brothers. Would it be okay if they helped me out for a few more days? If they get bored or tired of the work, I'll send them back home."

Happiness replaced the anxiety in her eyes. *"Nee,* they won't be bored. Hard work is *gut* for them, Josiah. They'll learn a lot from you."

Josiah wasn't sure about that after how he had treated them this morning, but he would feel better knowing he'd done something to make up for yelling at them. "Take care of your *mamm*," he couldn't resist adding as he opened the back door.

"I will."

He looked at her for one last moment, unable to pull his gaze from her pretty face. If only things were different. "*Ya*. I know you will. She couldn't be in better hands."

Chapter Ten

AMANDA STOOD AT THE BACK DOOR AND WATCHED AS Josiah made his way over to Andrew and Thomas, who were sliding down the plastic yellow slide attached to the swing set. Thomas listened at perfect attention, but Andrew hung back. After a few moments Josiah reached out and touched Andrew's shoulder. Her brother responded to the gesture by moving a little closer, then finally stood beside Josiah. Soon all three of them disappeared from view as they headed for Josiah's house.

She grinned, the tension draining from her. *Mamm* would be all right, as the Lord had watched over her today. Josiah had made amends with her brothers. Most important, he seemed to have opened up a little bit to her. She touched her cheek where his thumb had brushed away her tears. Such a kind gesture, and an unexpected one for so many reasons. Her skin still tingled from his gentle touch.

Turning away from the door, she went back and checked on her *mamm*. Her eyes were closed, and Amanda was glad to see her resting. She had been terrified when she'd seen her mother lying on the floor, unconscious.

Guilt pricked at her, and she realized she should have been here helping her *mamm* instead of over at Josiah's, who hadn't even wanted her there in the first place. If she had been here at the house, then her mother wouldn't have overdone it.

Amanda pressed her lips together. She wouldn't leave her mother alone again, not until the baby's birth. Even though Hannah and Rachel had been here to help, her mother clearly needed more rest.

"Amanda?"

"Did you need something, *Mamm*?"

Katharine shook her head. "Don't worry, *Dochder*. I'm still okay." She reached up and brushed back a strand of Amanda's hair that had escaped her *kapp*. "I just wanted to thank you for your help."

"I didn't do nearly enough." Amanda looked down at her hands. "I shouldn't have gone over to Josiah's."

"You think this is your fault?" Katharine tilted her head and gave her a gentle smile. "Amanda, these things sometimes happen. A person can pass out for any number of reasons. And I haven't been drinking water like I should. The doctor said to watch out for dehydration. So it's really my fault. Besides, you were right to go to Josiah's."

"He doesn't think so. He doesn't want my help anymore. Although he did tell Andrew and Thomas they could work with him for a few days."

"That's *gut*," Katharine said. "I'm sure he'll keep them busy."

"He plans to sell the house when he's finished."

Katharine appeared surprised. "He's selling it?"

Amanda nodded. "Then he's moving to Ohio."

"So that's where he's been."

"*Nee*. He lived in Indiana, but he's not going back there."

"Sounds like he has everything planned out."

"*Ya*," Amanda said, unable to hide the disappointment in her voice.

But if Katharine noticed her tone, she didn't mention it. "It's near lunchtime. Are you sure I can't help?"

"Positive. You rest."

"*Danki*, Amanda. You have been such a help to me."

"I'm happy to help."

"I know you are. You've been that way since you were a young child. And when we had Hannah, then the other *kinder*, I don't know what I would have done without you." She sobered. "But I worry I'm keeping you from your own life."

Amanda shook her head. "This is my life. Taking care of you and *Daed* and the children."

"But don't you ever think of having a family of your own?"

She paused. "Sometimes." More often than she wanted to admit. "But it seems God's plan is for me to stay right here, at least for now, until I meet the man He has set apart for me."

"Perhaps you've already met him."

"Oh, *nee*," she said, shaking her head vehemently. "Peter Yoder is not the man for me."

"I wasn't talking about Peter."

Amanda lifted her brow. "Then who?"

Katharine leaned back on the couch and closed her eyes. "You'll have to figure that out yourself."

❦

A short while later Amanda had lunch prepared and served to the children. She took a tray of chicken soup and a cheese sandwich, along with a large glass of water, to her mother, but she was asleep. Setting the tray on the coffee table in front of the couch, Amanda tiptoed out of the living room.

As she made her way back to the kitchen, her mind began to whirl. What did her mother mean about her already having met the man God had set apart for her? Thank goodness she hadn't meant Peter. She thought about the other young men in her community. While there were some very nice ones, none of them had stirred any feelings inside her. Unlike Josiah.

Surely her mother hadn't meant him. That didn't make any sense, especially after Amanda had just told her that he wanted to sell his house and move to Ohio. Besides, Josiah had been back a total of three days, and they had barely rekindled their friendship.

But she couldn't deny that romantic feelings for him had started to grow.

How did everything get so complicated?

❧

Josiah ran a brush through his hair, smoothing his bangs over his forehead. He needed a haircut, and maybe he would take the time to get one next week. But he couldn't worry about that now, not when he had to pick up Amanda in fifteen minutes.

Two weeks had quickly passed since Peter's visit. The more time passed, the more he regretted his snap decision to take Amanda to the singing. Everything had gotten too complicated too quickly. It wasn't that he didn't want to spend time with her—he did, more than he had a right to. But taking her to this singing meant facing even more of his past. He'd see people he grew up with, and they would undoubtedly ask him a lot of questions he didn't want to answer. At least with others he could be vague and not have to worry about them pressing the issue. Unlike Amanda.

He hadn't seen much of her the past two weeks except at a distance, when she and her sisters were working on their garden patch, pulling up dead weeds and spreading piles of compost on top of the garden to enrich the existing soil. To his chagrin he had spent more time watching her toil than he should have. But he couldn't help it. Her beauty stunned him, and she worked with such spirit and vigor. Any man would be proud to have her as his wife.

He would be especially proud. But he was also realistic.

Taking a deep breath, he slid his arms through his suspenders, then went downstairs to retrieve his hat. A worn-out brim, and a small stain near the hatband. He wished he had a new one to wear, but this would have to do.

A blast of brisk air greeted him as he stepped outside. It was near the end of October, when days were shorter and the air cooler. The temperature dropped a little bit as evening approached, cool enough to wear a jacket over his light blue long-sleeved shirt.

He glanced at the Grabers' house. Should he walk over and get Amanda, or hitch Tater to the buggy? Josiah didn't particularly care for the name Thomas had chosen, but the boy had a spark of pride in his voice every time he mentioned her by name.

Before he could make his decision, he heard the sound of a screen door shut and turned to see Amanda striding toward him. His mouth went dry as he gazed at her, taking in her dark green dress and white prayer *kapp*. She smiled as she neared, and it tugged at his heart.

He was in for a long night.

"Missed seeing you at church this morning," Amanda said as Josiah guided the buggy onto the road.

He shrugged, keeping his gaze straight ahead. He hadn't said more than two words to her since she'd met him at his house a few minutes ago. She glanced down at the plastic container filled with fresh-baked monster cookies—packed with oats, chocolate chips, and M&M's and rolled in powdered sugar. She had taken care with her appearance, knowing that the green dress brought out the green in her hazel eyes. But she shouldn't have bothered. She doubted Josiah even knew the color of her eyes, he so rarely looked directly at her.

Silence filled the space between them, and not for the first time she thought this was a bad idea. She hated feeling awkward around Josiah. After a few more minutes of only the sound of the passing cars and the clip-clop of Tater's hooves, she couldn't stand it anymore.

"You were right about Peter," she said.

He turned to her. "What?"

Finally, she had gotten his attention. "I expected at church this morning some of my friends would ask about our going to the singing together, but no one mentioned it."

"I'm not surprised. Like I said, Peter hates to lose."

"I'm not a prize, Josiah."

"Peter thinks so."

"Well, I don't care what he thinks." She settled against the seat. "I just hope he leaves me alone after this."

Josiah pulled on the reins, guiding the horse to make a right turn onto the road where Peter and his family lived. "You let me know if he doesn't."

She hid a smile at his protective tone. She'd never figure this man out. "I remember you spending a lot of time at your aunt and uncle's. I didn't realize you and Peter didn't get along."

"It's a long story."

"We've got time."

He glanced at her for a brief moment, then focused on the road ahead. "I suppose you'll keep asking until I tell you."

"You know me so well."

His lips quirked, but he didn't smile. "We were okay when we were younger. Then when I turned ten, I started helping my uncle in the shop. Peter wasn't old enough to do much more than clean up and be our gopher, which he hated. I think he resented the time my *Onkel* John and I spent together. And since Peter has five sisters, *Onkel* John appreciated the extra help."

"But then Peter worked in the shop too, right?"

Josiah nodded. "He wasn't quite as angry at that point, but we still didn't get along. Peter always had everything he wanted or needed, but he still never seemed happy. Then *Mamm* died." He swallowed. "My *onkel* was there for me more than my own *daed* was."

"I'm so sorry," she said, seeing the stricken look on his face. "I had no idea."

"I didn't want to talk about it. There's the house." He nodded toward a large white house several hundred yards away.

Amanda had only been to the Yoders' a few times before, for church services over the years and when Peter's oldest sister, Esther, had gotten married a couple of years ago. As the beautiful house came into view, she couldn't help but be impressed. Although there was nothing ostentatious about it, the size of the house, shop, and property bespoke of wealth. She had heard stories over the years of how generous John and Vera Yoder had been to families in the community that were struggling financially. She hoped Peter would keep up that family tradition.

Numerous gray buggies were parked in the large area near the shop. She spotted a volleyball net in the backyard behind the house, and several young women and men were already playing with a bright yellow ball. The scent of grilling meat greeted her as Josiah squeezed his buggy into the last space near the hitching post. Hamburgers, or maybe chicken, she couldn't tell. Her stomach growled.

They disembarked from the buggy, and Josiah tethered Tater. Amanda clutched her cookies while Josiah shoved his hands in his pockets. One look at his uncertain expression, and she knew they shouldn't have come here together.

"I'll take these cookies inside to your *aenti*," she said.

"I'll come with you." He fell in step beside her as they went to the house. "I want to say hello to her and *Onkel* John."

They entered through the side door and passed through a large mudroom before reaching the spacious kitchen, where plates and trays of desserts covered the oblong table. Giving the spread a cursory look, Amanda noticed at least four different kinds of cookies, a baking dish filled with date pudding, chocolate-frosted brownies, a huge hickory nut cake, and two double-crust apple pies.

"Looks *gut*," Josiah said, his hands still in his pockets. He nodded his approval, then glanced around the kitchen. "Wonder where *Aenti* Vera is."

Amanda looked out the large, multipaned window that exposed the Yoders' expansive backyard. Two more tables were set up near the gas grill manned by Josiah's uncle. Those tables were also filled with platters of food. "We won't starve here," she commented.

"*Nee. Aenti* Vera always makes sure everyone has plenty." Josiah walked over to the window and stared outside.

After shifting a few of the desserts around, Amanda made enough room for her container, then moved to stand by him.

"I don't know anyone here," he said, still looking outside. "Then again, I suppose most of our old friends are married by now."

"*Ya*, they are." She peered at a young woman and man standing off to the side, watching the volleyball game. From the way they stood close to each other, everyone could see they were a couple. "You remember Ben Weaver and Rebecca Miller, don't you?"

He hesitated, then nodded.

"Her twin sister drowned in a skating accident." Amanda shook her head. "Such a tragedy. Rebecca had a hard time dealing with it, not that anyone could blame her. She's found happiness with Ben, though."

"I can see that."

"They're getting married in a few weeks." She nodded toward another couple just arriving. "Leah and Aaron Lantz are here too. Leah Lantz was formerly Leah Petersheim. They married last year."

"I don't know them very well," he said.

"You'd like Aaron; he's a great guy."

Josiah didn't say anything for a moment. Then he looked at her. "I have to admit, I'm surprised you're not married yet."

"I could say the same thing for you."

He looked out the window again. "I don't plan on getting married."

Amanda did a double take. Choosing to remain single was almost unheard of among the Amish. She started to ask him why, when his aunt bustled into the kitchen.

"I know I put the extra napkins somewhere," she mumbled, tapping her chin with her index finger. Then she glanced in the direction of the window, and a wide grin appeared on her face. "Josiah!" She went to him, squeezing between the chairs around the table and the wall. "I had no idea you were here! When did you arrive?"

"Just a few minutes ago, *Aenti*. Amanda dropped off a dessert."

Vera looked at Amanda and smiled. "*Danki*. I hope you found room for it."

"I did. Everything looks wonderful."

"It's nothing," Vera said, batting away the compliment with her hand. "I just hope everyone has a *gut* time." She looked at Josiah and smiled. "Especially you."

Without replying, Josiah averted his gaze.

Apparently not noticing her nephew's reticence, Vera said, "Now, you two *geh* outside and have fun. They're starting up another volleyball game. You used to love to play, Josiah." She moved toward them and made shooing gestures with her hands. "Get out there before the game starts."

Amanda hid a smile as she and Josiah left the house and entered the backyard. Fragrant smoke drifted from the gas grill, scenting the air and making her mouth water. The Yoders had a large concrete patio, and several young people were sitting in plastic chairs, talking and watching their friends playing horseshoes and choosing teams for the volleyball game. She and Josiah stood on the perimeter, still unnoticed by everyone else. She turned to him. "Do you want to play?"

"*Nee*, not today."

"Oh, come on, Josiah," Amanda said. She enjoyed volleyball and remembered what a great player he'd been. Without thinking, she reached out and grabbed his hand. "It'll be fun."

Chapter Eleven

JOSIAH STARED AT HER SMALL HAND IN HIS LARGE ONE. Warmth traveled from his palm throughout his entire body as he reveled in Amanda's touch. The way she had grabbed his hand had been so smooth, so natural, he doubted she had thought twice about it, or that she had any idea how her touch affected him.

"I'm not taking no for an answer," she said, tugging on his hand. "Your *aenti* told you to have fun, and I'm going to make sure you do." She smiled at him, her cheeks rosy from the cool air, the ribbons from her prayer *kapp* fluttering around her shoulders.

Those ribbons weren't the only thing fluttering. Despite his efforts, he couldn't calm his heart rate.

Several girls and guys on the patio turned and looked at them, and he realized he either had to follow her to the volleyball net or risk making a scene. Taking off his coat, he took a few steps forward. "All right, you've convinced me. Or should I say you didn't give me much of a choice."

"Either one works for me." She grinned and released her grasp.

His hand had never felt so empty.

The underlying anxiety he'd felt since leaving his house threatened to surface as he approached the group of people near the volleyball net. He had spoken the truth to Amanda: he didn't know very many of them. Then his gaze landed on Ben Weaver, and he felt a little relief at seeing another friendly face.

"I see my cousin has decided to join us." Peter suddenly appeared and stood beside a pretty young *maedel* Josiah didn't recognize.

So much for relief.

"You all remember Josiah, don't you?"

A couple of people nodded, although Josiah wasn't sure who they were. Then he saw Ben tossing the volleyball up and down. Ben gave him a wide grin. "Hey, Josiah. Heard you were back in town. Glad you could make it."

Josiah nodded. He and Ben hadn't known each other all that well; Ben was a couple of years younger. But he'd always been friendly, and Josiah was glad to see that hadn't changed.

"We just finished picking teams," Peter said in an even tone, but Josiah could see a tiny spark of resentment in his cousin's eyes. "Since I'm one of the captains, I choose Amanda."

"We'll have Josiah," Ben said.

The teams assembled, and soon they started playing. Before long Josiah had shed any self-consciousness and immersed himself in the game. He hadn't played in a long time, but soon he fell into a comfortable rhythm and scored a couple of points.

At game point, it was his turn to serve. He tossed the ball in the air and executed a perfect serve—directly at Amanda.

"Mine!" she yelled, extending her arms and clasping her hands together in position to bump the ball either over the net or to one of the players on her team. Josiah watched her, hoping she would make a clean hit.

She missed the ball.

Josiah's team hollered and celebrated their victory, and a couple of the guys clapped him on the back. He accepted their congratulations and walked toward Amanda to tell her good game, but paused as he saw Peter moving to stand next to her.

"How could you have missed that?" His tone wasn't overly loud, but loud enough for Josiah to hear him.

Amanda, to her credit, didn't cower. "It was a *gut* serve. I misjudged it."

Josiah ducked under the net and went to Amanda. "Is there a problem here?"

"*Nee*," she said, looking straight at Peter, appearing a little upset.

"Food's ready!" *Onkel* John called out.

Peter walked away without another comment, but Josiah's anger continued to simmer. He wanted nothing more than to grab his cousin and knock some manners into him. But that wasn't the Amish way, and even if he were still living an *Englisch* life, he wouldn't have done anything to embarrass his aunt and uncle. He clenched his jaw, took a deep breath, then looked at Amanda, grateful everyone else had abandoned the volleyball court in favor of eating. "Sorry about that."

"You shouldn't apologize for your cousin's bad behavior." Glancing at Peter again, she added, "Maybe one day he'll grow up."

"We can hope."

Amanda turned and faced him, a smile on her face. "You haven't lost your touch at volleyball, I see."

"And you're still a graceful loser." He took a step closer to her, her gorgeous smile drawing him in. She had an adorable dimple in her left cheek. He had to fight the urge to bend down and kiss it.

"What?" She brought her hand to the dimple. "Is there something on my face?" She wiped at her cheek. "I wouldn't be surprised if it's grass or something."

He reached out and touched her hand, stilling her movements. "*Nee*," he said, bringing his hand up to touch her dimple with his thumb. "You're perfect."

❧

Amanda nibbled on her fingernail during the trip home in Josiah's buggy. The singing had ended fifteen minutes before, fortunately without any more confrontations from Peter. In fact, the rest of the evening couldn't have been better. Josiah sat next to her the entire time, even during the hymn sing. And although he had remained fairly distant since the end of the volleyball game, she couldn't get what he said out of her mind.

"You're perfect."

But it wasn't just the words that had made her emotions dance. His gentleness as he touched her hand and her face, the warmth in his eyes as he spoke—all those things made her dizzy with delight. Whether he meant to or not, Josiah had allowed her a glimpse into his heart.

She gazed straight ahead, taking in the beauty before her. Long narrow clouds streaked the pastel evening sky, as if God had skipped a paintbrush across the heavens. The sun had hidden behind the horizon a short while ago, leaving behind remnants of lavender, peach, and pink. The sharp clip-clop of Tater's shoes sounded against the pavement. There weren't many cars on the road to disturb the peaceful scene. The night was perfect.

"You're perfect."

She looked at Josiah's profile. His expression remained impassive, as usual. But she couldn't get the image of the way he looked at her out of her mind. Her body suddenly went hot, then cold as realization dawned. She shivered, hugging her arms around her body, despite the relative warmth of the evening.

It's Josiah, isn't it, Lord? He's the one You've set apart for me.

Perhaps she had always known, even when they were younger. That had to be the reason she'd been devastated by his leaving, and why his rejection upon his return had hurt so much. There had always been that hollow part inside her heart. Now she knew why she had never married, why no man had ever piqued her interest. Only one man held her heart, one man she loved completely, and one she suspected loved her in return.

Now if only she could figure out why he held those feelings back.

She waited for him to say something. Normally she would pepper him with questions and demand answers, but she had learned that method only pushed him further away. *Lord, what should I do?*

A short while later Josiah guided the buggy onto their dirt road.

Their houses came into view, and he still hadn't said anything to her. When he reached his driveway, he hesitated, clearly unsure whether to turn in or take her to her house.

"I can walk from your barn," she said, deciding for him.

He nodded and turned the buggy, making his way up the driveway.

Her frustration climbed as he yanked on the reins, signaling Tater to stop. "Josiah, you haven't said one word to me since we left. Is something wrong?"

"*Nee.*" He shrugged, then moved to get out of the buggy.

"I hate when you do that!" She knew she sounded as immature as Peter, but she couldn't help it. She was tired of Josiah being cold toward her one minute and hot the next.

"Do what?" He turned and looked at her.

At least she'd gotten his attention. "Shut me out. Don't you think we should at least talk about what happened tonight? And don't act like you don't know what I'm referring to."

He let out a long sigh. "I know what you mean. And I definitely don't want to talk about it."

She put her hand on his arm, her fingertips resting lightly on the bare skin of his forearm. The muscles twitched underneath her touch, spurring her courage. "Josiah, there's something going on between us. I feel it. I know you feel it."

"Amanda," he said, pain streaking his tone.

"Why are you running away?"

"Because that's how it has to be." His gaze bored into her, filled with intensity. "What I said to you tonight . . . it was a mistake."

He couldn't have hurt her more if he had tried. "A mistake?"

"*Ya.* I didn't mean it the way you thought I did."

"And how was that, exactly? Have you suddenly become a mind reader?"

"You've always been easy to read, Amanda. Look, I didn't mean to lead you on. I might have said . . . something . . . to make you think

I had feelings for you. But it was only out of friendship." He gave her a half smile. "We used to say goofy stuff to each other all the time, remember?"

She moved to withdraw her hand from his arm, her feelings stinging from his admission. But then she searched his face, met his eyes. "You're lying," she said softly, more confused than ever. "You've never lied to me before, Josiah Bontrager. Don't think you can start now."

He moved his arm from beneath her hand. "I've got to put Tater up." He turned his back to her and jumped out of the buggy.

Amanda clamped her lips together. He wasn't getting off this easily. "Josiah," she said as she got out of the passenger side. "You can't just walk away from this. From us."

He unhitched Tater from the buggy and started to lead her to the barn. "There is no us, Amanda."

She followed him. "There has always been an us, Josiah." She paused, waiting for him to lead Tater to her stall. When he latched the door shut, she continued. "We were inseparable as kids."

"We were friends," he said, his palm lying flat against the stall door.

"*Ya*, that we were. But when you left . . ." She took a deep breath, her body shaking with emotion. "You took a part of me with you."

He didn't say anything, only leaned his forehead on the stall door, his hat tilting back on his head.

The light continued to fade in the barn, and she had difficulty seeing his face. She moved closer, until only inches separated them. "You're still holding that part of me, Josiah. I don't know if you even realize it."

He drew in a sharp breath and stepped away from her. "Mandy," he whispered, his voice thick. "Don't . . . don't do this."

"Do what? Be honest with you? Tell you how I feel?" She had exposed her feelings this far, she might as well lay bare her soul. "Tell you I love you?"

Clamping both hands on his head, he exclaimed, "Don't say that!"

"I'm not like you, Josiah. I can't turn feelings off and on whenever it suits me."

He dropped his hands. "Is that what you think I'm doing?"

"That's exactly what you're doing. And I don't understand why."

"You want some understanding? You've got it. And when I'm finished, you'll wish you'd never known me."

◦⦣⦢◦

Josiah gulped for air as Amanda looked at him, love brimming in her eyes. "Nothing you could say would drive me away, Josiah. I told you that before, and I meant it."

"That's because you don't know the facts." He took off his hat and tossed it on the stack of hay bales nearby. Then he ran his fingers through his hair, because if he didn't do something with his hands, he'd lose his mind. Why was she pushing so hard? She said she loved him, but he didn't deserve her love. He had to make her understand that.

He watched as she moved to the door of the barn. He thought she might leave, until she picked up one of the old lanterns hanging on a peg near the door. She retrieved a match from the match holder bolted to the wall and lit it.

She walked toward him, her beautiful face illuminated by the soft yellow glow. "I want to see your face when you tell me, Josiah," she said, moving closer to him. "And I want you to look at me. Because when you're finished telling me your secrets, I want you to see that I still love you."

His throat hitched. Unconditional love. That was what she was offering him, even before she knew what he had done. He did not think he could love her any more than he did at that moment. But it

KATHLEEN FULLER

would only take a few words from him to destroy what she felt for him.

"Things were bad when *Mamm* got sick," he said, his memory sending him back to that terrible time when he had just turned twelve and he found out his mother had cancer. She had survived for almost a year before she succumbed. "*Daed* was angry all the time, especially when *Mamm* went into the hospital that last time. He'd always had a temper, but I never saw him raise a hand to her, ever. But . . ."

"He hit you?" She brought her hand to her mouth, her eyes widening. "Josiah, I had no idea."

"No one did. He'd always say he was sorry afterward. And he really didn't do it all that often . . . usually when I broke a rule or didn't do my chores."

"That's no reason to strike a child."

"I know that now. But when *Mamm* got sick, he started smacking me harder. More often. Sometimes he'd bring me out here." He glanced over his shoulder at the far corner of the barn, where the horse whip and stool remained. "He didn't always use his fists."

"Josiah, that's awful." Tears shimmered in her eyes.

"After *Mamm* passed, *Daed* just broke down. He stopped going to work, stopped caring about anything. He only spoke to me when I got in his way. After a while I avoided him as much as I could, and worked at my *onkel*'s shop every chance I got. Pretty soon the only income we had came from the money I made working there. I resented him for that, and it wasn't long before we were arguing all the time.

"Then one day I came home from the shop, and *Daed* told me to pack my clothes, that we were leaving. He didn't tell me where, or why, just that we had to *geh*. We drove into Paradise and met a man who had arranged to buy our buggy and horse, and then he hired someone to take us to Indiana. He planned it all out and didn't tell me anything." He paused and looked at her. "That's why I didn't tell you good-bye. I would have if I'd had the chance."

"I know, Josiah." She sniffed and wiped her cheek. "I never resented you for leaving. I just wished I had known what was going on."

"What could you have done about it? No one knew what *Daed* did to me. He made sure not to leave any visible marks. I don't know if my *aenti* and *onkel* had any idea either. Besides, at that point I figured I deserved what I got."

"How can you say that?"

"I was young; he was my dad. I believed him." Josiah started to pace the width of the barn. "I could never do anything right. I was in the way. Everything was my fault." He stopped and looked at Amanda. "You hear that enough, you begin to believe it's true."

Chapter Twelve

AMANDA COULDN'T BELIEVE WHAT JOSIAH HAD JUST TOLD her. How could she have lived next door to him all those years, been his best friend, and not known that his father abused him? But as more and more memories came to the front of her mind, she realized there were subtle signs. The fact that he never wanted to go near his barn. That the year after his mother died, he never invited her in his house. The underlying sadness she had attributed to grief over his mother's death.

"Did my parents know?" she asked, dread pooling in her belly. "Please tell me they didn't know."

"I'm not sure. It doesn't matter anyway. They couldn't have done anything."

"They could have confronted your *daed*! They could have gone to the bishop!" The lantern shook in her hand as she spoke.

"*Daed* would have just denied it. Besides, it would have made things worse for me."

"I don't see how they could get any worse."

"Trust me, Amanda. It did."

Her arms ached to hold him. She couldn't stand thinking about what he had suffered at the hands of his own father, and she could see by the tortured look in his eyes that he was reliving those memories.

"When we got to Indiana, we didn't know anyone. I think *Daed* thought the move would give us a fresh start. For a time things were okay. He got a job working in one of the RV factories there, and I did some odd jobs for some of the Amish and *Englisch* that lived near us.

He bought a small trailer, and we moved in. At least he stopped hitting me for a while. But that didn't last very long. A couple years later he started drinking. A lot, which made his temper worse."

"Oh no," Amanda whispered.

"I was almost seventeen and ready to move out anyway. I was sick of him yelling at me and smacking me around, and I had made some friends with a few *Englisch* guys. I moved in with them for a couple years. I tried living their fancy lifestyle—I even bought a car—but it wasn't for me. By this time my *daed* had drunk himself sick." Josiah went and sat on one of the hay bales, his shoulders drooping. "I ended up having to take care of him."

Amanda went to him and sat down, letting the handle of the lantern dangle from her fingers. "Josiah, why didn't you get in touch with me?"

He looked at her with a sad smile. "You couldn't fix this, Amanda. Although I have no doubt you would have tried."

"What happened to your father?"

"He died when I was twenty-two. He got drunk one night, and on his way to the bathroom he tripped and fell. Hit his head against the corner of his dresser. When I found him, he was dead."

"Josiah, I'm so sorry."

"I'm not." He stared straight ahead. "At least a part of me isn't. I didn't recognize him anymore. He wasn't my father by that point."

She reached for his hand, but he moved. "Josiah, don't pull away from me. Not now."

"I'm not finished. What I didn't tell you is that I not only didn't recognize my father anymore, I didn't recognize myself."

"What do you mean?"

He popped up from the bale. "I'm just like him, Amanda. Sometimes I get so angry I can feel it boiling inside my veins, running through my body. My temper is just as bad as his."

"But you're not him, Josiah. You would never hurt anyone."

"That's where you're wrong. I know how important it is for the Amish to be peaceful. To swallow their anger and turn the other cheek. Even though I didn't see that with my father, I understood that controlling those impulses is a basic tenet of the faith. And that's the problem. I can't control them." He looked at her, and she saw the shame in his eyes. "I hit my *daed*, Amanda. And not just once, either. We didn't just argue, we fought."

Amanda shut her eyes against what he had just revealed. She could barely fathom that gentle Josiah, the boy who wouldn't even step on a spider or squash a bug, would ever hit another person, much less his own father. Yet she couldn't doubt his words either.

"Now you see why I can't stay here. Why I keep pushing you away. Why I can't marry." He squatted down on the floor and held his head in his hands. "I can't risk hurting anyone else."

Heat emanated from the lantern, so she set it on the floor of the barn, well away from the hay bales and anything else that might catch fire. Tentatively she knelt down and put her arm around his shoulders, glad when he didn't pull away. "Josiah, listen to me. Everyone gets angry."

He looked up at her, his gaze narrowing. "Don't patronize me, Amanda. I know everyone gets angry. The difference is they can control it. I can't."

"With the Lord's help you can."

"The Lord's help?" He let out a bitter laugh, then sat on the ground, slipping out from beneath her embrace. "God abandoned me long ago."

"God is faithful, Josiah. He would never abandon us."

"Easy for you to say. Your *mamm* didn't die and your *daed* didn't beat you on a regular basis."

Amanda cringed, properly chastised. "I suppose it does sound like a platitude. I didn't live your life, and I can see where you might doubt God's presence." She said a silent prayer for the Lord to give her the right words before she continued. "But, Josiah, He was with you. You had to have amazing inner strength to survive what you did. That type of strength comes from God."

"I did what I had to do." He looked at her. "I'm still doing what I have to." He rose from the floor and retrieved his hat, then put it on. "I've told you everything, the whole sorry story."

She stood and faced him. "I know. And I'm still here."

He looked at her for a long moment, a myriad of emotions crossing his features. Shame. Anguish. And for a fleeting instance, hope. Then his expression hardened. "*Geh* home, Amanda. Forget we ever had this conversation."

"I can't just forget what you told me, Josiah."

"You have to. I'll be gone soon, once the house is sold."

"You think running away is going to fix everything? That didn't work out so well for your *daed*, did it? You can't keep running from the past, or from God. You'll never be free if you do."

"Maybe I don't deserve to be free. I hit my own *daed*, Amanda. What kind of *sohn* does that?"

"A *sohn* who was abandoned by his *vatter*, and who thought everyone else had abandoned him too."

He didn't look convinced. "I know you want to fix this, Amanda. To fix me. But you can't."

"Oh, I know I can't. Only God can do that." She reached for his hand, squeezing tightly when she sensed him pulling away. "I want to pray for you, Josiah. Will you let me do that much?"

❧

Pain like he'd never experienced welled up inside him. He had thought, or at least sincerely hoped, that when he had confessed everything to Amanda, she would leave him alone. But he should have known better. Amanda Graber never knew an underdog she couldn't champion or a lost cause she wouldn't support. She just couldn't understand he wasn't worth saving.

That thought had hit home when she had admitted she loved him. The words lifted up his heart while crushing his soul. Other than his mother, and for a short while his uncle, Amanda had been the only good thing in his life. Then when he moved, when she had been taken away from him, he knew God had written him off. Somehow he'd managed to go through the motions of life since then, not feeling much of anything except rage at his father, a rage he had expressed with his fists, just like his *daed*. He'd only punched his *daed* twice, but the look of shock and betrayal on Levi Bontrager's face was permanently stamped on Josiah's memory.

Why couldn't she see how dangerous he was? Even if he could afford to entertain the thought of a future with her, she could never trust that he wouldn't lose his temper with her or their children. Yet she stood strong, wanting to pray for him. "It won't do any *gut*," he muttered, knowing if he refused she would persist until he gave in.

"I think you'll be surprised at how much *gut* it will do." She gripped his hand and bowed her head. The words of her prayer skimmed over him, having little effect on his emotions or his opinion of himself. When she finished, she looked up at him, her eyes consumed with anticipation.

Her hand felt so soft and warm in his, he never wanted to let go. But he did. "It's late, Amanda. You need to get home."

She'd obviously expected some kind of miracle from her little prayer. He knew from experience that prayer didn't work. He'd said enough prayers after his mother became ill to last a lifetime.

"All right, I'll *geh*." She started for the door, only to turn around and rush toward him.

She threw her arms around him, drawing him against her. "This isn't the end, Josiah," she whispered in his ear. Her embrace tightened. "I still love you. God loves you too. One day you'll believe both of us." She released him, then turned and fled.

He stood in the center of the dusty barn, his arms slightly lifted. He realized he had been about to return her embrace. Although her hug had been brief, her warmth had flowed straight through him, and he ached to hold her again.

Tater whinnied, pulling him out of his stupor. The horse had been amazingly quiet during his conversation with Amanda. Weariness suddenly overcame him, both emotional and physical. He wanted to fall into bed and try to get this entire evening out of his mind.

But as he headed for the house, he realized that wouldn't happen. He couldn't put Amanda's reaction out of his mind. She truly believed in God's faithfulness, and a part of him wished he had her conviction.

~∽◠~

Sleep didn't come easily to Amanda that night. She tossed and turned, her emotions somersaulting as she tried to process everything Josiah had told her. She felt so clueless, so sheltered. Were there others in their community suffering the same fate as Josiah? Would she be able to tell if they were?

Unable to rest, she left her bed, walked to the window, and opened it. From here she had a clear view of Josiah's house, although a large oak tree that stood between the two properties partially obscured the barn. The lights were out in his house, and she wondered if he was already asleep.

Despite her confusion about everything else, her love for Josiah hadn't wavered. She had no idea how to convince him of that, or how to convince him of God's love. After spending a few minutes breathing in the fresh air, she returned to bed. As her eyelids closed, she prayed not only for Josiah, but for herself.

~∽◠~

The smell of smoke pulled her out of her fitful sleep. *Fire!* Panic shot through her as she jumped out of the bed. She ran to her brothers' room and woke them up. "Outside, now!"

"What's wrong, Mandy?" Thomas said sleepily.

"Don't ask questions, just *geh!*"

She woke up the rest of her siblings and chased them down the stairs. Where was the fire? Where were her parents? Her terror increased as she realized the fire might be downstairs where she had sent the children. But if that was the case, why didn't she see smoke?

"Amanda, what are you doing?" Her father met her at the foot of the stairs, his hair standing up in disheveled tufts all over his head. "Why are the *kinder* down here?"

"Can't you smell the smoke, *Daed?*" But even as she spoke the words, she realized the scent wasn't as strong down here. Maybe the fire was upstairs after all.

Daed inhaled deeply. "*Ya*, I smell something. But I don't think it's in our house." He dashed to the front door, Amanda dogging his heels. He threw open the door and both of them stepped out on the front porch. The thick scent of smoke filled the air.

"Josiah!" Amanda exclaimed, realizing the smoke was coming from his property. She ran toward his house, ignoring her father's calls. When she reached Josiah's driveway, she saw huge flames coming out of the slats of the old barn. Her head jerked back and forth as she searched for Josiah, or a sign that Tater had escaped the fire. When she saw a dark figure dash inside the barn, she rushed toward the burning structure.

"Amanda! *Halt!*" Her father came up behind her and put his hands on her shoulders, holding her back. "You can't go in there."

She spun around. "Josiah's inside!"

"I called the fire department from our call box. They'll be here in a few minutes. There's nothing else we can do."

"If Josiah's in there, he doesn't have a few minutes." Her nerves were stretched to their limits. "I can't lose him, *Daed*. Not again."

"You can't save him, either, Amanda."

Tears and smoke clogged her throat. She saw no sign of either

Josiah or Tater. She grasped at a thin thread of hope that she'd been seeing things. He might be in his house, safely away from the fire. But seeing the fierceness of the blaze in front of her, she knew Josiah couldn't possibly be in the house. He would be in the barn, trying to save his horse.

She folded her hands and tucked them under her chin, praying harder than she had ever prayed in her life. She squinted, willing him and Tater to come out. *Please, Lord. Save them!*

Then, in a direct answer to her plea, she saw them exit the barn, Josiah clinging to Tater's bridle as he hunched over and coughed. As soon as he was clear, he let the horse go and fell to the ground.

"Josiah!" She ran and knelt next to him. Even though they were well clear of the blaze, she could feel the heat searing her back through her thin nightgown. The shrill sound of fire sirens pierced the air.

"Josiah," she said again, cradling his head in her hands. Soot colored his face, and he remained very still. She leaned down and kissed his cheek, her unbound hair falling in a curtain around them both. "Say something. Please."

He opened his eyes slightly, then coughed, his chest heaving from the effort. "Tater?" he asked in a hoarse voice.

She glanced up to see her father guiding the horse farther away from the burning barn. "*Daed*'s got her. She looks all right."

Two fire trucks pulled alongside the driveway, engulfing Amanda and Josiah in their swirling light. Suddenly two men in paramedic uniforms hovered over her.

"Let us take a look at him," one of them said. "Step back and give us room."

She acquiesced, silently praising and thanking God for bringing Josiah out alive. His cough sounded horrible, and his T-shirt and pants were black. The paramedics helped him to a sitting position and gave him an oxygen mask. After he settled, one of the men came over to her.

"Looks like he'll be all right. We wanted to take him to the hospital to get checked out, but he refused. Your husband is a very lucky man to have gotten out of there alive."

Amanda started to correct him, then stopped. "*Ya*, he is. He's a very lucky man."

Chapter Thirteen

Josiah stood a few feet from the barn, staring at its charred remains, watching thin tendrils of smoke snake up in the air as they greeted the rising sun. The firefighters had extinguished the blaze over an hour ago, but there were still a few hot spots in the rubble. They had assured him the fire had been completely put out. Not that it mattered anyway. The entire structure had burned to the ground.

He took a deep breath and felt a catch in his lungs. He coughed, the burn in his throat and chest mixing with his despair. The barn was a total loss. And while he supposed he should be grateful the fire hadn't spread to the house or the Graber property, and that his horse had been spared, he couldn't summon a speck of gratitude. He couldn't afford to replace the barn. Even if he could, it would take him months to do it himself. He could sell the house and property without it, but without the barn he would take a significant loss.

His gaze landed on his buggy, which had caught fire after the fire department arrived. It also sustained damage, although it hadn't been completely destroyed. Scorch marks streaked the gray enclosure and oak frame. He could probably do the repairs himself, but he would have to purchase the materials. Another expense he couldn't afford.

"Josiah?"

He didn't respond. When Amanda stood beside him, he couldn't bring himself to look at her. He vividly remembered hearing her voice when he collapsed after leading Tater out of the barn. How she knelt beside him and kissed his cheek, her soft brown hair brushing against his face, keeping him from slipping into unconsciousness. If he allowed himself a single glimpse of her, he might fall apart right there.

"We just finished breakfast. I saved some for you." She stepped closer to him, apparently waiting for him to answer.

"Not hungry."

She hesitated a moment longer before saying, "*Daed* said Tater can stay in our barn as long as you need her to."

"Tell him *danki* for me." His voice sounded flat and emotionless to his own ears, reflecting how he felt inside. Empty. Hopeless.

"Did they tell you how the fire started?"

"The lantern exploded. I forgot and left it lit in the barn last night."

"Josiah, I'm so sorry."

He shrugged. "No need for you to feel sorry. It was my own *dumm* fault."

"But if I hadn't lit the lantern—"

"It was *my* fault," he snapped.

Amanda moved to stand in front of him. "I know you're upset—"

"*Upset?* Why would I have any reason to be upset?"

"You can replace the barn, Josiah."

"*Nee*, I can't. I don't have the money, Amanda." He looked over her shoulder at the pile of black remains. "Or the will." His gaze found hers again. "I guess God let me know how much He cares about me."

"Surely you don't believe this is God's fault."

"He didn't stop it, did He?"

"*Nee*. But, Josiah, you're alive. Your horse is alive." She gestured to the burned barn behind her. "This pile of burnt wood and ash can be replaced. You can't." Her hand went to her mouth for a moment, and she swallowed. "I don't know what I would have done if I lost you last night, Josiah." She wrapped her arms around his waist and leaned her cheek against his chest.

He stood motionless for a second before succumbing to her embrace. Closing his eyes, he rested his chin on the top of her head, touching the stiff fabric of her *kapp*. Fatigue seeped into his bones. He was tired of the struggle, of fighting against everything—his feelings for Amanda, his past, his uncertain future. Only now, as he felt her tighten her arms around him, as he breathed in the sweet scent of her freshly shampooed hair, did he feel a semblance of peace. He longed to hold her forever, to tell her how much he loved her. But he didn't dare. She'd said he had amazing inner strength, but compared to her, he had none.

"Amanda! Mr. Josiah!"

They broke apart as Andrew and Thomas neared. His first instinct was to send them away. They didn't need to bear the brunt of his foul mood again. Yet he couldn't bring himself to do it. Instead he walked toward them, meeting the boys at the edge of his driveway and the grassy yard.

"Wow," Andrew said, gaping at what little remained of the barn. "That was some fire."

"*Mamm* made us stay in the house." Thomas rubbed his nose with the palm of his hand. "I wanted to come over, but she said *nee.*"

"I wanted to come over too!" Andrew stepped in front of his brother. "But we had to watch from the window." His eyes grew wide with amazement. "Never seen a fire that big before."

"Or so many fire trucks." Thomas moved to Andrew's side, not content to remain in his brother's shadow for very long. He took in a deep breath. "It sure does stink! What are you going to do about the barn?"

"Not much I can do. It would cost me too much to fix it."

The young boy's face fell. "I'm sorry, Mr. Josiah." Then he leaned over and whispered something in Andrew's ear. Andrew nodded, and both boys took off running toward the house.

"Wonder what that's about," Amanda said.

"With those two, there's no telling."

"They think the world of you." She moved closer to him. "So do I."

He looked at her, incredulous. "Even after everything I told you?"

She nodded.

"Amanda, I can't be trusted to hold my temper in check. I'm afraid . . . I'm afraid I might hurt you."

"I'm not. I could never be afraid of you, Josiah." She reached up and brushed back a lock of his hair from his forehead. "If I have to, I'll spend the rest of my life convincing you of that."

"Mr. Josiah!"

He turned at the sound of Thomas's voice. The boys bounded toward him, each of them holding something in his hand. As they neared, he saw that each held a small, clear plastic baggie halfway filled with coins. The change jingled as they ran.

"Here." Andrew held out his baggie to Josiah, and Thomas followed suit. "It's all we got, but you can use it to rebuild your barn."

Josiah crouched down in front of the boys, unshed tears burning his eyes. The bags were filled mostly with pennies, and he doubted they had more than six dollars between them. He could only imagine how long it had taken for them to save such a meager amount. Yet they were ready to part with it willingly, expecting nothing in return.

"*Danki, buwe*," he said, then cleared his throat. He closed his hands over each of theirs, gently pushing the money back toward them. "I appreciate the offer, but keep your money. Spend it on something special."

"But we are," Thomas said.

"You have to have a barn, Mr. Josiah," Andrew piped up. "Tater needs a place of her own." He shoved the money back at Josiah.

"Take it," Amanda said quietly as she crouched beside him. "I'm not the only persistent one in my family."

"I can see that." He accepted the small bags.

Andrew grinned. "I can help you clean up the mess, Mr. Josiah."

"Me too!" Thomas added.

Josiah's spirits suddenly lifted, and he nodded, smiling back. "You know I can use the help. I've got a broom in the house, but the shovel was in the barn."

"I'll get the broom," Thomas volunteered and dashed to the house.

Not to be outdone, Andrew said, "And I'll fetch *Daed*'s shovel. He won't care if we borrow it for a little while."

When the boys disappeared, Josiah turned and looked at Amanda. The scent of smoke still hung heavy in the air, but things didn't seem as bleak as they had moments before.

She gave him a small smile. "The *buwe* will be back soon, eager to get started."

"*Ya*." He couldn't move away from her, not yet.

"I have to get back home and help *Mamm*. Today is supposed to be washday, but I think we'll wait until the smoke clears completely."

"*Gut* idea. You don't want to smell like a barbecue."

"*Nee*, we don't." She reached up on tiptoe and kissed his cheek. "I love you," she whispered. "Just wanted to remind you of that."

He turned and watched her walk away, wondering what he had done to deserve her love. Then he realized he had done nothing, because he didn't deserve it.

"I found the broom, Mr. Josiah."

"*Gut*," Josiah said, still watching Amanda, waiting until she disappeared inside. He didn't know how he would be able to walk away from her, from everything here.

But somehow he had to.

⤴⤵

Josiah woke up the next morning to the sound of hammers pounding nails. He popped out of bed and ran to the window, rubbing his eyes as he tried to fathom what he saw. Amish men, at least twenty of them, were in his backyard, working in perfect sync. They had already nailed several beams of wood together where the south side of his barn had been, creating a partial wall.

They were raising a new barn.

He threw on his clothes, dashed downstairs and out the door. A few of the men looked at him. He recognized Ben Weaver and Aaron Lantz, who both waved at him, then continued their work, with Ben holding up one of the six-by-six square poles while Aaron nailed a two-by-four to the base of the pole at an angle for support. Several of the other men were doing the same. To his shock he even saw Peter pitching in, although he didn't look too happy about it.

"You look surprised, Josiah." Uncle John came up beside him.

"I am." He pushed his hat back on his head, surveying the scene in front of him. "I truly am."

"You shouldn't be." John clapped a hand on his shoulder. "You know our ways. When a person loses something in our community, the rest of us help out."

"But I'm not part of your community."

"That could change, you know. It's up to you. You're family, a part of ours, and a part of the Lord's." He dropped his hand from Josiah's back. "Better get to work. Here," he said, handing Josiah a hammer. "*Geh* and help Ben and Aaron. I don't think that beam is straight."

The beam looked straight enough, but he eagerly joined the others, still incredulous that so many had turned out to help him. As the day progressed, even more men showed up. By the noon hour the women had arrived and were setting up tables of food on the Grabers' lawn. It seemed the entire community had put their own lives on hold for a day to help him build his barn. And while he knew this was the Amish way, their generosity humbled him, a generosity he doubted he could ever return.

"Beautiful day for a barn raising, *ya?*" Leah Lantz stood to Amanda's left and unwrapped a huge bowl of chicken salad. The faint scent of chicken, celery, and salad dressing wafted through the air.

"*Ya,*" said Rebecca Miller, on Amanda's other side. She placed a tray of thinly sliced ham, turkey, and roast beef on the table. "That chicken salad smells delicious, Leah. Did you make it?"

"That's the only thing she knows how to make," Leah's sister Kathleen said from the other side of the table.

Leah smirked at her. "I'll have you know Aaron loves my chicken salad."

"He'd better. He'll be eating it every day for the rest of his life."

Leah just responded to the dig with a soft smile.

Kathleen left to help some of the other women inside, clearing Amanda's view of the men working on the barn. Her gaze zeroed in on Josiah, who was working near Ben and Aaron. Still holding the hammer, he pushed his hat back and wiped his forehead with the back of his hand. He had rolled his shirtsleeves up, exposing his tanned forearms.

"The barn is coming along quickly, isn't it?" Rebecca asked.

"It always does when everyone helps out," Amanda replied. She tucked the ribbons of her white *kapp* into the front of her dress and waved her hand in front of her heated face. The day had turned sultry, but the heat didn't impede the men's progress.

"Don't get me wrong," Leah said, moving closer to the other two women. "I'm not glad Josiah's barn burned down, but I love a *gut* barn raising."

"Me too," Rebecca echoed. "It's *wunderbaar* to see everyone come together to help someone in need."

Amanda nodded, glad Josiah had accepted the community's help without an argument. Maybe this outpouring would help him see God's hand in his life. She had prayed almost continually for that to happen after leaving him yesterday morning. She knew she couldn't convince him herself, that her words about God's faithfulness had passed right through him with no effect. She had to let Josiah go and let God take over. It hadn't been easy, but when she woke up this morning, she felt the Lord lift that burden from her.

She surveyed her yard and Josiah's, taking in everyone who had shown up for the barn raising. The turnout was nothing short of amazing, considering it was a last-minute event. Yet so many men and women had taken part of or even the whole day off to come and help. Many children were there, too, running around the Grabers' backyard and playing on the swing set. She saw Sarah Fisher chasing after her toddler. She called out for her father, who was busy sawing a long section of wood into pieces. She also saw Miriam Fisher talking to her sister, Lydia King. Their husbands, Seth and Daniel, had spent the morning working alongside Josiah, Aaron, and Ben.

"Here come the men," Rebecca said a few moments later. "They look *hungerich* too!"

"Aaron's always *hungerich*." Leah stuck a spoon in the chicken salad.

They lined up at the end of the table, and the women served them buffet style. When Ben reached them, Amanda noticed the tender look he gave Rebecca, and how she blushed in response. Aaron stood right behind him, and he lingered longer than he should have in front of Leah and her chicken salad.

"Hurry up, Aaron," Peter called from farther down the line. "The rest of us need to eat too."

Aaron winked at Leah and moved on.

In between dishing out spoonfuls of colorful carrot salad, Amanda glanced around for Josiah but didn't see him in line. Then she caught a glimpse of him still working on the frame of the barn. Her father walked over to him, carrying a plate of food and a drink. The men spoke for a few minutes, then Josiah dropped his hammer and headed for the food line.

Since he was the last in line, some of the other women had already stopped serving and gone inside to help with the cleanup. Only Rebecca and Leah had stayed, and when Josiah approached them, they quietly disappeared.

Josiah thrust out his plate, which held two fresh yeast rolls and a large pat of butter. Amanda scooped some of Leah's chicken salad onto the plate, then a generous helping of carrot salad.

"*Danki*," he said, picking up a plastic fork and piling on slices of ham. He glanced at her, his face red and streaked with dirt from working. "Are you to thank for all of this?"

"*Nee*," she said. "Your *Onkel* John organized everything. I happened to mention it to him yesterday."

"Because you just *happened* to be over there."

She merely smiled.

"Is there enough for seconds?" Seth Fisher approached the table, flashing a charming grin.

"For you, always." Amanda served Seth, who had a reputation for being a bottomless pit when it came to food. She then turned to talk to Josiah again, only to find he had disappeared.

Chapter Fourteen

JOSIAH WALKED THROUGH THE FRAMED-IN POLE BARN, breathing in the scent of fresh oak. Everyone had left a little over an hour ago, making sure they got home before dark so they could do their own chores and take care of their families. Plenty of work lay ahead, but the men had managed to frame the barn and put up the supports for the roof. He could do the rest of the job himself.

As he examined their handiwork, he marveled at the gift they'd given him. Before his uncle left, Josiah tried to find out how much the materials had cost so he could pay everyone back. His uncle refused to say, reminding him that the materials and labor were donated. He didn't owe anyone a dime.

He paced off the length of the barn, stopping at the back corner. The frame of the barn extended at least four feet on all sides beyond its original size. Another gift.

As he sank to his knees, it took a moment for him to realize he'd knelt down in the exact same spot where his father had beaten him with the horse whip shortly after his mother had died. He ran his hand on the dirt ground in front of him, then looked at his palm. Brown dirt mixed with black ash and sawdust. Not a trace of the short stool his *daed* made him sit on before applying the punishment. Not a sign of the horse whip anywhere. Both had burned up in the fire.

Josiah closed his eyes, tears streaming down his cheeks. The heaviness that had weighed on his heart and soul for so many years slowly drained away. He could sense God's presence now, in the midst of the ashes of his past. Now he knew why he had returned to Paradise. Not to fix up an old house and sell it so he could keep running away from the relentless memories. God had brought him back here to face those memories—and let them go.

I'm ready, Lord. Please take this pain from me . . .

He didn't know how long he prayed, but when he opened his eyes, it was nearly dark. His father's image formed in his mind, the man's face contorted with anger as it usually had been during the last years of his life. But instead of the usual resentment and guilt, Josiah experienced peace. "I forgive you, *Daed*," he whispered into the darkness. He not only said the words, he felt them. "I forgive you."

◦◦◦

Although she was tired from helping with the barn raising the day before, Amanda had difficulty sleeping that night. Right before sundown she had gone outside to check on Lucy, who had given birth to four kittens earlier that morning in the barn. On the way she had spotted Josiah kneeling inside the barn, and she had fought the urge to check on him. But a niggling inside her soul held her back. She couldn't keep rushing to his side all the time, attempting to fix something she wasn't equipped to fix. She had to let him go, and if that meant his leaving her for Ohio, then she'd have to deal with it.

Yet as she tossed and turned, fighting the tears and praying to the Lord, she knew letting Josiah go would be the hardest thing she'd ever have to do.

She rose even earlier than usual, well before sunup. Quickly she donned a long-sleeved light gray dress, brushed her hair and pinned it up, then secured her *kapp* to her head. Picking up her flashlight off the nightstand, she quietly slipped out of the house to the backyard. While she wanted to check on Lucy and her adorable kittens again, she didn't dare go in the barn and disturb the animals. Instead, she walked to the swing set and sat down on a swing.

Amanda closed her eyes. A few birds were twittering in the surrounding trees, getting ready to start their day. The scent of smoke that had been in the air yesterday had disappeared completely, and she breathed in the sweet scent of grass. The chilly morning didn't bother her. She started to hum a hymn as she gently swung back and forth. When she finished the song, she opened her eyes, startled to see Josiah there. She hadn't heard him approach.

"Don't stop on my account," he said.

Dawn had started to break, but she couldn't make out his features clearly. He wore a coat over his white T-shirt and gray pants, but he'd left his hat at home. How long had he been standing there listening to her?

"I was finished anyway." She dug the toe of her shoe into the dirt and pushed the swing back. "You're up early."

"Had trouble sleeping."

"Me too."

Josiah stood next to her. "You mind?" he asked, pointing to the empty swing.

"*Nee.*" What was he up to? She'd become used to him fleeing from her or outright avoiding her, not seeking her out.

He sat down on the swing, which hung lower than the other two so the smaller children could reach it. His knees came halfway to his chin, but he didn't seem to care.

Neither of them spoke for a moment, but instead of the silence feeling awkward between them, it felt natural. Like it had been when they were kids. From their vantage in Amanda's yard, they had a perfect view of the sunrise. Amanda sighed.

"Something wrong?"

"*Nee,*" she said, twisting in the swing so she could see him. "God's gifted us with another *brechdich* morning."

Josiah looked at her and smiled. Beams of new sunlight lit up his face.

Amanda stared at him for a moment, content to take him in.

Then she realized it wasn't just the sun that made him shine. Tears sprang to her eyes. "Josiah?"

His grin widened. "I get it now, Mandy. You were right. All that time I thought God had left me. Turns out I ran away from Him. I lived in fear of becoming like my father, and I tried to steer clear of everyone because of that. But it didn't matter. Running away, blaming God, being afraid . . . I had already *become* my father. Maybe I wasn't as openly cruel, but I had turned bitter inside. But God and *mei* . . . we had a long talk yesterday. I know I don't have to live like that anymore. I finally forgave my father and let the past *geh*."

Happiness surged through her. "Oh, Josiah! I'm so happy for you!"

"I don't think I would have figured it out on my own. Not without your help." He took her hand. "I'm sorry, Mandy," he said softly. "I'm sorry for everything."

She glanced down at their hands as they hung suspended between the two swings. Their fingers entwined together, the intimate clasp sending a pleasant wave of emotion through her body. "It's all right, Josiah. I understand why."

"*Nee*, it's not all right. You've never been anything but honest with me, and I should have told you the truth a long time ago. Maybe if I had said something, everything would have been different."

"And maybe it would have stayed the same. You can't spend your life second-guessing the past."

"I know. I'd rather talk about the future."

"What about the future?"

"There's a Realtor coming here later on today. I talked to him a few days ago. He seemed really excited I was fixing up the place, but he thought it would go for a *gut* price even without the renovations. Of course, I'll have to finish the barn, but I only have to do minor repairs on the house."

"I see." She removed her hand from his grasp and stared at her lap, fighting the lump forming in her throat.

KATHLEEN FULLER

"He even quoted me a number. It's a lot of money, plenty enough for me to get started in Ohio."

"That's . . . great." So she'd been wrong about his feelings for her after all. So very, very wrong. Pain seared her heart as she comprehended what he'd just said. He really was leaving. It wouldn't take long to complete the barn and address the minor problems in the house. A week, maybe two at the most, then he'd be gone.

Wrapping her arms around her body, she wished she could disappear. She thought she had prepared herself for this, but she could barely contain her heartache. She never should have told him she loved him—she never should have let herself fall in love with him. And she'd been wrong about God, too, at least about His setting Josiah apart for her. Somehow she'd find the strength to mend her heart, but right now she couldn't even look at him. If she did, she'd burst into tears.

She rose from the swing, her arms still crossed over her chest. "I've got to get inside. *Daed*'s probably up already, and I'll have to make breakfast. I'll send the boys over when we're done." Unable to stop herself, she faced him. "Just do me one favor, before you leave."

He jumped up from the swing. "Amanda—"

"Make sure you say good-bye." Whirling around, she started for the house, only to stop in her tracks when he gently grabbed her arm. He tugged her toward him, and before she could say a word, he kissed her.

A few seconds later, they parted. "Just for the record, that was *not* a good-bye kiss." His gaze lingered over her face. "I'm not going anywhere."

Her lips still tingling, she said, "But the Realtor—"

"Is making a trip out here for nothing."

Joy surged through her. "You're not leaving?"

"*Nee*. I love you, Mandy. That's something else I haven't been honest about. I've loved you for a long time, I think even before I left Paradise. You've always been the only woman for me."

Her eyes widened. "I had no idea."

"I never let on. I didn't want to ruin our friendship, for one thing. Also . . . I thought you'd laugh in my face if I told you."

"I would never do that."

"I know that now. I've made a lot of mistakes, Mandy. I'm not a perfect man. I still have a temper, but I'm hoping with God's help I can control it. I also don't have much to offer. I only have this house and part of a barn to my name. I'll never have money like Peter does."

"You know I don't care about that."

He grinned. "It's one of the reasons I love you. One of many." He ran his thumb over her cheek. "I love your enthusiasm, your spontaneity, your spirit, your unconditional belief and love." Then his expression grew somber. "I've spent the last ten years longing for something I never thought I'd have. A wife. Family. A place of my own."

"You can have all of those things, Josiah." Her voice trembled as she put her arms around him.

"I can?"

"*Ya,*" she said, resting her cheek against his chest. "All you have to do is ask."

An Amish Gathering
READING GROUP GUIDE

*Guide contains spoilers, so don't read before completing the novellas.

For reading groups with five or more members,
the authors will participate in the discussion
of this collection. If you're interested,
go to www.Amishhearts.com.

A CHANGE OF HEART

1. Leah's father worries throughout the story that Leah will not master the skills necessary to become a good Amish *fraa*. At what point does he begin to realize that Leah's stories are much more than just a frivolous waste of time?

2. Aaron agrees to read Leah's books as a way to get close to her. What are some of the things Aaron learns about Leah by reading her stories?

3. Auntie Ruth nudges Leah and Aaron together by writing notes to each of them. What do you think would have happened if Ruth hadn't done this? Would they eventually have found their way back to each other? If so, who do you think would have initiated a get-together?

4. Leah's *Englisch* friends, Donna and Clare, are not at the same spiritual place in their lives as Leah. Can it be in a person's best

interest to avoid people with whom they are unequally yoked, as many Amish believe? Have you ever been friends with someone with whom you were unequally yoked spiritually? How did it affect you?

When Winter Comes

1. Rebecca has felt for years that she isn't as attractive or interesting as her twin. Do you have siblings to whom you feel you come in second in some way? Why?
2. As the oldest child in the family, Rebecca feels she has to be the caretaker. What role do you think birth order plays in a person's development?
3. How do you personally know when something is God's will for your life? When have you been right about this? When have you been wrong?
4. It takes a long time for Rebecca to make peace with her sister's death. What would you say to someone who is having trouble coming to terms with the death of a loved one? What do you feel God wants us to learn from the death of someone we love?

A Place of His Own

1. When Josiah arrives in Paradise, he's determined not to depend on anyone else. Has there ever been a time in your life when people let you down? How did you learn to trust again?
2. Amanda is a "fixer"—she's eager to solve everyone's problems. What lesson did she learn in the story?
3. Although it's not stated in the story, do you think Josiah asked for and accepted God's forgiveness? Why or why not?
4. Sometimes it seems easier to blame God for our troubles than to ask Him to help us during times of hardship. Why do you think we tend to do this? What should we do instead?

Amish Recipes

MARIAN PETERSHEIM'S TOMATO PIE

1. Mix until right consistency to press into bottom of pie dish:

> 2 cups Bisquick
> 1/2 cup milk

2. Slice 2 medium tomatoes and line the crust.
3. Sprinkle with:

> 1 teaspoon basil
> 1 teaspoon parsley flakes
> 1/2 teaspoon thyme leaves
> 1/2 teaspoon oregano
> 1/2 teaspoon onion powder
> 1 teaspoon brown sugar
> Salt and pepper

4. Mix together and spread over tomatoes and spices:

> 1 cup mayonnaise
> 3/4 cup shredded American cheese

5. Bake at 350 degrees for 35 to 45 minutes until golden brown.

REBECCA MILLER'S CHICKEN AND CORN SOUP

1. Bring to boil in chicken stock and simmer for 1 hour:

> 1 1/2 pounds chicken with bones attached
> 1 quart chicken stock

2. Remove chicken. Cool. Debone and dice. Return meat to pot.
3. Add following ingredients and simmer for approximately 30 minutes until celery, carrots, and onion are tender.

> 1/2 cup each diced celery, carrots, and onion

$1/2$ teaspoon celery seed

1 (16 ounce) package frozen corn (or fresh corn if available)

2 (16 ounce) cans creamed corn

1 ($10\,3/4$ ounce) can cream of celery soup

4. Mix *rivvel* (dough ball) ingredients in bowl:

1 cup flour

1 egg

$1/2$ teaspoon salt

$1/4$ teaspoon baking powder

5. Rub mixture between your fingers and drop into bubbling soup a little at a time. *Rivvels* should be pea-sized. If they're larger, you have dumplings! When *rivvels* are cooked, serve the soup in bowls.

Amanda Graber's Monster Cookies

1. Cream together:

$1^1/2$ sticks butter

1 cup white sugar

1 cup brown sugar

2. Add:

4 eggs

1 pound crunchy peanut butter

3. Mix until blended. Add:

$2^1/2$ teaspoons baking soda

$1/4$ cup flour

$4^1/2$ cups quick oats

4. Mix in:

$1/2$ pound M&M's

12 ounces chocolate chips

5. Dough will be stiff. Form teaspoon-sized balls and roll in powdered sugar.

6. Bake at 350 degrees for 10 minutes. Do not overbake.

Acknowledgments

BETH WISEMAN:

Special thanks to my husband, Patrick, and my family and friends. I'd never make it without your support and encouragement. To Barbie Beiler, thank you yet again for reading the manuscript to verify authenticity. You're the best! Thanks also to nurse Melissa Gips for verifying medical accuracy. Much appreciated!

To my fabulous fiction team at Thomas Nelson, you guys and gals are awesome. Kathy and Barbara, such an honor to work with both of you on this project. And special thanks to LB Norton for your editorial assistance. Thanks to my agent, Mary Sue Seymour.

My most heartfelt thanks goes to God. Without Him, there would be no books.

BARBARA CAMERON:

I'm so grateful for my family and my friends for their love and their support of my writing. Thanks to Linda Byler and Dr. Beth Graybill, agent Mary Sue Seymour, Natalie Hanemann, editor at Thomas Nelson, and to LB Norton, who along with Natalie helped make *When Winter Comes* a stronger story. And most of all, thank You, God. You heard the desire in my heart to write when I was a teenager and have blessed me with so many opportunities to write.

KATHLEEN FULLER:

My deepest thanks to Natalie Hanemann and LB Norton for helping me bring this story to life. Their expertise and insights were invaluable. As always, thanks to my family for their patience and understanding, especially during deadline time!

DEAR READER:

We hope you've enjoyed this Amish collection.

Your feedback as a Christian Fiction reader is extremely valuable to the entire Thomas Nelson Fiction team. We'd like to invite you to participate in a brief on-line survey where you can share your opinions about Christian Fiction. The survey itself should take no more than 10 minutes.

For the first 500 readers who go online and complete the survey, we'll express our gratitude by mailing you a free full-length Amish novel as a thank you for your time. Visit www.nelsonfictionfeedback.com to begin the survey.

Thanks for believing in the power of story—and for helping us create the stories you most want to read.

PUBLISHER, THOMAS NELSON FICTION